A DARK DESIRE

His patience snapping, he strode toward her. She cowered into a corner of the wing chair as he bent over her and gripped the armrests. Charles knew he was frightening her, knew he should play the gentleman and back away, but she'd blithely opened a wound that stung far too deeply to be denied some form of balm.

"What can you possibly expect of me, Tess? You tossed me out with the kitchen scraps ten years ago. What makes you dare contemplate making convenient use of me now? Did you honestly believe I'd jump at the chance to do your bidding?"

Leave it alone, his conscience murmured, *stop bullying the woman*. Yet it wasn't a need for revenge that pinned him there, but the ragged puffs of breath escaping her lips and grazing his cheek, subtle reminders of the intimacy they'd once shared. A dark, curling flame licked through him, unexpectedly, astoundingly.

Her lips were so close he felt their warmth, all but tasted their sweetness. She met his gaze, eyes wide and brimming with apprehension until their radiant blue all but encompassed him, made him dizzy. He might have been a wounded gull, spiraling out of control between sky and sea, plunging to a sodden death and glad for it.

BOOK YOUR PLACE ON OUR WEBSITE AND MAKE THE READING CONNECTION!

We've created a customized website just for our very special readers, where you can get the inside scoop on everything that's going on with Zebra, Pinnacle and Kensington books.

When you come online, you'll have the exciting opportunity to:

- View covers of upcoming books

- Read sample chapters

- Learn about our future publishing schedule (listed by publication month *and author*)

- Find out when your favorite authors will be visiting a city near you

- Search for and order backlist books from our online catalog

- Check out author bios and background information

- Send e-mail to your favorite authors

- Meet the Kensington staff online

- Join us in weekly chats with authors, readers and other guests

- Get writing guidelines

- AND MUCH MORE!

**Visit our website at
http://www.kensingtonbooks.com**

Mostly Mayhem

Lisa Manuel

ZEBRA BOOKS
Kensington Publishing Corp.
http://www.kensingtonbooks.com

For fellow authors
Cynthia Thomason, Nancy Cohen, Charlene Newberg,
Sharon Hartley, and Zelda Benjamin,
for encouraging me to pursue the dream all these years.

And especially for Paul,
my modern day warrior, my hero, and my best friend.

Prologue

The night heaved its fetid breath in Gwennie's face and she cringed, longing to retreat indoors. Her forearm throbbed, still tender from when Madam Sophie flung her out the brothel door. Landing hip first in the gutter hadn't helped. She'd have new bruises in the morning, new aches.

She'd begged Sophie to let her work from inside the house from now on, rather than having to venture out to find customers. Only last week, another girl disappeared. Not a soul in Stepney saw what happened.

The thought produced shivers that aroused a fit of coughing. Doubling over, Gwennie pressed a corner of her shawl to her mouth. When the clawing in her chest subsided, she squinted down into the tattered wool and breathed a sigh of relief. No blood this time.

She pushed away from the tenement's rotting framework and moved into the sputtering halo of a gas lamp. Stepney lay quiet tonight, the streets nearly deserted after the evening's downpour. But if Gwennie listened hard, she could hear giggles and the rustle of cheap taffeta in the alley across the street, the uneven clod of footsteps, the murmur of business dealings in blackened doorways.

At the sounds of an approaching coach she stepped closer to the street, hoping the vehicle might convey an opportunity her way. But it rolled on past, spraying the foul contents of the gutter onto her legs. Her shivers turned to quakes. Yet it wasn't so much the cold and wet she minded, but the fog boiling off the river like steam from a witch's cauldron.

Gwennie hated the fog. It smelled like dead fish and wet rats and dank, scary places. It wrapped people in a pall and muffled their voices until they resembled the ghosts in her nightmares, and she feared any one of them might be the Midnight Marauder, come this time for her.

She pricked her ears at the rumble of another coach. Within seconds a phaeton's black shape emerged from the haze. It creaked to a halt a few feet away, and a cloaked and hooded driver swung down from the box, raising a splatter of rainwater around his boots.

Strange cold eyes peered out from the hood like distant ship lights piercing the mist. Gwennie stiffened against the lamppost, glad of the iron support shoring her up. She tried smoothing her fears away, tried feigning the worldliness of the other girls. But as the coachman moved closer, her chin tucked low of its own accord, seeking escape from his roaming scrutiny.

"W—What's your master's pleasure, dearie?"

"You, cherie." His smile chilled her. He swung the carriage door open. "Get in."

Hugging her sides to conceal her trembling, she ducked to climb inside, then froze. A figure draped in black occupied a corner of the seat; clutched in one gloved hand, a lily glowed like a bloodless heart. Gwennie's heart careened into her ribs. "I—I've changed my mind . . ."

"You have nothing to fear." His breath hot on her neck, the servant nudged her forward. Every instinct urged resistance. She gripped the edge of the roof, but he reached his arms around her and encircled her wrists, prying her hands loose with an ease that made her despair of escaping him. When she tried, he spanned her waist and without ceremony dumped her on the phaeton's floor. The door slammed behind her.

Fear clogged her throat. Her vision swam dizzily in the darkness. She scrabbled to find her legs but fell again when the vehicle listed to one side. A lurch drove her shoulder into the seat in front of her. The painful jab radiated through her as the coach lunged forward.

"Please . . . I haven't done anything to you," she pleaded to the shrouded, faceless figure looming above her. "Please let me go. I . . . I won't tell."

The figure leaned forward and the lily sailed overhead, out the window. Gwennie's entreaties rose to shouts. The gloved hands gripped her face. "Hush."

Gwennie fell silent.

Chapter 1

Tessa James Hardington departed her Mayfair home that evening with the same futile hope as always, a hope that was dashed—as always—the very instant she reached her destination.

"Everyone's staring, Helena, leering at me as usual." And, as usual, making her quite regret the impulse that had sent her from the shelter of her solitude. She considered an about-face and a brisk ride home in her carriage, but Tess rallied every shred of courage she possessed to continue on toward the gates of Vauxhall Gardens.

Tonight began a brand new Season, and why, why should she miss the excitement?

She suspected, however, that it was her cousin Helena's presence beside her and not any store of inner fortitude that impelled her feet forward. Was she such a frightful coward, then, to cling to Helena's arm and draw closer to the very source of her strength? "Tell me, do you think our peers will ever tire of searching for horns at the top of my head?"

"Perhaps you've grown a forked tail, dear. You could hardly blame them for staring in that case."

Tess emitted a laugh, tempted to peek over her shoulder to see if Helena was right. Nearer the turnstile the surrounding crush grew tighter, but suddenly the disparaging looks and snide whispers didn't seem nearly so menacing.

"Still," she said, "London must be a shocking bore these days if a staid widow such as me is worthy of this much attention."

"Oh, pish posh on them." Helena flashed the brilliant smile that had, since her entrance into society two years ago, grown almost legendary among the *ton*. Men and women alike vied for that smile whenever Helena Holbrook was among them, but tonight it belonged to Tess alone, filled with love and sympathy and infinite understanding.

And, yes, something more. That little quirk in her brow showered more disdain on Tess's detractors than any of them would ever suspect. Helena held her fan over her mouth and whispered, "These tiresome sots only gawk because they're envious of you."

"Of me?" That raised a guffaw of surprise. "Of my enormous popularity, I suppose."

"They envy your courage, your perseverance."

"You mean my stubborn refusal to tuck tail and run as any rational person would." Tess released a breath. Five years had passed since her sister's death—five long years. But the *ton* had neither forgotten the rumors surrounding the last months of Alicia's life nor grown the slightest bit more understanding.

Or tolerant. Tess knew it was a commonly held belief that she would one day follow her sister's example. Blood always tells—how many times had she heard that adage strategically whispered within her hearing?

Ah, but such broodings. Giving them rein only permitted the gossipmongers one more triumph over her, a triumph she wouldn't allow. At least not here, not tonight.

She and Helena continued arm in arm into the wide expanse of the Grove, glittering with the Season's newest silks, lace, and gems. Gilded by the brilliance of a thousand gas lamps, it was a scene of noisy, swarming, colorful gaiety set to music—Handel's—by an orchestra perched high on the circular Gothic Stage.

The aromas of melting chocolate and roasting nuts curled through the air, enticing new arrivals further into the evening's magic. Tess's mouth watered. She might almost—ah, so very nearly—forget she was not, indeed, a welcome and valued member of the assemblage.

Well, never mind. "It's breathtaking, Helena. I'd forgotten how so. Walter and I used to come here nearly every week during the Season."

Her cousin slipped an arm about her waist. "You miss him."

"I do. Oh, I can't pretend my marriage was a great love match, you of all people know better. But Walter and I were . . . well suited."

"And you're lonely now he's gone."

By lonely they both knew Helena meant vulnerable. While married to the influential Walter Hardington, Tess had at least enjoyed a measure of relief from society's more obvious rebukes.

She squared her shoulders. "Lonely or no, I have little choice but to be strong and move on with my life. My niece deserves the very best and if I don't provide it for her, no one else will."

"Someone else most certainly will." Helena snapped her fan shut. "I am Blair's godmother, after all."

"I stand corrected."

"How is our darling girl? Did she receive my package?"

"She did and she loved everything, especially the bells for her pony's bridle. My leaving Highgate Court was quite another matter. She grabbed my skirts and demanded I take her to London with me." Tess winced at the recollection of Blair's tiny voice barking orders like a warrior commanding surrender. "Oh, Helena, am I wrong to keep her hidden in the country, to go on shielding her from the truth?"

"Wrong to raise her with a sense of self-worth and protect her from the people who would . . ."

"Do to her as they do to me?"

Helena's face sharpened, yet even the fierceness of her expression couldn't diminish the perfect symmetry of her features. "You've done exactly right by Blair. You've given her a safe childhood, and a happy one at that. Someday, when the time is right, our little girl shall command this town. She'll set fashions, inspire poets and break countless hearts."

Tess laughed. "As you do each time you enter a ballroom?"

"The only heart I'm concerned with is my husband's." She opened her fan and fluttered it in a show of feigned indignation. "If I'm not mistaken, our Blair will outshine even the most accomplished London debutante."

"She's an extraordinary child, isn't she?" Tess's chin inched higher. "I'm so proud of her."

"And Alicia would be proud of what a wonderful mother you've been to her daughter." Helena embraced her quickly, then pointed her fan toward the horseshoe-shaped Chinese Pavilion. "I'm famished. Shall we join our friends and have a bite before the concert? Father and Wesley are waiting there for us as well."

Tess appreciated the abrupt change of subject. Helena knew exactly how far to tread on the subject of Alicia. "You go ahead. I'm going to take a turn down the Grand Walk."

Eyes as vivid as the morning sky regarded her. "All alone?"

So perceptive, this cousin of hers. Tess nodded. "The Grand Walk is about the only place in London I *can* walk alone and not be ogled. People are far too engrossed in who might be watching them to pay any mind to a lone matron. Besides, it's such a lovely night and Vauxhall . . ." She drew a breath laden with the mingled sweetness of perfume, delicacies and fresh spring flowers. "Vauxhall never fails to dazzle, does it?"

"All right, dearest, but mind you don't tarry. Everyone is eager to see you." Helena touched her fingertips to Tess's cheek. "Remember, you're not without friends. You have me and Father and Wesley and all the ladies of the Friends of the Bard Society. As my sister-in-law, Charity, would say, we're an odd scrap of family but a family all the same."

Tess kissed her cousin, then caught her in a tight embrace. Helena had been one of only a handful of acquaintances brave enough to stand by her through the worst of the gossip. For that alone she'd earned Tess's deepest devotion.

She continued by herself to the Grand Walk, holding her skirts above the ankle straps of her velvet slippers to prevent her hems dragging on the gravel. Helena's words rang in her ears: *Alicia would be proud . . .*

Would she? Blair's tantrum that morning played back in her mind. Beyond doubt, she'd spoiled that child. But how could she not have done, with those tremendous eyes so like her mama's, and that imperious tone the child took when she wanted her way—so contrary to her tiny stature it drew laughter from Tess when she should have been cross. So like Alicia when she was small. . . .

Her eyes misted. She tried blinking the tears away but too late—a great big one rolled down her cheek. Oh, it had been far too long a day. She should have stayed home. Should have stayed in the country with Blair.

And how mortifying that someone might discover her weeping, here in Vauxhall's pleasure gardens. The walkway blurred as she quickened her step to evade the glow of the paper lanterns suspended from the elms.

"Oh!" Loose gravel rolled beneath her shoe. Her ankle turned with a slice of pain. "Ouch. Oh . . . hang it."

Limping, she groped for a tree trunk, a statue, anything to catch her balance. Her fingers made contact with sleek cloth that covered something quite solid beneath.

"Are you all right, madam?" A male voice rumbled beneath her fingertips. She pulled back with a start. "Do you require assistance?"

Recognition, astonishing and inconceivable, closed a debilitating fist around her. She gasped and might have staggered off the path had the gentleman not placed a steadying hand beneath her elbow. Her startled gaze met cool gray eyes and the strong angles of chiseled features, features with the power to trip the beat of her heart. Her reply drowned in sheer incredulity.

"May I . . ." Then he, too, gaped. "Good heavens. That is to say . . ."

"Good evening, Charles." Her voice fluttered, as thin and trembly as a moth's wings.

He released her elbow. His hand hovered in the air uncertainly before raking through his hair. "How . . . how are you, Tess?"

"I'm—ah—quite well."

"Are you sure? You seemed, I don't know, distressed just now." He leaned closer, searching her face in the shadows. "Still do, in fact."

Good heavens, could he still read her so easily? Something far too familiar—the starch of his shirt, his shaving soap—curled beneath her nose and released a tumble of conflicting sensations: warmth, affection, happiness . . . heartache, loneliness.

Regret.

"I-I've twisted my ankle." A limping step backward put space between them. "It's nothing really, already feeling better. I should be on my way. My party will be wondering where I am. Delightful to see you again."

"Nonsense. You're injured." A firm hand girded the small of her back, guiding her whether she will or no toward an iron bench beside the walkway.

Within the crook of his arm, she marveled at how large he seemed, how much more muscular than she remembered. She felt impossibly small in comparison, as small and uncertain as the day he left her, all those years ago.

Left her? Had he? Or had she been the one, ultimately, to send him away with words that shattered both their hearts, their dreams, their future?

"Sit a moment," he said, "I insist. It's been a long time, Tess. You look . . ."

Older? Weary? Was he comparing her to the girl she'd been? As they settled side by side his gaze caressed her. "You look lovely."

Ah. Suitable. Polite. But what more could she expect—or deserve—than cold, common civility?

"And let me offer my belated congratulations. My mother mentioned you'd married in one of her letters."

"Did she?" And had the news wounded him to his very soul? He nodded with a nonchalance that pinched her throat.

"Have you? Married, that is?" Her hands wrapped tight around her reticule until something inside—her comb?—snapped.

"Me? Good heavens, no."

An irrelevant sense of relief swept through her. "I married Walter Hardington," she said, "but I was widowed just over a year ago."

"Oh, I . . ." His aplomb slipped a fraction. For the briefest instant the boy she'd known peered out from the man's face. "I'm indeed sorry to hear it, Tess."

"Thank you. I've only recently emerged from mourning. Walter and I were wildly happy together."

Good heavens, what on earth had made her add that? True, she'd developed a warm affection for Walter, had been infinitely grateful to him for offering a sense of haven from a less than hospitable world when Alicia died. But why pretend there'd been more?

Perhaps because her life might have been so very, very much more, not with Walter but with Charles.

"He was a good man, this Walter Hardington?"

"Oh, the best of men. Solid and steady and true . . ." Charles's face went taut and she could have bitten her tongue. She'd once accused him—wrongly—of lacking those very qualities.

Ah, but there had been so much neither of them understood at the time. Swallowing a sudden urge to sob, she forced herself to view his handsome features and see only the man he was now, nearly a stranger.

But even in this she failed. The torchlight brought a copper glow to his auburn hair, sparking a recollection. She used to tease him about its being fiery red in the sun, a charge he adamantly denied each time.

"Ah, but your ankle." A roguish twinkle entered his eye, a look she remembered of old. It set her on her guard, albeit irrationally. Surely he wasn't about to tickle her. He slapped his thigh. "We must attend to it. Put it here."

"Goodness, Charles, no. Really, there's no need . . ."

"Come now. I've proved a fair medic when necessity dictated." To her utter chagrin he lifted the injured appendage, bringing it to rest across his thighs. This caused her bottom to rotate on the seat until she half reclined in the most undignified manner against the arm of the bench. "Now then. Does it hurt when I touch it here?"

Hurt? His fingertips, steady and firm, spread a quivery sensation through her leg, sent a hot rush of embarrassment to her cheeks. She shook her head mutely. Couples strolling past turned their heads to gawk at her questionable position. Charles acknowledged them with a stern nod. "Sprained ankle here. Proceed with caution."

Looking chastised for having been caught staring, the group hurried along. Charles turned his attention back to her injury. "How about when I turn it this way?"

She winced, though less from pain than because her skirts slid upward to reveal her calf. He showed no signs of noticing either her compromised state or her discomfiture.

"So I, er, understand you're *Captain* Emerson now," she said in a weak attempt to make conversation, to pretend his touch meant no more than a physician's would.

"Past tense." His palm slid up and down her inner ankle, raising shivers no physician's hands ever could and sending her pulse for a tumble. "I've resigned my commission."

"Resigned?" She tried to appear unconcerned as her skirts slipped another inch. Through her stocking and his trouser, she felt the hardness of muscle honed from years in the saddle. "Wasn't military life wonderfully adventurous?"

"I suppose."

"You . . . er . . . served in India, yes? What was it like there?"

She hoped the question would distract him while she slid her leg free.

He didn't give her the chance. Inclining his head, he cupped both hands round her ankle as if to trap it there. "India is a place of contrasts," he said, "enticingly exotic in places, predictably tragic in others. Its people know great opulence but even greater poverty, with few if any bridges between. As soon as the chance arose I left, ended up in the West Indies and finally Australia."

His face turned serious, a little sad. "The world is a fascinating place to a young man's eyes, Tess, but of late I found myself pining for the ordinary, the familiar."

So then, he'd come home for England, for the comforts of home. Her gaze drifted to the flowerbed across the Walk. As if his affairs were of little consequence, she asked, "Have you been back long?"

"A week today, though I've yet to see my family. I thought to surprise them with my homecoming but the surprise was on me. They're all scattered about the country just now."

"How disappointing."

He didn't comment. His eyes strayed to her mouth, lingering until her lips tingled with the remembered heat of his kisses. His hand brushed absently along her shin, fingertips all but disappearing beneath her hems.

This was all too much. Pulling upright, she swung her leg from his lap and placed her foot safely on the ground. "Much better now, thank you."

She fully intended to stand and bid him good evening when he said, "My father and brother established an architectural firm a few years back. Perhaps you've heard of it?"

Her mouth fell open for the briefest instant. "Emerson & Son? Good heavens, I've always thought the name a coincidence."

Everyone had heard of Emerson & Son, whose talents were revered only slightly less than those of the famous John Nash. Why, with new streets and squares being developed in London with astonishing speed, Richard Emerson's star must surely be soaring.

"I plan to join them," he said. "I only hope they haven't grown too set in their ways to accept my intrusion into the business."

"Intrusion? They're hardly likely to consider it that."

Why would they? For so many years she'd have welcomed his intrusion back into her life. She'd hoped for it, yearned for it so keenly she'd have accepted him under any circumstances. Now . . . now it was too late. Her life had changed in too many ways and besides, he hadn't come home for her, had he?

"Your family must have missed you terribly these ten years." She flexed her injured ankle, trying to wiggle away the pain that lingered despite her assertion to the contrary. "Such a long time to stay away."

"I've been home occasionally, though never for long. There wasn't much to keep me here in London." His hand went to his chin, chafing lightly against his evening growth of beard.

A shudder passed through her, a rippling awareness of how his strong hands had once held her, caressed her, slipped briefly between linen and lace to forbidden places, places she had only ever intended to share with him.

His words suddenly struck her. He'd been home, and had never once made inquiries into her welfare. She would have learned of it if he had, someone in even her small circle would have informed her. Under the circumstances she supposed she shouldn't have expected otherwise. He'd left England to forget her, but even so the knowledge stung.

"If you had little to come home to," she blurted before considering the wisdom—or lack—of her words, "perhaps it was because you'd tossed your prospects away."

"Did I?" he asked, low and even and maddeningly unperturbed, "or was I the one tossed away?"

The question aroused years-old guilt, and with it, defensiveness. "It wasn't me that ended our engagement. You know it was my uncle's doing."

"Ah, yes." His sardonic chuckle made her regret dredging up the past. "Because an Emerson would never be good enough to marry a James. Tell me, how is dear old Uncle Howard?"

Tess felt the old shame rising in waves to scorch her face. Charles's father had been a merchant then, a middle class commoner just beginning to invest in real estate. Tess was the daughter of a gentleman and the great granddaughter of an earl. The James family boasted a pedigree encompassing nine generations. The Emersons were upstarts who didn't know their place. Or so Uncle Howard, her guardian at the time, had argued.

"I never agreed with him. I didn't care a fig about pedigrees or trade or . . ." Her throat closed around the rest. After a decade, how could she look Charles Emerson in the eye and claim their love had been all that mattered, or renew the assertion that once she had come of age she would have defied Uncle Howard and his lofty notions. She had pleaded as much then, and Charles had scoffed.

He had wanted her to run away with him, to forsake her fortune, family and the life she knew. Oh, she might have done without the money, and certainly without Uncle Howard. But Alicia, still a child at the time, had needed her. Surely Charles should have understood.

But no, her refusal sent him marching off across the world with the king's army. So like a man. They hadn't the faintest notion what it meant for a woman to disregard convention and court scandal.

Ah, but we do, don't we, Alicia?

Beside her, he sat stiffly, brow etched and brooding.

"Oh, Charles, surely after all these years, the past should no longer have the power to hurt us." It took an effort to inject a ring of truth into the words.

His features smoothed. "No, and I certainly didn't return to England for the sole purpose of upsetting you." He offered his hand and, after an instant's hesitation, she took it. "Forgive me for being a cad."

"You've been nothing of the sort." Her fingers instinctively tightened around his reassuring strength, until she realized she was squeezing and released him. "The important thing is that we're both content with the choices we've made."

"Of course. How young and rash we were then." He shook his head as if at a distinct memory, though Tess couldn't remember a single rash moment beyond his urging her to elope. "Too young to know what we wanted in life."

"Indeed." Sadness seeped like an ague through her. There'd been no question in her mind, all those years ago, of what she wanted. She looked away down the Grand Walk at happy, chatting couples. She should have been among them, one of them, but at some point she had swerved off the proper path and ended up all alone, or nearly so. If only she'd had some hint of the consequences, might she have avoided that misstep?

"I'm sorry, but I must be on my way." She stood, ready to be off. Regret burned a painful rift through her heart; she inhaled deeply and hoped the pain left her when she left him.

"Give your sister my regards."

She froze, her mouth hanging conspicuously open. Charles merely stared back, unaware that he'd said anything amiss, one eyebrow cocked in a quizzical way.

"Don't you know about Alicia?" she finally managed in a whisper. "Did no one send you word, not even your mother?"

"No, she never mentioned your sister." Misgivings shadowed his handsome face. "Alicia hasn't been ill, I hope?"

"Alicia has lain in her grave these five years. She died of lung fever."

Charles paled. "Good God, Tess. I'm so sorry."

Remorse nudged at her conscience for the abrupt way she'd announced the news. Still, she longed to be away. She should not have ventured to Vauxhall tonight. She should have stayed home, alone, safe from the painful memories. Only the shocked dismay on Charles's face prevented her pivoting on her good heel and fleeing.

"Forgive me for saying it as I did." She placed a hand on one straight, solid shoulder, meaning to console but arousing another palpable memory instead. How well her cheek had once known the strength of that shoulder, how often she'd sought shelter there. "I know you were fond of my sister. I remember how you used to let her cheat at bridge." This recollection almost made her smile. Tears pulsated behind her eyes. "I really must go."

"Tess, wait, I . . ."

His voice faded, lost beneath the hum of the crowd and the airy notes of Handel. The harmonies of violin, harp and pianoforte clashed with the uneven crunch of gravel beneath her favored ankle.

Relief cooled the burning threat of tears as Tess's friends' faces came into view, illuminated and softened by some two dozen tapers lighting their supper booth. She slowed to a stop several paces away, taking time to smooth her hair, shake out her skirts, don a cheerful facade. She would not for the world be a damper on the evening.

The Friends of the Bard Society comprised twelve members in all, some married, some spinsters, each eccentric in her own way and equally dear in Tess's estimate. Helena's misfits, she privately—and fondly—termed their little group.

The aromas of baked goods and nutty ratafia liqueur wafted from the open-air booth. As Tess approached, animated snippets of conversation greeted her before anyone noticed her arrival.

"Have you heard," Beatrice Aimes said, leaning forward to address the others until her double chin all but disappeared, "the Midnight Marauder has struck again? Plucked another unfortunate right off the street before at least a dozen witnesses." Her raspy voice plunged to a confidential whisper nonetheless audible to all. "This one vanished only three doors down from her brothel. Hasn't been seen or heard from since."

"And did he leave a lily in her place?"

"On the very spot where she disappeared, just as always."

"I tremble to wonder what he does with the poor creatures." The Viscountess Morely, once accused of murdering a husband who'd merely absconded to the Americas, gave a little shudder. "Has no constable discovered any clue leading to this villain?"

"Sadly, I believe not." Helena popped a brandied cherry into her mouth.

"Well, I for one find it scandalous how London treats these crimes as an adventure story," Nora Thorngoode said in a tone of righteous, if youthful, indignation. She regarded the others with the slight squint that had lately become her habit. "Have you seen the sketches in the papers? It's as if this Marauder were some kind of rogue knight."

"You're quite correct," Beatrice Aimes agreed. "We can only hope he doesn't harm the girls or worse, yet I'm afraid that's merely wishful thinking. Do you suppose perhaps he's set up a heron somewhere, you know, with carpets and plush pillows and gilt mirrors . . ."

"That's *harem*, dear."

"Oh, yes, harem. Do you?"

"Good evening, everyone." Tess stepped into the booth, putting an abrupt end to the speculation.

Helena waved her to the empty seat beside her. The gentlemen stood, and Helena's husband, Wesley Holbrook, held her chair for her. Along the table, platters of parchment-thin ham, roasted hens, biscuits, cheese and bowls of fruit lay in disarray, picked over and more than half consumed. Tess turned her gaze from the sight; her appetite lay in equal shambles.

"What kept you so long?" Helena murmured. "I was about to send in the Bow Street Runners."

"I'll explain later."

"Good to have you back, Tess." Wesley Holbrook resumed his seat at his wife's other side. "You're needed here in London. Perhaps you'll succeed where the rest of us have failed in keeping my wife out of mischief."

"I'll certainly do my best, my lord, though we all know it's no easy task."

"Oh, pish." This came from Helena, her cheek protruding around another brandied cherry. "Ever since Wesley won his seat in the Commons, he feels he can order everyone about, including me. And you needn't call him 'my lord' anymore, dearest. He's your cousin now by marriage. I won't have my family members standing on ceremony."

After nodding his approval of the sentiment, Wesley slanted a disapproving eyebrow at his wife but spoke again to Tess. "Only last week she ran off to Southwark and nearly got herself killed."

"I beg your pardon, I did not go 'running off' to Southwark." Helena paused to dab her napkin at the corner of her mouth. "I was delivering food and blankets to an orphanage. And neither was I nearly killed. Three gentlemen merely asked if I might care to make a donation to their charitable establishment."

"Yes, and thankfully our coachman happened to have brought along a firearm that day." Wesley tweaked his wife's chin. "You *will* be more careful from now on."

"Of course I will, darling. I'll bring my own firearm next time." Helena reached for a quick kiss, bringing a broad smile to her husband's face. He leaned in for a second.

Tess's gaze darted away. The Holbrooks' open affection for one another had always been a source of amusement, but not tonight. Their display only served to remind her of what her life might have been . . . with Charles . . . if things had only been different.

"Good evening, Tess," Helena's father called from across the table. He flourished a broad hand in the air.

"Uncle Joshua, you're looking well." Indeed he was. For many years Sir Joshua Livingston's health had been a matter of great concern to his daughter, but events at their country home in Wakefield, followed by Helena's marriage to Wesley and the birth of their son, had rallied the old gentleman in ways that astonished them all.

The portly man was seated beside Miss Emily Canfield, a

self-proclaimed spinster and proud of the fact. The two of them were sharing a plate of petit fours.

Lady Beatrice turned to her. "As a matter of fact, Tess, we were discussing you just before you arrived."

"Not in the same breath as the Midnight Marauder, I hope."

"Heaven forbid." Beatrice tittered and shook her head, jiggling the blue-gray sausage curls hanging beneath her lace cap. "No, my dear, we're all so pleased to have you back in London. The Friends of the Bard Society has not been at all the same without you."

"Speaking of which," Helena said, "we're having our first meeting of the Season next Friday at two o'clock, my house. Do say you'll come. We've decided to begin with the sonnets rather than a play."

"Of course I'll be there." Tess cast a fond glance at the faces around the table. "A good choice, the sonnets. I've always loved them so."

She regretted the words as soon as they left her lips. On summer evenings long ago, she and Charles often sat side by side in the garden, reading the sonnets out loud. *Thy sweet love remember'd such wealth brings*. . . Ah, Charles . . . How sweet her life had once been. How utterly it had changed. Another line from the same sonnet made her throat go tight and stinging. *I all alone beweep my outcast state*. . . .

Unaware of her dismal musings, Helena beamed at her. "Oh, it *is* splendid to have you back."

Her forced smile felt as cold as a stone, but then warmed with an ember of hope. She was not completely alone, after all. She did have her cousin.

After supper, the ladies and their escorts filed from the box and set out for the Prince's Gallery, where a crowd was gathering for the evening's performance. Tess knew better than to entertain fruitless thoughts but there it was: would Charles attend the concert? If so, would he be alone, or . . . had he come to Vauxhall to meet someone?

"Tess, are you listening?" Helena's hand closed around hers.

"Yes, and I'm looking forward to the performance."

"No, goose, look there." She pointed her fan over the sea of heads. "Isn't that your Uncle Howard?"

"Oh dear, is it?" Tess barely had time to spot the tall, reedy figure of her uncle, Howard James, before the tide of concert-goers delivered him to her side.

"Tessa, my dear, an unexpected pleasure. I hadn't received word that you'd returned to London."

She gave a little shrug, quite aware she'd sent no such word to him.

"And good evening to you, Lady Wesley." Howard tipped a bow. "Are you both enjoying the festivities?"

"Indeed we are, thank you," Helena replied. "In fact, we were just about to take our seats. See you afterward?"

He ignored the hint, clearing his throat loud enough to be heard above the clamor. "I'd like a word with you, Tessa, if you please."

"Oh, but Uncle . . ." She gestured toward the stage. "The entertainment is about to begin."

"It's important." His lips thinned to a condescending smirk. "The singer is an unknown. You'll miss nothing."

"That's not true," Helena protested, but Tess hushed her.

"As you wish, Uncle Howard." To her cousin she said, "I'll join you later. Give my apologies to the others."

If the radiant Helena Holbrook were capable of producing an expression one could call tetchy, she did so now in Howard's direction before starting up the aisle.

Tess followed her uncle out to the now quiet Grove. He preceded her up the steps of a gazebo, its latticework sides enclosed by clinging ivy. After gesturing for her to sit on the circular bench inside, he leaned against the center pillar, staring down his nose at her.

"You know, my dear, you should really thank me. I not only saved you from an unremarkable performance, but rescued you from those irksome creatures you spend so much of your time with. Your cousin Helena aside, they are hardly fit company for a woman of your background."

"They are my friends, Uncle," she replied, managing not to grit her teeth but only just. "What is it you wish to speak to me about?"

He studied his fingernails. "You know I always have your best interests at heart."

A cloud of foreboding gathered around her. "What interests might those be, Uncle Howard?"

"It seems I've been quite neglecting my responsibilities toward you. You've been widowed for over a year now, but since you've been rather reclusive in that time, I don't suppose your whim has resulted in any great harm."

"My whim?" Her stomach knotted.

"Yes, that of managing your finances without a man's guidance."

"I am not a child, Uncle Howard."

"No, but you are still a woman." His gaze traveled her length.

The knots in her stomach gave a twist. She shrank beneath Howard's scrutiny until she remembered the importance of showing a valiant front. "What has that to do with anything?"

"A woman of your rank and fortune must not be left to her own devices indefinitely. As stated in the terms of your father's will, God rest him, I am trustee of your inheritance unless you are married."

"And I have been married, so you need no longer concern yourself with my affairs."

"Ah, but my dear, my solicitor has recently informed me that we have misinterpreted the will." His triumphant gleam wrapped Tess in a sense of doom. "Your father didn't appoint me trustee of your inheritance *until* you are married, but *unless* you are married, or reach the age of thirty."

She gained her feet in an instant. "You have no right. When Father wrote his will, he had no inkling of how you'd misuse your authority."

Howard flinched but held his ground. "It isn't so much a

matter of right as responsibility. I owe it to my poor deceased brother to ensure the well-being of his daughter."

"The way you ensured Alicia's well-being?" Anger coursed through her until her limbs trembled.

"Alicia made her own bed and then chose to lie in it."

"You mean die in it. And it was *not* her choice. You literally shoved her out the door."

"That was only after she ruined herself by taking up with a man and then refusing to divulge his identity. Anonymous love letters, midnight trysts. . . . She behaved despicably."

A crimson haze obscured Tess's vision. She shut her eyes and willed a steadying breath into her lungs. "It was your refusal to allow either of us to marry before we came of age, not to mention all your lies that drove away potential suitors, that compelled her to do as she did."

"That is enough." Howard's sallow complexion darkened to a ruddy scowl. "I cannot be blamed for Alicia's disgrace. But I would be remiss if I neglected my duty toward you now."

"How dare you speak of duty. My inheritance had dwindled to barely more than half its size by the time I married Walter."

"Tessa . . ." Her name ended on a warning note she ignored.

"I suppose we are only having this discussion because Alicia's money is all gone and now you need mine."

"How dare you speak to me that way." His hand flexed and Tess's throat closed. Uncle Howard had never struck her before, but neither had she ever uttered such charges aloud. She considered darting beyond his reach and escaping down the gazebo steps, but knowing she'd spoken the truth lent her the courage to face him.

His eyes smoldered for an instant more, then cooled. His hand relaxed. "You always were a spoiled child, Tessa."

"You'll soon find, Uncle, that you are not dealing with a child." Though relieved his temper had calmed, her voice shook. She swallowed, attempting to collect her composure. Any further show of emotion would only reinforce his claim that she was an irrational female incapable of seeing to her own affairs.

She needed her money, every last penny. Her father's will named Howard James trustee of her inheritance until she reached the age of thirty. That was a year away. Her mind reeled at the amount of damage he could wreak on her finances in that time.

Perhaps she should appeal to Wesley Holbrook for help. After all, a member of the House of Commons should wield enough influence to sway her case in her favor. But that would mean legal proceedings . . . questions . . . unwanted attention. If her private affairs suddenly became public, not only would her own designs be thwarted, but Wesley's political aspirations as well.

Then what should she do—what? So many people depended on her and here she was, about to let them down.

Unless . . .

"Silly me." She laughed as if at a secret jest. "Why am I arguing with you this way? To be frank, Uncle, the entire discussion is rather a moot point. I am not living without male protection. My affairs are quite well looked after by . . ."

"Yes? By whom?"

"Ah . . ." *Make up a name, any name.* She could devise a story tomorrow, perhaps even hire an actor willing to play the part until she found a more permanent solution.

And then she saw him, strolling from the Chinese Pavilion toward the Prince's Gallery. He was alone and seemed in no particular hurry. Heart in her throat, Tess gathered her skirts and scurried down the gazebo steps, ignoring her sore ankle.

"Here he is now. Charles!" She raised her arm and waved frantically. "Over here, darling."

Charles Emerson lurched to a halt. The lamplight above him illuminated the incredulity creeping across his features. He glanced over one shoulder and then the other. He turned full around, searching behind him. Facing Tess again, he touched a finger to his chest and frowned.

"Yes, dearest. Do come and greet my Uncle Howard."

And please wipe that suspicious look off your face. The crease between his brows only deepened. Seeing her scheme about to fall apart, she swept down the walkway and slipped her arm through his.

"If you ever cared about me the teensiest bit," she hissed, "you'll play along. Please." Louder she said, "Darling, have you been looking for me long?"

He eyed her askance. "What are you about, Tess?"

"No time to explain. Just come with me and for heaven's sake, smile."

As she led him to the gazebo, she became all too aware of his presence beside her, his closeness, solid and warm where their arms linked, their thighs brushed. For an instant she felt hurtled back to that happier, gentler time when she belonged at his side, before circumstances had destroyed their dreams.

"Here he is, Uncle Howard," she announced brightly. Perhaps too brightly, for her uncle's eyes narrowed. "Surely you remember Charles Emerson."

The older man moved to the top of the steps, his lined features sharp with cynicism. "What the devil is going on? Surely, Mr. Emerson, you don't expect me to believe you'd return to Tessa after the way we dismissed you the first time?"

"Now see here, Mr. James." Charles's voice emerged as a growl. Tess dug her fingers into his arm. When his face swiveled in her direction she pleaded with her eyes for silence. Then she smiled up at her uncle.

"You needn't be so formal—Mr. James and Mr. Emerson." Her brittle laugh skittered across the empty Grove. "We're one big happy family now. Uncle Howard, Charles is my husband."

Chapter 2

That single word struck Charles like a jab to the windpipe.

Husband? Had the world gone mad? Surely the woman gripping his arm as though her life depended on it couldn't be the same Tess Hardington who had dashed off to escape him less than an hour ago, who had made it clear she had little interest in ever laying eyes on him again.

And suddenly they were married?

He might have laughed, had he discovered anything amusing in this bizarre development. Instead, he nearly choked on the irony. Ten years ago, he'd begged Tess to be his wife. He'd been so sure of her love, so positive she'd overcome her fears and take firm hold of the hand he offered.

But perhaps fear hadn't, after all, been the force that drove them apart. Perhaps Tess simply hadn't been the woman he'd believed her to be; perhaps she had secretly agreed with her uncle that he'd never be rich enough, noble enough or good enough to be her husband. In the end, the reasons hadn't mattered. She'd rejected his suit. Rejected *him*.

His response had been so instinctive he couldn't remember giving it the slightest thought before abandoning his studies at Cambridge. Within the week he'd donned his country's uniform and boarded a ship bound for England's most distant colonies, all in the effort to forget the lovely young Tess who would never be his.

Or would she?

"Your husband?" The shrillness of Howard James's voice yanked Charles firmly back to the moment. "Since when?"

Charles studied the man who had changed the course of his life with a word: *no*. Beyond doubt Howard James still held money and position above all else—above honor, loyalty, and most importantly love, all of which would have been Tess's in rich abundance had her uncle—and she—but consented to their marriage.

"Confound it, one of you had better start talking." A thread of fury rippled through Howard's words. Charles had indeed been about to answer the question—with a succinct and emphatic denial. But as an ominous vein throbbed in the elder man's temple, Charles's protests died unspoken. There was more here than a simple family dispute. Far more.

Whisking his cloak about his lanky form, Howard James descended the gazebo's wooden steps, raising a conspicuous thunk-thunking in the quiet. "Well?"

"It hasn't been quite a week," Tess said with a light note of laughter, as if the announcement had been received happily all around. Her hand trembled against Charles's coat sleeve. She turned her face to him. Her nose was pinched, her eyes fever bright. "Has it, darling?"

This was as close to panic as he'd ever seen her. His pulse quickened with an old reflex: she needed him. His blood surged, readying his body to do battle if necessary.

Ah, but then logic spoke, reminding him it was no longer his place to champion Tess James, nor his right.

The ruffled hem of her gown inched over his right shoe. Her heel followed, pinning his smallest toe to the leather beneath. "*Has* it, dearest?"

Good God. Why not deny it all and end the farce now? Yet he wavered, gazing into a face every bit as compelling, as befuddling as he remembered. The truth struck him a violent a blow: ten years of trying to forget her had amounted to ten years of failing miserably.

He opened his mouth and plunged headfirst into a current certain to drown him. "Indeed, my love, barely a week."

Her foot moved away. "Charles and I renewed our acquaintance through correspondence well over a year ago, Uncle. He initially wrote to convey his sympathies over Walter's passing, and things progressed from there."

A muscle in Howard's cheek contracted. "Assuming any of this is true, exactly where did this wedding take place?"

"In Surrey, of course, at Highgate Court. Such a charming setting for an elopement. It was just the vicar, his wife, and a couple of servants as witnesses."

Charles remembered hearing of Highgate Court, the country estate Tess and Alicia had inherited from their maternal grandmother. He, however, had never once set foot there.

"We've told no one as yet," Tess surged on, "not even Charles's family. I suppose we're waiting for the right moment to make our announcement."

As she warmed to the task of providing details, Charles watched her, amazed at how readily the lies came, equally astonished at how the movement of her lips could still captivate him.

An insidious thought crept into his mind. Perhaps she had lied to him in the past, and he none the wiser. The unsettling notion left him pondering the validity of memories that had chased him throughout a decade.

"As your guardian, Tessa, I must express my disapproval of this hasty union." Spittle gathered at the corners of Howard James's lips. He compressed them to a thin, hard line.

"Yes, but the trusteeship aside, Uncle, you are not my guardian." Releasing Charles, Tess clutched fistfuls of skirt and swept forward, a fierce if elegant arsenal of dark curls and silk-clad curves. "That was *not* part of my father's will. At twenty-nine I am free to do as I please. I'm afraid your disapproval won't undo the vicar's handiwork. Now, if it isn't too late, I'd very much like to hear that soprano I've been told so much about. If you'll excuse us, Uncle. Charles?"

Every ounce of logic urged him to make his excuses and seek the nearest exit. Her dilemma, whatever it was, shouldn't matter, not to him. But of all people, he understood Howard James's talent for reducing a person's life to shambles. If Charles abandoned Tess now, what would she do? More to the point, what might Howard James do to her?

Ignoring his better sense, listening instead to the foolish gallant that should have learned his lesson ten years ago, he offered the crook of his arm. "Mr. James, we look forward to seeing you again soon."

"One moment." Howard surprised Charles by smiling, albeit without a trace of warmth. "When you do, be sure to have the marriage license on hand."

Charles nearly stumbled over a loose cobblestone. Tess, on the other hand, didn't miss a beat. "Why, of course, Uncle Howard."

He felt Howard James's ire blistering his back as they started away. At the entry to the Prince's Gallery, he steered Tess past with a resolute tug on her arm.

"But the concert . . ."

"Will proceed without you, madam."

"Where are we going? Don't pull me like that."

"I'll pull you any way I wish. I am your husband, after all." But he eased his hold, replacing his grip on her wrist with an arm about her waist. "Come along, *darling*. You have a mountain of explaining to do and I can't wait to see what you come up with."

"Come up with?"

He hurried her toward the Bridge Street turnstile. She started to protest but he cut her off. "Not a peep from you till I say so. I let you have your say back there and look where it got me. For pity's sake, woman, not another word."

On elegant Aldford Street in Mayfair, Tess's three-story townhouse loomed before Charles like a closely guarded fortress. Guarded, because Tess's servant stood on the foot pavement with arms folded and legs akimbo, blocking the steps to the front door.

Charles supposed he might have brushed past the compact figure easily enough, but something in the young man's dark features—a cool confidence that hinted at hidden, and possibly dangerous, abilities—held him in check. It felt akin to being greeted by a growling dog and not knowing if the beast would snap or slink away.

"It is late," the manservant drawled, stretching each syllable in a manner distinctly French yet tinged with other, more exotic influences. "Madame needs her rest."

"Mrs. Hardington invited me," Charles replied, bewildered at this show of insolence and wondering why he need explain himself to a footman.

"Madame does not always know what is best for her." Perspiration on the servant's forehead caught the moonlight with a stubborn gleam. A silver earring in his left lobe winked within inky black hair tied in a queue at his nape.

Charles studied the resolute features. The upsweep of the eyes and sleek black hair were undoubtedly Indian. The wide lips and chocolate skin spoke of Africa. The aquiline nose implied European ancestry as well. Such a blending of traits, he guessed, could only have originated in a place like America. So how the devil had this person found his way into Tess's service?

"Good gracious, Fabrice." She crossed the foot pavement and started up the steps, her skirts swishing in time to the sway of her hips. "Do leave Mr. Emerson alone and open the door. It is late, I am tired and I'd like to slip inside without waking the entire neighborhood."

The servant grumbled something unintelligible but undoubtedly flippant. He sauntered up the stairs to do his mistress's bidding. As he stood aside to allow entry into the foyer, his unnerving gold eyes followed Charles's every move.

"I'll bring the carriage around back," he said, "then make Madame tea."

Tess tossed her wrap onto the hall table. "I don't want any."

"You'll drink anyway."

"Yes, all right." She let out a huff. "We'll be upstairs in my sitting room."

"Madame should entertain the gentleman in the downstairs parlor."

She plunked her hands on her hips like an obstinate child. "One of these days I'm going to scribble Australia across your forehead and deliver you to the nearest transport hulk. My sitting room is warmer and that is where we'll be."

Her footman harrumphed, and Charles's temper surged along with his incredulity. Then, like a shifting shadow, the rascal named Fabrice slipped out the door.

"Sorry about that." Tess gripped the banister and started up.

"He's an impertinent fellow. How do you tolerate him?"

"Do forgive him. He's quite devoted to me and tends to take his responsibilities rather too seriously." Her expression turned pensive. "He makes ferocious noises but is really quite harmless, I think."

"You think?"

"It's never been put to the test. Well, once . . . but for good reason." She flicked her hand in a dismissive gesture. "Anyway, he's been with me since . . . well, for several years now and I can't imagine getting on without him."

"Is that so?" He caught up with her on the stairs. "Then perhaps you should have made him your husband tonight, rather than me."

In the flickering glow of a wall sconce, Charles watched rich color blossom on her cheeks; it made her look younger, vulnerable. Again the old impulse to take care of her reared up. He held his arms stiff at his sides to prevent them reaching for her and offering reassurances she'd yet to earn.

"I suppose it's time I explained," she said.

"Indeed, madam." He cleared the huskiness from his throat and continued in a firmer voice, "Don't leave anything out."

She nodded. "Come this way."

At the top of the stairs she led him across a narrow gallery and through an open doorway. The street lamps beyond the windows illuminated a good portion of the room, catching the sheen of blue damask furnishings, the gilded frame of a wall mirror, the more than occasional glint of crystal and porcelain. The well-appointed room reiterated the tale of wealth told by the house's Mayfair address.

"Impressive." He tried but did not quite succeed in quelling a troubling thought: he could not have provided her with such things had she married him, at least not then.

"Thank you, I'm quite comfortable here." She turned up the gas on a wall lamp and lit the wick. Soft highlights sprang to life in her hair.

An unbidden image flashed in his mind of her dark glorious tresses tumbling in the wind as he tipped her chin for a kiss. He had once determined her hair to be the color of aged mahogany caressed by candlelight. And her eyes . . . her eyes were the fathomless sapphire of the twilight sky on a crisp winter's eve.

He stifled a groan. What a lovesick sot he'd been. But that was long ago; he had no business dwelling on any of it now.

Nor had he any business dwelling in Tess Hardington's private sitting room. Through a pair of open double doors, he spied the enticing corner of a canopied bed, draped in ivory satin and wispy lace. As ethereal and diaphanous as the silk evening gown that hugged Tess in certain places and skimmed her in others.

His chest tightened, as did a part of him somewhat lower. He turned and focused on the empty hearth. A deep breath helped clear his head.

"I'm glad to see Walter Hardington left you with the means to be comfortable," he said, meaning it. Never once during his years away had he wished misfortune on her.

Oddly enough, she bristled. "Walter saw to my needs. For

that I am grateful." She plunked her reticule on a tufted ottoman and eased into the matching wing chair.

The anxiety he'd glimpsed earlier at Vauxhall flickered again in those brisk blue eyes. As he stood watching her, she huddled between the wings of the chair as if seeking protection.

From what? Her uncle, yes, but why? He swung his cloak from his shoulders and draped it beside her purse. He'd stay long enough to discover what demon could drive a woman to such desperate lengths, and then he'd leave.

He settled at the edge of the settee opposite her, leaning forward until he might have reached out and cupped the shapely knee beckoning from beneath her skirts. "Perhaps you'd be good enough to explain how the devil you and I progressed from near strangers to man and wife in less than an hour."

That raised a frown, followed by a hasty effort to smooth it. "You must think me mad."

He said nothing. She heaved a sigh, providing him an opportunity to savor the rise and fall of her décolletage. Her breasts were fuller now than years ago. He'd had only the faintest knowledge of them then, stolen caresses through layers of linen and silk. Still, the memory singed his palms.

"It's a long story," she said, "one that began years ago."

He stopped her with a wry chuckle.

She blinked. "What?"

"Do make it a true story, madam."

"Are you calling me a liar, sir?"

"And a clever one at that."

Her expression turned grave. "The culprit of this story is my Uncle Howard."

"I'd never have guessed."

"If you wish to know the truth, please hold your sarcasm till the end."

He settled back and gestured for her to continue.

Her hands plucked and smoothed her skirts, worried the arms of her chair, hovered in her lap. As he watched her fidget, he struggled to subdue his impatience, his frustration, and the temptation to lose himself in the vast, winter sky depths of her eyes.

Pay attention, old boy, you're about to find out how the blazes you became a married man tonight.

"He's after my money," she said quietly, "as much of it as he can lay his greedy hands on. That's always been his game, even when Alicia and I were young. While my parents were alive he very cleverly played the part of 'dear old Uncle Howard,' with gifts and charming compliments at the ready. Even after Mother and Father died and he became our guardian, he seemed so kind, so caring."

Her face drew tight. "An act, all of it, meant to distract us from the truth while he squandered our inheritances. He'd already depleted his own."

"The man's a rogue, undeniably." Charles crossed one leg over the other in a display of patience he felt not in the least. "But what part does your inheritance play in tonight's fiasco?"

"Don't you see? Father's will names him trustee of my inheritance unless I'm married. Now that Walter is gone, Howard plans to retake control of my finances. He told me so tonight. I can only suppose he's spent all of Alicia's money in gambling and extravagant living."

"But didn't your sister's inheritance revert to you when she passed away?"

Her chin quivered as she shook her head. She turned a grim countenance toward the cold hearth. Obviously her knack for pretense did not extend to her grief over Alicia's death. But then, for the second time that evening he, too, experienced a painful stab for the lively young sister that might—in a kinder world—have been his.

Sitting taller in her chair, looking firmer of countenance, she turned back to him. "Part of that is my own fault, I admit. Much of Alicia's inheritance had already been spent by the time she passed away, mind you. And then I . . . I only wanted Uncle Howard out of my life. I didn't fight him for the money. I married Walter soon afterward and . . . well, I believed I'd be safe from Howard's greed from then on."

Charles hesitated over his next question, not wishing to upset her further. Her sorrow over her sister and her desperation over Howard's threats seemed genuine enough, but he'd stake his life she was holding back, offering up only as much, or as little, information as she believed he'd accept.

"What of Walter's fortune?" he asked.

She held his gaze, unblinking. "The bulk of it went to his son by his first wife. I have the use of this house and a modest annuity. And Highgate Court, of course, but the place barely produces enough income to support itself."

"And so you find yourself backed into a corner." And he with her. The absurdity of the notion propelled him to his feet. He made a round of the room, running his palm over the smooth surface of a freestanding globe, the spines of several gilt-edged books. "Surely, Tess, you don't believe this ruse you pulled tonight can solve your predicament."

"Why can't it? The will stipulates that once I'm thirty my inheritance is mine, free and clear whether I'm married or not."

"If I remember correctly, your thirtieth birthday is at least a year away. You can't mean to sustain this charade for that long." He began pacing in front of the fireplace, his exasperation rising. "And why, for heaven's sake, did you tell such a whopping lie? Why not simply claim we were engaged? A more plausible fabrication, don't you think?"

"Plausible, perhaps," she replied with irritating calm, "but hardly adequate."

"Why in Lucifer's name not?"

"Because Howard can control my finances right up until the moment I say 'I do.' If I told him we were merely engaged, he'd be drawing funds Monday morning and off to a gambling hell by nightfall."

"Aren't you forgetting something?" Ah, yes, he had her now, and once she admitted the folly of her endeavor he'd be a free man. "The matter of the marriage license. Your uncle demanded to see it. He's certainly within his rights . . ."

A faint but infuriating smile curled her lips. "I can arrange it." Her gaze wandered past him as she considered, then eased back with a composure that set his anger pounding for release. "I'm certain there must be a way to protect what is mine. Until I find it, won't you please play along?"

"Play along?" He paused to unlock his throbbing jaw. "Marriage is no game, Tess. Have you considered the damage to your reputation when your friends and neighbors come to believe our so-called marriage has failed?"

"Why should I care what people think?" She dismissed the notion with a shrug that made him want to grasp those delicate shoulders and shake sense into her. "And anyway, our little charade is for Uncle Howard's benefit alone. No one else need ever hear of it."

"You think not?" He circled back to the ottoman and reached for his cloak.

"Where are you going?"

"Home."

"But I need you."

"Need me?" Flinging the garment back down, he glared. Good God, did she think him made of stone? Or were his feelings of no consequence at all? "You have the gall to utter such a thing to me."

His patience snapping, he strode toward her. She cowered into a corner of the wing chair as he bent over her and gripped the armrests. He knew he was frightening her, knew he should play the gentleman and back away, but she'd blithely opened a wound that stung far too deeply to be denied some form of balm.

"What can you possibly expect of me, Tess? You tossed me out with the kitchen scraps ten years ago. What makes you dare contemplate making convenient use of me now? Did you honestly believe I'd jump at the chance to do your bidding?"

Leave it alone, his conscience murmured, *stop bullying the woman.* Yet it wasn't a need for revenge that pinned him there, but the ragged puffs of breath escaping her lips and grazing his cheek, subtle reminders of the intimacy they'd once shared. A dark, curling flame licked through him, unexpectedly, astoundingly.

Her lips were so close he felt their warmth, all but tasted their sweetness. She met his gaze, eyes wide and brimming with apprehension until their radiant blue all but encompassed him, made him dizzy. He might have been a wounded gull, spiraling out of control between sky and sea, plunging to a sodden death and glad for it.

He shoved away, shaken to the core. How could she still have the power to affect him that way? How could he let her? Certainly after all these years he should no longer feel these appalling tugs at his heart. Damn it. Damn it to hell.

Damn her.

He dragged air into his lungs. "I am not the besotted youth I was. I won't play this mad game with you."

"But—"

"Enough." He grabbed up his cloak and flung it over his shoulder. Without another word he strode to the door.

"If you leave now," her desolate voice scrambled after him, "I stand to lose everything."

Chapter 3

She didn't think her feeble plea would bring him back. It had slipped from her lips, the first completely honest thing she'd uttered thus far. Admittedly too little, too late.

Yet there he stood, his formidable figure filling the doorway. An equally formidable emotion turned his eyes to steel—glacial, implacable—and brought Tess trembling to her feet.

A misgiving shimmied through her. After ten years she barely knew Charles Emerson. What had possessed her to seek his help, to involve him in ways that could prove her undoing?

Just as she might have wished him away, he stepped back into the room, into her life. He would want answers now. Explanations. The hair on her nape rose. Once she weeded out her many secrets, there would be precious little she could tell him.

He stared her down until her chin sagged and her shoulders shrank. She would have preferred shouting, ranting, anything to this unnerving silence with its sizzling undercurrent of fury.

"Please, Charles." Please what? *Do this for me simply because I ask it?* That would have been sufficient once.

She looked him full in the face, searching for the young man she had known, the beau who had pledged to clear the sky of clouds and rearrange the stars to her liking. The rapid rise and fall of his chest rumpled his starched shirtfront. Otherwise he stood pillar-still, his demands for truth unspoken but inescapable.

"There are people who depend on me," she said weakly, inadequately, but wishing beyond all hope that it would suffice. "Servants, my tenants at Highgate Court . . ."

And little Blair, Alicia's beautiful but illegitimate daughter, tucked safely away at her country estate. There the child would remain under the watchful eyes of Mrs. Rutherford and Reverend Coombs until enough time had passed that people no longer remembered Alicia's disgrace. Only then might Tess introduce the girl into society as her ward, perhaps as a distant cousin.

But she dared not reveal Blair's existence to Charles, for then she'd have to explain about Alicia—her affair and all the ugliness that followed. That would lead to further disclosures about Tess's present life, to the endangerment of everything she'd worked so hard to establish over the years.

Secrecy had always been the key to her success. She must not lose sight of that.

"If you won't help," she whispered in sheer desperation, "I'll lose everything." *Everything in life that means anything to me*, she added on a silent prayer.

"And you seem to have so very much to lose," he replied with a pointed gaze around the room.

Good heavens, did he think her no better than Uncle Howard? Had the love they'd once shared amounted to nothing more than bitterness? Exhausted from the night's pressures, she sank into the wing chair, quite at the mercy of a man who had no good reason to show her any at all. "Will you help me or not?"

She counted it a small miracle that he returned to the settee and flung his heavy cloak over its carved back. "You ask quite a lot of me, Tess, and offer so little in return."

He held up a hand when she started to speak. "Not that I want anything from you other than the truth. You're not being at all honest with me. Not about tonight and not about the past. I can feel it in my bones, Tess."

Was she that transparent? Had her skills of deception slipped, or had she finally met her match in Charles Emerson?

She tried to smooth her features into a semblance of genuine honesty, not the feigned kind she'd become so adept at producing over the years. "There is something else I can tell you, something that concerns my uncle and our past, though you may not wish to hear it."

"Trust me, my dear, I'm interested in everything you have to say tonight."

"Very well, then." She clutched her hands in her lap, squeezing till they ached. "When Uncle Howard refused to allow our marriage years ago, he said hurtful things about your family—"

"I remember well," he interrupted. "You needn't repeat them."

"I wasn't about to. There would be no need, for you see, those were merely excuses. Uncle Howard wouldn't have cared a fig if you were a beggar or a duke. It was all about my inheritance, about his maintaining control over my finances, which he would have lost had I married. So you see, Charles, he used and manipulated us both to his own purposes."

He took in this information with a nod.

"Have you nothing to say?"

"What did you think I'd say? That it made a difference?"

"Doesn't it? His greed interfered with both our lives. He—"

"No, Tess, his greed didn't, not in the end. I admit this is a bit of a revelation after ten years of believing my family's social position had come between us, but I'd given you a choice. You dismissed it."

"I was barely more than a child. I was not of age." She gripped the arms of the chair until her knuckles whitened against the satinwood frame. "Running away with you meant forsaking my family and friends. I couldn't abandon Alicia. She was so young, she needed me. We had no parents, only each other." A burning in her throat rose to prick the backs of her eyes, threatening her last shreds of dignity. "Why won't you understand?"

"Understand?" He chuckled, a harsh and derisive sound.

With a sudden heave, he pushed away from the sofa and came toward her as he had minutes earlier. But infinitely more alarming, this time he crouched at her feet and seized her hands.

"Have you the faintest understanding of the consequences of your decision ten years ago, Mrs. Hardington?" He placed mocking emphasis on her name. But it was the heated urgency of his large hands over hers that spread an indignant confusion through her—indignant because he had no right to hold her in that manner; confusion because, Lord help her, his touch released a multitude of sensations, all of them sensual, none of them proper.

"I don't mean those that only involved you," she heard him press on over the roaring in her ears, "but that might have affected say, me, for instance."

She snatched her fingers from his grasp. "I see you feel the need to mock me. Tell me it's the price I must pay for your help and you may taunt me all you like."

"Who dares taunt Madame?" To the accompaniment of jangling silverware and rattling teacups, Fabrice shouldered his way into the room carrying a tray of refreshments. He aimed a blistering glare at Charles.

"It's all right, Fabrice," Tess hastened to say, at the same time silently thanking him for the interruption. Her heartbeat thumped to its natural pace. "Mr. Emerson and I are having a discussion."

"Is the room so small Monsieur must sit upon Madame's lap to have a discussion?"

Charles pushed to his feet. "All right, I'll retreat to my corner and await the bell for the next round."

Fabrice set the tray on the cart beside the hearth. "Would Madame like me to escort Monsieur to the door?"

"No. Just wheel the cart here and leave us, please." She noted his look of disapproval, his hesitation. "I am perfectly fine."

Seeming disinclined to believe her, he crossed the room and lit the lantern on the writing table, adding its flare to the glow of the wall lamp. The hissing flame gilded Fabrice's bronze features, accenting the defiant jut of his lip, the rigid plane of his brow.

Tess couldn't help smiling at her servant and his uncanny intuitiveness. He sensed the discord between her and Charles and took no pains to conceal his hostility. She considered her earlier claim that he was harmless. In truth, she wasn't at all sure.

"Thank you, Fabrice. You may go now."

He cut a path to the door, pausing to hurl a final, unspoken warning at Charles. She made a mental note to speak to him about his manners.

"Quite a watch dog you've got there," Charles commented with a smirk.

"He's a pussy cat, really, though loyal to a fault. You needn't worry about him."

"No," Fabrice's voice swept in from the hall, "no worry so long as the gentleman remains a gentleman to Madame."

"Good night, Fabrice."

His footsteps receded.

"Where the devil did you find him?" Charles's mouth twisted. "Devil being the operative word."

"He found me," she said, meeting the challenge in his tone with a heft of her chin. Lifting the teapot, she poured steaming liquid into a cup so delicate the tea shimmered through the porcelain. "I had a frightening encounter with a footpad some years back. If not for Fabrice's intervention, I don't know what might have happened." She glanced up. "Tea?"

"No."

Ah, still angry, still unyielding. She spooned sugar into her cup, leaning to impede his view of her face. She'd omitted as much from Fabrice's story as she had from her own. Would Charles guess that Fabrice was more than a servant, so very much more? Her accomplice. Her friend. Her dark angel.

She lifted her cup but instead of drinking, worried her lip between her teeth while making a conscious effort to halt the thudding of her foot on the rug. She'd already played her one card, flimsy though it was, and the uncompromising look on

Charles's face had yet to ease. He recognized her for a liar and no mistake about it. What if he stood to leave? How would she stop him?

If her plan fell apart in the next few moments, the very next time she wrote a bank draft she would need Uncle Howard's signature beneath her own. And then what would happen to Blair? What would become of the others?

Charles watched Tess blow into the steam rising from her teacup, his gaze drawn to the moisture clinging to her lips when she sipped.

Ah, he'd once explored those lips so thoroughly he might have mapped their every curve, every sensuous dip and depression. Yet tonight, had all his senses not proclaimed otherwise, he'd swear this was not the Tess he'd known, the girl whose delectable lips were incapable of spouting such bitter deception.

Good God, why was he still sitting there?

If you don't help me, I'll lose everything. That much he believed. The words—and the desperation behind them—pierced his defenses and shot straight to the core of his honor and deeper, to the very heart of his guilt.

He was a thief and a scoundrel and could pretend no less. Yet his were crimes for which he'd never stand accused, never be condemned. On the contrary, he'd been commended more times than he could bear to remember. Ten years in the king's service—ten years of invading and occupying. Ten years of following orders and shutting his eyes to the consequences.

The truth had finally confronted him, not during the violence of an uprising but in the silent, brimming gaze of a mother leading her children from the only home they'd ever known. His command had cleared and then razed the aboriginal village in New South Wales, because the inhabitants had been in the way of the expanding penal colony. True, the order to remove them had originated with a superior officer, but that day it had been

Charles's hand that swept away a thousand years of tribal tradition.

It galled him that he or anyone else believed it justifiable to do such things. In India, the West Indies, Australia, he and his countrymen had laid claim to what simply wasn't theirs, using force when they met with resistance.

He'd resigned his commission and escaped with what little soul he had left. Or had he? Could he sit by now and watch Howard James treat Tess in similar kind? Wouldn't that heighten his sin of indifference beyond all redemption?

When he rose from the settee, panic flickered across her face. Her cup landed on its saucer with a clatter and a slosh of amber liquid. "Charles, please . . ."

He held up the flat of his hand. "Don't bother. Nothing you can say will persuade me. What I do, I do for reasons of my own."

Her face contorted with dismay, with the threat of tears. Part of him dreaded the possibility. Another, more cynical part felt half-inclined to let her go on that way. Serve her right for all the trouble she was about to cause him.

"You have your motives and your secrets, Tess. I have mine." Disregarding a thousand misgivings, he extended his hand. "Or shall I call you . . . Mrs. Emerson."

"You mean it?" She sprang from her seat. He thought she might throw her arms around him, even braced for it, but she stopped short an arm's length away. "Oh, Charles, really?"

"For as brief a time as possible," he admonished, trying to look and sound his sternest. But Tess's enthusiasm angled like a ray of sunlight through all his misgivings; he couldn't help feeling, well, glad he'd agreed to help her. She always could melt his resolve with one of her smiles. "I'll contact a solicitor first thing Monday and have him work out a solution. Meanwhile, we stay quietly out of society's way and attract as little attention as possible."

She grasped his hand in both of hers and pumped it. "You're a dear. A prince. I promise you won't regret this."

"Madam, I already do. This is certain to be the mistake of a lifetime. Now if you'll excuse me, I've had enough excitement for one evening. I'm going home."

"Oh, but you can't." Her grip tightened until his knuckles complained of the pressure.

"Indeed I can, if you'll unhand me."

"What if Uncle Howard should stop by unannounced? He might come early in the morning or late at night. If you're not here he'll grow even more suspicious than he already is. If we're to convince him we're married, he must believe we're living under the same roof."

As she apparently realized the implications of her words, a blush fanned across her cheeks, one Charles rather enjoyed. The notion of living as man and wife had its effect on him as well; a flood of heat coursed to the juncture of his male anatomy.

He lifted a hand, trailing his fingertips along the curve of her jaw. When his thumb brushed her lower lip, it trembled in response.

"As you wish, then, Mrs. Emerson," he murmured. He tipped her chin until she looked up into his eyes. "Shall we retire for the evening?"

Her mouth fell open with a little quiver. Her blush deepened, but Charles sensed it was no longer the flush of embarrassment but of memory—the recollection of stolen kisses and impassioned embraces. Memories too vivid to be forgotten or ignored. She might have been eighteen again—innocent, virginal—and he twenty-one and driven by a torturous knot of love and lust twisting inside him.

A sharp pain spiked his chest even as he remembered, in a foggy corner of his brain, that he didn't believe in this thing suddenly gripping his heart—didn't indulge in fairy tales where love could be lost and ultimately recovered.

If only she had pulled away or scowled or voiced even the slightest objection. She did none of those things, but met his gaze wide-eyed, mirroring the wonderment he felt that after so many years, the two of them should find themselves at such a crossroad.

It seemed only natural, lowering his lips to hers with a whisper of warmth, a gentle pressure of flesh against flesh. The result was anything but gentle as desire roared to life inside him, as Tess emitted a moan and her arms surged around his neck.

Mouths opening, their tongues met with a fierce need, a burning hunger. Hearing his name like a storm-ridden gust from her throat—*Charles, ah, Charles*—he seized her, hands seeking purchase in the folds of her gown, in the glossy ringlets of her painstaking coif. He knew he'd bring her meticulous eveningwear to ruin. He didn't care in the least.

How right her body felt in his arms; how thoroughly familiar. Fueled by her breathy noises of acquiescence, his erection came on with the blazing glory of the rising sun. He might have taken her right there in the middle of her sitting room before the gaping door, with the lamps bearing illuminating witness to his loss of control.

"Tess," he murmured, drunk with the fragrance of her hair, the warmth of her skin. "It's been so long and I've—"

A sound in the doorway stopped him short. "I have prepared a guestroom for Monsieur. Shall I show him the way?"

In disbelief Charles peered over his shoulder, at the same time attempting to block Tess from her servant's view. Christ, had the rogue been lurking in the hallway all this time?

She shoved out of his arms. "Y-yes, thank you, Fabrice." Fingers shaking, she pressed the backs of her knuckles to her mouth, a reddened and glistening testament to the past moments. "Charles, it's best you go with Fabrice."

She was embarrassed, of course. Seeking to reassure, he caught her chin on the ends of his fingers. "I'll go if you wish. It's late. We can continue our . . . discussion in the morning."

"No." Her barbed reply took him aback. She swung away, putting distance between them. "We've quite exhausted the subject, I'm afraid. I'm very sorry if I conveyed the wrong impression just now."

"What wrong impression?"

"I kissed you to . . . express my gratitude. I hope you didn't think it anything more."

"Gratitude?"

"Yes, of course. I'm very grateful for your help."

"Madam, I'm familiar with the sentiment and believe me, that wasn't it."

"Charles, I'm afraid you were acting on impulses some ten years old. I appealed to you for assistance, not seduction." She raised a decidedly haughty eyebrow and started toward her bedroom.

Charles stared after her feeling empty handed, cheated. Foolish.

Dismissed? For the second time that evening, the absurdity of the situation nearly made him laugh. He'd just consented to a sham marriage in order to commit inheritance fraud with a woman who had once thrown him out on his ear. Who apparently had just done it again. And who could not piece together three honest words, especially about that damned kiss.

Common sense urged that he not waste another scrap of energy on the inexplicable Tess Hardington. Only the past prevented him from striding out the door. Not *their* past but his own, events that transpired long after he and Tess had parted. During his years as an officer he'd been on the wrong side, had done the wrong thing and had known it to be so.

Perhaps coming to the aid of this querulous woman was both his just punishment and his chance for redemption. As he traipsed down the hall behind the irascible Fabrice, he had no trouble accepting the former notion. He entertained serious doubts, however, about the latter.

Tess waited an hour, perhaps more, until Charles must have fallen asleep. Then she pulled a hooded cape from her wardrobe, stole through her sitting room and tiptoed to the stairs.

As her foot touched the top step, her resolve faltered. Charles might awaken and discover her gone. He might hear the coach roll away and decide to follow.

What if he demanded explanations? Or claimed a husband's right to stop her? Had she forfeited a portion of her independence with this brash arrangement?

Oh, and why, why had he kissed her?

She pressed her fingertips to her lips and relived the fire of his kiss. Even now a smoldering weight melted over her lower regions, while her breasts ached to feel his solid form against them. All that from a simple kiss. She had forgotten it was possible.

But *why* had she complicated everything by kissing him back? Thank goodness Fabrice interrupted when he did. She should have been stronger. Should have remembered how much was at stake. Should have considered the misery that inevitably befell any woman who lost her head over a man.

Not her, by heaven. It would not happen to her.

Renewed determination surged. Swinging her cape over her shoulders, she hurried down the stairs, skipping lightly over the step that creaked.

She found Fabrice waiting below in the kitchen. Ah, he knew her so well.

Perched on a bench before the glowing remnants of the hearth fire, he drained the contents of a mug cradled in both hands. At her approach he turned his head but said nothing, awaiting her orders. So steady, so loyal. Her dark angel. A tiny lump pushed against her throat.

"Thank you for waiting up," she said.

He answered with a nod.

"Once more unto the breach, dear friend."

His lips pursed. His strange gold eyes held her in an aura of resigned forbearance, if not quite disapproval. A muscle worked in his cheek. She thought he was about to object, but instead he rose and crossed to the garden door. "I'll bring the carriage round," he said.

Chapter 4

Dreams of Tess taunted Charles throughout the night. In them he was younger, laughing, pushing her on the garden swing while studying the flirty ripple of hems against slender ankles. Each upward swoop gave torturous hints to the wonders concealed beneath her skirts—the swell of calves, the contour of knees, the sleekness of thighs.

With no more than fleeting guilt, he whisked his gaze from her legs only to become lost in the sheen and shadow of unbound hair tossed about delicate shoulders. Catch me, she suddenly cried, and he sprinted around to the front of the swing. With a yelp she pushed off the seat, laughing and trusting. He caught her against his chest, stumbling backward for balance and laughing at the ticklish vibration of her lips on his neck, his cheek, his. . . .

"Ouch!" Charles's hand went to his nose, fingering a tender spot to the right of the bridge. What the devil? He opened his eyes.

An unfamiliar ceiling blurred above him. As he blinked away the bleariness, his hand found the corner of a satin pillowcase beneath his head. Not his. Nor were the carved oak posts reaching toward the ceiling at either end of the headboard.

Something warm and fuzzy nuzzled his chin. Startled, Charles peered downward. Bright green eyes in a tufted gray face leered back. Whiskers twitched as a pink tongue darted to the corner of a feline mouth.

"Well, good morning, little fellow. Where did you come from?"

A paw lashed out—*swhack!*—striking Charles square on the nose. Again.

"Confound it, what was that for?"

With a screech the cat bounded to the floor and streaked through the partially open door.

"Good grief." Charles felt his nose for scratches. "Little demon," he called to the empty doorway. "Fabrice sent you, didn't he?"

But a cat that can open doors? The unsettling notion fit with the image of Fabrice appearing out of thin air when least expected—or needed. Then he spotted the mist rising from a pitcher on the wash stand in the corner. Fresh linens, a shaving cup and soap brush awaited him as well. The maid must have been in and left the door ajar.

On a table near the wide sweep of a double casement window, a silver coffeepot sent dollops of sunlight shimmering through the room. The aroma of freshly ground brew rose on thin wisps of steam.

He spied a dressing gown draped across the foot of the bed. Judging by the midnight-blue fabric and notched lapels, a man's dressing gown. He grabbed it and held it up.

What the devil was Tess doing with a man's dressing gown? The blasted thing couldn't belong to Fabrice or any other servant; the tailoring declared it too fine an item for anyone but a gentleman.

So who had the proper and oh-so-dignified Tess Hardington been entertaining lately that she kept his dressing gown on hand? He flung the robe onto the coverlet, and noticed the initials embroidered beside the left lapel: WH—for Walter Hardington.

That consoled him only slightly. Scowling, he traced the serpentine monogram with his forefinger. Walter Hardington had died well over a year ago, yet Tess maintained his possessions in the house they'd shared. When Charles had first heard the news of her wedding, he'd assumed it a marriage of convenience like most everyone else's. But perhaps not. If Tess couldn't bring herself to dispose of her husband's personal effects, she must have loved him deeply indeed.

His better sense said what of it, while a murmur from somewhere in the vicinity of his chest suggested an altogether different sentiment.

Flinging the bedclothes aside, he swung his feet to the floor. He shoved his arms into the dressing gown's cuffed sleeves and had only just secured the sash when a soft tapping sounded at his door. "Come in."

Tess poked her head into the room. "Ah, you're awake."

The sound of her voice brought the sensations from his dream flooding back. His body's reaction was immediate, involuntary and, coupled with the flow of blood a man typically experienced in the morning, obvious. Luckily for him, Walter Hardington had been a portlier man than he. His robe afforded enough folds of fabric to maintain a modicum of dignity.

Luckily, too, Tess appeared preoccupied, evidenced by the little ridge above her nose as she made a quick survey of the room. "I see Becca has been in. Do you have everything you need?"

"As long as Fabrice hasn't poisoned my coffee, I'm sure I'll be fine."

"Very funny." She turned a face smudged with fatigue in his direction.

"You look tired," he commented. "Didn't sleep well?" He suddenly remembered waking to the sound of carriage wheels sometime before dawn. "Was that your coach I heard last night? Off to some secret rendezvous, were you?"

"Certainly not." Her chin came up. "I'm sure I was asleep long before you."

Quite possibly. Frustration and mutinous desires had kept sleep at bay for hours. "I was only joking," he said. "You needn't get your dander up."

She stifled a yawn with little success. Perhaps she had lain awake regretting her denial of their kiss. He'd known enough women in his lifetime to recognize mutual desire when he encountered it, or so he had thought. She'd certainly fooled him—and made him feel like a scoundrel.

Well, he wouldn't make that mistake again.

She crossed the threshold and came to a sudden halt, eyes widening as they traveled his length. Her brows gathered in a display of perplexity he couldn't help but enjoy. This was, after all, the first time she'd ever seen him with more than his neck cloth and top button undone. A wash of color tinged her otherwise pale features. "I'll, er . . . come back when you're decent."

"Nonsense, madam, we're man and wife after all." He grinned when her nostrils flared in the delicate way he remembered. "No need for false propriety."

"We are not married, Charles Emerson, and you know it." Despite the protestation, she perused him from his head right down to his bare feet sticking out beneath the hem of the robe. If he wasn't mistaken, she paused just a second or two over his, well, lower middle section.

"Not married?" He sighed innocently, shifting the folds of Walter Hardington's robe to conceal his body's keen response to her scrutiny. "In that case, my dear, I'll grab my clothes and be on my way like a proper gentleman." He started to untie the sash but she stopped him with an outraged squawk.

"Don't you dare or I'll call Fabrice."

He dropped the ends of the belt and threw up his hands. "Truce. I'll behave. Join me while I break my fast?"

"I've eaten, thank you." But she ventured further into the room with small, hesitant steps. "I do need to speak with you, if I may."

"By all means, my dear. I believe in open and honest communication in a marriage. Makes for a more blissful life together." The green leather chair beside the window creaked as he settled into it. He adjusted the robe around him, not wishing to frighten Tess away before she revealed the cause of that anxious expression she seemed so determined to hide.

"Now then," he said, "what might I do for you, my darling?"

She folded her hands at her waist and took several more prim steps across the carpet. He couldn't help but admire the snug fit of her morning gown, a salmon-hued affair that brought out the dark luster of her hair. Her neckline dipped, while a lace inset allowed a veiled but enticing view of the valley between her breasts. Charles tilted his head to enjoy the sight. "Well?"

"For one thing, you might stop calling me 'my dear' and 'my darling.'"

"I'm sorry. You never minded before."

"Yes, but then it was without mockery."

"I wouldn't dream of mocking you, Tess." He grinned. "And I merely wish to fulfill my role as husband. You do want me to be convincing, don't you?"

"Not when we are alone."

"As you wish, madam." He affected a wounded expression. "Have a seat."

She chose the armchair opposite, draping her skirts just so around her legs. Stalling, he concluded.

"How's the ankle?" his inner rascal asked, hoping to arouse a response.

He was not disappointed. Looking startled, she tugged her hems lower over the tops of her shoes. "Fine. All better, in fact."

Did she think he might make another grab for her? Not an altogether disagreeable idea. He'd rather enjoyed the weight of that curvaceous leg across his lap last night, its warm, silk-clad contour filling his palms.

Of course, he'd started out with the best of intentions. Her ankle might have been sprained or worse. But the mere act of touching her had triggered powerful memories, memories that made him yearn for the old trust, the old familiarity. He'd detected neither. Tess had only wanted to pull away, reclaim her dignity and rush back to the friends who occupied her present life.

He sighed in an attempt to dispel the memories, the yearnings, the disappointments. "So then, what did you want to speak to me about?"

She fussed a bit more with her gown, brushed lint from her sleeve, made a little noise through her lips. "We have a teensy problem," she said at length.

"You don't say." He gestured toward the coffeepot, growing amused when she hefted the pot by its carved handle and filled his cup. A wifely duty to be sure, but he had only meant to offer her refreshment while he rang for a second cup and saucer. She lifted the sugar bowl and questioned him with a glance. "None, thank you. A spot of cream, if you would. How teensy?"

"Oh, teensy weensy." She trickled cream into his coffee, stirred it round and handed it to him.

"Thank you. Do elaborate."

Her hand disappeared into a satin pouch pinned at her waist. "This arrived earlier." Between two not-quite-steady fingers she offered a folded sheet of parchment. Charles took it and read:

> *Tess dearest,*
>
> *The cat is out of the bag, you sly thing. How could you have been so naughty as to keep such a secret from me? Did you think I'd disapprove? Dearest, I desire only your happiness and am quite willing to forgive you, provided you and the mysterious Captain Emerson join us for supper tonight. Just an intimate gathering. Do say you'll come.*
>
> > *Fondly,*
> > *Helena*

"A teensy problem?" The blood tapped at his temples. "This is exactly what I insisted we avoid."

"I know, but we have to go." Her hands came up, open and empty. "What will they think otherwise? Oh, but don't worry. It'll only be the Holbrooks and a few friends."

"Define what she means by 'intimate.'"

"The members of the Friends of the Bard Society. And their spouses, of course."

He groaned.

"Perhaps I could send our excuses. It's still early, and if Helena hasn't gone to any trouble yet . . ."

"To what end? They've all apparently heard the happy news." He set his coffee cup down with a clank. "There's nothing for it but to come clean."

"No!" The whites of her eyes gleamed. "I never thought Uncle Howard would blabber like this. Ordinarily he keeps to himself and his gentlemen friends. When I married Walter he went sulking off to the Continent for nearly a year. I assumed he would do the same this time, leaving me free to work on a solution to this problem with the will."

"Obviously, madam, Howard is proving quite capable of making this charade as complicated as possible. I don't know what possessed me to . . ."

"Charles Emerson, don't you dare go back on your word. As a gentleman—"

A gentleman? He stopped just short of hurling the word back in her face. For ten years he'd believed Howard James had forbidden the marriage based on his *not* being a gentleman in the social sense of the word. That, however, he'd been able to live with. Far more troubling had been the notion that Tess might have agreed. Now he realized even that would be preferable to the more likely reason: she simply hadn't loved him enough to place her future in his hands.

He leaned to retrieve his coffee cup. "I said I'd help you and I will. But the moment this gets out of hand I'm putting a stop to it. Understood?"

Looking relieved, she nodded and pressed a hand to her bosom, to the tempting spot where her breasts began their

gentle swell, where he might have placed his lips had circumstances been different.

"Now," he said. "About what I expect in return."

"Remember our bargain." Charles's voice grated in coun-
terpoint to the rumble of the coach wheels.

As passing street lamps chased the shadows between them,
Tess caught glimpses of his profile—the straight line of his
nose, the sturdy angle of his chin. Her fingers flexed with the
urge to caress his freshly shaven cheek. It was the sort of gesture of endearment she'd once lavished on him liberally.

His shoulder brushed hers as the carriage jostled over a
bump in the road. The brief contact of masculine broadcloth
against her bared shoulder raised simmering gooseflesh that
had less to do with memories than with the solid strength of
a man who simply sparked her desire.

After a decade she should have been over him, yet their
meeting at Vauxhall had thoroughly tossed that assumption
out the window. Sitting so close to him now, she discovered
it wasn't so much the past tormenting her but much more recent recollections. The ghost of his kiss—their kiss, for all
she denied her part in it—shimmied hotly across her lips.

"You're to explain the truth to the Holbrooks and the rest
of your friends immediately," Charles ordered, interrupting
her thoughts. Her eyes were drawn to the grim line of his lips.
"The sooner we nip this marriage rumor in the bud the better."

This produced a lick of panic. She hadn't at all liked the
way he had taken command of the situation that morning, the
way he'd issued his first decree with all the authority and arrogance of a husband. *You'll honor me by telling me the truth
from this moment on, and you'll obey me without my having
to repeat myself.* It hadn't helped that they'd been sitting in his
bedroom, or that he'd only just climbed out of bed. The memory of it made her insides contract, leaving her breathless, a

little afraid. In what other ways might he decide to press his rights?

"I'll take Helena aside at the first opportunity," she replied. "I promise. But as for the others, we mustn't tell them anything yet. What if someone inadvertently blurts the truth to Uncle Howard?"

"Can't you trust your friends?"

"Of course I trust them. But you know how secrets are. They always find a means of slipping out."

"You ought to have considered that sooner." He grasped her chin and turned her face to his. "I'll play my part for Howard, but no one else. Make no mistake, my dear. I intend to hold you to the promises you made earlier. I may not be your husband, but you'll honor my wishes as if I were."

There were those words again: husband and honor. Beginning where his fingers curled about her chin, heat spread to engulf her. Suddenly she couldn't draw a breath that wasn't suffused with his scent, with the very taste of him.

"I have an idea," she said unsteadily. "We'll tell the others we haven't yet announced our elopement to your family. They'll think it a romantic little secret and be extra careful not to chatter about it."

He held her another moment while his gaze raked her face. Then his flinty eyes softened. His hold relaxed but his fingertips remained on her, trailing down her neck to the pulse in her throat. Tess could do nothing to conceal its frantic thrashing. A faint smile curled Charles's lips.

She fell against him again as the carriage bumped round a corner. His hands quickly found her shoulders, steadying and righting her. The carriage slowed to a stop.

When Fabrice opened the door and set down the steps, Charles caught her hand. "Remember. At the earliest possible convenience, you'll speak with your cousin."

"I said I would, and I will."

The conviction of that promise sputtered like a spent candle as the butler admitted them into the foyer. A clamor of voices tumbled down the stairs from the drawing room, so many Tess barely heard Stenson's greetings as he took her wrap and Charles's hat and cloak.

She frowned. The Friends of the Bard Society never raised such a din, not even with their husbands in tow.

Charles tapped her shoulder. "Sounds like a mob."

Yes, it did. Her feet turned leaden as they followed Stenson up to the first floor of the Holbrooks' lavish townhouse. If she'd only contacted Helena first thing that morning, she might have forestalled these well-meant but surely disastrous intentions. Now there was nothing to do but face. . .

More people than she'd encountered in one room since her wedding to Walter. More than usually spoke to her in the course of an entire Season.

"Good heavens," she murmured. "What *has* Helena done?"

"Assembled a select few of your friends, it would seem." In mutual dismay, she and Charles lingered on the drawing room threshold.

"I don't have this many friends," she whispered while trying to affix a smile. A faint gnawing beside her drew her attention to the fact that Charles was grinding his teeth. "Stop that. Look happy. We're supposed to be in love."

His breath hissed between his teeth. Tess could only guess at the admonishments forming in his mind. The butler cleared his throat.

"Captain and Mrs. Charles Emerson," he trumpeted, effectively stifling a dozen conversations at once.

Gazes converged on the doorway, seeming like hands around Tess's throat. She struggled to breathe while fighting the urge to retreat at a vigorous pace. Beside her, Charles mumbled a brief protest about having resigned his commission.

"Tess, dearest." Helena hurried toward them, the rattle of her jewelry startling in the silence. Despite being several years younger, she enfolded Tess in a motherly embrace and kissed her cheeks. "My most heartfelt felicitations. Captain

Emerson, I do hope you realize how extraordinarily fortunate you are." She clasped his hand and offered the brilliant smile that had made her the toast of London for two Seasons running. "Our Tess is a rare and precious prize. We expect you to take the very best care of her."

Just before bowing over Helena's hand, Charles aimed a threatening scowl at Tess. "I'll do my best, Lady Wesley."

"Now, now, none of that nonsense. We are family. You'll call me Helena or nothing at all."

She slipped between them, linking an arm through each of theirs. As she drew them into the drawing room, colorful silks and formal black eveningwear blurred at the corners of Tess's vision. She felt immersed in a sea of expressions ranging from delight—her few friends—to wariness and thinly cloaked hostility. The heavy silence threatened to suffocate her.

Wesley Holbrook cleared a path through the room. "Tess, wonderful news. All the best." He kissed her and extended a hand to Charles. "Captain Emerson, a pleasure. Where are you stationed now? We'll have to compare war stories later."

"Actually, I've resigned my commission . . ."

"Darling, don't be such a goose." The delicate bridge of Helena's nose crinkled. "The captain is our cousin now. Call him Charles. But where's Father? Ah, there he is. Father, do come greet Tess and her new husband."

"Indeed, indeed." In the knee breeches and frock coat of the previous king's reign, Sir Joshua Livingston made his way forward with only minimal use of his ivory-handled cane. His waxed mustache, a new acquirement of which he seemed exceedingly proud, poked Tess's cheek when he kissed her. He chuckled as she reached to straighten the resulting kink.

"You look scrumptious tonight, my dear. And very happy indeed." With a throaty chuckle she interpreted as approval, her Uncle Joshua pumped Charles's hand. "Your father's work is commendable, Captain Emerson. A true asset to this city."

Tess did a double take. Had she been the only soul in all of

London ignorant of the connection between Charles and the architectural firm of Emerson & Son?"

"Yes, thank you, sir," Charles replied. "But it's *Mister* Emerson. Charles, if you please."

"What's that?" The old gentleman held a hand to his ear, at the same time adjusting the pipe clenched between his teeth. Though he was rarely seen without it, he never lit the thing; his daughter wouldn't have it, for until very recently his health had been precarious at best.

"Heard you've explored the empire from top to bottom." Sir Joshua turned to address the nearest clutch of guests. "Did you all know Captain Emerson's been abroad for a good number of years? Come, my boy, entertain us with your exploits. There's a good fellow."

"I'm told you've been all the way to Australia," a gentleman said as he flanked Charles's side. Tess's eyes went wide. How had these veritable strangers learned so much about Charles while she had known so little?

"Tell us, Captain," said yet another addition to the growing circle of men, "is it true the Aborigines are as fierce and uncivilized as Africans?"

"Both claims are rubbish," Charles shot back, clearly irritated.

Oh, dear. Tess chewed her lip. How would they ever survive the evening? How would she? The storm tossing in Charles's lustrous gray eyes sent a chill down her back. Oh, he'd surely take her to task at the first opportunity.

"Tess, you wicked thing," Helena whispered at her shoulder, "to keep such a secret from me. I can't think how you accomplished such a coup, but rest assured I'm elated at how it's turned out. And Charles is . . . well, nearly as devastatingly handsome as my Wesley."

"Helena, we must talk."

"And we will, dearest. Later, after the triumph of this evening. I've quite decided to launch you and Charles into society."

Tess only just suppressed a yelp of dismay. Charles would have her head for this.

Hands gripped her shoulders from behind. "Tess, darling, how marvelous!" Miss Emily Canfield turned her about and caught her in a hug so fierce Tess gasped. Emily released her. "Sorry, love, but this is all so exciting. A clandestine wedding—how utterly romantic. And such a dashing bridegroom."

When Beatrice Aimes and the Viscountess Morely nudged their way through the crowded room to add their congratulations, Tess found it difficult to look either lady in the eye.

"Wait until you see all the splendid gifts," Beatrice said with a jiggle of her ringlets.

Young Nora Thorngoode appeared at Tess's side. "For my present, Tess, I should like to paint a portrait of you and Mr. Emerson. In the meantime, I do hope you like Sevres porcelain. Mama insisted that only Sevres would do for a new bride."

"And I would be quite correct, would I not?" Nora's mother, Millicent Thorngoode, turned to Tess and curtsied. Tess cringed at the gesture while the others traded amused glances. "Many felicitations on your marriage, Lady Hardington. Oops!" Mrs. Thorngoode pressed a hand to her mouth. "Dear me, I meant to say Lady Emerson."

"Thank you, Mrs. Thorngoode," Tess replied with a little sigh. The woman, determined to join the ranks of London's upper crust and tolerated only due to her husband's considerable wealth, nearly always got it wrong. If she wasn't addressing a member of the House of Commons as 'your grace,' she was mistaking a plain missus for a countess. Poor Nora blushed several shades of crimson. Tess reached for her hand and gave it a sympathetic squeeze.

Ah, but Mrs. Thorngoode's idiosyncrasies had provided a welcome if all too brief distraction from her predicament. Then the reality sunk in. Parties, expensive gifts—where would this all end? "Ladies, I thank you all so much, but you shouldn't have gone to so much trouble and expense."

"Don't be a goose." With a fond smile, Helena straightened the pearl brooch affixed to Tess's delft blue bodice. "We want you to have everything a lovely young bride dreams of. For you are young and lovely, dearest, even if this is your second time at the altar."

"Yes, but . . ."

Peals of laughter drifted from a few feet away. Tess's stomach sank. One of society's worst gossips, the twenty-year-old Lady Justina Reeves, turned away from her companions and reached for Helena's hand. "Lady Wesley, do come hear what the Princess Von Haucke endured during her journey here from Austria. It's enough to convince a body never to stray from home again."

Drawing Helena from Tess's side, Lady Justina maneuvered her fashionably flared skirts to prevent anyone else joining her circle. It was a subtle rebuke Tess understood well enough.

Not that it mattered. Justina Reeves reigned over an entourage of spoiled, overgrown girls with few thoughts beyond which balls to attend, how to catch a husband and, upon achievement of that, how to attract a desirable lover. It troubled Tess not a whit to be excluded from their set. But she wondered what on earth her cousin had been thinking to invite these people.

At supper, she found herself seated between Sir Joshua Livingston and the pale young Earl of Wrothbury. She did her best to be an engaging dinner companion, truly she did, but her brief efforts to join in the conversation were half-hearted at best. More intent on devising a way to elude Charles's anger later, she simply couldn't work up an interest in idle chatter. Until. . . .

"I suppose there's some element of romance to be found in an elopement," Justina Reeves proclaimed to the balding marquess beside her. The marquess nodded, making some inaudible comment. Justina sipped her wine and sniffed.

"Yes, well, I for one find the notion of furtive weddings quite sad, really."

Glances, both sympathetic and not, flittered over Tess. Embarrassment tingled along her spine. Oh, she wanted to slide beneath the table. What *had* Helena been thinking?

Only one person seemed not to have noticed Justina's unkindness. Tess had expected Charles to sit stiff and silent among all these aristocrats, yet there he was, holding his own in an animated discourse with the Princess Constanza Von Haucke on his right and Arabella Stewart on his left. Several times during the meal, his easy laughter resounded across the table. Through furtive glances Tess witnessed how his attentive courtesy gradually loosened the ladies' haughty pouts and replaced them with simpering smiles. Charles had clearly charmed them.

No mistake, he was not part of this set and never had been. Through a series of clever investments in London's growing real estate market, his father had amassed enough money to send his eldest son to Cambridge, where he'd met and was befriended by several of Tess's longtime acquaintances. Then, as now, he'd moved among the *ton* with ease, with the confidence one usually associated only with the gentle born. Tess couldn't help a surge of pride.

And a teensy twinge of envy. By rights, she was a member of the *ton*, yet they held her at arm's length. She peered across the table at his handsome face and sighed. Perhaps in the coming days she might gain a trace of his confidence, his dignity.

But no. Charles wouldn't be in her life long enough to affect changes.

A giggle skittered across the table. Princess Von Haucke, leaning on Charles's arm, trailed freshly manicured fingers along the back of his hand as she murmured into his ear. Something heavy and uncomfortable settled in Tess's stomach. Her gaze narrowed as the pretty Viennese princess pursed her lips and made dimples dance in her cheeks. She whispered again in Charles's ear, eliciting a chuckle in return.

Tess stabbed her fork into the fricassee of pheasant on her plate. She stole a glance at the dark-haired earl beside her. He and the princess were considered practically engaged, but he appeared oblivious to her behavior, rambling on as he was about deed polls and patents.

Her opportunity to speak privately with Helena came soon after supper. When the men remained around the dining table for port and cigars and the ladies made their way back to the drawing room, Tess whisked her cousin behind the plush amber curtains that swathed the doorway of the Chinese Parlor.

Helena's vivid blue eyes regarded her with surprise. "Is something wrong, dearest?"

"Wrong? No. It's . . . it's just that . . . well, you see . . ." Oh, dear. How the blazes was she supposed tell her sweet, trusting cousin that the man she was living with—*living with*, for heaven's sake—was not, in fact, her husband?

"Oh, pish, Tess. Thanks aren't necessary."

"Yes, but . . ."

Helena patted her cheek. "I've been blessed with a doting husband, a darling, robust son and my father's restored health. That leaves me wanting for one thing only—a sister. Yet even there I'm blessed. We may merely be cousins but I've always thought of you as a sister and I can only hope that . . . that I might in some small way make up for your losing Alicia."

A lump the size of a fist pressed against Tess's throat. "In truth, Helena, you've been my anchor. I don't know where I'd be without you."

"Then allow me to do this for you."

Oh, but there was one quite compelling reason why she must not, and even Helena's loving enthusiasm could not change the facts. "Helena, this is all simply too much, you see, because . . . all these people and gifts and . . ."

Grinning, Helena shook her head. "Stop. I know what you're about to say."

"You do?"

"Of course, goose. Some of our guests tonight are the very same who've turned a cold shoulder toward you these past several years. And that's exactly why I invited them."

"It is?"

"Indeed." Helena grasped Tess's hands and swung them up and down. "It's past time you rejoined society. Enough is enough. While many of them consider me the tiniest bit dotty—"

"They do not."

"Oh, yes, they do. But they don't dare shun me. Ever since Wesley won his seat in the Commons, he's performed countless favors and learned equally as many secrets concerning our peers." Her garnet earbobs winked like co-conspirators. "They owe us."

"So you plan to extort their good graces on my behalf." Tess regarded the hands enfolding her own, creamy, flawless hands that nonetheless possessed the strength to smooth away hurt feelings and restore courage to the most downhearted wretch. "Do you think that will work?"

"Eventually." Helena chortled, an unladylike sound that somehow gleaned refinement through her lips. "Society's a biddable lot. Consider how they follow the dictates of fashion, how they sit about waiting for someone of influence to instruct them on how to think. Well and good. I've decided to be someone of influence and you, my Tess, will be the latest rage. Along with that charming husband of yours."

"Yes, about that," Tess tried again, but Helena's face lost its dreamy look and turned somber.

"Have you told Charles about . . . you know what?"

"No. Of course not." The very notion set off a charge of anxiety. Charles's place in her life was temporary. The less he knew, the better for everyone. "And don't you dare breathe a word."

"I wouldn't do any such thing." Helena looked affronted. "But dearest, I think you should. He's your husband, after all. There isn't a matter in the world I wouldn't trust my Wesley with."

"Yes, on the subject of husbands—"

"Ah, there you two are."

Tess let out a yelp as, with a sudden yank, the curtain was swept aside. Wesley Holbrook peered into the doorway. "What are you doing here, telling secrets?"

Helena swatted her husband's arm. "Don't sneak up on people that way."

"Who's doing the sneaking?"

"It's women's talk." Helena took a superior tone, even as she leaned in to kiss the corner of his mouth. "You wouldn't be interested."

"Humph. Time enough for gossip later. Come along, you two. Arabella Stewart has agreed to play the pianoforte." He pivoted on his heel and marched across the hall.

Helena held the curtain open, a satisfied twinkle in her eye. "You see, we've achieved our first victory already. Arabella Stewart has decided to lower her nose from its lofty heights to play the pianoforte at your wedding celebration."

"Yes, but, Helena . . ." Too late. Her cousin was already halfway to the music room. Tess trotted to catch up.

Chapter 5

"You should have told her last night."

"I tried."

"You should have tried harder." His frustration rising, Charles scowled into his coffee.

"It wasn't my fault." Seated across the breakfast table, Tess flipped the page of her newspaper. "We were continually interrupted."

He clenched his teeth while she perused the morning news with an innocent air that didn't for one minute fool him. Was she so interested in current events, or simply hiding behind the pages to avoid him?

He stared across the table at the top of her head. Sunlight slanted through the morning room's vaulted window, shooting glints of dark fire through her hair. She had pinned it behind her ears but allowed its rich, gleaming waves to tumble down her back. Silky, touchable, inviting. The way she'd often worn it years ago.

This was damn near killing him, sitting down to breakfast with her and realizing how many breakfasts they might have shared these past ten years. How many moon-drenched nights they might have spent within the caress of warm bed linens, happily immersed in the wonders of each other.

The regret would chip away at his soul if he let it. Seizing a soft-boiled egg from its porcelain holder, he rapped his spoon angrily against it, as if the crackling shell were somehow responsible for his predicament, his mistakes, his lost youth.

"I couldn't very well announce the truth before all those gawking guests, could I?" she said, abruptly breaking into his thoughts. He angled a gaze at her; she just as quickly dropped hers, the downward sweep of her lashes the very picture of modest virtue.

"Humph. Lord only knows what else your cousin may be up to." He flicked eggshells onto his plate, eliciting little pings against the porcelain. "Intimate gathering, my eye. Before long the all of England, nay madam, the entire bloody empire, will be celebrating our so-called nuptials."

"You needn't exaggerate so."

"Needn't I? Last night has left me wondering why I agreed to this madness at all."

Her lips pursed in preparation of certain protest. Ah, when they rounded like that, it made him want to toss self-control aside and silence her with one furious, unbridled kiss. Instead he used simple logic. "It wouldn't have taken much legal maneuvering at all to have your Uncle Joshua appointed trustee of your inheritance."

She tossed the newspaper onto the table, shook her head and emphatically said, "No." Then she drew a breath and visibly calmed, leaving Charles wondering exactly what made her so jumpy today, besides their fiasco at the Holbrooks's last night.

"Uncle Howard would fight it in the courts," she said, "and I fear the kind of harm he could do both Joshua and Helena. You see, until quite recently Joshua's health had been of great concern to us all. Not just physically, but his mind as well. His thoughts . . . tended to wander. I won't have him humiliated or risk a setback with any sort of competency hearings."

Charles couldn't refute such an argument. He'd genuinely liked the old gentleman. "What about Wesley Holbrook, then? He's a member of parliment. Surely his influence—"

"No, Charles." The words were sharp, insistent. "I will not

risk Helena's well-being for the sake of mine. Only two years ago, Wesley abandoned a military career to take on the responsibilities of the duchy of Wakefield when his brother was believed dead. Then his brother returned and Wesley was left with nothing. He's finally found his passion in Parliament. I won't jeopardize that with any sort of scandal."

He studied the heightened color in her cheeks, the almost hunted gleam in her eyes. "What scandal, Tess?"

She snatched up her newspaper, not quite concealing an alarmed expression. "Oh, why can't you understand? I suppose you've been away from English society too long to realize how delicate such matters can be."

And yet she'd risk the scandal of a supposed annulment. He smiled inwardly, perversely amused and determined to find answers. "All right, my dear. But tell Helena the truth this afternoon or I will."

"Don't you dare breathe a word." Her newspaper crumpled between her hands. "I said I'd tell her and I will."

"And I intend to make certain you do."

"What does that mean? Surely you don't plan to be here when she arrives later."

"I certainly do."

He was backing her into a corner and they both knew it, though the fact left Charles mystified. Years ago, not a soul on earth would have been able to hold such sway over the confident, innocent Tess James. She'd had nothing to hide then, nothing to regret.

"Don't be ridiculous." She fluttered her hand at him. "Go for a ride. Go to your club. Go anywhere. Just don't be here."

"For your information, I don't have a club. I do however intend going home for a few hours. But not to worry, I should be back in plenty of time for Helena's visit."

"Home? Where? Your parents' house?"

He shook his head. "I have a suite of rooms on St. James."

"You can't go there." Her brow puckered. "You can't be seen hanging about your flat like some free-and-easy bachelor."

So she thought she could rule him, did she? Believed his reluctant cooperation meant she'd somehow managed to resurrect the blind devotion of a young man eager to please and prove his love?

He eyed her levelly. "Believe it or not, Tess, I have a life of my own. I never agreed to put my affairs on hold while I masqueraded as your husband."

Indeed, he itched to return to the drafting table he'd set up in his cramped study. Before this debacle began, he'd begun laying out plans that could very well change the manner in which his father did business. In fact, Charles's ideas could conceivably alter the face of London itself. But not if he tarried his days away here, with a woman who made demands and offered virtually nothing in return.

"I suppose you're right." Looking duly chastised, she stared down at her newspaper. Her eyes went wide.

"Something important in the news?" Peering across the table in an attempt to read the headlines, he made out the bold lines of a caricature. It depicted a man in a hooded cape seizing what appeared to be a distressed—and half-undressed—woman. "What the devil is that?"

"Oh, nothing," she murmured without looking up. "Just that Midnight Marauder nonsense."

"Ah. I've heard of him. Doesn't seem like nonsense to me. More like the worst sort of villainy."

"Oh, I agree." She plucked the corner of the page and flicked the image away. "It's the mythology built around him that exasperates me. People seem to have so little else to occupy their minds."

"So true," he said, noting how she riffled page after page without reading a word. Ah, woman. Didn't she realize her elusiveness was the very thing that piqued his fascination? That the more she evaded his questions, the deeper he'd search? Did she really believe she could enlist his help, and then conceal her reasons for doing so?

Ah, Tess. Think twice, my dear.

* * *

As two o'clock approached, Tess hovered at the parlor windows, glancing nervously out to the street. Charles hadn't yet returned. With any luck, he'd be detained for another hour or two at least. Long enough for Helena to come and go; long enough for Tess to explain the situation in the gentlest terms possible without interference from him.

Interference. The man was a master at it. Why, the very idea of Charles Emerson playing the convivial husband while minding his own business was ludicrous. Too late did she realize her mistake in drawing him into her affairs. Between deceiving Uncle Howard and preventing Charles from learning too much, the situation had become a juggling act that could come crashing down on her head at any moment.

Of course, duping Uncle Howard weighed lightly enough on her conscience. Charles was another matter entirely. Oh, she wasn't fooling him, she knew, but so far she'd managed to keep him guessing. And at a distance. A painful one. One she longed to broach and would have, if she had only herself to consider.

The very worst of it was that he deserved the truth. She owed it to him, certainly. But neither reason proved compelling enough to break her silence. Not now. Probably not ever.

The echo of carriage wheels drew her attention back to the street. A phaeton of simple but costly design rolled to a stop before her front steps. With a surge of relief, Tess hurried to the foyer to greet her cousin.

The flaxen-haired beauty beamed at her as she climbed to the threshold. "Good afternoon, dearest. Look who I found on my way here."

Tess peered over Helena's shoulder to the street. Backing away from the carriage with an armful of parcels, Charles turned and nodded up at her. "I told you I'd be home in time, Tess, and I never break a promise."

She heaved a sigh.

"My feet are positively throbbing," Helena moaned as she stepped inside. "My own fault, I suppose. I've been down on Regent Street all morning but, oh, Tess, I found the most delicious things. You won't believe the little chapeau I picked up at Godierre's. A work of art. Oh, thank you so much, Charles." As he followed her inside, she hefted a beribboned hatbox from the top of his burden.

"I'll set the rest down in the parlor," he said, stepping between them.

Helena leaned close to Tess and murmured, "He's so dashing in that dark blue suit. And such a gentleman. I do so approve of this match."

Of course Helena found him attractive and charming. What woman wouldn't? But his return home couldn't have been more ill timed, for a difficult task would now be unbearable. Why couldn't he have understood and stayed away until later? Why couldn't he simply trust her to tell Helena the truth?

Perhaps, a little voice suggested, because she hadn't given him any reason to.

He reappeared in the parlor doorway. Arms at his sides, he leaned lightly against the jamb, one eyebrow raised to an expectant slant.

"Charles, surely you have no interest in Regent Street's latest hats and frocks. Why don't you go for a drive," Tess suggested with a tight smile. "I'll have Fabrice bring round the curricle."

"But I've only just arrived home." He smiled and held out his hand. "For now, ladies, I'd rather enjoy the pleasure of your company."

"Splendid." Helena swept across the hall and linked her arm through his. "I'm never one to shun the company of a handsome gentleman. Such broad shoulders you have, sir. Doesn't he have broad shoulders, Tess?"

"Hmm," she commented and followed them into the parlor.

Halfway into the sunny room, Charles grunted and stumbled to an abrupt halt. He looked to his feet. "What the blazes is that?"

A pair of furry gray paws clutched his ankle in a vise grip, while two sets of thorny claws hooked into his trouser cuff. "Good grief."

The cat hissed.

"Tanya!" Tess clapped her hands. "Naughty kitty. Release at once."

Tanya meowed. Threads ripped as her claws retracted.

"So sorry about that." After shooing the cat, Tess stooped to brush at the back of Charles's trouser. Through the lightweight wool, her fingers traced the hard outline of a muscled calf. Her pulse jumped and she pulled away.

She discovered him staring intently at her. Sadness tinged his gaze. Perhaps they'd shared a similar thought: that only a wife touched a man that way, just as she might smooth his lapels or adjust his cravat. It was an act of familiarity, even intimacy—the sort shared by married couples. Despite Helena's presence, the moment held only the two of them, sealed in a world of mutual memories and broken promises. And regret; most of all that.

"I . . . don't know what got into her." Tess tried to smile, to appear as though her cat's behavior was all she need apologize for.

"I suppose it's her way of showing affection." Charles smirked. He settled into an armchair, smoothing his coat and dignity both. The heat of his leg lingered on Tess's fingertips.

She and Helena sat on the settee opposite him. Apparently oblivious to the tension between them, Helena compressed her lips, trying but not quite succeeding in hiding her amusement of the past few moments. She turned to Tess. "What did you wish to discuss with me? Your note this morning seemed rather urgent, even if you did say not to come until this afternoon."

"She was hoping to be rid of me by then," Charles put in.

"She what?"

"He's only joking." Tess glowered in his direction, still wishing he'd go away and leave this to her. She turned back to her cousin. "It's nothing overly pressing, really."

"Yes it is," he interrupted with a sharpness that made her flinch. "It's quite pressing."

"Do let me handle this, please."

"Handle what?" Helena looked from Tess to Charles and smiled. "I do hope you're not going to thank me again for the party."

"No, dearest, it's not about that. Although it was so very sweet of you. Charles and I enjoyed ourselves immensely. . . ."

He cleared his throat.

Helena's gaze darted back and forth between them. "Tess, do stop hedging, won't you?"

"Yes, all right." She fidgeted with the gold locket hanging round her neck. "The truth is, Charles and I aren't married."

"What?" The word came as a gasp.

"Bloody brilliant." Looking heavenward, Charles whistled between his teeth.

Helena blinked. "I surely heard you wrong."

"No, dearest, I'm afraid you didn't."

Slinking out from beneath the side table, Tanya sprang over the rounded arm of the sofa and thudded into Tess's lap. She raked her fingers through ashen clouds of fur. Purrs rumbled in the silence.

"You shouldn't joke like that," Helena finally said.

"Oh, this is no joke." Tanya batted her head against Tess's palm when it hovered in mid-stroke.

"Tess, kindly put that animal down and look at me." Helena folded her hands in her lap and pulled up as straight as a sentry on the alert. "What *can* you possibly mean? You are *living* together, aren't you?"

"Hmm," Tess admitted with a nod. She nudged Tanya to the carpet.

"'Hmm'? Is that all you have to say?" Helena's voice

surged. Tess winced. Helena almost never, ever, raised her voice. To anyone. But she regained her control, if not quite her patience, soon enough. "Dearest, this is a civilized society. People *cannot* live together without first standing before a minister and promising to love and honor till death do them part!"

Tess cast Charles a pleading look. No help at all, he raised open palms. She frowned at her cousin. "It isn't what you think."

"I don't know what the bloody blazes to think!"

"Do stop yelling. I didn't mean to upset you. We aren't actually doing anything wrong. Not actually."

"Tess. Dearest." Helena reached for Tess's hand, holding it so tight her knuckles rubbed painfully. "I'm well aware that being widowed allows you certain liberties other single women cannot enjoy. But this is not one of them. You'll be forever ruined. You'll be ousted from society once and for all, and then what will happen to Bl—"

"Helena!" Tess's free hand shot up, and she'd have clapped it over Helena's mouth before she allowed that sentence completion in Charles's hearing. Helena fell to a baffled, somewhat seething silence. Tess drew a breath. "Please, let me explain."

She felt Charles's curiosity on her, sensed his conjecture. Oh, his mind was already working it over—what will happen to . . . who . . . what? Oh, yes, he'd be searching for the answer to that one, wouldn't he?

But dear Helena provided the perfect, if momentary, distraction by aiming an accusing finger at him. "You, sir, should know better than to drag a fine, upstanding woman like Tess into such a compromised position. I know how you urged her to run off with you once before. Oh, yes, she's told me all about it. And here you are again, with an officer's fancy epaulettes to help turn her head. . . ."

Charles gained his feet, startling the cat who had been licking her paws beneath the sofa table. With a yowl that made them all flinch, Tanya darted across the room and into the hall.

"First of all," he said, "I've resigned my commission." He paused, jaw beading with tension. "Secondly, I am not the villain here. Tess's virtue will suffer no harm at my hands, you may be sure."

Helena gripped the armrest of the settee and pushed to her feet. "If you are not the villain in this matter, sir, pray tell me, who is?"

Tess sighed, tipped her head back and spoke to the ceiling. "Uncle Howard. Who else?"

Helena looked down at her. "Dear me, I might have guessed." Understanding smoothed away lines of vexation on her brow, only to raise new ones. "What the devil's he done now?"

The late afternoon sun streamed through the hired coach's windows. Charles shaded his eyes with his hand and watched lavish homes give way to fashionable storefronts as the driver maneuvered from Park Street onto Oxford. They soon headed east out of Mayfair and north toward Bloomsbury.

There'd been a note waiting for him at his rooms earlier. His mother had arrived in London ahead of the rest of the family and wished to see him at his earliest convenience, meaning of course he should drop everything and come at once. Ah, well, mothers were like that.

Still, he might have waited until tomorrow rather than set out after Helena's visit. His reasons had less to do with his mother's summons, however, than with his need to put distance between himself and Tess. After her cousin's departure she'd voiced quiet and—for her—humble gratitude for his patience. It was those words of thanks that drove him from the house. He couldn't quite explain it, except to admit that while he wanted a host of things from her, the very least of them entailed her gratitude.

Upon entering Bloomsbury, the coach slowed to join the more leisurely stream of residential traffic. This irked Charles not in the least. He needed the time to think. A dozen various explanations for his fraudulent marriage had already sifted through his mind, each dismissed as not nearly clever enough to fool Blanche Emerson.

Something in her missive had raised his guard, leading him to suspect the gossip had already penetrated his parents' circle. Though the wealthy middle class families of Bloomsbury had few obvious connections to the aristocracy, the lines between classes were blurry at best. As fortunes soared and plunged, social sets overlapped more than many liked to acknowledge. And somehow, rumors always managed to spread through London like fire through a parched forest.

More than any other member of his family—even more than himself—his mother had never forgiven Tess for spurning him. Even when he had declared the matter closed, she'd continued to scoff and assign blame. If she thought he and Tess were married. . . .

Good grief, these days it seemed he ran headlong into trouble each time he encountered a woman. This afternoon's confrontation with Helena Holbrook had been no exception. Yet, for all his protestations concerning Tess's virtue, a flood of heat at the time had privately pronounced him a liar. In truth, wouldn't he relish the chance to lay waste to Tess's genteel propriety, especially as she'd looked during her cousin's visit: flushed, a little breathless, and not nearly as imperious as she liked to pretend.

At a sign heralding Chelmsford Square, the driver turned right and eased to a halt. Charles peered out at a town house indistinguishable from its neighbors but for the numbers fashioned in wrought iron beside the paneled front door: twenty-eight.

This homecoming would take place in a house that had never been his home. He'd grown up in the City proper, his father then a successful merchant just starting to diversify into real estate. It had been those investments that allowed Charles to attend Cambridge, where he'd befriended the sons of noblemen, through whom he'd eventually met Tess.

After paying the driver he surveyed the building's façade of whitewashed brick, contrasting black shutters and leaded casement windows. Glancing three stories upward, he saw four chimneys reaching toward the sky. His father had prospered in recent years. If he'd boasted such a home years ago, would marriage to Tess have been such an unreachable goal? Or would Howard have denied his suit regardless?

A brass doorknocker gleamed in the sun, indicating someone in residence. As the coach eased away, the front door opened upon a familiar sight, his first since entering the neighborhood. Rodgers, the Emersons' steward since Charles was a boy, looked a tad older but no less dignified in his somber suit and silver-framed spectacles.

Charles took the steps two at a time. "Good to see you, Rodgers," he declared, and pumped the other man's hand.

Clearly startled by the familiarity, Rodgers grimaced but quickly recovered his dignity. "And you, Master Charles. Welcome home, sir."

Charles's gaze traced the columns on either side of the door. "Quite a place."

"We're all proud of it, sir." He ushered Charles into a foyer tiled in marble, draped in silk and illuminated by a crystal chandelier. It wasn't quite Mayfair, but still worlds away from the wide-board floors and whitewashed walls of his boyhood home.

"Is my mother in?"

"Eagerly awaiting your arrival, sir."

"How'd she look to you, Rodgers? Perturbed at all?"

A ridge grew between the butler's lush brows. "She looked her best as always, sir."

"Of course. Well, nothing for it, then, but to go on in and—"

"Charles!" She appeared beneath the swoop of an archway,

her startled image captured in the broad mirror on the opposite wall. "I didn't expect you this soon."

"Did you think I'd keep you waiting, Mother?"

In the few seconds it took her to cross the polished floor, he took in everything about her, or nearly so. Silver vied for dominance now in her auburn hair, though only the faintest lines traveled the planes of her fine-boned features. Petite hands, just beginning to slacken about the knuckles, reached for him.

He opened his arms and returned her embrace. The fresh scent of floral dusting powder enveloped him and he knew he was home. His mother planted kisses on either side of his face and held him at arm's length.

"Darling, can it be a mere three years? Seems like three decades." She surveyed him with a look of approval, then hugged him again. "I rushed from the country the moment I received your letter. George and your father will come as soon as they can, in a few days or so."

"There's no hurry, Mother." He grasped her shoulders. "I'm home to stay this time."

She blinked away tears. "That is the best news I've heard in quite the longest time. Do come into the drawing room, darling." She took possession of his arm with both hands. "You must tell me all about your recent adventures. But first, I heard the strangest rumor yesterday and I'm certain there can't be a grain of truth to it. Perhaps you can enlighten me as to where such a preposterous story might have originated."

He braced for battle with yet another female.

Balancing a stack of books in her arms, Tess shouldered her way out the door of Hookham's Lending Library on Old Bond Street. Her trip had yielded enough reading material to keep her quietly at home and out of trouble, according to Charles's latest edict.

After Helena's visit, he'd admonished her to find some harmless and inconspicuous employment, then excused himself and strode from the house without a word as to where he was going. Oh, whatever made her think she could control him?

Of course, he was right about being inconspicuous. After witnessing Helena's reaction to the truth, she trembled to consider how much further she stood to fall in the *ton's* estimate. If anyone ever learned she was living with a man. . . .

Living with a man. With Charles. The thought sent goose bumps traveling down her arms—arms that lately yearned to reach around him, rediscover the feel of him and seek the strength she'd once taken for granted.

Ah, but momentary weakness spawned thoughts such as those, thoughts not to be dwelt upon. The Charles she'd known and loved no longer existed, just as she was no longer the naïve young girl of years ago.

She squinted into the sunlight, dazzling after Hookham's subdued interior. Fabrice had dropped her at the front door but continued down the street to wait with the barouche. Cradling the books against her, she set off west along the foot pavement in search of him. She wondered, would Charles be home when she arrived? Or would he stay away and try to avoid her from now on, as many genuine husbands avoided their wives but for occasional public appearances together.

She couldn't blame him if he did.

After only a few paces she ground to a halt. Even from a distance, she recognized the long-legged stride of the man advancing through the throng of afternoon shoppers. A wave of dread blanketed her senses, obliterating all but the loathsome face that so often haunted her nightmares. It was Sebastian Russell, the demon who wooed, deceived and discarded Alicia. He was headed Tess's way.

A young redhead, little more than a girl, strolled on the crook of his arm. Her eager, exuberant smiles proclaimed to passersby: *look at me, see who I'm with.*

Yes, I do see, Tess thought with a sad shake of her head, *and I know what he's capable of doing to you.*

Contempt coursed through her as she studied his impeccable suit and polished shoes. His smug grin made her blood
sizzle. He was horrible—*a snipe; all spleen and nothing of
a man*.

And how dare he appear so carefree, so . . . unaffected by
the past. True, his family cast him out after Tess informed
them of what he'd done. He'd inherit his title someday but little else. But the Russell family had also persuaded Tess to
preserve their honor by keeping their son's name a secret.

He spotted her and slowed his steps. The girl looked up at
him, clearly puzzled. From behind, a distracted pedestrian
jostled them, mumbled an apology and continued on his way.
The villain took no notice. His gaze flickered over Tess in
consternation before his pale lips curled.

When she'd last seen him she'd been with Walter, and Sebastian Russell hadn't dared look at her, much less form an
impudent smirk.

Anger pummeled through her. Oh, in that moment she
could have done violence. Veering to the center of the foot
pavement, she blocked their way. "My dear," she addressed
his companion, "if you possess any sense you'll run as fast as
your feet can take you."

"What?" A nervous giggle bubbled in the girl's throat. "Do
I know you?"

"Come." Nudging Tess aside, the awful man hurried the
demoiselle past. "Poor demented woman. I've no idea what
she could have meant."

Tess's armful of books tumbled from her trembling arms,
scattering on the foot pavement. Gaping pages fluttered in the
breeze. A sense of foolishness and self-reproach descended,
heavier for her having allowed Sebastian Russell to manipu-
late her into a futile display of temper.

"Blast." She crouched to retrieve the volumes. Seconds
later a brown hand appeared from above, reaching for her
own. "Fabrice. Thank goodness."

"I saw that man who made you drop your books," he said, helping her rise. "Who is he?"

"No, you're mistaken. It was an accident."

"It was no accident. Fabrice saw." He bent to gather the texts.

He arranged them neatly, spines facing the same direction. "Madame should say who this gentleman is and what he has done. Fabrice will attend to it."

"No, Fabrice will not." She turned her face away, knowing he'd read the remaining rancor as easily as the titles stamped on the book covers. She couldn't tell him the truth, couldn't risk testing his loyalty. It would only end with Sebastian Russell permanently maimed or worse and Fabrice consigned to a penal colony clear across the world. "Where is the coach?"

"This way." He indicated the direction with a nod.

When they reached the vehicle she opened the door and climbed in unassisted. Fabrice piled the books on the seat beside her. His gaze held her but she pretended not to notice. Pretended nothing was wrong while bitterness toward that monster mounted like a fever inside her.

There was only one cure and she burned for it: a midnight ride through Stepney, St. Giles, or any of London's rookeries. But Fabrice knew her too well. He might connect such an excursion with today's encounter outside the library. She'd confided only minimal details about Alicia, careful not to reveal the identity of the scoundrel involved. Even if Fabrice had tried ferreting out the information among Mayfair's network of servants, Alicia's affair had been conducted in secrecy in an attempt to fool Uncle Howard. Precious few people knew the facts.

Still, if Fabrice ever guessed the truth, could she prevent him from seeking revenge? She dared not take that chance.

Chapter 6

Charles reached to cover his mother's hand with his own but on second thought pulled back. She had that look on her face, one that said, *do not touch me or attempt to console me. Just tell me this isn't true.*

Choosing each word carefully, he'd got as far as confirming that he and Tess had reunited. That small disclosure had raised tense white lines on either side of her nose.

He doubted she'd find the truth of his marriage any more palatable than the rumor. And while he'd understood her enmity toward Tess ten years ago, the severity of her reaction to this latest revelation left him frankly baffled.

"Perhaps it's time to let bygones be bygones," he suggested, wondering, however, if he'd quite taken his own advice.

"After the way she sent you packing for lack of an acceptable background?" She shuddered, a melodramatic gesture if ever he'd seen one. "Never."

An oak buffet dominated one corner of the room. He went to it and picked up a leaded crystal decanter. Sliding the stopper free, he sniffed the contents and poured a small portion of chestnut liquid into a glass. He brought it to his mother.

"To think that . . . that . . . woman," she spat, taking the offered stemware between her fingers, "actually believed herself better than us, better than anyone for that matter."

"It was her uncle who came between us," Charles said, the words firmer than the conviction that fueled them. Perhaps then, as now, he'd been little more than a convenience in

Tess's life. When his services were no longer needed, she'd likely show him the door as peremptorily as she had then.

"Perhaps, but darling, that's the least of it." His mother paused for a sip of sherry. "I've never told you the rest because . . . oh, because it's too tawdry for decent people to speak of." She made a face as if her glass contained curdled milk instead of fine liqueur. "It began with that sister of hers."

"Alicia?" Still standing, he drifted from the sofa, crossing to the window overlooking the square. He stared off into a cloud-filled sky above the rooftops. "She was just a child."

"Child, bah!" Her vehemence spun him about. Dark triumph flickered in her gaze. "Tess hasn't told you, has she?"

"She told me Alicia died some years ago. Consumption, I believe. Poor girl."

"Oh, Charles, before Alicia James died, she ran off with some man like a common harlot, disgracing herself utterly."

"Don't be absurd." The very idea of Tess's sweet, vivacious sister falling to such depths defied reason. He retraced his steps and resumed his seat on the sofa. "You know better than to listen to gossip, Mother."

"It's all true, I'm afraid." She raised her chin with a long-suffering air. "I heard the tale in the usual roundabout way, but the facts were clear. I'm sorry Charles, but your late sister-in-law disappeared with a rake for months without benefit of marriage, engaging in God only knows what kind of debauchery that destroyed her health."

As much as Charles didn't want to believe it, his mother's story rang with a peal of truth. He thought back to that first night at Vauxhall; the mere mention of Alicia's name had all but reduced Tess to tears. An excessive reaction considering her sister had died several years ago, unless. . . .

He sat back, stunned, picturing Alicia as he'd last seen her: young, vital, without a care. Then he attempted to reconcile that image with the one his mother described. To his consternation, his reeling mind instead conjured Tess—the Tess of today who spoke in circles, who piled lies and secrets so high he despaired of ever climbing to the truth.

"Who was this man, Mother? Do you know his name?" Because, by God, if he ever found the cad he'd. . . .

"No, the girl refused to tell anyone. But what does it matter? Alicia James possessed neither heart nor conscience, or she'd have considered her family's honor before garnering such disgrace." Blanche set her glass on the side table and reached for Charles's hand. "Darling, she and Tess are of the same blood and blood *always* tells. That's why you must leave that . . . that . . ."

"Woman?"

She nodded, face bent over his hand. Charles knew the time had come to dispel the myth of his marriage. Despite his mother's unfairly biased opinions of Tess, she at least deserved to know the truth. "Mother—"

"This marriage will never do," she interrupted. "Tess actually defended her sister, then had the audacity to bring the creature back into their Mayfair home before sneaking her off to the country. Her neighbors were offended beyond words."

He slid his hand free. "It shouldn't have been any of their business."

"Tess Hardington isn't received in any home of consequence," she continued, seeming oblivious to his mounting anger. "She goes about with her cousin and a few foolish friends, but nearly all of London society shuns her. You must obtain an annulment at once. If you act quickly, our reputation will suffer very little harm, I should think."

"Now see here." She blinked at his sharp tone. He dredged up a remaining shred of patience and continued more calmly, "Even if Alicia did do these things, I see no reason to blame Tess for it, nor do I perceive any crime in Tess coming to her sister's aid."

"Oh, but Charles . . ."

He shut his eyes and pinched the bridge of his nose. He'd had enough. He felt drained and more than a little confused

about why he still hadn't told his mother the truth, especially
when doing so would have made his life infinitely easier.

He stole a glance at the crocodile tears gathering in her
eyes. Women. They were supposed to be the weaker sex yet
when it came to swaying a man to their purposes, they knew
exactly which weapons to wield.

"I won't be manipulated, Mother, not by you nor anyone
else." He couldn't help wincing, albeit inwardly, at the
damned irony of that claim. For all appearances Tess *had* manipulated him into helping her. The odd thing of it was,
neither Tess nor his mother understood that his decision was
entirely his own. No amount of persuasion on Tess's part
could have coerced him against his will, just as his mother's
exhortations would not now deter him. He'd given his word.
It was a matter of honor.

Or was it? Did integrity keep him at Tess's side, or the
prospect, however remote, of losing himself in the delights of a
body that tempted him beyond the pain and loss of ten years?

He shook the thought away. "If I choose to be Tess Hardington's husband—or Tess Emerson's, I should say—it's my
affair. Either congratulate us, Mother, or say nothing at all."

She gasped. "Why, Charles, how can you speak to me that
way, your own mother . . ."

"Leave off the dramatics, they won't change a thing." He
pushed to his feet, wanting to be away. "Howard James once
judged the Emersons as not good enough to marry a James. It
cut you deeply. I remember. Yet now the tables have turned and
here you are, discarding Tess for reasons equally as shallow."

She stared mutely back. He studied her face a moment
longer, searching for remorse but finding only the consternation of a defied parent. So be it. "I must be going, Mother. I'll
see myself out."

Arriving back at Aldford Street as dusk descended, Charles
hurried upstairs, intending to change for supper. Upon reach-

ing the upper landing, he discovered the door to Tess's sitting room ajar, and through it he spied the tip of a satin slipper propped on the cushion of the settee.

He moved noiselessly across the gallery and peered in. He knew he shouldn't, knew he should continue on to his guestroom and prepare for supper. But the sight of her held him, tucked as she was against a pillow in the corner of the sofa, one leg drawn up beneath her skirts, the other stretched to reveal the contour of an ankle.

As he watched, she bent her head lower over a book in her lap, her graceful neck elongated by the upsweep of her hair. Her parted lips made tiny movements while her bosom rose and fell in a rhythm only she could hear. Pensive, absorbed, she seemed utterly unaware of anything but the words on the page.

Poetry did that to her. Ah, yes, they used to read together sometimes, she for the sheer love of it and he for the fascination of watching her concerns melt away into the perfection of words and form and meter. It had been at those times, just as now, that she looked her most radiant.

He shifted for a better view and the floor creaked beneath his weight. Tess's gaze flicked upward. Her tranquil expression vanished and the Tess of today reappeared, the one with secrets and sorrows and undecipherable moods.

"Sorry to disturb you," he said, knowing he'd been caught staring and helpless to devise a clever excuse.

She flipped the book closed, holding her place with a forefinger. Her expression wary, she smoothed her skirts in place and swung her feet to the floor. "Were you spying on me?"

He shoved his hands into his trouser pockets. "I suppose so. Sorry."

"Why?"

"Why was I spying or why am I sorry?"

She smiled. "The first."

"Something about the look on your face," he admitted, pushing the door wider and leaning against the jamb. "It reminded me of . . . when we were young."

He expected her to chuckle or dismiss the notion with a shrug. Instead she brushed a palm across the tooled leather cover of her book. "You and I wore quite a path through these pages back then. It's the sonnets. Will's, of course."

"Are there any others worth reading?"

"These are special." A cloud settled over her face. "They calm me when nothing else can."

"Has something upset you, Tess?" He stepped into the room, compelled by that old impulse to pull her into his arms and shield her.

Only just keeping from gritting his teeth at the sentiment, he recovered his better judgment several feet shy of the settee.

"Not having a very good day, then?" he amended hoping to sound more offhand, less fiercely protective.

"I'm fine." Her voice rose with artificial brightness. "Perfectly fine."

"Liar."

"I beg your pardon."

"Don't bother to deny it."

"Humph. I fail to see any reason why I should deny or affirm anything."

"No? What of our bargain?" He circled the sofa table, coming to a halt directly in front of her. "You promised you'd be honest with me. Completely honest."

"You would throw that back in my face." As if giving herself time to think—as was no doubt the case—she reached around him to retrieve a satin bookmark from the sofa table. She placed it between the pages and laid the book on the cushion beside her. "What makes you so sure of yourself?"

"Sure of myself? Madam, I'm certain of one thing only: that I don't know the half of what's really going on here." When he settled on the sofa beside her, alarm sparked in her eyes. Would she find an excuse to bustle him from the room, ring for Fabrice, or employ one of a dozen other tactics meant to avoid his proximity?

Her nose tilted in the air. "I'm sure I don't know what you mean."

Ah, stubborn woman. And so transparent. Not to mention possessive of such an adorable nose, he compressed his lips to stifle the urge to kiss its tip.

He contemplated the book between them, bound in dark green leather and emblazoned with gold block letters. He touched a darkened smudge in the gilding the size of Tess's fingertip. Perhaps he'd achieve with gentleness what he'd surely never bully out of this formidable opponent.

"What happened today?" he asked quietly.

"It's silly of me, really." She gave a little shrug. "My path was darkened by someone I'd be content never to lay eyes on again."

Those dogged instincts to protect rose up again. "Did this person say or do something to offend you?"

"No, nothing of the sort." She smiled weakly. "Merely seeing him dredges up unpleasant memories from a few years back."

Charles nodded, taking note of the small fact she'd revealed. The person in question was a man. Alicia's lover perhaps? No, that would be too much of a coincidence, certainly. Charles tensed, waiting for her to continue. The clock on the writing desk ticked loudly in the silence.

"So who is this person?" he prompted at length. "Anyone I'd know?"

"Surely not." She fell into another maddening silence, her fingers tapping a taut rhythm against the book.

"You never know. What's his name?"

"I'd rather not say."

"Why on earth not?"

She shrugged. "I just wouldn't."

Charles's frustrations simmered to boiling. He sucked in a breath, fighting the urge to shake her and demand she trust him.

He settled for placing his hand over hers and stilling the erratic tapping of her fingertips. But touching her ignited something powerful and compelling inside him, a blending of past desires and newfound attraction so tangled he could barely discern where one left off and the other began.

An audible breath, a little outpouring of emotion she couldn't quite contain, suggested she was not entirely impervious. He curled his fingers around hers, on impulse bringing her hand to his lips and brushing a faint kiss across her knuckles. Proper, nothing a lady might object to, yet in the instant of contact he inhaled her essence and filled his mouth with the taste of her.

But now was not the time for indulgences, no matter how heady.

"Will you at least tell me what set you at odds with this man?" he asked, fingertips making little circles against the pulse in her wrist. She was tense, jumpy, very much on her guard.

"Nothing of consequence, Charles, really." She frowned down at their joined hands. Or was she merely regarding the book between them, perhaps wishing he'd leave so she might return to her reading? Was she glad the volume prevented him moving any closer, or did she share his desire to fling it across the room so they might sit knee to knee, thigh to thigh?

"Ah, Tess," he whispered, leaning close, so close stray hairs tickled his lips, "why not take a leap of faith and tell me what happened?"

She pulled a little away, as far as the settee's arm would allow. Just as Charles cursed himself for pressing too far too fast, her lips parted. "He . . . inferred things about . . . me, when I married Walter. I suppose because Walter was so much older than I, many people thought I married him for his money. Nothing could have been further from the truth, of course. I knew when I married him that I'd inherit very little of his fortune."

Glaring at the works of Shakespeare, Charles was reminded of a line from Hamlet: *The lady doth protest too much, methinks*. People married for money all the time. Why would anyone blink an eye if Tess Hardington chose to follow suit? Oh, no, this story was an obvious ruse.

"Surely such impudence is not to be taken seriously," he said.

"You're quite right but—" What began as a shrug became a convulsion of her shoulders, a rigid twitch accompanied by a catch in her breath that explained, if not the why, at least the extent of that other man's rancor and her vulnerability to it.

The book thudded to the carpet and he ignored it, intent on slipping an arm around her. "You know, Tess, it's perfectly acceptable, upon occasion, to not be strong."

She murmured something about loathing weakness, a sentiment not quite completed. Her resistance held them apart for an instant more, until the heave of another half-suppressed sob brought her against him. As the heat of her soft curves penetrated layers of fabric and spread through him, lies and secrets ceased to matter. He wanted only this—their arms entwined, breath mingling, no barriers between them.

But even as desire ripped through him, she broke away, brushing back wisps of hair from her face. He didn't attempt to hold her. He knew better.

"Forgive me, I'm being foolish," she declared with a stoic sniffle. "I merely glimpsed a man on the street. And I suppose I likely wouldn't have given him a second thought if I weren't already so upset over Uncle Howard's threats."

Back to that again. They'd come full circle and Charles had learned precious little. Only that some man possessed the ability to reduce Tess Hardington to tears, albeit briefly. That she'd sooner tell some outlandish lie than reveal a particle of truth to him.

The latter notion should have piqued his anger but, oddly, not so. Despite her duplicity, those abrupt tears had just as quickly dried—against his collar. Could that mean—dared he entertain the notion?—that perhaps she needed him for something more than money?

Damned if he didn't look forward to discovering the answer.

Chapter 7

"Fabrice, are you there?"

Pausing halfway down the service staircase, Tess leaned over the banister to peer into the kitchen. The first hint of dawn sent ashen light creeping along the whitewashed corridor. She squinted into the gloom and descended to the landing.

She knew she'd find Fabrice awake; he always rose well before dawn. She had an errand for him in Surrey and wanted him to set out before the rest of the house stirred. Before Charles awakened and began asking infernal questions.

Oh, that man was relentless and all too perceptive. Not to mention dangerously irresistible, so much so she regretted the wild impulse that had impelled her to draw him into her private affairs. If only he hadn't come walking down that path at Vauxhall, at the very moment she needed a means of evading her uncle.

And yet . . . and yet. . . . If Charles hadn't appeared when he did, she'd be free of his prying, true enough. She would be free of *him*. Rather than slumbering at this very moment beneath her roof, he'd have faded from her life, forever this time.

Was that what she wanted?

Gathering her dressing gown more tightly about her, she continued to the kitchen threshold. "Fabrice, are you—"

A breath of air swept her nape. "Oui, Madame."

Nearly shrieking, she whirled. He stood a foot away. "Don't do that."

"You were looking for me."

"Yes." The dim light revealed the outlines of his riding coat and breeches. She narrowed her eyes and shook her head. "How did you know?"

The lift of an eyebrow mocked her.

"Never mind. I need you to ride to Surrey." She handed him the letter she'd written and sealed the night before. "This is for Reverend Coombs. He'll have something to give you before you return to London."

He tucked the envelope into the pocket inside his coat. "What will he give me? Nothing too burdensome, I hope."

"You *are* an impertinent fellow, you know that?" She clasped his wrist and drew him into the kitchen. The windows were shut, the hearth cold, the room hushed and vacuous. "A marriage license," she whispered.

His tawny eyes flickered. "It is a complicated game Madame plays."

"It's always been complicated."

"You have brought in an outsider. That is dangerous."

"Oh, trust me, my friend, there's nothing dangerous about Charles Emerson. He'll help me for a time, then go on with his life. He's no threat to us, I promise." A tremor of doubt robbed the words of their conviction.

"The threat, I think, is to Madame. Monsieur will not vanish as though he never existed. You would be foolish to think it." He stepped closer, angling a shrewd look through the darkness. "But Madame is no fool, is she?"

A fair question. Logic had certainly deserted her if she ever believed Charles Emerson would provide an easy solution to her problems. There were times she yearned to tell him everything. Just yield to those strong arms and confess all her secrets against a broad shoulder, a solid chest.

But Fabrice was right. Charles was an outsider. Intuition whispered that he would not betray her, but wisdom warned against confiding in anyone beyond her circle of co-conspirators. The smaller that circle remained, the safer for everyone.

"We're wasting time."

He nodded. "Fabrice goes now. But supposing Reverend Coombs will not give me this thing you seek? You are asking a man of God to commit a falsehood."

"He'll do it. He knows how much is at stake. We cannot allow my uncle to rob us of everything we've been working for." She opened the cupboard where candies and baked goods were stored. "Is there anything special I might send for Blair?"

"You," he said to her back.

Regret and longing tumbled inside her. "Not just now, I'm afraid. In a few weeks, when things have settled down."

"Glazed walnuts." Reaching over her shoulder, he slid a small wooden box off the middle shelf.

"Of course, she adores those."

He nodded.

"Do take her for a ride this evening, won't you?" Blair loved horses, loved to sit astride her saddle and urge her pony faster, ever faster.

"I will," he promised.

"Go now, my dark angel." She squeezed his shoulder. "And Godspeed."

An hour later, Tess sat down to breakfast with Charles. They shared only the briefest of words, for he seemed preoccupied. When he made an offhand remark about Fabrice's absence, she told him only that her servant had gone on an early errand.

Thus her means of obtaining the marriage license became one more secret kept from him.

Lying had become instinctive, deceit as easy as thought. She despised that necessity in her life. But if she told Charles about the license, he would inevitably demand to know how the devil she convinced a clergyman to falsify a legal document. From there, he'd attempt to wear her down until he learned all he wished to know—and all she wished to conceal.

He left the house soon after breakfast. He didn't say where he was going and Tess bit her tongue rather than ask. Doing so would have been rather the height of hypocrisy, after all.

She passed the next hours staring at the pages of her library books, gazing out the rain-soaked parlor windows and . . . oh, she knew better . . . missing him. The house had seemed so much less empty these past several days. Less lonely. Last night, passing his door on her way to the linen cupboard, she'd heard the even rumble of his breathing within and felt . . . safe.

Why did she find his offer of friendship so compelling, his embraces so tempting? Why did the very scent of him—masculine, mysterious, never masked by cologne—unfurl a yearning she felt helpless to resist?

Ah, but wasn't the answer obvious? Charles Emerson hadn't simply been her first love; to date, he was her only love.

Her marriage had been mutually satisfying on certain levels, but she hadn't loved Walter Hardington any more than he had loved her. He had found her attractive and engaging, a comfort in his latter years. Had she been plain and shy he would not have married her. And neither would she have married him, had he not offered protection from society's rebuke. To his credit, Walter had known about Alicia *and* Blair and hadn't cast judgment. For that alone he'd earned her respect and gratitude, even a measure of genuine affection.

But her heart . . . ah, Charles Emerson alone had claimed it, known it, set it to racing. And, whether he meant to or no, left its broken pieces in his wake.

From behind her, a scampering sound dispelled the sodden memories like a scattering of raindrops. She turned from the window to see Tanya dart across the room. The cook's daughter followed, luncheon tray in hand. Usually Fabrice carried Tess's meals up from the kitchen, but today Becca took his place.

The girl smiled shyly. "I thought you might be more comfortable dining 'ere this afternoon, ma'am, since Mr. Emerson's not at 'ome."

"At *home*," Tess corrected with gentle emphasis on the H. She gestured toward the sofa. "Thank you, Becca, here would be lovely."

"Here," the young maid repeated, this time succeeding in making the H heard. She set the tray on the sofa table, then bent to stroke Tanya's fuzzy head. With a loud purr, the cat vaulted onto the sofa cushions.

Tess smiled and joined the pair. "You know, dear, I don't mean to be a nuisance but little things like proper pronunciation can be so important. It might make the difference someday between working below stairs or above, or becoming a teacher or entering into trade."

"Yes ma'am." Becca's hand hung suspended above Tanya's twitching ears. "But a trade, ma'am? Surely you don't think—"

"I do indeed. You're bright and a very hard worker. Anything is possible. You must always remember that, Becca. Always . . ." She broke off. Poor Becca. She'd only intended bringing her mistress luncheon, not enduring an impassioned lecture on how not to fall prey to life's injustices. Tess smiled. "Thank you, Becca. That will be all."

The girl curtsied. "Ring if you need me, ma'am."

Tess watched her go. Besides her other attributes, Becca was pretty, with her wheat blond hair and clear complexion. Though London born, the girl might have been plucked off a summer mountainside. Tess hoped she'd never learn to rely on those traits, hoped she'd someday discover that women possessed talents and ambitions just as men did.

Glancing at the covered dishes on the tray and deciding she hadn't the appetite to care what lay beneath, she ambled back to the window and began tracing patterns with her finger in the fogged panes. Swishing through the air, Tanya sprung over the sofa's arched back and leapt to the windowsill. The morning's drizzle had burgeoned into driving rain, slapped against the panes by gusty winds. Tanya chased the drops with a paw, blinking in frustration when she failed to capture any against the glass.

Was Charles out somewhere soaked to the skin? He might have used the curricle but no, not with one horse gone. She regretted sending Fabrice to Surrey today of all days. Without the use of a coach, both men ran the risk of a thorough drenching. She wouldn't forgive herself if either fell ill. Lately, even her very best intentions seemed to go awry with disturbing frequency.

"Ah, Tanya, what's happening to me?" A ghostly reply took shape on the window. She stared at it, taken aback, then scoured her palm across the swooping C she'd unconsciously drawn in the condensation.

Heavy clouds obscured the sky over Mayfair that evening. As twilight settled over the neighborhood, Charles let himself into the coach yard of Tess's property through the delivery gate. A few minutes later and the wrought iron entry, set between the garden's high brick walls, would have been locked for the night. He felt thankful to have slipped in, glad to avoid Fabrice's watchdog scowls at the front door.

Dripping rainwater broke the stillness. As he rounded the gazebo, pigeons roosting beneath its roof cooed and rattled their wings as they settled in for the night. Through the trees, flickering terrace lanterns illuminated his way.

Today had proved his most productive since returning to England. He'd visited one of his father's projects in the City, then holed up in his flat for hours. By the end of the afternoon, his future, and perhaps that of London, had taken shape on the sheets of parchment strewn across his drafting table. His plans wanted only his father's approval. Would Richard Emerson embrace Charles's vision, or believe his eldest son had taken leave of his senses?

He'd worry about that another time. The work had consumed him, exhilarated him, and for hours he'd all but forgotten the existence of wills, secrets and mad schemes.

But a certain beautiful schemer? Not for an instant. His first thought, upon completing his designs, had been to race home and share his innovative ideas with Tess.

Race home to Tess. A mawkish sentiment, to be sure, leftover from the past. This was not his home, nor did Tess seem particularly interested in sharing ideas or anything else with him.

As he neared the house, he caught an unexpected glimpse of her, an indistinct shape through rain-splattered glass. In a gown of flowing saffron, she drifted down the hothouse's center aisle like a flower amid the foliage, pausing here to touch a plant, there to adjust a vine.

He watched her, captured by the rain-blurred contrasts of bright gown and dark hair, vivid eyes and pale skin. A twinge of guilt pricked his conscience. He supposed he was spying again. But when she didn't know she was being watched, everything about her changed. Became softer. Calm. Ingenuous. The Tess of his youth.

He rapped his knuckles on the glass and the illusion vanished. She started like a frightened doe, craning her neck to peer through the reflections. He rapped again and waved. Seeing him, she hurried down the aisle to unlock the door.

"Good evening, madam." He shook rainwater from his shoes and stepped inside.

"I very nearly jumped out of my skin." She sounded out of breath. Her brow furrowed. "What in the world are you doing sneaking about the garden in the rain?"

"I was not sneaking and the rain has stopped, for the moment at least." He smiled at her scowl, a fair imitation of Fabrice's. Of course, Fabrice wouldn't have presented such a fetching vision in that tarnished gold frock. Charles couldn't resist taking her hand and turning her in a slow pirouette. "You look lovely, my darling. Ah, forgive me, I'm not supposed to employ such honeyed terms when we're alone, am I?"

"You're in a frolicsome mood." Reclaiming her hand, she moved away to adjust a stake that supported a flowering stalk.

He followed her. "Would you like to know why?"

"I suppose you're bent on telling me whether I will or no." She sidestepped into a narrow aisle. Despite the less than enthusiastic response, he detected a teasing melody in her voice.

She halted by a grouping of potted trees. Tiny green buds promised to burgeon into some kind of fruit. She fingered several.

He moved to her side. "If you must know, I was planning for the future."

"How very conscientious of you." Gathering her skirts and crouching, she pressed her fingertips to the soil in one of the pots. As she started to straighten, the tip of a branch caught in a lock of hair and pulled it from her coif. Hairpins tinged on the tile floor.

"Oh . . . blast." Hunched at an awkward angle, she gave a little tug that only succeeded in securing the tree's grip.

"Allow me." Ignoring her little noise of protest—not quite a sigh and not quite a groan—he moved behind her, following the curve of her arm with his own. But good intentions somehow weren't enough, not with the heat of her back warming his chest and her bottom a scant few inches from his groin. His fingers worked clumsily at best as his gaze settled, not on his task, but on the fragrant nape of her neck.

His lips pursed with the desire to melt over each little protuberance of a graceful spine, lower and lower to the top button of her dress, and beyond.

Raising his gaze, he discovered her staring an entreaty over her shoulder. "If you wouldn't mind . . ." She nodded toward the source of her dilemma.

"Of course." He sighed. It wouldn't have been much of a conquest, after all, to seduce a woman caught helplessly in a tree. Little by little, he slid the tangles free. "You are released, madam."

"Thank goodness." Roses as vivid as those damasks growing by the window bloomed on her cheeks. Abruptly she swung away and strode to the end of the aisle where it turned along the hothouse wall. Was she running from him?

He circled the opposite way, heading her off in front of a wooden stand that on first glance seemed to be covered in cotton or clouds or a parade of tiny robed virgins. Upon closer inspection he discovered rows of the same white flower, rather bugle shaped and tinged with only the faintest violet at their tips. Charles breathed in their light perfume and experienced a deep and disconcerting tug.

"My lilies," Tess explained, looking perplexed to discover him once again beside her. "The bulbs came all the way from China."

"Did they?"

Disheveled strands of hair lay against her neck. He reached out, combing his fingertips through them, knowing but not caring that she'd likely scowl at the familiarity. Well, he *had* just rescued her, hadn't he? And—ha—he had his reward: at his touch, the pulse in her throat lashed visibly, a silent communiqué that spoke directly to the part of him that craved her most.

A deep breath meant to subdue his desires—produced the entirely opposite effect. He might have pressed his nose and open mouth to her warm bosom and inhaled the very essence of her. Mystified, experiencing a baffling rise in his trousers, he gazed down at the lilies and was struck by a realization.

For days now, he'd been surrounded by this subtle but unmistakable scent. It clung to Tess's clothes, her hair, hovered in the rooms of the house.

He inched closer to her, breathing her in and finding her infinitely more tantalizing than the flowers. "Magnificent."

"Yes. Fabrice and Becca help me with them. Lilies take quite well indoors, actually, although the timing can be tricky depending on when you want them to flower."

Smiling at her schoolmistress tone, he held her gaze while tracing a velvety petal with his fingertip. "Sensual little devils, aren't they?"

"Oh, I . . . suppose." She moistened her lips. With an air of efficiency, she shifted a pot an inch or two to the right, as if this change would make all the difference in the plant's progress.

He leaned in closer, pretending to study the flowers from

over her shoulder but actually enjoying the tickle of her hair against his chin. "I'd like to learn more about them."

"Would you?" She pivoted out from under him.

"Or perhaps I'd be prying into a gardener's revered secrets?"

"No. But I'm surprised that you're interested. Men usually aren't."

"Oh, I'm interested, all right." What healthy male *wouldn't* be utterly fascinated by growing things beneath a twilight sky, especially when shared with a beautiful woman whose sable hair lay all askew as though he'd taken her for a tumble?

An image stole into his mind of Tess on a stack of hay, skirts rucked and straw sticking out from her hair. And he beside her, leaning in for a kiss. . . .

As if she'd read his thoughts, she made a dismissive sound—a breathy harrumph—and started toward the door that led into the house. Charles quickly decided he was in no mood to spend the remainder of the evening alone. Catching up with her, he reached for her hand.

"Come out with me, Tess."

"What on earth are you talking about?"

"We'll go out for the evening. That's what married people do."

"You said we were to stay quietly at home."

"That's a moot point now that Helena has announced our marriage to all of London."

"It wasn't *all* of London."

"It was nearly so but never mind. Tell me you haven't been cooped up all day and wouldn't enjoy an outing beneath a starlit sky."

She sniffed. "It's raining."

"No, it has stopped." He pointed up at the glass roof. When she raised her head, he used the opportunity to admire the smooth expanse of bosom hugged by her low cut evening dress. "You see?" he murmured, entranced. "Stars. Sparkling white and touchably . . ."

He jerked his chin up at the same instant she lowered hers. Caught again. He answered her suspicion with a look of feigned innocence. "Will you come out?"

She surveyed her skirts. "I'd have to change."

"No, Mrs. Emerson, you're perfect as you are."

"Hardly. But where would we go?"

"Can you get us into Almacks?"

"I'm afraid not." Her derisive chuckle reminded him of his mother's scathing comments and the revelations about Alicia. If they were true, Tess was undoubtedly blackballed at London's social clubs.

"Never mind," he said. "I hear it's quite the bore nowadays. We'll go to Vauxhall."

"Well . . ."

"Great. Grab a wrap. Shall I have Fabrice bring round the curricle or would you rather be ostentatious and go in the barouche?"

"You'll have to hail a hackney."

"A hackney?" Suspicion reared up. "When you've two perfectly elegant vehicles in your carriage house, not to mention a handsome pair of horses?"

"One handsome horse, I'm afraid." With a deft twist, she slipped her hand from his. "Fabrice took the other."

If she had tried to elude him during their chase through the hothouse, she was doing it again with words, or the lack of them. He eyed her up and down. "His errand is taking a rather long time. Where exactly has he gone?"

She studied the air above his right shoulder as though perusing a list of possible answers. Charles wondered if the one she chose would in any way resemble the truth.

"To Surrey," she said. "On estate business."

"I see." Damn. Once owned by her maternal grandmother, Highgate Court belonged to Tess free and clear of the terms of her father's will. Which meant the goings on there were none of his business.

His mother said Tess brought Alicia there after her ordeal.

It made him wonder. . . . But no, that was years ago. Surely Fabrice's errand had nothing to do with that.

"Very well," he said, "I'll hail a hackney."

She looked infinitely relieved when he didn't question her further. Did she think that was the end of it? Not on her life, it wasn't. As she swept away in her trailing yellow skirts, he came to a decision. He would unravel this woman's secrets if it killed him.

Chapter 8

The mood at Vauxhall Gardens proved less than festive, the turnout half-hearted at best. In the Grove, a thin crowd surrounded the Gothic Stage where a chamber orchestra proceeded through the Winter Concerto of Vivaldi's *Four Seasons*. The piece made a vigorous backdrop for a decidedly listless audience. Even the trees seemed downhearted, drooping with rain and the weight of their lanterns.

As Tess and Charles walked through the Grove, she began to regret the outing. Even more so when she caught sight of the spoiled Justina Reeves, standing near the stage with her gloved hand draped possessively over the arm of her latest beau, Sir Robert Bessington.

The girl's parents hovered near the couple. Tess felt Justina's gaze descend upon her, then saw the pointed glance she exchanged with her mother. Thin eyebrows drawing tight, Justina whispered something in Sir Robert's ear. He glanced their way and nodded slowly, thoughtfully.

Tess sighed. *Not tonight.* Oh, how she wished the whispers were of admiration or even envy that Tess Hardington walked on the arm of such a dashing gentleman. At one time, long ago, that would have been the case.

As if Charles had a particular purpose in mind, he steered her in the group's direction and acknowledged them with a smart bow. Had he noticed Justina's rancor that night at the Holbrooks'? Would he see it now and demand to know why?

Sir Robert returned the greeting with a polite nod and Tess

felt a twinge of hope. But Justina's nostrils flared like pretty little trumpets announcing her scorn. "Good evening, Mr. and Mrs. Emerson. How enchanting you both look tonight."

Prickles of embarrassment traveled straight down to Tess's toes. Neither she nor Charles had changed their clothes, and appearing in a place such as Vauxhall in a muslin at-home dress was nothing short of scandalous.

She held her chin high. "Why, thank you, Lady Justina. So lovely to see you here."

Why should she let this disdainful child ruin her evening? Why not give full rein to her fantasy of happier days? Indeed, some people might find their state of dishabille charming, the rashness of a newly wedded couple too enamored to waste a thought on anything as mundane as eveningwear.

And despite Justina's unpleasantness, being out was preferable to staying home—alone—with Charles. She'd acted the fool earlier, twittering about the hothouse like a nesting sparrow. What, after all, had he done to prompt such ridiculous behavior? Not a blessed thing beyond admiring her plants, expressing interest in her lilies, untangling her hair.

Yet there had been more to it than that. On the surface he'd exhibited impeccable manners, but the undercurrents had all but sucked the oxygen from the room.

"Wine?" he offered as the orchestra's tempo mounted with the fury of a winter storm.

"Please."

The instant he walked away she felt the lack of him, felt exposed and vulnerable in the milling crowd. Her muslin dress stood out as hopelessly shabby in the midst of the surrounding silks and, ugh, the color. Yellow? So inappropriate for this time of evening. She felt gauche, a vulgar blotch amid the elegance. Despite the evening's warmth, she shivered.

"Here you are, madam."

Oh, thank goodness. The sensation of being so indefensibly alone slipped away with Charles's return. Yet, as he handed her a goblet of wine, the heat of his hand thrust her into a whole new realm of jeopardy.

"To a long and happy marriage?" He raised his glass. She viewed him askance and he laughed. "All right then, to a mutually satisfying partnership."

"Mutually satisfying?" She shook her head. "That's a bit of a stretch, too. I'm afraid I'll owe you a great debt when this is over."

"'*Afraid*' you'll owe me?" His grin turned devilish. "Are you worried I'll demand some unspeakable payment in return?"

Her heart fluttered at his proximity, at the way his voice rumbled when he said 'unspeakable.' Instinct urged her to step away, to create a comfortable distance between them. She stood firm. In the hothouse she'd unwittingly cast him in the role of pursuer, a subtle advantage she'd not allow again.

"Don't be silly," she said, and sipped her wine. "Nothing about you frightens me."

Was that a shadow of disappointment flitting across his brow?

"I do hope to repay you in some way," she added, meaning it. He'd already done her more favors than she had any right to expect.

"My payment, madam, comes in knowing I may be of service where I'm needed."

A flippant, lopsided smirk accompanied the words. Still, something in his tone, an involuntary note of sincerity, arrowed deep inside her. Her throat tightened and she looked away, trying to conceive words adequate enough to convey her gratitude. He recaptured her attention with a clink of his glass against hers.

"To you." His gaze drifted across her face, lingering, she thought, on her lips. Dear Lord, did he intend kissing her? The notion sent the blood racing to her pulse points. She braced, helpless to avoid the inevitable or devise a quip clever enough to stop him.

She didn't wish to stop him, any more than she had wished

to avoid his kiss that first night in her sitting room, any more than she had wished to escape him earlier in her hothouse.

Some force beyond her control seemed intent on driving them together. Was it the allure of their past relationship, or nothing more mysterious than the attraction of a handsome man whose masculine heat was augmented by the warm, moist evening? Suddenly she felt too weary to deny the obvious or stand strong another moment. As her belly tensed around ripples of anticipation, she let her eyes fall closed and raised her chin.

"Cheers," he said. She opened her eyes. Charles's face lingered close to hers, intimate, inviting. She found her gaze drawn to the fine lines framing his smile, the imprint of sun and wind and time—time they might have shared, if only . . . He raised his glass to his lips, then turned to watch the orchestra.

Dumbfounded and disappointed—even slightly peeved— Tess gaped at his profile. In three gulps, she drained half the contents of her glass.

A sudden jolt pitched Tess from an otherwise comfortable stupor. She pulled upright, dismayed to discover that her cheek had found a sturdy pillow against Charles's shoulder. Shadow and light flickered across his fuzzy image beside her. She blinked, attempting to bring the strong lines of his nose and chin into focus.

Those slightly craggy features turned toward her. A corner of his mouth quirked. "Are you all right?"

"Fine. Per—fect—ly fine." Her voice droned; the words slurred. Good grief.

And where *was* she? Gazing through half-closed lids—her eyes felt like cracked marbles—she took in the less-than-spotless interior of an unfamiliar coach.

Ah, yes, another hackney. She and Charles must be on their

way home. Oh dear, she hoped that was right. She pressed a hand to her brow, cool and clammy against her fingertips.

"Are we almost there?" she asked, hoping *there* was indeed her Mayfair home.

His open palm descended on her thigh. She regarded it, undecided whether to smack it away or simply enjoy the intimacy of the gesture, until she realized he was only trying to prevent her sliding off the seat as the coach listed. An instant later he released her. "Just rounded the corner of Aldford Street."

"Thank goodness." Her head pounded. The coach's swaying sent the threat of illness spiraling from her head to her belly and back. She swallowed, gripped the door handle and wished for the return of Charles's hand, wished she could cling tight to him until the vortex inside her ceased spinning.

Good gracious. How many glasses of wine had she consumed? She glanced at the fingers of her right hand. More? Less? She didn't know.

Moments later she became aware of Charles helping her—no, half-carrying her—up the front steps of the house. She wanted to protest that she could make it on her own but couldn't quite work her tongue around the words. Besides, the weight of his arm securing her to his side was not an entirely unpleasant sensation.

At the door she fumbled with her reticule, rattling the contents as she searched for her house key. She thought she had located it when the smooth satin purse slipped through her fingers, hitting the brick stoop with a jangle. Giggles bubbled in her throat. She stared down at the bag, wondering how on earth to retrieve it. It didn't seem to want to fly back up into her hands.

Charles scooped the wayward purse off the step, found the key and opened the door.

Amazing man.

"In you go, my dear." His open hand settled between her shoulder blades, warm and steadying, guiding her across the threshold. She stumbled on the doormat but he caught her elbow and righted her.

Such a gentleman. "What would I do without you, Charles?"

When he didn't reply she realized she had only thought the words. She considered trying them aloud when she experienced the oddest sensation of being lifted off her feet. "What the blazes are you doing?"

His handsome, chiseled, intensely male face hovered mere inches from her own. "We can do this the hard way or we can have it done quickly." His arms supported her around her back and beneath her knees. If she leaned just a little to the right, she might snuggle her forehead against his neck. Entirely tempting. She was so very tired and he was so warm, so strong. "I opt for the latter," he concluded. "Hold on."

Yes, she could not but agree the staircase presented an arduous climb. In truth, she probably couldn't have managed it alone. Might have even curled up on the bottom step and made do there. Before that last thought reached completion she and Charles arrived at the upstairs landing, he catching his breath and she smiling and thinking Helena had been right about him. He did have the broadest shoulders.

She pointed the way to her sitting room. "Might as well complete the job, sir."

"You're no featherweight, madam."

"Oh!" While her brain sifted through possible insults to toss back, he carried her into the sitting room and deposited her on the settee. Plunked her, actually. The down cushions puffed up around her and settled with a hiss. Sliding horizontally, she rested her head on the sofa's arm and allowed her eyes the luxury of drifting closed.

"Are you all right?"

She hefted heavy lids. With only the light of the candelabra on the hall table behind him, his face was shadowed and featureless, his expression a mystery. "Yes. Why on earth wouldn't I be?"

"You're rather deep in your cups."

"Am not." She considered sitting up to demonstrate both her indignation and the truth of her denial but couldn't summon the energy.

"Are too. You don't feel ill, do you?"

" 'Course not." That intolerable weight over her eyes forced them shut again. The ottoman creaked, she assumed beneath Charles's weight as he sat. At the murmur of fabric she peeked at him through one eye. He'd untied his cravat and tossed it to the chair behind him.

Hmm. She thought it prudent to mention the impropriety of a man untying his cravat in a lady's sitting room. After all, it could lead to . . . the unbuttoning of his collar.

She opened her mouth to tell him so, but other, unexpected words slipped out. "Thank you for tonight. I had a lovely time. You're a good friend, Charles Emerson."

"Yes, well, I can't help feeling remiss in having refilled your glass as often as I did."

"I am not drunk, I tell you." A tide of nausea proved her wrong. She tipped her head back and groaned. "Maybe just a little. What of it? Don't I deserve a night of fun without having to be so painfully aware of the gawking and the whispers and the pointing fingers?"

"Do people point fingers at you, Tess?"

The disarming question startled her. Oh dear, what had she said? Confound it, more than she'd meant to. But she couldn't quite control her tongue or her thoughts enough to prevent the one from betraying the other. "Never mind," she said. "Just the ravings of a woman in her cups."

"No." The hassock creaked again. She slitted her eyes to see him slide off it and crouch beside her. His large hand settled over hers where it lay across her abdomen. "You aren't raving, not by any means. People treat you unkindly, don't they, Tess? Why?"

She balked at trying to explain; it was too much of an effort. Unkindness had become part of her life, an unpleasant fact she had learned to withstand over the years. But kindness, especially from Charles, was too new, too astounding in its earnestness, too undeserved. She didn't know how to accept it or trust it, or how to maintain the illusion of a strong, independent person in the face of it.

A tear traced a burning path to her ear. Exhaustion, she reasoned. She needed to reach her bed. Or perhaps sleep there on the settee.

"Tess," he whispered, nudging her shoulder. "What happened while I was away? What could you possibly have done that was so unforgivable?"

"You credit me, sir, with more integrity than I possess," she murmured back, hating the admission but unable to deny it.

"That's absurd." His hand tightened around hers. "Why would you say such a thing?"

"Oh, Charles. If I'd had any strength of character, I'd have acted sooner. I wouldn't have been such a coward. I might have . . ." The memory of how she'd failed Alicia squeezed her throat, then gripped higher, pinching her mouth and lips and halting speech. It wrung the numbing alcohol from her system and left her smarting, throbbing, inside and out.

"You might have what, my Tess?" His voice came as a temperate tide, inviting, soothing. Yet she resisted the inducement to let the truth pour free, knowing if she did she might very well drown in grief. "Tell me, Tess. Trust me."

"Alicia." It slipped out before she could dam the current of guilt.

"Her death wasn't your fault."

It was. So much of it was. Charles didn't know, didn't understand. If only she'd found her courage sooner, Alicia might have lived and the *ton* with their loathsome judgments be damned. None of their foul opinions would have mattered, but now . . . now their accusations echoed with a peal of truth she could not ignore. Could not escape.

Escape. The word reverberated through her brain as the tide roared over her, sweeping her along in its swirling wash. Struggle though she might, she could not find her arms and legs in time to fight the swell. It wasn't until the settee fell away beneath her that she realized Charles had lifted her in his arms.

Even as she buried her face in his collar she cursed herself for a weakling. She should be stronger, strong enough to heft her chin and laugh away the pain. But muscle and sinew proved an irresistible refuge. Her nose tickled with the scent of starch, while his evening growth of beard chaffed a reassurance against her temple. She felt wrapped in safety, cloaked in masculine strength. Her arms twined about his neck, tight and desperate. It had been so long—so very long—since she'd felt truly protected.

She awoke in her bed sometime later, the coverlets tucked securely around her. Her brain felt encased by a dry cotton haze. For several moments she wondered how on earth she had gone from Vauxhall Gardens to her bed without a single memory along the way. Then vague images took shape. Music and wine, rain and weeping trees. A weeping Tess . . .

Oh, dear God.

Then came a further and more disquieting revelation. It was not the weight of the coverlet pinning her to the mattress. It was an arm. Charles's arm.

And he was propped on his other, gazing down at her. She stifled a cry.

He flinched. "I'm sorry. I didn't mean to startle you. Are you all right?"

She had the distinct impression he'd asked her that numerous times during the evening. She nodded, not yet trusting her voice. Trying not to attract attention to her movements, she slid her hand beneath the bedclothes to feel what she wore, or didn't wear. Had he . . . had they . . .?

No. At least not if her frock, undergarments and stockings were any indication. As her eyes adjusted to the darkness, she made out the snowy linen of Charles's shirt, albeit without his collar.

"You were so distraught and, well, out of sorts," he explained, "I was loath to leave you alone."

"Out of sorts," she repeated, glad of the darkness that hid her embarrassment. "A tactful way of putting it. Thank you."

She didn't so much see his smile as hear the parting of his lips. The small sound echoed like a kiss inside her. Oh, she remembered his kisses from years ago, from just a few nights ago. And she remembered how she had wanted him to kiss her this evening at Vauxhall. Would he kiss her now?

He delivered, not a kiss, but a touch equally sweet, equally unsettling. The callused tip of his forefinger traced her cheek, leaving a trail both rough and gentle and so essentially male her heart wrenched.

Had he noticed the resulting quiver in her chin, the catch in her breath? Would he think her a skittish fool? Lying supine on her back beneath his scrutiny, she felt at a distinct disadvantage. Intending to roll to her side and face him, she shifted and somehow—she doubted either of them would ever be able to explain it—his hand was suddenly on her breast.

She gasped.

His arm swept to his side but not before Tess experienced the full impact of his brief but potent touch. Lust streaked through her, piercing and exquisite.

"Forgive me," he stammered. "I only meant to give your shoulder a squeeze, but you turned and—"

"It's quite all right." She fought to control her voice, calm her heart. "No harm."

"Clumsy of me."

"No, my fault."

He sat up uncertainly. "If you're feeling better, perhaps I should leave."

Her heart froze at the thought. If the past hours had proved anything, it was that she was in no condition to face her demons tonight. Releasing them even briefly had left her bruised and defenseless.

But no, that wasn't it, not really. It wasn't reassurance she needed, it was Charles . . . Charles beside her as he should have been these many years.

"Please stay," she whispered. "Only . . ."

Only what? Despite her weak yearning for his caresses, after ten long years they were little more than strangers. Anything beyond an affectionate hug would be wrong, simply wrong. Oh, but if he'd only stay, she'd cherish each moment in his arms the rest of her life. "I need a friend tonight."

"Not a seducer," he finished for her. "I daresay I promise to behave myself." He found her hand beneath the coverlet and brought it to his lips. "I'm your man, Tess. Consider me a shoulder to cry on, a chest to beat upon, whatever you will."

She felt almost able to smile. "And what for you?"

"As I told you earlier, though you may not remember, the satisfaction of being needed should soothe my ego nicely."

"Ah, Charles, you are a gentleman. I wish . . ." She clamped her mouth shut, aghast at what she had very nearly voiced: a ridiculous yearning to change the past and undo their mistakes, to be young and happy and in love again, and wise enough to stay that way. Ah, wistful, impossible dreams.

Chapter 9

Upon awakening the next morning, Charles discovered nothing but cool sheets beside him. He should have expected it, should have known Tess would manage to slip out without waking him and leave the house long before he descended to the morning room.

Hours later, she arrived home claiming she'd spent the afternoon with Helena and the Friends of the Bard Society. After a light supper she pleaded a headache and retired for the evening.

Yet here she was now in the middle of the night, fully awake, fully dressed and stealing off with her equally elusive servant. The barouche, its black lacquered lines barely visible across the garden, stood ready beside the carriage house. Revealed by the coach lamp hanging from the vehicle, Fabrice opened the door to assist Tess inside. The servant had returned from his mysterious errand late that afternoon, managing to avoid Charles after a terse, "Bon jour, Monsieur."

Leaning against the upstairs hall window, Charles was careful not to ruffle the white lace curtain lest they notice him spying. It was becoming a deplorable habit, one he wasn't proud of but which he seemed unable to avoid.

The grandfather clock in the downstairs foyer had chimed midnight a few minutes ago. He pressed his lips together, burning to know where those two were headed.

An unwelcome prickling raised the hairs on his neck. So far he'd found Tess to be deceptive and too clever by half. But dishonorable? Until now, he hadn't entertained that possibility. No, he'd chosen to believe a reasonable explanation for everything would eventually materialize.

An odd shadow on the garden wall caught his eye, changing shape as if with a life of its own. What he first took to be a trick of the moonlight soon revealed its more earthly nature. Raising up on four slender legs, the creature elongated with a luxurious arch before settling into a comfortable perch.

Tanya. Of course—the perfect accessory. Charles would have wagered his finest cravat pin that she knew exactly what her mistress was up to. Before he fully acknowledged the absurdity of the thought, a clap echoed its sharp report across the garden. Like boiling fog, the shadow that was Tanya poured down the side of the wall and scurried into the coach.

Fabrice swung up onto the driver's box with the same nimbleness. The horses lurched into motion, clip-clopping down the cobbled drive. Charles pushed away from the window, certain of one thing: he *had* heard Tess's coach his first night here. He'd asked her about it the next morning but she'd denied it, of course.

Angry strides propelled him to his bedroom with the urge to slam the door behind him. He glared at the furnishings and pondered how much of a fool Tess Hardington would make of him in the end. After all his patience, damn it, his chivalrous understanding. How many other men would have kept their promise to hold her and nothing more throughout an entire night?

He'd learned one important lesson in the process: compassion made a rotten bedfellow. He'd lain awake for hours fully clothed but for jacket, cravat and collar, God help him, but clothing had done precious little to insulate him from the fullness of her breasts, the curve of her hips, the warmth of her skin.

It had been excruciating. Teeth clenchingly so. But she had *needed* him, rendering seduction out of the question. Odd thing though—her need had proved as much an aphrodisiac as the most alluring of smiles.

As the coach wheels echoed along the street, he considered following the unwitting little temptress. Unfortunately she had taken the barouche and both horses. By the time he hailed a hackney she'd be long gone.

An insidious suggestion pitched in his gut. Women who stole off in the middle of the night usually had one destination in mind.

A rendezvous with a lover.

For the briefest instant, he experienced a blinding desire to break another man's legs.

Lifting one hand from the reins, Fabrice pulled his hood forward in an effort to shield his stinging eyes. Coal smoke hung thick in the air tonight, drifting like jaundiced ghosts beneath the street lamps. Worse, the Thames lapped its banks at low tide, releasing a fetid stink from the mud beneath. It reminded him of the tepid bogs surrounding his native Baton Rouge, with their rising vapors that brought typhus and malaria in the hot months.

The streets were relatively hushed tonight but by no means empty. At the bottom of Nightingale Lane he turned the horses east onto High Street, lined on either side with the gaunt silhouettes of the shipping warehouses. Shoved here and there between them, the squat huddles of lodging houses and taverns tossed squares of light across the road. Beyond, a forest of masts scraped the night sky.

Madame had left their destination to him, and he had chosen to hug the riverbank east of the Tower, near the London Docks. Garbled voices and drunken laughter mingled with the shrill clangs of the buoys, discordant notes that traveled under Fabrice's skin. Handfuls of sailors and dockhands stalked the street, staggering from one sagging building to the next. Giggling, ill-clad doxies beckoned from second story windows.

Fabrice received more than one proposition along the way. Emerging from the mist, wraithlike figures picked their way across the mired lane to offer up suggestions, most of which were swallowed up by the vibrations of the coach wheels.

It did not matter. One look at them told their stories. They had spent years on the streets plying their trade. They were too old. Too jaded.

Too risky.

But the one he had come to find was new to the game and still innocent enough to remember a different way of life. Still young enough to believe in happy endings.

Some minutes later he spotted her, with her sharp shoulders and faltering gait, shuffling toward the bridge that spanned the conduit from the river into the dock basin. There were fewer people about here; the street grew darker, quieter. Farther along, beneath the bridge itself, a small bonfire illuminated a circle of hunching figures. A tavern tune's writhing melody surged on the fog, its bawdy chorus flung out over the water on licks of laughter. Were they sailors? Almsmen with nowhere else to go? Or simply thieves?

The thought of that young girl selling herself to such a band sickened him. He tucked his chin into his cloak collar and swallowed against a bitter taste.

When he pulled up beside her, she started violently and stumbled over her own unsteady gait. Only through luck did she catch her footing and regain her balance.

After a moment's hesitation she settled into the nuances of her trade, propping her fists at her waist and hoisting her chin. When Fabrice stepped down from the driver's box, the desire to flee flickered in her eyes, soon extinguished by her greater need to survive.

"Bon soir," he murmured, sweeping her with a glance that feigned admiration but in truth took in the ravages of the streets. While he detected no consumptive wheezing, her flesh hung about her bones like an ill-fitting robe. The shadows beneath her eyes stood out darker than the brown irises above. Starvation was a leisurely assassin, he knew, but a thorough one.

"Am I for you, luv," she drawled in a voice more frail than seductive, "or is there a gentleman within?" A skeletal arm gestured toward the coach.

He reached for her, his hand easily encircling her wrist. Her pulse lurched against his fingers. "Relax, mademoiselle. You have much to gain tonight."

Doubt peered fearfully from those doe eyes as he drew her toward the coach. Her hair, nondescript in the darkness, hung lank on her shoulders. Her dress was suitable for little else but the trash heap.

Looking at her, thoughts of another filled his mind. Almost a month had passed since they had snatched Gwennie from the streets. He remembered her resistance. Her terror. Her loathing of him. But he would do it all again.

He would do it tonight.

"What is your name?"

"Eleanora."

He quirked his mouth.

She shrugged. "Ellen."

He turned the door handle, but at that moment a door across the street creaked open. Urgent footsteps charged in their direction.

"You shameless hussy," a woman's voice shouted. Its echo slapped the building fronts. Seconds later a tall woman, her thin features pinched with rage, rounded the back of the coach. With a scowl of simmering contempt, she shook a fist at Ellen. "I've warned you to stay clear of this stretch of road. This here is my stretch, and if you know what's good for you you'll . . ."

"The lady and I have business to conduct." Fabrice stepped in front of the girl. "It is nothing to do with you."

"Lady, bah! A lowdown gutter whore is what she is." Her

tirade stopped short. Her expression eased as she studied him. "If it's a courtesan you're looking for, sweeting, you've come to the right place."

She leaned a shoulder against the barouche and cocked her hips. "I know how to satisfy a man's needs. Why don't you tell your master," she thrust her thumb toward the coach window, "to forget this scarecrow and hire the services of a professional."

When she tried to peer into the window, Fabrice grasped her shoulder and pulled her back. The curtain was drawn but a gap at one side revealed Madame huddled tight against the seat.

"Your services are not needed here," he growled in a voice meant to frighten.

She jerked from his hold. "Don't you paw me, you scurvy goat. I ain't some slattern you can toss about."

"Buck! Buck!" she shrieked. She started back across the road but stopped half way. "Come out here, Buck. That little tramp's at it again. And there's a bloke here thinks he can cast me aside."

Before Fabrice could shove Ellen into the carriage, a heavier set of footsteps pounded from the house. Their owner proved a mammoth of a man, taller than Fabrice by a head, his thick neck set between powerful shoulders.

"There a problem 'ere?" Shifty eyes narrowed on Fabrice and Ellen. "You want 'er, do you? That's well and fine." He ignored the indignant grunt of the woman behind him. "But this 'ere's my territory. You'll 'ave to pay me a fee, like." With a predatory grin, the man called Buck inched closer. Fabrice could smell the sheer malice emanating from him.

He easily envisioned the terms of this fee: any money he or Madame had on them—their jewelry, shoes, even the buttons on their clothing. Not to mention broken bones for him and God only knew what unspeakable things for Madame.

A glance over his shoulder assured him Ellen stood the necessary few feet away. As he had done in countless similar situations, he widened his eyes, drew an audible breath and put just enough quiver in his chin to make it visible. Then he waited until Buck's sneering countenance advanced within arm's reach.

When it did, Fabrice's hand and leg shot out simultaneously. His fingers found purchase around the huge man's neck, cutting off the blood to the brain. His knee swung upward into an unsuspecting gut. Sputtering, Buck groped to pry Fabrice's fingers from his throat. It was already too late.

Fabrice watched consciousness ebb. The man's legs wobbled before collapsing beneath him. He toppled, though not before treating Fabrice to a look of gawking astonishment. A scream from the tall woman skittered across the river.

The coach door swung open. Madame's arms snaked out, grappling at the air. Fabrice wasted no time in pushing Ellen into them. The moment Madame dragged her inside, he slammed the door and clambered to the driver's box. A fleeting glance registered several figures from the bonfire moving toward them. He clucked to the horses and urged them in a tight arc, heading back the way they had come.

Tess lurched as the coach pitched forward and then veered sharply. The momentum tossed her sideways; she hit her head against the doorframe. A weight far too slight for a grown person fell against her knees. Fingers poked like sticks at her legs, grasping for leverage.

With shaking hands Tess gripped frail shoulders, holding tight to prevent the girl being flung about more than she already had. On the floor near her feet, a small tattered heap glowed in the darkness: the lily she had intended to leave in Ellen's place. There had been no time and besides, two eyewitnesses rendered such a statement imprudent.

Beside the lily, Tanya bunched into an agitated ball. The fur spiked on her arched back while a complaint vibrated in her throat. When the barouche jolted over a rut, she screeched and leapt onto the seat beside Tess.

Ellen screeched too, startled by the feline's sudden appearance. The coach righted and settled into a brisk if bumpy pace, and Tess used the opportunity to haul Ellen onto the seat. The girl's mouth gaped. Tess feared she might start yelling, but then she clamped her lips shut. Perhaps she realized the futility of calling for help in a neighborhood such as this.

"Are you all right?" Tess asked her, holding the girl's hand in an attempt to reassure. To the same purpose, she stroked Tanya's neck. This had been a close call. Too close.

Ellen nodded, eyes wide and staring.

"You're taken aback," Tess said in the same soothing tone she often used to placate Tanya. "You didn't expect to discover a woman in this coach."

Another nod. Ellen retreated along the seat.

"You're wondering," Tess went on, "what kind of strange predicament you've found yourself in."

No nod this time. Ellen placed another several inches between them and tried to disentangle her hand from Tess's.

"You needn't worry. Fabrice and I aren't going to hurt you." She smiled. "Neither is Tanya for that matter. We've come to offer our help."

"Why?" The word shivered in the air.

"I have my reasons. Just as you have yours for doing what you've been doing. How long has it been?"

Ellen gazed into space before answering. "A few weeks."

"Would you like to stop?"

Suspicion and resentment glittered at Tess through the shadows. Over the years, she had learned about this kind of fear. Girls like Ellen dreaded the streets, dreaded the men who used them, but dreaded the unknown more. Early on Tess had realized that approaching a streetwalker and nicely offering assistance achieved no more than a smirk and a toss of the head.

In Ellen's mind, Tess presented the unknown, with possibilities so unthinkable she might rather take her chances with the evils she knew. Tess maintained her hold on the girl's hand. Physical contact at least ensured her continued attention.

"You needn't do anything you don't wish to do. I can take you somewhere safe where you can have decent clothes and enough to eat, and no one to make you do hurtful things." Tess leaned, shrinking the space between them. "Would you like that?"

Tanya stepped onto Tess's lap and sniffed the air in Ellen's direction. Purring, she offered her ears for the girl to scratch. A cautious hand reached out.

"Wh—what would I have to do in return?" Her voice teetered between hope and fright.

"A good question." Tess nodded. "There is something expected of you in return. Most definitely."

"I knew it."

"In exchange for my help," Tess continued as if she hadn't heard the girl's cynicism, "you will be required to study and learn skills that will enable you to live a decent life, so that no one—no man or anyone else—can ever hurt you or take advantage of you again." She took Ellen's chin between her thumb and forefinger. "Ever."

Tears traveled down Ellen's sunken cheeks. Her fingers convulsed around Tess's. "Why would you do this?" she whispered. "You could have been killed back there. Why would you risk yourself for the likes of me? Who are you?"

"If I tell you, you must swear never to reveal the truth to any living soul, other than those you will meet over the next several days. Can I trust you?"

Open-mouthed, Ellen nodded.

"My dear girl, I am the Midnight Marauder."

Chapter 10

Tess arose later than usual the next day, dragging her weary body out of bed beneath the weight of a crushing headache. Please let Charles already have gone out, she thought, for she didn't believe she could put up a brave front for him for several hours at least. She felt a surge of relief sometime later upon entering an empty morning room. An inquiry with young Becca confirmed his scarcity in the house.

Ah, but her relief would not last long.

"Good morning, Mrs. Emerson." Charles's sudden appearance in the doorway startled her. She hadn't heard his approaching footsteps. Perhaps he had tiptoed down the corridor just for the purpose of catching her off guard. Which was exactly what he'd done.

She whisked her hand over the note she'd been reading. "I thought you'd gone out. Becca told me so."

"Yes, good morning to you, too, Charles."

"Oh, quite right. Good morning." Hoping her smile held his attention, she inched the note beneath her plate. Helena had written earlier to report on her temporary charge. Ellen seemed recovered from last night's escapade and quite likely to eat the Holbrooks out of house and home. Well and good. Later today, they would send the girl on to Highgate Court in one of their carriages.

Charles picked up his plate and sauntered to the sideboard. Tess used the opportunity to slip the note into her bodice.

She hadn't liked involving the Holbrooks again. If the truth ever came out, the scandal might very well cost Wesley his seat in the Commons. But there were times, like now, when she couldn't manage alone, when the Marauder needed accomplices. Odd thing, the otherwise fiercely protective Wesley had proved surprisingly cooperative, even eager to help, providing his wife took no midnight rides along with Tess.

Charles returned to the table, his plate laden with eggs, sausages and a scone slathered in preserves. Feeling his gaze heavy upon her, Tess wished she had asked Fabrice to bring the morning newspaper so she might bury her face behind its pages. Earlier, her dressing table mirror had announced the stark truth: she presented a dismal image this morning with swollen, bloodshot eyes and a distinctly gray cast to her skin.

"Enjoy a restful night, did you?" Charles asked as he picked up his knife and fork.

"Quite well, thank you." She frowned. An innocent enough question to be sure, but something in his tone raised her guard.

"You look much better than when you arrived home last evening."

"Do I?" What did he mean? What did he know of last night? She had waited until long after he'd retired for the evening, until she'd heard his restful breathing from beneath his door. Only then had she and Fabrice ventured from the house.

"When you returned from your visit with Helena," he said, prodding his eggs with his fork, "you complained of a headache."

"Ah, that." She bit into a slice of currant bread. "All better now, thank you."

"Glad to hear it. So where's the cat?"

She glanced up in alarm. Why would he ask about Tanya? Had he heard her yowling in the garden after they'd arrived home last night, as she'd chased a mouse around the gazebo?

Becca saved her from having to answer by entering with the coffeepot. As Charles held out his cup, Tess studied his face. Despite his amicable concern for her welfare, a grim shadow hovered about his mouth.

He suspected; she knew he did. And soon he'd ask questions she would not be able to answer. If the Midnight Marauder's identity ever became common knowledge, she'd be forever unable to secure positions for her girls once they were ready to leave Highgate Court. No one in respectable society would hire a former prostitute.

"What are your plans today?"

She flinched at the sound of his voice. What had he been saying? She reached for her coffee. Though she hadn't yet added sugar or cream she endured a bitter sip, buying time to gather her composure. "You were saying?"

"I was asking about your plans."

"Plans? Today? None to speak of."

"Good. A note came a little while ago . . ."

She heard little explanation of this note as her thoughts again drifted. The situation was becoming impossible. With Charles residing in her home, her normal, hectic double life threatened to dissolve into chaos beyond her control. Ah, but he couldn't be blamed, could he? She had asked—no, begged—him to stay here in a desperate attempt to ensure the Midnight Marauder's continued exploits.

But what of Tess Hardington? Had she any future to look forward to? Sometimes she felt as though that ordinary woman barely existed, was little more than a ghost haunting—and haunted by—the happiness of her past.

"Tess?"

Her thoughts scattered. His gaze keen upon her, Charles rose and circled the table. Standing beside her chair he dwarfed her, filled her vision. She found herself contemplating the checked weave of his waistcoat—its snug fit across a trim abdomen and powerful chest—until he grasped her chin and raised it.

"What's going on inside that lovely head of yours?" His thumb smoothed back and forth below her bottom lip. "You're worlds away."

More than the most relentless questions and fiercest demands, his gentle touch had the power to melt her resolve. *Tell him. Just tell him.*

"I—I'm a bit preoccupied."

He studied her a long, silent moment that bordered on unendurable. "You didn't sleep at all well last night, did you?"

The question resounded with accusation, but with invitation, too. It provided the perfect opportunity to confess the truth, to seek shelter against that broad chest and admit that not only had she not slept well, she'd hardly occupied her bed at all because she'd been out most of the night.

He released her and logic came sweeping back. Charles Emerson was not her husband. No genuine commitment existed between them, no binding pact on which to base loyalty. In a corner of her mind, Alicia's memory whispered caution, reminding her that Charles had left her once before, when she so very much needed him to stay. Reminding her, too, that her secrets were not hers alone. They belonged to countless others who might suffer for her weakness.

"Excuse me." Scraping back her chair, she gained her feet and attempted to squeeze between Charles and the table. But he stood his ground, and her hand knocked her bowl of blueberries and clotted cream. Frothy blots scattered across the table linen and onto Charles's sleeve. He regarded his ruined morning coat in silence.

"Oh, dear. Oh, I am sorry." She snatched a napkin and swatted at his arm. "Do forgive me."

"Quite." He stayed her hand with his own. "That is if you'll stop hitting me."

She tossed the napkin to the table and massaged her temple. "I'm afraid this headache never completely left me." She started for the door. "Do excuse me."

"No."

She stopped and turned. "I'm sorry?"

"Come out with me."

"But my head . . ."

"A brisk ride in the open air would do you wonders." The

authority in his voice brooked no argument. "Have Fabrice harness the curricle and off we go."

"I don't think so."

"Go on. I'll change quickly and we'll be on our way. As your husband, madam, I insist." The corners of his mouth tilted with too cunning a slant to be termed a smile.

Apprehension settled in Tess's stomach, crowding the meager breakfast she'd consumed. What was the man scheming this morning?

Within the hour, Charles steered the curricle from Park Lane into Hyde Park. The previous night's fog lingered despite it being well past noon, creating the illusion of disembodied trees presiding over ethereal gardens and miasmic pavilions.

But the man beside Tess was substantial enough, warm and solid against her shoulder, her arm, her thigh. His scent drifted, raising a strange tumult inside her, a spinning ball of anticipation and a little bit of fear.

"Feeling better?" He bent his head to see beneath her bonnet's wide brim. His gaze held hers with a dark intensity, sending that ball inside her careening all the more wildly.

"Quite restored, thank you," she said and hoped he wouldn't study her closely enough to know she was lying. Folding her gloved hands in her lap, she scanned the meadow beside the lane. "Do we have a plan or are we to wander aimlessly?"

"Indeed we do have a plan." A light wind scuttled the clouds apart and rays of sunshine began burning through the mist. Other coaches soon became visible up ahead. Charles shaded his eyes and peered toward an open tilbury. "Isn't that the Princess Von Haucke's carriage? Let's pay our respects."

"Must we?" But he had already clucked the horse to a trot.

In moments they caught up with the fashionable two-seater. Hazy sunlight glinted off the Von Haucke coat of arms with its incorporated Habsburg crest emblazoned in blue and gold on sleek black lacquer. The princess held the reins. Beside her sat Arabella Stewart, her lovely violet eyes widening with interest at the sight of Charles. Both ladies boasted the very latest in carriage dresses, with sweeping collars and flared hems trimmed in bold braid.

"Good afternoon, ladies," Charles hailed as he pulled the curricle up beside them.

Miss Stewart brandished a gloved hand. "Why, Mr. Emerson, what a pleasure." Her agreeable expression dissolved. "Good afternoon, Mrs. Emerson."

Tess managed a taut smile.

"Good afternoon, Mr. and Mrs. Emerson." Catching Charles's eye, the princess flashed a dimple and shook her ringlets. "How lovely to see you again. Where have you been hiding yourself? People are beginning to wonder."

"Are they indeed?" Charles exchanged a glance of mild astonishment with Tess, an entirely fabricated one by her estimate.

The princess laughed coyly into her hand. "It isn't at all fashionable for newlyweds to keep to themselves, Mr. Emerson. Why, people will begin to believe the two of you are smitten." She traded giggles with her companion. "It so happens I have extra tickets to Almacks tonight. Would you like one? Oh, dear me, I meant to say would you like a pair, for Mrs. Emerson and yourself, of course."

Oh, of course. And what sort of welcome would Tess find at Almacks? Sneers and tight-lipped greetings, insults designed to humiliate while being too subtle to warrant open acknowledgement.

Charles dismissed the offer with a cluck of his tongue. "I'm afraid we must decline. We've other plans for this evening."

They did? Tess couldn't remember any.

"Can't you change them?" Arabella asked with a tinge of impatience.

"I'm afraid not. People may wonder what they will and I daresay they won't be far off in their suspicions. I know that sounds hopelessly gauche and you must forgive me for it, but Mrs. Emerson and I are far too blissfully wedded to worry about what anyone thinks of us." He aimed a sly wink at the ladies before turning an expression of sheer adoration on Tess.

Her pulse lurched. She'd not seen that look in many, many years, yet it evoked memories that seared her heart.

When he winked again for her eyes only, she understood. His sudden ardor had been affected for Arabella's and the princess's benefits, not hers. Disappointment vied with common sense. Longing with caution. Wishes with truth.

The ladies exchanged sullen pouts. "Good day," they chimed in unison and drove on.

"Habsburg coat of arms, indeed," Charles muttered when they once more had the lane to themselves. "Is she even really a princess?"

Tess studied his profile, wondering whether to scold him or kiss him. "You did that on purpose, didn't you? Just to raise their dander."

"You mean hackles. And they more than deserved it after the shameless way they flirted with me at the Holbrooks' supper party. Besides . . ." He broke into a grin filled with boyish mischief. "Thought you could use a bit of cheering up this morning."

She hid a grin of her own. "You should be ashamed of yourself."

"I'm not."

"Neither am I."

"Good. Now then, about our plans." He flicked the reins lightly over the horse's back. "First an excursion through the park to see and be seen, so it might be reported to your uncle that we were abroad together as newlyweds should be. The ladies should prove useful in that department."

She laughed. "Despite your principles, Mr. Emerson, deception isn't quite beyond your ken, is it?"

"Not when I have the example of a master to follow."

She tucked her chin, taking cover beneath her bonnet. To change the subject she asked, "Where to next?"

"Into the City for a visit with my father," he said evenly,

"and afterward I thought we might dine at the Clarendon Hotel. If you've no objections."

Tess's pulse centers tapped out an alarm. "What was that first thing?"

"Heading into the City."

"To visit . . .?"

"My father."

A tentative throb heralded the return of her headache. "Why on earth would we want to do that?"

"I told you at breakfast, goose, weren't you listening? My father's returned to London and he'd like to see me as soon as possible. I thought we'd go to his office together."

"Are you mad?"

"He said he'd like to congratulate us."

"He knows about us?" She could have bitten her tongue; her question sounded far more suggestive than she'd meant. "I mean about our arrangement?"

Charles's eyebrows shot up and Tess realized she'd attached even more lewdness to their situation. "I mean our *agreement.*"

"Ah. I assume he knows only what my mother has told him."

"And what the blazes might that be?"

He shrugged. "That you and I are married."

"You told your mother that?" Her voice became shrill but Charles didn't flinch.

"Actually, no." Damnably calm, he paused to consider. "I believe it might have been her dressmaker or some such person, who heard it from a friend, who heard it from her maid, who heard it at the market and so forth."

"Why didn't you tell her the truth?"

"What, that we're not married but merely living together? Considering Helena's reaction, I hardly considered that a sound idea."

"Charles, how can you let your family believe we're married? What will you tell them when we, you know . . ."

"Divorce?"

She shuddered. "Don't use that ugly word. And we won't divorce because we are not married."

"Separate then."

That term held no more appeal than the first. Yet they'd do exactly that, eventually. Sooner than eventually, because once they discovered a way to elude Uncle Howard's claims on her inheritance, she'd no longer need Charles.

Not need Charles? Oh, but when he left, who would hold her on those nights when the grief and guilt became too much to bear? Who would claim she looked perfect in her everyday clothes and escort her to Vauxhall Gardens? Who would stand between her and the unkind stares, the well-aimed snubs?

"I can't help but remember," he said after a moment of silence, "that you took quite the cavalier attitude when I brought up these very same concerns at the outset of our little debacle."

She chose to ignore that last word. "I was only thinking of casual acquaintances, people whose opinions don't matter. I never thought your family would become involved."

"And why not?" His shoulders went rigid; his fists tightened around the reins. "Did you think my family so removed from polite society they wouldn't hear of their own son's elopement?"

"No, of course not." A breeze fluttered against the straw brim of her bonnet. She tugged it lower over her brow. "I'd thought . . . I don't know what I thought. I suppose that's the problem. Come, I've seen enough of the park. Let's go and do what we must."

"As you will, madam."

"It's certainly not my will and you know it. Obviously this excursion through the park was merely a ruse to convey me to your father's offices."

"Such a charge, madam. And wholly unfounded."

"Oh, pish. Let's get this over with."

He made an adjustment to the reins and the horse picked

up its pace. Tess watched the terse motions with which
Charles steered east at the next fork and headed back toward
Park Lane. She despaired of understanding his moods today.
The gamut of suspicion to playfulness to his now obvious ir-
ritation had left her weary and bewildered.

Yet the day was far from over. How would she gather sufficient courage to face Richard Emerson, a man whose son
she once spurned and whose family her uncle maligned so
unforgivably? How would such a man receive her?

It was not the sudden pitch of the curricle that sent her
stomach plummeting to her toes.

Chapter 11

In the shadow of St. Paul's dome, Charles steered the curricle onto Cannon Street and stopped in front of the offices of Emerson & Son. And none too soon, in his estimate.

Thus far he'd given Tess ample opportunity—not to mention blatant prodding—to utter at least one truthful remark in his hearing. Another few minutes alone with her and he might have stopped the curricle, seized her face between his hands and demanded to know where she'd gone last night, who she'd been with and what she took such great pains to hide from him. And then, just to prevent any more lies slipping through her luscious lips, he more than likely would have kissed her speechless.

He was angry, damn it, and far too obsessed with this woman's mysterious antics for his own good. This trip to Emerson & Son should serve as a solid reminder, to him and Tess both, that he had plans and goals of his own.

They stepped into the cool green and teak tones of the lobby to find the establishment bustling at a brisk pace. Waiting patrons sat ranged along leather settees while workers scurried from office to office carrying rolls of plans beneath their arms. In response to Charles's inquiry, a clerk directed them to the narrow corridor that spanned the building from front to back.

They discovered Richard Emerson in the large rear office. Rows of drafting tables stood oddly empty for that time of day. Charles soon surmised the reason for the absence of the draftsmen. Near the alley door, his father stood speaking with a man dressed in the coarse, durable clothes of a laborer. The two men appeared embroiled in some sort of debate, a heated one by the looks and sounds of it.

As he and Tess looked on unnoticed, the roughly dressed chap grew red-faced and made aggressive gestures in the air. Charles caught sharp-edged references to vandalism and missing building materials. Unperturbed and holding his ground, his father answered each complaint with a commendable show of patience.

Charles experienced a surge of pride toward his parent. Like his mother, Richard Emerson hadn't changed much in three years. A little grayer about the temples, a bit more lined around the mouth. But still tall and straight in his conservative but well-tailored suit, his bearing still the steady mingling of confidence and modesty that had always won him the trust of workman and wealthy businessman alike.

At a particularly harsh reproach from the workman, Tess gasped. Charles cupped her elbow and turned her toward the door, at the same time stepping between her and the offensive fellow. "I'm sorry. Come, we can wait in the private office."

"Not on your life," she whispered back. "This is far too interesting."

Before he could ponder the wisdom of humoring her, the argument hit a crescendo and reached its conclusion. Shaking the workman's hand, Charles's father promised to appear at the site in question before the day's end. With a mollified shrug, the worker left through the alley door.

It was then his father saw Charles, holding him in his gaze a long moment as if unsure whether to trust his eyes. Then he crossed the room. "Son."

That was all he said as he clasped Charles's hand. His embrace was equally brief. Charles hadn't expected more, nor did there need to be. The sentiments spoke from the glimmer in the elder man's eyes, from the firm set of a mouth doing its utmost to remain dignified.

"Sorry about that." He hooked a thumb toward the alley door. "On-site problems, you know."

"Is it resolved?" Charles knew the best way to return his father's stoic affection was to show concern for the family business.

Richard beamed at him. "It will be, soon enough. Now tell me," his voice dropped to a confidential undertone, "can I finally add the S?"

"You can, Father."

"The S?" Tess poked her head out from behind Charles's shoulder. "Whatever is that?"

He moved aside as she swept forward, her tentative smile barely concealing an apprehension he shared. Remembering his mother's reaction to the news of their marriage, he wondered what to expect now.

His father reached for her hand. "Forgive me for not greeting you properly, my dear. I was so pleased to see my son that I momentarily forgot my manners. How are you, Miss—" He broke off with a shake of his head. "I almost called you Miss James."

"That was long ago, sir."

"Indeed. And now you're my daughter, an Emerson." He raised her hand and kissed it. "Welcome to the family, my dear. I wish you and Charles all the happiness in the world."

"Do you?" She seemed taken aback, her smile both wistful and uncertain.

"I most certainly do." The emphasis placed on the words hinted at the row he must have endured with Charles's mother. He frowned over Tess's hand, still grasped in his own. "We'll leave the past where it belongs, shall we? I'm happy for you both."

"But . . ." She glanced up at Charles, her eyes imploring him to come clean.

But as his father placed a hand at her waist and declared the backroom no place for a celebration, Charles couldn't find the proper words. As they proceeded to the private office and passed round small glasses of sherry, Charles could not muster the heart to halt the good intentions. When his father raised his glass and toasted the radiant bride, it moved beyond Charles's power to gainsay those words.

It was too rare a treat to see someone other than the Holbrooks show her true kindness. And its effect on her—she positively would have glowed were it not for the imperative looks she shot him each time his father turned his back.

For the briefest moment he questioned his motives, especially when Tess might in fact be cuckolding him in the most brazen manner.

Where the blazes had she gone last night?

Yet, with his anger dulled by his father's generosity as well as by sherry, he conceded the absurdity of his suspicions. If Tess had a lover, why would she have appealed to Charles for help in the first place? Not to mention that a woman could not, by definition, cuckold a man who was not her husband.

Which brought him back to the present matter. "Father, there's something we must tell you." But his resolve withered again when the sunlight fell full on the elder man's features.

Had Charles believed his father hadn't aged much? Ah, now he saw his mistake, plain in the pallor of the other man's skin, the fatigue clouding his eyes. It was gone—the last of Richard Emerson's youth—faded behind the etchings of responsibility, in employing every shred of energy to ensure his family's welfare.

Charles experienced a pang. He should have been here. All these years, he should have been helping, sharing the burdens. He was the elder son. He should have taken his place in the family business, at his father's side, long ago. His years in the military had been wrong on so many levels.

"We're very sorry, Father, to have married in secret," he lied, ignoring Tess's ill-concealed groan of frustration. "Sorrier still you were not there to share in our happiness."

"Ah, son, I understand." His father waved a dismissive hand. "It's your time to be young and impetuous, mine to be old and wise." Grinning, he raised his glass. "In the latter case, I at least try."

"With great success, sir," Tess said, and Charles was sure she blinked away a tear. "But you still haven't told me what the S means."

"Ah, the S. Perhaps you noticed our sign out front, the one that reads, 'Emerson and Son', the son being Charles's younger brother, George. For years I've waited for Charles to return home and join us. Now that he has, I can change the sign to read 'Sons'."

"Speaking of George," Charles said, "did he return with you to London?"

"Not yet. He detoured to Suffolk, but he and Caroline should arrive here by Wednesday. Did you know she's increasing again?"

"I didn't. That's wonderful. George must be beside himself."

"Only just found out, and yes he is. Why don't you and Tess join us for supper Wednesday night? We'll have George and Caroline as well and the four of you can exchange congratulations."

"Oh, dear, I . . . I don't believe we can," Tess stammered.

"Why on earth not?" His father placed his sherry glass on the desk. "It's the perfect opportunity to reunite the family. Except for Charles's sister, Jane, of course. You remember Jane, don't you, Tess? She married Andrew Carlyle—don't know if you ever met him. They have four children. All off touring the Continent at the moment. So you will come, won't you?"

"We'd, ah, like it very much, Father."

"Charles," Tess murmured in a little singsong voice. Her expression accused him of having lost his wits.

And she might be right. Considering his mother's attitude, bringing Tess to a family supper would surely be nothing short of a disaster. He'd be mad to chance it.

"I'd forgotten, Father. Tess and I have prior plans for

Wednesday." His father's obvious disappointment stabbed at his conscience. "Tentative plans, that is. If they change, we'll let you know."

"Yes," Tess said brightly, "if they change, we'll let you know."

"Yes . . . do," Richard said with a perplexed frown.

"But I would like to speak with you and George both as soon as he's back, Father. It's business."

"By all means. You're part of this enterprise now."

"Thank you, sir. I suppose we should let you get back to work now."

"Yes." Tess was on her feet, smiling and extending her hand. "We don't wish to keep you."

"You'll let me know about Wednesday evening?"

"Of course, Father."

They shook hands all around, his father lingering over Tess's for an added moment. As she walked out to the lobby, Richard detained Charles with a hand on his shoulder.

"You mustn't think you aren't welcome at home."

"Of course I don't, Father."

"Your mother will come around. She always does."

Hardly convinced of that, Charles nodded.

The worry lines around Richard's eyes deepened. "Please try to come Wednesday night. It would mean the world to me."

Charles hesitated.

"Yes, I know, son. You'll try."

"Now you have me lying to my father," Charles muttered minutes later as he eased the curricle away from the foot pavement. He felt abominable.

"I have *you* lying?" Indignation flared Tess's nostrils.

"Yes, about joining my parents for supper."

"Never mind that. You should have told him the truth about us."

"I tried."

"You should have tried harder." Her lips pursed in disapproval, though their plump pout would have served equally well for a kiss. A good, sound one to keep her quiet for a few moments at least.

Well, he supposed he did deserve to have his own words thrown back in his face after the way he had upbraided her about not being truthful with Helena at the outset.

"It's better this way," he said.

"How so?" she asked sullenly, adjusting her hat.

"Let my parents believe what they will for now. It'll be easier to explain everything after the fact than during." A flimsy excuse, even he had to admit. He'd managed to find extenuating reasons to leave both his parents ignorant of the truth. For their sakes? He'd like to think so. His damned conscience suggested otherwise, that perhaps not telling them was his way of indulging in past hopes that hadn't quite been left in the past.

Tsk-tsking beside him, Tess tugged on the braided cords of her reticule. "Now what are we to do?"

"I've plans to see a solicitor later today." Squinting in the sunlight, he steered the horse past St. Paul's Cathedral and onto Ludgate Street. "If he can find a loophole in your father's will, matters may be resolved soon."

"One can only hope."

"Eager to be rid of me?" He looked away. Her offhand statement rankled, a fact that forced him to acknowledge he harbored more than the simple wish to help an old friend. He flicked the reins and guided the curricle around a slow moving cart. He wanted much more, damn it, than Tess seemed willing to give.

"You needn't scowl so." Her hand came down on his forearm, a delicate entreaty that inflamed him, fanning a desire to feel all of her against him. "I'm not eager to be rid of you," she said. "All I meant was that I hope we're soon free to return to life as normal. This is taxing for both of us." She paused, searching his face. "Isn't it?"

"Indeed." More than she'd ever know. More than he could have guessed.

"So," she said, brightening, "who is this solicitor we're going to see?"

"*I'm* going to see."

Her shoulders squared in a troops-to-the-offensive manner. "I am most certainly going with you."

"It would be better if I saw the man alone."

"Why?" Not so much a question as a drawing of battle lines.

He knew she wouldn't readily accept his reasoning. He would try anyway. "This is a delicate matter and the man I have in mind is an old friend from——"

"I fail to see how that precludes me from being involved in my own affairs."

"I thought it might make things easier since——"

"You thought wrong, my friend."

Exasperation set in. His fuse was becoming considerably shorter with each passing day. He blew out a breath. "You're not going to let me finish a sentence, are you?"

"Not until you utter the words, 'Tess, we are going to see the solicitor together.'"

"Good grief, have it your way."

"Say it."

He gritted his teeth. "Tess, we are going to see the solicitor together."

"Splendid," she exclaimed. "Now, who is the chap and how do you know we can trust him? After all, there are precious many facts we don't want sneaking out just yet."

"Such as our sham marriage?"

"Precisely. We need our aces all in a row before we come clean."

"More like a mopping up, I should think," he muttered.

"What was that?"

"Nothing. Kenneth Fortier is an old military friend. He returned to private life a few years ago and has done pretty well for himself. He's sharp, shrewd and knows how to keep his mouth shut."

"Sounds like our man," she declared. "Let's see him now, before going to the Clarendon."

"Whatever you say, my dear." He shook his head and wondered if he'd ever feel in command of his life again.

They rode on in silence, lost in their separate thoughts, shoulders occasionally bumping with the jostling of the rig. That seemed to fairly well sum up their so-called marriage, he thought. Two people living separate lives, bumping shoulders every so often as life jounced them about.

It wasn't much to boast.

Chapter 12

The Clarendon's dining room was packed and noisy, and Tess enjoyed the pleasure of disappearing into the anonymity of a lively eatery. The other patrons hardly noticed her beyond a few perfunctory glances. Perhaps Charles's solid presence warded off the ill will. Or did the wide brim of her hat simply prevent anyone recognizing her?

"You going to eat that or redesign it?" From across the café table, Charles gestured toward her plate with his fork.

"Very funny." She regarded the venison pie she'd all but dissected with knife and fork. "I'm not very hungry."

"Thinking about what Kenneth said?"

"It all keeps spinning around in my mind. Codicils, entailments, escape clauses . . . all of it sounds highly unlikely and not very encouraging."

"There's always Ken's main suggestion." Charles didn't look up as he spoke. "Which is to make real what we're already pretending."

Her heart fluttered, just as it had when Mr. Fortier first made the recommendation. Married to Charles, *really* married. To plan their days together just as they had today: a ride through the park, a visit with family, dining out. It all seemed so natural. Comfortable. Even their occasional bickering had taken on the rhythm of old habit.

But when Charles looked up again she saw the amused quirk on his brow. The subject of marriage had merely become an ironic jest between them.

Their time had passed ten very long years ago. He had his own life to lead now; he had his work with his father and brother. To her dismay, she realized that this, too, constituted another insurmountable difference between them. The Emersons transformed old squares and alleys into posh neighborhoods, while the poor families that lived there found themselves evicted from their homes. As Tess well knew, such circumstances led to many more women walking the streets at night.

"Don't give up hope." He raised his voice as the surrounding clamor increased in volume. "Ken will find some loophole in the papers we left him."

She nodded but thought perhaps she'd detected a skeptical note in his reassurance, as if he were less than resigned to their plan. She wondered. . . .

"Tessa. *Teeessssa*."

Startled, she glanced all around, searching for the source of her name weaving a thin path through the tangles of conversation. "Oh dear, that sounds rather like . . ."

Uncle Howard. His lanky figure stood nearly a head taller than every other occupant of the hotel lobby. As Tess sank in her chair he caught sight of her, hailed, and started through the arched doorway into the dining room.

"Of all the restaurants in London," she muttered in disbelief, "he had to pick this one." She fingered the buttons on her carriage jacket. "It's almost too much to bear."

Charles's brow furrowed. "One would almost believe he's been following us."

"I swear the man hangs about me like a disease."

"A fine time to be quoting Shakespeare. What do you suppose he wants? I hope not the . . ."

"Marriage license. What else?" She drew a fortifying breath. "Never fear, I'm ready for him."

"What do you mean?"

She hadn't time to answer. Howard James arrived at their table and treated them to a decidedly malevolent smirk.

"Good afternoon, Mr. and Mrs. Emerson." The *missus* dripped with sarcasm.

"Good afternoon, Uncle Howard." Tess raised her chin and met his predatory gaze. "I trust you are well."

"Quite, thank you." His sneer persisted, a wolfish baring of the teeth. "How fortunate running into you. It may save me a trip to your home."

"Oh? Is there something we can do for you, Uncle?"

"Yes. The marriage license. You wouldn't happen to have it with you?"

It was a moment she'd anticipated and dreaded, for it would either buy her the time she needed or cut her deception short. She willed her fingers not to tremble as she lifted her purse from her lap.

"As a matter of fact, Uncle, I do." Rather than savoring his dumbfounded expression, she focused on her reticule as she untied the cords and opened it wide. He thought he had her cornered, did he? She pursed her lips to keep from smiling. As long as Howard didn't find anything in the document to make him question its validity, she'd be in the clear.

She handed him the paper with as benign an expression as she could manage. "I'm sure you'll find everything in proper order."

"Of course," Howard mumbled. He pulled a pair of spectacles from his waistcoat pocket. Setting them on his nose, he began perusing the contents.

Charles shifted in his chair, trying to peer around the edge of the page. He looked as stupefied as Uncle Howard, even more so when his gaze locked on the sight of his own signature near the bottom of the document.

Oh dear. She really should have discussed the matter with him after Fabrice returned from Highgate Court, but there had been neither the time nor the opportunity.

No, that wasn't it. She just hadn't rallied sufficient courage.

But do close your mouth before you make Uncle Howard

suspicious. Compressing her lips, she settled for a more subtle warning—a swift tap with the toe of her shoe beneath the table. Charles flinched—more from surprise than pain, of course, because she'd barely grazed him. He positively glowered. She flashed him another silent but imploring message from beneath her lashes: *just play along*.

A begrudging nod conveyed his understanding while his continued scowls promised a thorough admonishment in the not-too-distant future.

Howard cleared his throat. "May I take this with me?"

And let you show it to a solicitor? "I'd much prefer not," she said, then added with a laugh, "I suppose I'm still too new a bride to let it out of my sight. But you may join us and look it over as long as you like. You have no objections, have you, Charles?"

She interpreted his grimace as permission. Apparently, so did Uncle Howard. He slid a vacant chair out from under the table and plunked down onto it. With a snap he straightened the license and hunched to continue his scrutiny. Tess held her breath.

"Don't let me stop you from enjoying your meal," Howard murmured without looking up.

"Hmmm." She poked at her ruined pastry, then exchanged another exasperated look with Charles, or at least tried to. He was staring over her shoulder into the lobby.

He tossed his napkin to the table. "If you two will excuse me a moment."

"Where are you—?" But he was already gone. She glanced over her shoulder to watch him disappear behind a boisterous gaggle of ladies who had just stood up from their table. A moment later she glimpsed the back of his coat as he crossed the lobby and vanished into the gentlemen's taproom.

Oh, that man. How *could* he abandon her?

She went back to watching Uncle Howard. As his eyes skimmed the certificate, his lips caught between his teeth,

Take A Trip Into A Timeless World of Passion and Adventure with Kensington Choice Historical Romances!
—Absolutely FREE!

Enjoy the passion and adventure of another time with Kensington Choice Historical Romances. They are the finest novels of their kind, written by today's best-selling romance authors. Each Kensington Choice Historical Romance transports you to distant lands in a bygone age. Experience the adventure and share the delight as proud men and spirited women discover the wonder and passion of true love.

Get 4 FREE Books!

We created our convenient Home Subscription Service so you'll be sure to have the hottest new romances delivered each month right to your doorstep—usually before they are available in book stores. Just to show you how convenient the Zebra Home Subscription Service is, we would like to send you 4 FREE Kensington Choice Historical Romances. The books are worth up to $24.96, but you only pay $1.99 for shipping and handling. There's no obligation to buy additional books—ever!

Save Up To 30% With Home Delivery!

Accept your FREE books and each month we'll deliver 4 brand new titles as soon as they are published. They'll be yours to examine FREE for 10 days. Then if you decide to keep the books, you'll pay the preferred subscriber's price (up to 30% off the cover price!), plus shipping and handling. Remember, you are under no obligation to buy any of these books at any time! If you are not delighted with them, simply return them and owe nothing. But if you enjoy Kensington Choice Historical Romances as much as we think you will, pay the special preferred subscriber rate and save over $8.00 off the cover price!

protruded, then skewed to one side. Oh, he was angry all right, and that made Tess hopeful. Hopeful enough to be bold.

"You see, Uncle?" She stabbed the meat pie with the point of her knife. "Everything is in order, just as I told you."

His throat made a grinding sound. His nose crinkled. "What about the banns?"

"Special license, as indicated." She pointed toward the certificate. "We saw no reason to wait."

"Hmm." He rubbed his chin. "Witnesses?"

"Signed right there at the bottom by Mrs. Rutherford and Anne, the groundskeeper's daughter." She twisted her knife into mangled meat and piecrust.

"Anne . . . how old is she?"

The knife fell to her plate with a clatter, attracting attention from nearby tables. Tess returned inquisitive glances with an apologetic shrug. "Old enough," she replied, gritting her teeth. "Anne's old enough to witness what Reverend Coombs made legal. Will you please accept it, Uncle?"

"Humph." He launched his chair backward, knocking the table with his thighs as he stood. Tea sloshed over the rim of Tess's teacup and dribbled onto the table linen. "I'll accept it," he said. "For now. Goodbye, my dear." He smacked the license onto the table and shoved it toward her. She snatched it up before spilled tea spread a stain across the seal.

She's gone too far this time, Charles brooded as he made his way across the dining room, dodging waiters and veering narrowly around tables. Not only falsifying legal documents but forging signatures. His signature. And a deuced good forgery at that.

But he wondered. Had she fashioned his signature to that paper? Knowing Tess, she'd simply have cajoled him into signing the damned certificate himself. No, this caper had Fabrice written all over it.

Crossing the lobby and stepping through the curtained

archway into the taproom, his mood calmed. Masculine colors and the resonant hum of male conversation produced a steadying effect. Charles's pace slowed, his footfalls eased. In a moment he spied the excuse for his sudden and admittedly rude departure from the dining room: the familiar face he'd followed. He crossed the room.

"If it isn't the Viscount Kirkwood. This seat taken?" He placed a hand on the back of an armchair. Seated in the wing chair opposite, a decidedly raw-boned man of about Charles's age shrugged and shifted long legs as though not quite sure what to do with them.

A pair of bored-looking eyes rose to take stock of Charles's attire, then his features. Recognition dawned. "I know you."

"It's been a long while." Charles grinned. "I'll give you a hint. A gang of quite foxed underclassmen decide to challenge each other to a midnight row across the lake. One boat tips over, and a spindly sot who hasn't the foggiest notion of how to swim goes under. I leap in after him, though I'm so deep in my cups myself it's doubtful I'll ever find my way to shore, much less drag you there."

"Emerson, you old dog." The man unfolded his long legs and stood.

"How are you, Kirkwood?" Charles shook his hand. "Still haunting pub rooms, I see."

"A man's got to have his comforts. Sit down. How's life treating you?" The viscount tucked his length back into his chair, one knee becoming a craggy peak inside its trouser leg, the other stretching awkwardly under the low table in front of him. "Such a coincidence seeing you here. You were the subject of a fascinating discussion only the other day."

Charles made a long-suffering face. "I dread to ask."

"Is it true? *Have* you entered a state of wedded bliss?" Elbows propped on the arms of his chair, Kirkwood bent forward in interest.

Charles shoved out a breath. "Where'd you hear it?"

"At my barber's."

Good grief, where *hadn't* the news of his marriage been heralded? "I suppose you could say it's true."

"You suppose?"

"It's been a hell of a few days."

"A whirlwind romance?"

Charles felt a sudden urge to confide. He and this man hadn't been more than casual friends at university. They'd been underclassmen together at Cambridge's Trinity College, but for the most part the viscount had run with a wilder set. Still, he'd had a reputation for discretion, a bloke who'd help a fellow out of a scrape and keep mum about the details.

But all Charles said was, "I sort of married the lady as a favor."

"A favor?" Kirkwood puckered his lips and whistled. "Remind me to ask you next time I need a good turn. But then, she's not a chore to look at, is she? You can't be suffering too badly from your philanthropy."

Charles was taken aback. "You know Tess?"

"You introduced me to her once. At the Winston's Christmas party, I believe, not long before you donned the king's uniform. How well I remember it. You went about boasting to any man who'd listen that Tessa James would be your wife before the next Season." Kirkwood leaned back thoughtfully and folded his arms. "I have to say, that was such a long time ago I was damned surprised to hear you'd hooked up with the lady again."

"It's a long story." And one he didn't have time for at the moment. He tugged his watch from his waistcoat pocket. By his estimate he'd been away from Tess and her uncle nearly ten minutes. With any luck, Howard had gone on his way. He felt a stab of guilt. Abandoning Tess hadn't been one of his more gallant acts.

He replaced the watch and stood. "I should be getting back to my party. Care to join us?"

Kirkwood waved the notion away. "I've eaten, thanks. And

anyway, newlyweds like yourselves hardly need a third wheel."

"Are you in London for the Season?"

"More than likely." Kirkwood reached into the pocket of his coat and extracted a card. "Here is my direction. I'm usually up by noon and home till two, although . . ." He covered his mouth with his hand as though relating something scandalous. "I wouldn't come by with the wife if I were you, the place is never presentable. A real bachelor flat."

"So you've never married?"

"Me?" Pale lips curled in mock horror.

Charles laughed. "Not to worry. If I come, I'll come alone." After all, calling on his old friend might provide a few moments of peace in an otherwise chaotic life.

"Or you can usually find me at my club in the late afternoons. It's Bartle's. On Arlington just off Piccadilly."

"I know the place." An establishment for men only. No women. No Tess. Sounded like heaven.

"Be seeing you then?"

"Count on it."

After paying the luncheon bill without so much as a word, Charles offered a rigid arm to Tess. "Let's go."

She chewed her lip as she stood. He was angry, even angrier, perhaps, than Uncle Howard. Rightfully so, she supposed. But surely once he understood. . . .

"Where are we going?" she asked, sliding her hand into the unyielding crook of his arm.

"Coach," he snapped. His biceps flexed, as rigid as hewn oak against her fingertips. Oh, yes, he was irked.

"Of course," she said, hoping normal conversation would take the edge off his mood, "but then where?"

"Home."

Right. Small talk had just acquired an entirely new meaning. As they crossed the lobby, she turned to him frankly. "You're upset."

"Out." He jerked his chin toward the street door. A porter hurried to open it for them.

"It's about the marriage certificate, isn't it?" Discussing the matter in a public place seemed far preferable to facing his wrath alone later.

His humorless chortle raised hairs on her nape. When they reached the carriage, a tiny bit of panic set in. Ignoring his offered hand, she planted both feet firmly on the foot pavement, lifting her chin to see him above the brim of her hat.

"I can explain," she said. "I meant to do so earlier but we had so many other matters to worry about. Your father and the meeting with the solicitor, for instance." She paused and swallowed, flustered by his heavy silence. "Perhaps I should have shown you the certificate yesterday, after Fabrice arrived—"

Thwack! Charles's palm came down on the side of the carriage. "Fabrice. I knew it."

"He shouldn't have signed your name—"

"Forged."

She ducked beneath the shelter of her hat brim. "Yes, regrettably that is the word for it. But he wouldn't have done so if he hadn't feared you might not cooperate."

"Why the devil should he think I wouldn't cooperate? Haven't I so far?"

"Of course you have. You've been splendid. But he thought that since, well . . ." She clutched her hands and retreated once more beneath her hat.

"That since the document itself is fraudulent I might balk at putting my name to it." His severe tone made her want to pull her hat all the way over her face.

"Yes." Feeling wretched, she studied the pavement until he nudged her chin. His gray eyes held storm clouds, threatening and oppressive. Her stomach sank. This could get worse. Considerably worse.

"You've gone too far this time, Tess."

"I know. I'm sorry."

"Are you? Sometimes I think the only thing you'd be sorry for is losing your fortune."

The accusation cut, deeply. Did he believe so little of her? "That isn't true," she whispered. "That isn't it at all."

"Then what is this all about?" His fingers tightened about her face, not hard or hurting, but demanding, insistent. "I know this involves more than just your damnable inheritance. But what? I wish to bloody hell you'd tell me."

He released her and the world stood still. Tell him. Just bloody tell him. How easy it would be. What an enormous relief. Perhaps he'd shoulder some of the burden for her. Become one of her accomplices.

The anger drained from his features. She watched, breath suspended, as the old eagerness to charge to her rescue fell into place, calling to her conscience and her heart.

He held out his arms. "You can trust me."

She wished nothing more than to fall into those masculine arms and feel safe. Fool. What was it about Charles Emerson that reduced her to a dithering, spineless schoolgirl? Had the past taught her nothing of self-sufficiency, of withstanding temptation and refusing to allow her weaker tendencies to gain the better of her?

Only by remaining clear-headed could she guarantee the safety of those in her care. She'd vacillated once, and Alicia had paid the price. Lingering desires for a man, no matter how dashing, held no place in her life.

And yet, she must allay his mounting suspicions somehow. A new lie formed in her mind, one that made her want to hide from the optimism lighting Charles's handsome features. She swallowed. "It does have to do with my inheritance, though the money's the least of it. Quite simply, Uncle Howard must not be allowed to win."

"Win?" His arms fell to his sides.

"Yes." She nodded and wondered if one more deception

would indelibly blot her soul. "Alicia's death was partly his fault, you see. They'd quarreled, badly, about a . . . a young man she'd grown fond of. Uncle Howard took the same stand as when you and I were, well, you remember. Anyway, he became so enraged he ordered her from the house. With no where else to go, she went to Highgate Court. It was there she became ill and . . . you know the rest."

"I see." His expression became shuttered, unreadable. He reached for her hand. "Shall we?"

His abrupt acceptance of her story took her aback, made her warier than ever. Had she finally silenced his questions, or raised new ones that would simmer to boiling? She found her answer in the granitelike set of his jaw, in the stiff hand that helped her into the curricle, gripping her own without a trace of warmth.

She watched him check the halter and bridle, pushing and tugging on the leather straps with a kind of singular determination. Nothing had been resolved in that stubborn mind of his.

And perhaps nothing ever would be, at least where she was concerned. What purpose would confiding in him serve? He'd soon be a wealthy London developer. By some miracle that eluded her, Charles Emerson seemed equally at home among common workmen and England's highest peers. She, on the other hand, fit nowhere, her only niche in life being that of a shadowy savior of other misfits. What place could she possibly hold in his life or he in hers? The idea was ridiculous, absurd.

Still, when he slid onto the seat beside her, silent and brooding and intent on maneuvering through the streets, a great emptiness opened up inside her, only to be filled to brimming with an aching regret.

Charging up the stairs, Charles headed straight to the top floor. When he achieved the landing he clutched the rail and paused, drawing in deep breaths while attempting to harness the burst of energy that had propelled him. It wouldn't do to appear distraught.

When he'd calmed, he crossed the hall and delivered three determined knocks to the closed door before him.

"Entrez vous."

Good. The villain was in. A delay might have squeezed the bluster from Charles's billows and lessened the impact of a well-deserved dressing-down. He turned the knob and swung the door inward.

Beneath the sloping eaves, Fabrice sat at the edge of a roomy sleigh bed. A book lay open on the coverlet beside him, spine up, the name Victor Hugo peeking up from the cover in slender black letters.

Fabrice gained his feet in the narrow space between the bed and a pine clothespress. He wore his shirtsleeves rolled up, his waistcoat unbuttoned. His strange gold eyes surveyed Charles without surprise. And without a trace of guilt.

How dare this reprobate refuse to show so much as a qualm for his illicit activities? Charles clenched his jaw to stop its pulsing; he clasped his hands behind his back to conceal their trembling urge to form fists.

"If you ever forge my name again," he said evenly, "I'll have you dragged before a magistrate and locked behind bars for more years than you'd care to count."

Was that a smile? Good grief, did the impertinent baggage possess no conscience whatsoever? Obviously, he'd swiped one of the letters Charles had placed on the post tray this morning and copied his signature. The man was a criminal. What was Tess doing with a criminal in her employ?

"Wipe that smirk from your face," he commanded. "Just what the devil do you find funny about this?"

Fabrice sobered—a subtle rearranging of his dark features. "Nothing, monsieur. Only your threat. You have not thought it through, have you?"

"What in bloody hell does that mean?"

"I did what I did to protect Madame. Perhaps I should have trusted you to do as she needed." His gaze sharpened as it skimmed over Charles with maddening impudence. "But you see, I trust few when it comes to Madame. I could not let Monsieur's scruples interfere with her needs." He shoved his hands in his trouser pockets and smiled that almost-smile again. "If you have Fabrice arrested, who will protect Madame at all costs, even by breaking the law?"

"Why must the law be broken?" Charles narrowed his eyes, trying to return the servant's disconcerting scrutiny. His efforts felt less than adequate. "Is Tess's life so complicated?"

"Complicated." He nodded, still smiling, almost. "An accurate term."

"Why?"

"That is for Madame to tell. But I ask you this. If you send Fabrice away, who will safeguard Madame? You?"

The question startled him. He hadn't given much thought to Tess's fate once he vacated her life. In fact, he hadn't thought that far ahead at all. Despite the turmoil of the past days, he'd begun to feel, well, permanent. Married.

Good God.

"Perhaps that is what Monsieur wishes." Fabrice's quiet voice blended with the breeze grazing the curtains at his open window. "To have Fabrice's job of caring for Madame."

A grunt of indignation erupted from Charles's throat. Of all the insolent, smug, unmitigated gall. He strode forward, fully intending to wring the servant's neck.

He stopped. Devil take it, the rogue had hit the mark exactly. And even if Charles did forego civilized behavior and land a punch, he doubted he'd so much as rattle the infuriating composure that made Fabrice seem so . . . damned superior to every other man he knew.

Pivoting, he strode from the room without the courtesy of closing the door behind him. Halfway down the stairs, he punched the wall.

Tess had confided to her servant every blessed detail she'd

denied him. The stakes, whatever they entailed, must be high indeed, but Fabrice's regard for his employer must be equally lofty for him to risk his very freedom to help her.

It nearly made Charles ill, this morass of loathing, envy and—damn it all—respect churning inside him. He was an adult, a former officer and a businessman. It shouldn't matter that Tess trusted her servant over him.

Ah, but it did.

Chapter 13

Over the next several days Tess developed an entirely new strategy for handling encounters with Charles—one that nearly drove him raving to the nearest madhouse.

For the sake of restoring peace and lessening the tension between them, he forgave her for the marriage certificate. He stipulated one condition: in the future she confer with him before involving him in any sort of criminal behavior, whether he be its victim or unwitting accomplice. She'd jumped to agree, promising up, down and every which way that he needn't fear such a transgression again.

Clever minx, using acquiescence in an attempt to blindside him to future schemes. Not that she fooled him with her niceties. Each conversation contained a maddening assortment of *please, thank you, so nice of you to inquire* and nothing at all of substance. In short, not a bloody thing had changed between them, and all he wanted to do was pull her into his arms and kiss her until her lips yielded all their confounded secrets. Until all her stubbornness melted away.

On Wednesday morning he donned his hat shortly after breakfast, hailed a hackney and gave the driver terse instructions: St. James.

Outside his flat, he asked the driver to wait while he ran upstairs. There he quickly bundled the sets of plans scattered across his drawing table and tucked them beneath his arm. Before leaving the building, he knocked on the landlady's door and paid the rent for the coming month. Ken Fortier was a damned astute solicitor and Charles might be taking up residence here again soon enough. He should have viewed the prospect with relief, yet his fingers tightened around the money just before he laid it in the woman's waiting palm.

The rolled plans reminded him he had a life, a real one, on which he could count long into the future. Upon arriving at the offices on Cannon Street, he found his father in the back alley issuing instructions to two of his foremen.

Given their gruff appearances, they might have been mistaken for cutthroats if encountered in that same alley in the dead of night. But appearances never intimidated Richard Emerson, who allowed the quality of a man's work to reveal the nature of his character. Charles felt confident these two could get a job done on time and to exact specifications. Emerson & Sons didn't employ any other sort.

Deciding to wait in the private office, he discovered his younger brother, George, hunched over an open ledger. Reviewing each figure and verifying every sum, no doubt. Charles knocked softly on the open door.

George's head jerked up. Annoyance turned to surprise and then pleasure. "You startled me, though it's not hard to do when I'm poring over the books." He slapped the ledger closed and came to his feet. "Egad, Charles, you look awful. What's that wife of yours doing to you?"

"Nice to see you, too, brother." They met at the center of the rug, grinning.

As of old, George had to tip his head back to meet Charles's gaze. But in every other sense his brother seemed altered. Older, more mature, more confident. A new quality existed in his very bearing, something in the flow of his movements inside the expensive cut of his suit. George's gaze didn't waver as he sized Charles up, not at all like a younger brother but as an equal.

Competitive. Even slightly predatory. It would seem that while Charles was away, George had grown fully into his manhood. The thought made him grin all the wider.

"That all you've got to say, that I look awful?"

George slapped his back. "Glad you're home."

"It's good to be. By the way, congratulations. How's Caroline feeling?"

"Fine, fine. Been through it all before, you know. Quite a trooper." George touched a hand to his pomaded hair, a pat to ensure all was in place. "Hoping for a girl this time. I'd like that. But hold on, where are my manners? I haven't congratulated you on your marriage." His fist made light contact with Charles's arm. "Rather sudden, wasn't it? Any special reason for the haste? I can keep a secret, you know."

"Who has a secret and why haven't I been told?"

The brothers turned toward the door as their father entered the room. "I have," Charles said, holding up his rolled plans, "and it's time I let you and George in on it. If you have the time."

"Looks like you've been busy." Richard Emerson angled his chin in interest. "Let's open those up."

"Wouldn't think the army gave you time to draw," George murmured as they moved ledgers, inkwells and other items off the desk.

"It didn't," Charles replied. "This is something I've concocted since returning to England."

"In between resigning your commission and getting married?"

"You might say that." Eagerness nearly made his hands shake as he smoothed open the first roll. "I've put a lot of thought into this."

"Heaven help us." George peered over Charles's shoulder. Charles waved both men closer.

"These are redesigned plans for the Coddleton Mews," he said. "I visited the site last week and came up with a few improvements that I think will—"

"What do you mean, improvements?" George frowned at the detailed sketch. "Father and I worked for months planning that site. It's some of the best work we've ever produced. How can you possibly hope to improve on our efforts?"

Before Charles could form a rebuttal, his father cupped his younger son's shoulder. "Let's hear what Charles has to say."

"Thank you, Father." With a deep breath Charles braced to deliver a proposal persuasive enough to win over Emerson & Son. "At first glance," he said, "there's nothing wrong with the work thus far. By ordinary standards, it's quite the norm."

"Ordinary standards?" George gave a snort. "I'll have you know that when completed, those mews will be far from ordinary."

"I'm sure they will be," Charles replied calmly. "But you see, you've overlooked certain matters. Matters which are habitually overlooked in the course of redevelopment."

"Such as?" his father asked, his tone and expression neutral.

"Such as the fact that there were—and still are—people already living in the mews."

"They'll leave as the work progresses," George said with a shrug.

"Precisely. And that's the problem. They're being forced from their homes."

His brother raised open palms. "They don't own the property. They'll have to rent elsewhere."

"Where?"

"I don't know." He exchanged a frown with his father.

"You should." Charles gestured toward the plans. "I've devised a solution. See here."

The two men flanked him at the edge of the desk, their gazes following the line of his outstretched arm. Though neither exactly sparked with enthusiasm, Charles knew he held their attention. His father, at least, seemed willing to hear him out.

"I've left most of the main residences as they already exist, allowing for the fact that walls are going to be knocked down and flats combined. But notice this area here." His finger traced a walkway between buildings leading to a smaller square behind the first.

"Brickel Close is in a state of disrepair and for the most part abandoned. It provides the perfect answer for Coddleton's displaced residents. The two courtyards have entrances on separate streets, making each distinct from the other, yet we can establish convenient homes for the very people who'll provide services for the much wealthier residents of Coddleton Mews."

"And what makes you think those wealthy residents will want their servants dwelling so close to their new, fashionable homes?" his brother asked.

"Why, George," Charles said quietly, "have you become a snob while I was away?"

"No," he snapped, "I've learned how they think. But aside from that, who is going to pay for the renovations in the second square? If anything, it'll be developed just the same as Coddleton—posh and expensive."

"Yes, but why? Why not buy Brickel Close and redevelop it for working class families, for people whose hold on a decent life is tenuous and constantly at risk."

"But how do you propose . . ." His father trailed off as he studied the plans for the two squares. Charles could see his mind working it over, looking ahead. "Interesting . . ."

"You're talking about financing the sales of these properties, aren't you?" George glared, his face reddening. "You're bloody mad."

"Now, George. Your brother's ideas are novel, but—"

"He'll ruin us. Put us in the poorhouse."

"Stop overreacting. I know how extravagant this sounds, but there's potential for tremendous profit in the long run." Charles set a hand on his brother's forearm. "The way I've worked things out, we can't lose."

George yanked away, scowling. "We'll lose plenty when we're left holding slum flats."

"That's not likely to happen. We can develop the square economically and set fair prices. Pride of ownership is a strong motivator. It's exactly what this city needs more of."

"This is damned absurd." George swung away from the desk. "How are we supposed to develop this square the way you want and not lose our britches?"

"By employing the very people who'll eventually live there to do the renovations."

His father cocked his head, and Charles knew his interest had risen several notches.

George huffed. "It's that woman, isn't it? She's turning you dotty, the same way she did ten years ago."

Something inside Charles crouched for a fight. "Don't, George."

His brother ignored the warning. "When she discarded you, you went running off to the military. Now she's married you—"

"George, let it go before you cause trouble where none exists." Indeed, Charles felt a sudden urge to throttle his brother as he hadn't done since they were boys.

"Yes, married you, for chrissake," George continued undeterred, "and suddenly you're running headlong into bankruptcy and trying to drag Father and me with you." George thrust his face close to Charles's. "We won't have it, big brother. Will we, Father?"

"I'd like some time to think it over," Richard said slowly, glancing over the plans again.

"Good grief." George ran both hands through his hair and uttered noises that didn't quite become words.

"Thank you, Father," Charles said with a pointed look at his brother. He experienced a small surge of triumph that his father wasn't ready to declare sides against him. "That's all I ask. Just consider my proposal."

"It's interesting . . ."

"You two can ponder fanciful possibilities." George cut a path to the door. "I'm going back to work."

"That's what this is, George," Charles called to his retreating back. He met his father's gaze. "He takes after Mother."

Richard gave a half nod, half shrug. "He'll come round. Eventually."

"Do I look all right? Is this dress completely wrong for the occasion?" Tess smoothed nervous hands across her skirts as the barouche rolled to a stop. The gown she'd chosen for supper at the Emersons was of simple, sleek design, its moss green taffeta overlaid with a netting of matching silk. She had thought it elegant and tasteful, but despite bands of beribboned lace at the hem and off-the-shoulder décolletage, perhaps it was too unadorned. Perhaps the Emersons would think she didn't consider an affair at their home worthy of her best finery. "Oh, it's entirely wrong, isn't it?"

"You look lovely," Charles assured her for at least the thousandth time. She didn't believe him any more now than she had at the first. He offered his arm to assist her from the carriage.

With no small amount of trepidation, she took in the imposing façade of the Emersons' home. The family might not have achieved nobility since she'd seen them last, but they'd certainly prospered. As her gaze skittered over fine brickwork and gleaming windows, she pondered what awaited her inside.

Her heart thudded as she recalled her last encounter with Blanche Emerson. Unknown to Charles, his mother had come to Tess's home armed with harsh words and recriminations. Tess had uttered some regrettable charges as well. At the time, neither had understood how their anger and resentment had been orchestrated by Uncle Howard's greed. They'd all been victims of his manipulation, while he—the undeserving lout—had prospered nicely.

Charles extended the crook of his arm. "Ready?"

She grasped it; perhaps if she held on tight enough she might keep from falling on her face.

What a thought. What a coward she was to think it, she who prided herself on her strength. Over the years, standing strong for the sake of others had proved not so difficult a task.

She'd simply set her own needs aside. Tonight would be different. Tonight she must maintain a brave front for her own sake. The Emersons wouldn't judge her based on her sister's actions but on her own, years ago when she hurt their son.

She touched a shaky hand to her hair and felt horribly inadequate. "I wish I'd had more time to prepare," she whispered, stalling. "I thought we'd declined your father's invitation. You might have given me more notice that you'd changed your mind. I might have sent for Helena's maid to dress my hair. Becca did her best but . . ."

"There's nothing wrong with your hair and your dress is perfect." With a tolerant grin Charles leaned in and brushed a kiss across her lips.

Merely a gesture of reassurance, quickly rendered and easily dismissed, or so it should have been. But his proximity rendered a breath laden with masculine scents, a rush of warmth, a desire for more.

"Ah, easy for you to say," she admonished with a laugh, hoping to conceal how much that kiss affected her. "You can run a comb through your hair, snap some fancy studs on your shirt, stuff a hanky in your pocket and off you go."

How true. Tonight, Charles presented . . . oh, a dashing image of perfection in his sapphire evening coat and gray trousers that tapered over muscled thighs and honed calves. In the gaslight he cut a tall, strong, dark figure, his face a wonderful mystery of planes, shadows and exquisite angles above a glowing white shirtfront.

"Rather plain, actually."

She started at his observation. "What's plain? Me?" Her hand fluttered to the gold locket hanging from her neck; she fingered the delicate chain. "Is it my jewelry? It is too plain, isn't it?"

"No, goose. My shirt studs. I didn't wear the fancy ones. For pity's sake, Tess, it's merely my family."

"Merely your family." She snapped open her fan and whisked it back and forth in front of her face. "Heaven help me. I wish you had told your father the truth."

"If you insist, I'll do so tonight."

She felt her eyes grow as wide as the full moon hanging above one of the Emersons' chimneys. "Don't you dare!"

"All right, then. Chin up." His right hand covered hers where it lay on his forearm, giving it a comforting squeeze. "This won't be as difficult as you think."

No. Far worse, probably.

They were met at the front door by the same butler Tess remembered from years ago. Hodges—no, Rodgers—a study in solemn dignity. Richard Emerson entered the foyer a moment later. He reached for her hand and kissed her cheek with all the warm sincerity she could wish for. Her spirits rose a notch.

But then her heel caught in the hall runner's fringed border. Losing her balance, she landed with an awkward lurch against Charles's chest. He caught her in a quick embrace.

"How clumsy of me," she murmured, her voice gone breathy with mortification.

Richard chuckled. "Newlyweds. Can't keep their hands off one another."

"Steady there," Charles murmured against her hair as his father turned away to hand her cape to the waiting butler. "Not that I mind you throwing yourself at me, but now might not be the proper time."

She administered a swift cuff to his shoulder, while the sensation of his arms around her and the murmur of his suggestion released a curling ache inside her.

Pulling away, she steeled her nerves with a breath and followed his father to the drawing room.

The Emersons were all there, waiting like a pack of . . . no, that was too harsh, a figment of her apprehensions. They were ranged about the room like a typical family awaiting supper.

Charles's brother, George, stood at the center of an elaborate arrangement of settees, side tables and delicately carved arm chairs, their rich scarlet upholstery repeated on the surrounding silk wall coverings. Gold accents brought a sense of established wealth to the room, one obviously designed to impress.

Or in Tess's case, intimidate.

"Everyone, our guests of honor have arrived," Richard announced.

George Emerson turned and acknowledged their presence with a raised eyebrow and a slight contraction of his facial muscles.

Not very promising.

Beside him, a woman Tess assumed to be his wife—young, blond, beautiful—smiled and then assumed what Tess would consider a carefully neutral expression. Tess wondered how much this woman knew about the past and whose opinions colored her own. A flawless hand drifted to her belly. Charles had mentioned the pregnancy but Tess saw little sign of it beneath the young woman's stylish silk frock.

Richard placed a guiding hand at her elbow and ushered her into the room. Charles followed close behind, his presence shoring her up with borrowed courage.

A rustling drew her attention to a high-backed chair that faced into the room. Blanche Emerson came to her feet and slowly turned. Her hair, swept into an elaborate coif, glittered with dozens of tiny jewels. An exquisite gown of silver silk, its bodice tucked with rows of painstaking needlework, hugged her slender figure to perfection. At her throat, a diamond necklace caught the flickering light of the chandeliers and thrust an icy flame into Tess's eyes.

As Blanche came forward, her gaze slashed once across Tess's face before softening and settling on her son. "Charles, darling, I'm so pleased you could come."

"We're delighted, Mother." He took her offered hand and planted a kiss on her lightly rouged cheek.

Seconds stretched like decades. Tess felt invisible—no, worse, like the most conspicuous of intruders. The scent of dusting powder tingled in her nose. She struggled not to sneeze.

Charles drew her to his side. "Mother, you haven't yet greeted my wife."

"Why, Mrs. Hardington, how do you do?"

"It's Mrs. Emerson now, Mother." His arm slipped securely around Tess's waist, his fingers imparting warmth through her dress. She stood taller and summoned a smile.

"Of course." Blanche's reddened mouth parted. A smile? Perhaps. "How careless of me. I trust you are well."

"Quite well, thank you, Mrs. Emerson. And you?"

She chortled, a sound like tinkling glass. "Three Mrs. Emersons! How confusing for us all."

Tess wanted to alleviate the dilemma by reducing the number to two.

Making clucking noises with his tongue, George crossed the room. His wife followed at his heel. "Three Mrs. Emersons will certainly keep the Mr. Emersons on their toes. I wonder if we're equal to the challenge."

"George," the lovely blonde murmured, "that sounded rather less than gallant, dearest."

"Did it, Muffin?"

"It did," Charles said. A warning edged his voice. His arm tightened around Tess.

"I certainly didn't mean it to." George gave his wife's hand a pat. "Tess is an old friend. Surely she knows when one of us is joking. Unfortunately, it would seem my brother does not."

Despite George's jocular tone, an undercurrent of hostility simmered. Why? Tess wondered. He'd been a boy when Charles went away. He could not have understood much of the circumstances, except of course what his mother had told him.

Still, he maintained an outward show of civility. "Tess, allow me to introduce my wife, Caroline."

"Congratulations on your impending joy," she said to the younger woman. "Charles has told me the happy news."

"Yes, we're quite delighted, thank you." Caroline's hand returned for an instant to her belly.

Blanche coughed, a tight, almost choking sound. The color drained from beneath her rouge.

What on earth? But the cause of the woman's sudden loss of composure, not to mention complexion, didn't elude Tess for long. The subject of babies. Surely Blanche Emerson found the very notion of Tess as the mother of her grandchildren appalling.

How then would the woman react to Blair, beautiful, intelligent and quite illegitimate? Tess could only assume Blanche would look upon her niece with abhorrence.

Rodgers entered the room with the curt dignity Tess remembered. "Supper is served."

"Splendid," Blanche said, though she didn't sound as if she found anything splendid at all. "Shall we adjourn to the dining room?"

Like a sentinel, Charles remained at Tess's side as they took their seats around the gleaming cherry wood table—the very same table at which she had once been a welcome guest. How very long ago that seemed. As supper was served, she found herself grieving for the happy young girl she had been, in love, naïve, unaware of what the future held.

Charles's mother presided over the meal with a grim propriety that nothing—not George's witticisms nor her husband's diplomacy—could lighten. On the surface, her behavior toward Tess remained free of rancor or anything blatantly spiteful. Obvious rebukes weren't necessary. The very emptiness of her gray eyes—similar to Charles's in color though not in depth—conveyed her sentiments with perfect clarity: *You are not welcome here, Tess Hardington, and you never shall be.*

Chapter 14

Charles peered out his bedroom window to the street below. The hired coach stood waiting two floors down. Good.

When he and Tess arrived home from his parents' house earlier, she'd rushed upstairs pleading exhaustion. The look on her face had told a different story. He'd seen the signs before—the anxiety, the restless energy. Unless he were greatly mistaken, her barouche would be pulling out within minutes.

He regretted the evening, regretted subjecting her to his mother and brother's blatant scorn. Going there had been for his father's sake really, for Richard's obvious delight at having Charles home again and for the way he'd welcomed Tess even when other family members had not.

But the evening had clearly left her wounded.

He pulled out his pocket watch. Five minutes to midnight. By his estimate she'd be tiptoeing down the stairs any moment.

Crossing the room, he carefully cracked the door just enough to hear her footsteps. He hated all this sneaking about but she left him little choice. Of course, one might argue that her secrets were none of his business. But, devil be hanged, if he had agreed to take on the role of husband, she should bloody well accept the role of wife. That did not include deceiving him at every turn.

Downstairs, the clock chimed twelve plaintive notes that echoed up the empty stairwell. Charles drew himself up against the doorframe and held his breath. A moment later he heard the soft thud of her door. His pulse made a leap of triumph, though a short-lived one. He'd rather have been proved wrong.

Through the narrow gap between the door and lintel, he watched her glide across the gallery, phantomlike in a dark cape that concealed the sensuous details of her body. At the landing she paused, turning. He could have sworn she stared straight at him. Resisting the impulse to draw back, he didn't move, didn't breathe.

After a second or two she shook her head. With barely a sound she started down the stairs.

He darted out to the landing. Leaning over the rail, he spied the corner of her cloak whipping out behind her as she hurried to the service staircase. The moment she disappeared from view he headed down, avoiding the step that creaked as she had.

He slipped out the front door as the sound of hooves and carriage wheels reverberated from the yard. Sprinting, he reached the waiting hackney seconds before Tess's barouche pulled onto the street. It ambled past him at a quiet pace, heading east out of Mayfair.

He had already instructed his driver to follow at discreet distance and to use other nighttime travelers as camouflage. The man had narrowed a curious gaze on him but a sovereign had silenced his questions.

The ride became a guessing game for Charles. First they traveled east out of Mayfair along Oxford Street, apparently headed toward the City until a sharp turn sent them south.

Covent Garden? Drury Lane? His bafflement grew as streets narrowed to muddy lanes and houses shrank in size and value; as the bright windows of mansions yielded to black portals in walls that sagged with neglect.

They were well into St. Giles before the barouche slowed its pace, turning off the main thoroughfare—if the squalid street could be so termed. The air turned thick and acrid, the result of low-grade coal burned in poorly ventilated stoves.

The sharp fumes mixed with the sour, yeasty odor from the breweries to the south. Charles pressed his handkerchief to his nose.

By the many turns the coachman made, he realized they were circling the neighborhood. They passed through Seven Dials on at least three occasions, each time veering onto another of the intersecting streets and then doubling back around.

Despite his singular reason for being here, Charles couldn't help a morbid fascination in the view outside his window. While working class neighborhoods slept at this hour, St. Giles teamed with all manner of sordid activity. He saw prostitutes openly plying their trade along the slimy gutters, some beckoning to his carriage. The only discreet thing about them was where they tucked away their earnings to elude the equally obvious cutthroats prowling the area.

Finally his vehicle slowed to a stop. He poked his head out the open window. This street was darker, quieter than the Seven Dials. Tess's barouche stood a few dozen yards away. He rapped on the roof to signal his driver to pull over and wait. Another coach rolled by. Not an elegant barouche like Tess's, but a glorified wagon with a cloth top. A rider passed on horseback, his face and figure concealed beneath a shapeless cloak.

Charles fidgeted with the window curtain, the door handle. Waiting set him on edge. Voices drifted from the tavern across the street, from the open windows above. He flinched at the explosion of smashing glass. A woman let loose a curse colorful enough to make a dockhand blush.

For what possible reason had Tess come to this miserable place?

The barouche rolled forward again, slowly rounding a corner. Charles opened his door to whisper to his driver. "Follow it, but stay well behind."

Before the man coaxed his nags to a walk, the rumble of Tess's coach fell silent. "Hold up." Charles swung down to the pavement. "Wait here."

Touching two fingers to his cap, the coachman stared straight ahead with the disinterest Charles had purchased.

Hugging the building fronts, he made his way to the corner. Tess and Fabrice were just around the bend, mere yards away but partly obscured by a gathering fog.

Perhaps now he'd have his answers.

When the carriage rolled to a stop, Tess stayed put and waited for Fabrice to come around to the window.

"She is finally alone," he murmured, pushing back his hood. He nodded toward a doorway partway down the lane. Within the shallow recess, a small fire lapped at the rim of a kettle. The flames illuminated a pair of hands above the heat but revealed little more of their owner than a series of hazy black outlines.

"You're certain her companions have left?"

"Oui, Madame. Shall we proposition her?"

The irony of his question brought on a wave of despondency. Tess had been propositioning women for five long years. The anticipation never ebbed. Each time, she saw her sister in the worst of her despair, abandoned by the man she believed had loved her, cast out by another who should have sheltered her, and abused by many from whom she sought means of survival.

Alicia's fall had been so very long and steep, from gentlewoman to . . . to that desperate creature huddled in the doorway. Who did that poor girl used to be before desperation drove her to the streets? Surely her life had been no less valuable than Alicia's.

"Drive closer first," she replied to Fabrice. "This lane seems quiet but we must not take chances. There could be trouble if she resists."

He pulled up his hood, giving his head a quick shake when his earring caught on the wool. His weight tilted the carriage as he climbed onto the box. When Tess expected the vehicle to ease forward, it instead bucked with a burst of speed, slamming her backward. She gripped the edge of the seat as they sped past their quarry and beyond, down streets, around corners, across squares. Like the barouche, her confusion careened out of control. She could only anchor herself with her hands and wait until Fabrice brought them to a stop.

When the door beside her finally opened, she recognized the vicinity of Charing Cross. Fabrice panted to catch his breath. His fingers trembled from the strain of controlling the horses at such a speed.

"What happened?" she demanded in a breathless whisper.

"We may have been followed."

Her pulse lurched. "By whom?"

He shook his head and frowned. "As we were about to drive up to the girl, I heard a noise behind me. Another coach had stopped near the corner, one I had seen only minutes earlier." Concern darkened his tawny gaze. "It was not worth the risk. We will find the girl another night."

"Yes." Tess relaxed against the seat, trying to ease the tension that traveled up her back and into her neck. "I doubt she's going anywhere, poor thing."

Fabrice's stare lingered. His silence resounded with unspoken assertions.

She sighed. "All right, my dark angel, what is it?"

"We have grown careless of late. We should not go again for several weeks at least."

"And while we stay safely at home, more young women will be hurt. No, Fabrice, I cannot live with that."

His bottom lip protruded. "If Madame goes, Madame goes alone."

"You know I can't—"

"Oui, Fabrice knows."

"Devil," she said, and treated him to a scowl.

"Oui. It takes a devil to be Madame's guardian angel." Grinning, he sauntered back to the driver's box and headed the barouche for home.

On the way Tess pondered the mystery coach that had thwarted her plans. A suspicion nudged. Had Charles followed her?

She would question Fabrice further about the vehicle as soon as possible. Was it hired, she wondered, or privately owned? If the latter, Charles couldn't have been the culprit. She had left the curricle at home with no horses to pull it. If the former, however. . . .

Perhaps Fabrice had mistaken mere coincidence for something more sinister. The thought comforted, but only briefly. Over the years, her dark angel's instincts had rarely proved wrong.

Charles raced back to his hired carriage, wondering what the devil had just happened. One moment Tess and Fabrice were approaching what appeared to be a lady of the night, and the next they were fleeing as if hell's flames licked their coach wheels.

Hissing to his driver to make haste to Mayfair, he dived headlong into the hackney. Two streets away from Tess's he exited and sprinted the remaining distance, glancing over his shoulder every few strides. Thank heaven it was too late for her neighbors to be out strolling.

He didn't know how much time he had, but the silence inside the house assured him Tess hadn't yet arrived and the other servants were abed. He took the stairs two at a time, shrugging off his coat, tugging his shirttails free and undoing his cufflinks as he went.

It wasn't long before he heard her tiptoeing up those same stairs, but by then he'd kicked off his shoes, changed into a nightshirt and dressing gown and tousled his hair. He flipped the bedclothes to complete the illusion. Just as she reached the top step he pushed his door open and stepped into the hall.

She let out a yelp.

He faked a gasp. His hand went to his chest for good measure. "Good grief, Tess, you nearly scared me out of my wits." Then, pretending to bring her into focus with bleary eyes, he added, "You're dressed. Have you been out?"

"I, uh, w—what are you doing up?"

She looked disheveled, rumpled, as though she'd just tumbled out of bed and threw on some clothes. No doubt the results of her hasty departure from St. Giles. A flame burst to life inside him. With her mussed hair and wrinkled cape slipping from her shoulders, he pictured her tangled in passion-tossed coverlets—his coverlets. He wanted to pull her against him, grab handfuls of her hair, tip her chin for a kiss, then more—much more.

Desire thrust, hot and sharp. He sucked in a breath. He had business to attend to, that of coaxing something resembling the truth from that lovely, lying mouth.

Shrugging, he said, "Something woke me and I couldn't fall back to sleep. A bad dream, I suppose. Thought I'd go downstairs for a nightcap. But you haven't answered my question."

"Question?" Her brows rose in a show of innocence that did little to conceal the nervous glint in her eye. He moved to the railing beside her. She tensed as though poised to run.

"Yes," he said, inwardly daring her to tell him the truth. "Why are you dressed for an outing at this hour?"

"Ah, that." She glanced down as though surprised by her attire. "Yes, well, a message came after you retired. From Helena. She needed me. It was Sir Joshua. He felt ill and . . . she feared it might be his heart. She was in quite a state when I arrived."

Involving her dearest friends in her deception—his blood ran cool at the thought. "Did she send for a physician?"

"Oh, yes. But Helena needed me for moral support. You understand."

"Of course. You should have woken me. I'd have gone with you."

Her hand fluttered in the air between them. "No, no, I didn't wish to disturb you."

"Nonsense." He eased closer. "I wouldn't have minded."

Her nostrils flared. "All's well now. He's feeling much better."

"Glad to hear it." He forced a smile he wished were real. "I don't know them well, but I've grown fond of the Holbrooks and Sir Joshua."

"Yes, they're all such dears." Her own smile was thin and fleeting. "Good night, then."

She started by him but he caught her wrist, encircling it within his fingers. The sensation of her tapering forearm trapped within his hold instantly transformed into something more, something that traveled straight to his loins.

This wasn't what he'd intended. But, ah, it was a fool's master, this lust, always hovering, ready to strike him unawares and send his world for a spin.

But perhaps she felt it, too. He pretended to ignore her sudden intake of breath. "How about a nightcap for both of us? After your ordeal, I'm sure you could use one."

"Ordeal?"

"Thinking Sir Joshua might be seriously ill, of course." He smoothed his hand along the inside of her arm beneath her cape, finding her skin warm and moist.

She shivered.

"Are you cold?"

"A little. Come, there's a decanter of brandy in my sitting room."

"Didn't know you kept it so close at hand."

"For colds and the occasional toothache," she retorted, eyes snapping at him in the darkness.

"Only joking." He slipped his hand higher, settling it between her shoulders. He stroked his fingertips across her nape and felt a tiny shudder in response. "You're the last person I'd accuse of nipping on the sly." No, he thought, she needed all her wits to carry out her intrigue.

Once through the doorway, she shrugged from his hold and went to the glass-paned cabinet near the bookcase. He heard the clink of a stopper, the trickle of liquid. She turned back to him holding two glasses of brandy, shimmering and darkly amber. The one she handed him held more than her own.

He moved to the sofa. When she paused, looking tentatively at the furniture as if debating whether to sit with him or seek the shelter of the wing chair, he patted the cushion beside him. "Come, Tess. Talk with me a while. Help me banish the ghosts from that bad dream I had."

There, she couldn't refuse that. She took longer than necessary to remove her cloak before settling beside him. He tapped his glass against hers, steeling himself to do battle with her conscience.

"To friendship," he said. "Despite our occasional disagreements these past few days, I feel we're on our way to a new level of trust."

"Trust?" A worried shadow crossed her face.

"And honesty." He sipped his brandy.

Her eyes widened above the rim of her glass. "Honesty?"

He nodded, caressing her gaze with his own. "And sincerity."

Taking her free hand in his, he smoothed his thumb across her knuckles, pausing an instant over the cool sheen of her wedding ring. A not-so-subtle reminder that he sat in Walter Hardington's house, drinking brandy with his wife in the very suite he and Tess once shared.

It pounded home the fact that neither the house nor the brandy nor the woman beside him were his, nor ever likely to be. He'd yet to determine whether it was the past that stood like a bulwark between them, or some dire secret from her present. He only knew that the closer he tread, the harder she pushed him away.

Well, tonight he'd push back and see what came of it.

She relaxed when he released her hand, only to tense again when his arm encircled her shoulders. He pulled her closer. "Warming up?" Ah, she'd never been cold in the first place, but what harm in making convenient use of her lie?

"Much better." She sipped her drink, her hand trembling slightly when she lowered the glass.

"I hope you gave them my regards."

"Who?"

"The Holbrooks and your Uncle Joshua, silly. You must have been terribly worried about the old gentleman. Poor Tess." His leaned his lips against her hair, breathing in the subtle scent of lilies. "This on top of all your other recent troubles. I don't know how you're coping."

"I'm perfectly fine."

"You're as tense as a harp string." Before she could protest, he grasped her shoulders and turned her away from him. After setting his snifter on the sofa table, he spread his hands wide and placed them at her nape, massaging with slow, deep, circular motions.

"By God, you're a jumble of knots. There, how does that feel?" He increased the pressure while maintaining a languid and, he hoped, hypnotic rhythm.

"Heavenly," she replied with an unsteady laugh. "Thank you." She attempted to turn but he held her firmly in place.

"I'm not done with you yet." Working his way down, he reached her lower back. The breath left him when his fingertips met the curve of her buttocks.

His plan, of course, entailed plying her with brandy, immersing her in relaxation and coaxing admissions from her. But an admission of his own raced through his brain. He wanted her. Badly. Almost without realizing it, he deepened the pressure of the massage, communicating a desire that slowly took control of him.

She didn't shrink away and that surprised him. Whatever had happened in St. Giles must have sapped her defenses. Her neck arched when he pressed his palm against it. She purred like a kitten. An invitation to move closer still? He chose to believe so and shifted until his thigh hugged her bottom.

His need intensified, became painful. He sucked air through his teeth. "Tess," he said, "I know how very troubled you are. I wish you'd let me help."

"You've already done so much." Her chin fell forward and

her nape, thus exposed, acted as a magnet to his lips. He could all but taste her.

"Helping an old friend out of a jam, that's all," he murmured. Lifting wayward strands of hair, he found the tiny mole he remembered, a tempting dot where her shoulder met her neck. "Then again, we're much more than old friends, aren't we? We shouldn't be afraid to seek one another's help, or hesitate to confide."

"I . . . yes, I suppose you're right."

He swallowed against a dry throat and slid his arms around her waist. Snuggling her against his chest, he sensed her momentary apprehension rise up between them, then felt excruciating relief when she relaxed against him. She released a tremulous sigh that rippled through him like the echo of a woman's ecstasy.

He stroked her hair, savoring the glide of silk through his fingers. "If I were in any sort of trouble, you'd come to my aid, wouldn't you?"

"In the span of a heartbeat."

"Yes, I knew that." His resistance shattered. Pressing his mouth to the curve of her neck, he ran his tongue over the diminutive mole that marked what he considered a perfect place for kissing.

With a moan she turned in his arms. He took the brandy glass from her hand and set it beside his own. *Please*, he thought, *don't let her prim logic awaken now*. But as he gathered her closer and lowered his mouth to her throat, her shuddering response assured him logic was furthest from her mind.

He slanted his mouth over hers, jubilant when her lips blossomed, wide and eager. She gave a little gasp that grazed his tongue and set it ablaze. Even so he leaned away, pausing for both breath and approval. Her eyes half-closed, she smiled. Before her lips reached their full tilt he pressed for more, kissing her deeper and allowing his tongue the thrill of exploration.

And yet her very pliancy and complaisance tempered his

pleasure. This was not typical of Tess. She should be resisting him, scolding him. That she'd yielded so easily spoke less about his seductive skills than about her reaching the limits of her endurance.

And for that he was partly to blame.

"I'm sorry my mother and George upset you tonight," he whispered against her cheek. "Their misguided loyalty toward me is no excuse for their behavior."

"I can't blame them for wanting to protect their son and brother." Her fingers slid through his hair, and she pressed his face to her warm and fragrant neck. "You deserved better ten years ago."

He nodded, only half aware of what he agreed to, focusing instead on the spectacular vista about to open before him. The swooping neckline of her mossy gown made firm, enticing mounds of her breasts. He lowered his lips to the smooth curve trimmed in ribbon and lace, kissing, stroking with his tongue. Her murmurs encouraged him; her ragged breathing inflamed him.

While his fingers struggled with the buttons down her back, his teeth caught the end of a ribbon and yanked. Her bodice fell open. Tess stiffened, pulling away a little.

"Charles, I—I'm not sure."

He wanted her to be sure, beyond all doubt. Kissing her softly, he lingered, waiting for her lips' response. When it came, intensely erotic in its sweetness, he delved his hand into the loosened gown and drifted in euphoria when her warm breast melted against his palm.

His other hand found her hems. Soon ankles, calves and more lay exposed to his touch, to the night air. Stroking her knee's inner angle, he discovered a trail of tiny goose bumps that led to the top of her stocking. His forefinger slipped between silk and flesh, in and out, in and out. Her half-bared leg slid over his thigh and her hands stole inside his dressing gown. She gripped his nightshirt roughly, greedily, nails biting flesh with exquisite torture.

He could have had her then. He knew it as he knew the sun would rise in a few short hours. One fluid motion would sweep her beneath him onto the cushions. Then he'd shove her skirts to her waist and finally—ah, God, finally—satisfy every fantasy that had plagued him throughout ten years of trying to forget.

Before he could roll, a second thought fired like a faulty musket: with the rendering of her body, she'd surrender her secrets. For once Tess trusted, she trusted completely. He would have succeeded in seducing the truth out of her.

"Darling . . . perhaps we shouldn't," he murmured and cursed himself for a damned fool. "Not now, while you're so clearly upset."

He straightened so abruptly she nearly slid from his lap. The ache of wanting, of knowing that want would go unsatisfied, seeped through him until his very joints moaned with pain. Why had he done it? He had feared Tess's qualms getting in the way only to fall prey to his own. But seduction had not begun this night's work. Deception had. Hers, his. Equal perhaps in guilt, but which of them bore the greater shame now?

As if she, too, wished to know, she turned a doubt-ridden face to him, her bottom lip seeking shelter between her teeth. Did she believe the sudden cooling of his ardor to be her fault? If she only knew the truth of it.

"Tess, forgive me, I—"

"Goodness." She cleared her throat and disentangled her legs from his. Putting a good foot or two of sofa between them, she shoved her skirts down over her knees and wrestled her bodice up to her shoulders. "What were we thinking?"

He felt like the greatest cad that ever lived. The memory of each caress scorched blame across his hands; each kiss branded him a liar.

How could he sink so low as to combine his pressing need to learn her secrets with his burning need to know her physically? He gulped air, filling his lungs with new resolve. No more spying, no more wheedling. He'd be a friend to her from now on. He'd trust her.

At least, he'd try.

"This was entirely my fault and I'm sorry." He stopped. This was damned awkward. He wouldn't blame her if she threw him out come morning. Or sooner.

"This night has been a trying one." She looked away, face blazing as her shaking fingers attempted to secure her dress. Failing, she simply held the bodice up against her breasts. "I supposed I longed for . . . a bit of comforting."

If she wanted to call what he'd done *comforting*, he'd be a gentleman and let her. Gazing at the floor, at his feet—anywhere but at the woman he'd nearly wronged in the most unforgivable way—he noticed that his dressing gown gaped around him. He tightened it, secured the sash and pushed to his feet.

"Forgive me for overstepping the bounds . . ." He trailed off. What could he say without making matters worse? Instead, he offered his hand to help her up, then realized both her hands were employed in salvaging her modesty. He watched, feeling futile and bloody despicable as she came to her feet unassisted.

"It wasn't your fault," she said. "There's no denying the attraction between us. Let's simply say goodnight and speak no more of it."

He nodded and glanced away, fearing the temptation to wrap her in his arms again. This time, he might not let go.

"I'm not angry. Really." She kissed his cheek before disappearing into her bedroom. He contemplated the tops of his slippers until her door closed.

A realization knifed his conscience. He was as contemptible a rogue as could be. Because he still hungered to know two things: what the devil she was up to, and exactly how she would feel beneath him, naked and writhing with delight.

Chapter 15

Tess woke with a start, a crash echoing in her ears. Harried footsteps pounded across the sitting room outside her bedroom. Bolting upright, she blinked away sleep. Becca would never enter her suite making such a racket. Charles? The thought sparked a flame of anticipation.

Her answer came with the bursting in of her bedroom door. She'd no time to react before the bed curtains were whisked aside and a newspaper thrust before her nose.

"We are in trouble," Fabrice said, and slapped the publication to the coverlet.

"What are you raving about?" She sank back onto the pillows, relief and disappointment at war within her. Had she really hoped for Charles? Could she face him after what they'd very nearly done last night?

Good Lord, Fabrice was right. She *was* in trouble. Last night had seen the annihilation of every conviction she had vowed these many years to live by.

Shutting her eyes, she attempted to clear her mind of the memory of Charles's kisses, of how readily her traitorous body had dissolved beneath his roaming hands. He had touched her as only a husband should, arousing exquisite longings such as she'd never known or dreamed of with Walter. With a tremor she recalled the sensation of his open palms across her bared breasts, her legs. The memory sizzled even now.

Oh, but then had come that awful change, when Charles

had pulled away and yanked the sash of his robe tighter, sapping her pleasure all at once and leaving her utterly mortified. How could she, for the sake of a moment's physical pleasure, allow integrity and caution to be swept away like so much dust?

He'd shouldered the blame of course, playing the gallant in the face of her half-hearted reassurances that it hadn't been his fault. In truth, she didn't know which of them had been more at fault, more eager to join their bodies as she'd once dreamed they would.

"Madame." Fabrice nudged her shoulder. "Are you awake?"

"Of course I'm awake." She shoved hair from her face and opened her eyes. "You made sure of that when you broke the door down. What on earth do you want at this hour?"

"Front page." He seized the newspaper and straightened it with a shake.

The headline filled her vision. MIDNIGHT MARAUDER STRIKES. BODY FOUND.

Body found?

Her heart hit her throat and stuck. *Dear God.* Snatching the paper with trembling hands, she skimmed the text: a prostitute who frequented the St. Giles area found in an alley at dawn, strangled and laid on her back in a doorway, a lily upon her chest.

The blood drained from her face in dizzying waves. If she'd been standing, her legs would have given way beneath her. She read the article again, shaking her head with each erroneous sentence.

"The girl was fine when we left her. I still had the lily when we arrived home." The paper sagged between her hands. As horror sunk in, she stared across the room. "There it is, in that vase."

"You should never have begun leaving the lilies."

"You know why I do it."

"Oui, Fabrice knows and understands. But now Madame

must understand." He perched on the edge of her mattress with a familiarity he'd never shown before. "I spoke true when I said we must cease our midnight rides for a time. Now we must also take pains to erase all trails leading here, to us."

"She's dead," Tess murmured, too shocked to follow his every word. She rubbed at a sudden and quite painful cramp in her neck. "This is dreadful. Appalling. If only we'd taken her while we had the chance . . . or perhaps this isn't the same girl? But then I suppose we failed this one as well, didn't we?"

"Madame," Fabrice said gently, "it is a tragedy either way, to be sure, but we must make certain you and I are not implicated."

Her eyes darted to his face. "Why should we be? The only people who can identify us are the women we've helped. They would never betray us."

"We may have been followed last night," he reminded her. "And whoever murdered that girl made sure everyone would think it the work of the Marauder."

The revelation sent her fist crashing against the mattress. "How dare they?"

Fabrice's amber gaze held her, then slipped away.

"What are you not telling me?"

"I might have lost something last night."

"Go on."

"My earring." His fingers disappeared for a moment beneath loose shanks of hair. "The silver and coral."

"The one that dangles, with the etchings?"

"Oui, that one."

"Do you have any idea *where* you might have lost it?"

"On the lane in St. Giles perhaps, when we stopped." He shook his head. "Or perhaps when we fled. If could have fallen anywhere. I've searched the coach—it isn't there."

Tess placed a hand on his forearm. "At least we know the one place it couldn't be. You and I never set foot in the alley where that poor girl was found."

"Madame is right. Perhaps we need not worry."

"Fabrice," she began, not liking the thought forming in her mind but needing to voice it, "do you believe the person who followed us is responsible for this murder?"

"It is possible."

She massaged the biting knot in her neck. "You don't think the person who followed us could be Mr. Emerson, do you?"

"How well do you know the man?"

"He's not the violent sort," she replied with conviction. "It's just that when I came upstairs last night, he was awake. He asked all sorts of questions. And I remembered that coach you said you saw."

"It had red rims and brass door handles. I spotted it first on Tower Street, then again on the lane where we found the girl. That is why I sped off."

"Seeing it twice could have been a coincidence."

"Perhaps."

"And Mr. Emerson's questions could have been a coincidence as well." She clasped her hands so tight they hurt. "I can't help but feel this is all my fault."

"Your fault? Why?"

"Because whoever this villain is, we led him to St. Giles and to that girl." Her chin sank to her folded hands. "Someone has used the Marauder's identity to commit murder. They've made a demented game out of all the good we've done over the years."

"That is not your fault." He grasped her shoulders. His grip was determined, his voice fierce. "You have helped countless people, including me. If not for you, I would have starved or swung from the gallows. You have done no wrong. You are not responsible for the actions of a killer."

She nodded, not because she believed him but because she wanted him to believe she did. When he released her, her hands went to her face to discover unexpected tears. Fabrice glanced away as if he hadn't noticed.

"What do we do now?" She should have been the one to tell him, but images of a defenseless girl and her terrifying end dulled her ability to think. She could only gaze at her dark angel and hope he'd provide answers.

"Nothing."

It wasn't the solution she'd hoped for.

"We live like normal people," he went on, ignoring her frustration, "and do nothing—*nothing*—to arouse suspicion." His voice softened. "Madame need not look at Fabrice that way, as though he will let you down. Has Fabrice ever?"

"No, dear friend. Never."

As Charles prepared to leave the house at midmorning, Becca informed him that her mistress had not yet stirred from her room. Not a surprise. It had been well past two in the morning before either of them had retired.

Angling his top hat before the hall mirror, he ruminated over his lost opportunity. If not for his ill-timed onslaught of principles, heaven help him, he might have spent the night in Tess's bed rather than his own. She'd seemed so willing, so ready to respond to his overtures of love with equal enthusiasm. The memory of it aroused him even now, in the glaring light of morning.

Love. Could he call it that after a mere week? Could their relationship a decade ago even have been termed love? Oh, it had felt so at the time, or had he been too young and eager to understand the distinction between driving lust and lifelong commitment? Was there a distinction, or were the two merely different strands of the same tangled web?

Within the hour he reached the offices of Emerson & Sons. George and their father were conducting a meeting with the owners of a property near Regent's Park. Charles might join them, the secretary informed him, or wait in the private office. He chose neither option, depositing his top hat on a convenient shelf and making his way to the drafting room. The time had come to familiarize himself with the firm's daily activities and the men who performed them.

The conversation that drifted to meet him partway down the corridor, however, had little to do with drafting or architectural styles.

"I'm telling you," a man's gruff bass insisted, "this Marauder has finally shown his true colors."

Charles halted a few steps short of the doorway. He pricked his ears.

"So you think he's been murdering all along?" a second and more youthful male voice asked.

"Of course," resumed the first. "Only up until now he hasn't left the bodies where they could be found. Probably been dumping them in the river."

"Isn't that what the magistrate was quoted as saying?" a third and decidedly husky voice inquired.

"Right, that and the fact that the Marauder made a big mistake murdering in his parish."

"Have to admire a man who stands up for a hell hole like St. Giles."

St. Giles. Warning bells clanged in Charles's mind.

"Admire him or consider him a lunatic?"

"Maybe a bit of both."

Subdued laughter followed. Charles sagged against the wall as if the wind had been knocked out of him. Implications and possibilities pitched through his brain. This murder took place in the very neighborhood Tess led him to last night. Good God, she might have stepped right into the killer's path.

Pushing away from the wall, he strode into the drafting room. The four men inside snapped to attention, grabbing pens and smoothing paper. Sheepish expressions conveyed their dismay at being caught in an idle moment. He waved a dismissive hand, signaling them to relax.

"Did I hear you correctly?" he asked. "The Midnight Marauder killed someone last night? In St. Giles?"

"Yes, sir, Mr. Emerson," said the youngest of the group, a youth with sandy hair and a fledgling mustache. "Strangled a streetwalker."

"But why assume it was the Marauder?" Charles propped an elbow atop a filing cabinet. "Thus far it hasn't been his style to leave behind victims."

"It was the lily, sir," the florid-faced senior draftsman said in his gravelly tone. "The Marauder's signature."

"The magistrate's determined to catch the fiend," the first one added.

"Is that so?" inquired a dubious voice from the hall. Charles's brother crossed the threshold. "One wonders why. No one of name or fortune has fallen prey."

"Good God, George." Charles whirled on his brother, incredulity mingling with disgust. Aware of the draftsmen's eyes upon him, he hustled his younger brother several paces down the corridor. "You really have become insufferable."

George assumed a patronizing air. "I'm not saying this criminal doesn't deserve to hang. I'm stating the obvious fact that unless the victim is someone of influence, the authorities do little."

Charles couldn't refute the claim. With a rueful nod he cuffed his brother's shoulder, much as they'd always apologized for their boyhood disputes. "How'd the meeting go?"

"Looks like a profitable deal all around. Come, I'll fill you in on the way to Father's office. He wants to talk to you more about the Coddleton Mews project."

Despite that encouraging news, a sense of foreboding raised the hairs on Charles's neck as he followed his brother. Tess had risked her welfare, perhaps her very life, by venturing into crime-ridden St. Giles last night. Why? The image of a lily flashed in his mind, followed by the memory of Tess cultivating her hothouse assortment. Their light fragrance hovered on her hair, her clothes, blending their essence with her own.

Was it mere coincidence the Marauder used the same flower as his signature?

Chapter 16

Friday evening found Tess in the least likely of places, one she thought never to set foot inside again. Yet the Almacks of her memory bore little resemblance to the one that greeted her tonight. Upon entering the main ballroom, she instantly noticed changes that disputed her recollections of creamy plaster walls, fine artwork, burnished floors and blazing chandeliers that transformed ordinary balls into glittering dreams.

Now, yellowing walls begged fresh paint while the once gleaming floors bore drab witness to the many heels scuffed across their surfaces. Overhead, dusty chandeliers sputtered, thirsting for sufficient gas to renew their brilliance.

"Why, the place is becoming shabby," she murmured to Charles beside her.

His hand settled on the small of her back, warm, protective, sending a tingle along her spine. "It certainly doesn't live up to its reputation."

Tess hadn't set foot here since before her husband's death. She would not be here tonight were it not for Helena calling in several favors and procuring extra tickets for tonight's ball. Helena meant well, of course, but sometimes Tess wanted to shake her cousin and insist she stop trying to fix her life. Helena's words came back to haunt her: *you, my dear, are to be the latest rage*. Well, tonight they'd see about that, wouldn't they?

"Shall we make a round or two?" Charles's murmur produced gooseflesh on her arms. His presence made her feel safe on one hand and very much at risk on the other. Until tonight's ride in the barouche, she'd managed to maintain a tolerable distance between them. That deplorable scene in her sitting room two nights ago had served as clear warning: she was a weak woman when it came to Charles Emerson.

Days later she still felt confused and embarrassed by what happened—nearly happened—at the same time experiencing an undeniable ache of regret. Surely Charles couldn't have meant for things to progress so out of hand, or he wouldn't have retreated so abruptly, leaving her to cool her passions in the lonely chill of her bedroom.

She forced her attention back to the ballroom. Beyond doubt, the elegance had faded from these rooms. Tess wondered how long before the *ton* ceased coming to Almacks; before the *ton* itself transformed into something altogether new.

"Times are changing, aren't they, Charles?"

"It's the illusion that's fading," he replied in a thoughtful tone. "An illusion fueled by silk and candlelight and all the trimmings money can buy."

"The notion frightens me a little. It makes me wonder what the future might bring."

"Society always finds ways to recreate itself. When an era wanes, a new one begins."

Something in his tone sparked her optimism. What might a new era mean for Blair, and for the many unfortunate women who passed through the doors of Highgate Court? Dared she believe the coming years might usher in a spirit of tolerance, of compassion?

They were just passing the smoking room when an undertone lashed her ear, as she immediately knew it had been meant to do. A derisive male voice spoke her name and made hurtful reference. A mean-spirited snigger followed. She cringed.

Charles went rigid and stony-faced. Pausing in the doorway, he glared with a vehemence that might have made Tess tremble had he aimed the look at her. The chortles withered to silence. Two men rose from their chairs and retreated further into the room. With fingers splayed across the back of her satin bodice, he hurried her along.

"Thank you," she whispered.

His craggy features softened. "You're very welcome. Don't ever put stock in anything those kinds of louts have to say."

Her heart did a little dance. She wanted to kiss him—long and deep. Gratitude, yes, but more . . . just as it had been more than gratitude when they kissed in her sitting room that very first night. Ah, but tonight they were at Almacks, where dignity mattered.

Across the room, the Holbrooks appeared in and out of view behind dancing couples. Helena, elegant in ivory satin, had the ear of the handsome Lady Palmerston, one of Almacks's chief patronesses. Nearby, Sir Joshua, his beloved pipe clutched between his teeth, was offering glasses of punch to Emily Canfield and Beatrice Aimes. Other members of the Friends of the Bard Society milled through the room as well, some dancing, others looking on and no doubt remembering younger days.

From the far corner, Nora Thorngoode, the Bard Society's only truly youthful member, squinted in Tess's direction. At the moment of recognition her face lit up with relief. Nora hated society affairs such as this; coming would have been her mother's idea, most likely facilitated by another of Helena's favors.

As the orchestra took up the opening notes of a waltz, couples rearranged themselves on the dance floor. Nora made a face as her mother approached, all but dragging a young man by his coat sleeve. Tess chewed her lip on behalf of her friend. Would Mrs. Thorngoode have the audacity to suggest her unmarried daughter waltz publicly with a man she hardly knew, without the permission of Almacks's patronesses?

Poor Nora. Having deemed it high time her daughter married, her mother had become almost predatory in her search for an eligible member of the nobility.

Charles broke her reverie by reaching for her hand. "Shall we?"

Unlike Nora and the other unwed ladies here, Tess, as a widow, might take the liberty. Spinning round and round in Charles's arms . . . the notion was heavenly, dizzying even before the dance commenced. He would of course hold her close, his muscular legs brushing her skirts, perhaps her thighs, while his open palm took firm possession of her waist. And all perfectly respectable, because that was how it was done.

But those sudden, twisting flames of desire were not respectable, not in the least. She shook her head. "Later perhaps, if you don't mind."

He tipped a little bow. "As you like, madam."

They drifted into one of several parlors that opened off the ballroom.

"What a crush," Tess commented. Indeed, packed in a dense circle that filled half the room, people stood on their toes and craned their necks to see over heads. Every so often someone shouted out a word or phrase, eliciting giggles and groans from fellow onlookers. Charles shrugged and shouldered a path through, until he and Tess stood near the front of the crowd.

To her dismay she discovered, at the center of that rapt audience, Justina Reeves and her beau, Sir Robert Bessington, making silent but exaggerated motions.

"Charades," she whispered to Charles. He nodded. She was about to suggest they move on. After all, Justina was no friend of hers. Then an odd thing happened. Justina caught her eye and waved; one might even say she smiled, or very nearly.

Surely the gesture hadn't been meant for her. But when Justina called, "Do join us, Mr. and Mrs. Emerson," Tess's uncertainty burgeoned to astonishment.

Helena had certainly outdone herself.

As the game continued, she slipped her hand into the crook of Charles's arm. "Should we stay?"

"Why not?" he whispered back. "Let's see if we can't decipher Lady Justina's attempts to dramatize the absurd." His fore-arm flexed beneath her hand. "But mark me, Tess. At the first sign of insolence, I'm whisking you back into that ballroom."

Through eyes that misted dangerously, she regarded his bold features. Had she wished to kiss him for his kindness moments ago? How infinitely dearer that wish now became, this yearning to thank him for compassion she knew she hadn't earned. She squeezed his arm and hoped he understood.

From the strength emanating through the masculine sleeve beneath her hand, she found the courage to chuckle and then laugh outright at the antics employed by Justina and Sir Robert.

"Up . . . top . . . sky?" the portly Lord Edgar Reeves called out, his already ruddy face darkening with each conjecture.

At *sky*, Justina nodded and held out her hands, urging her father to further his guesses.

"Sun? Stars?"

Justina's nods became vigorous. She began prancing back and forth with her arms extended as if holding something above her head.

"Kite?" the Princess Von Haucke ventured. "Are you flying a kite?"

Justina cupped a hand to her ear, indicating the word she sought rhymed with kite.

Sir Robert fished in his coat pocket. Extracting a shining gold coin, he displayed it with an eager expression.

"A sovereign?" a young man asked. "How does that fit with flying a kite?"

Justina and Sir Robert exchanged exasperated glances.

"You're stumping us," Justina's father bellowed.

"Act it out," her mother urged.

Flashing a diabolical smirk that set Tess chuckling again, Sir Robert wrapped his hands around Justina's slender neck. Though startled for an instant, she soon warmed to the performance with rolling eyes and an expression mimicking terror. Snickers and scandalized giggles erupted from the onlookers. Even the card players across the room paused their game to watch.

Sir Robert pretended to wrestle Justina to the floor. In actuality he laid her out gently on the carpet and tucked a sofa pillow beneath her head before resuming his stranglehold on her neck. Justina faked a series of gasps and went still.

Her mirth fast dissolving, Tess's eyes widened with dismay. She began taking tiny steps backward, until she trod on the toe of the man behind her. Sir Robert extracted the boutonniere from his lapel and placed it on Justina's bodice.

A gasp pierced the laughter. Horrified, Tess realized it had escaped her own lips. Her hand flew to her mouth; she stared from face to face to see if anyone had noticed.

"Why, I've got it," Miss Alberta Granville cried. She thrust a triumphant finger into the air. "It's the Midnight Marauder!"

"Just so." Justina sat up. Grasping Sir Robert's hands, she came to her feet. "About time someone got it. I didn't think our clues so terribly abstract."

"But what's a sovereign got to do with anything," a gentlemen asked.

Sir Robert made a disgruntled sound. "It's also called a quid, you numskull. Which rhymes with mid, as in midnight."

"Ahhhhh."

Instinct urged flight. But Tess knew that doing so would only draw suspicion where none existed. Neither Sir Robert nor Justina, nor anyone else at Almacks tonight possessed the slightest inkling that the Midnight Marauder came from among their ranks. Except for Helena and Wesley, of course, but they were nearly as much a part of the Marauder's identity as Tess.

No, this reference to her midnight crusades had been innocent enough. Tess must tolerate it with as guileless an expression as the young earl sitting in the corner, fumbling with the fob of his late father's pocket watch.

But the new Earl of Wrothbury proved less naïve than he appeared. Having arranged the watch chain to his liking across his waistcoat, he thrust out his chin. "He killed again last night, you know. The Marauder, that is. In St. Giles, just a few streets over from the time before."

"You don't say." Sir Robert gave a low whistle.

"Good gracious," exclaimed his cousin.

Tess felt the breath knocked from her lungs and struggled not to show it. Charles inched closer. Had he noticed something amiss? His arm hovered at her back as if waiting to catch her.

"He'd better not set foot in Mayfair," the Princess Von Haucke declared, "or I'll book passage on the very next ship bound for the Continent."

Several ladies nodded.

"Are they sure it was the Marauder?" Charles asked, making Tess want to cover his mouth to silence him. "Did he leave his signature at the scene?"

"As plainly as Bessington did just now," Lord Wrothbury said with the air of one who knew his facts. "Not only that, an odd piece of jewelry turned up as well."

Tess's throat squeaked. The blood pounded at her temples. She tried listening to the details of this piece of jewelry, but between constant interruptions and the roaring in her ears, she made out only a few words.

It didn't matter—she *knew* the discovered bauble was an earring, etched silver with a dangling coral teardrop. What she couldn't fathom was how on earth it had found its way to the scene of this latest crime.

"Are you all right?" Charles's hand settled at the small of her back.

She allowed his touch to steady her before trusting her voice. "Of course. Perfectly fine."

His eyes narrowed. "Why do I never believe you when you say that?"

"Don't be a goose." Panic edged her attempted cheerfulness. Perspiration trickled down her sides.

"Let's dance then," he said, and grasped her hand.

She let him convey her into the ballroom, her mind too jumbled with images of murdered girls and Fabrice's glaring clue to protest.

Princess Esterhazy, another of Almacks's patronesses, announced a quadrille. The woman had at one time been among Tess's most outspoken detractors, and a principal reason she had ceased coming to Almacks.

"Perhaps we shouldn't," she mumbled to Charles.

"Nonsense. We most certainly should."

His insistence didn't surprise her. He was always insisting she do one thing or another. What shocked her was Princess Esterhazy's approach, and the correct if not warm smile fixed on her face.

"My dear Mr. and Mrs. Emerson." She offered her hand to Charles. "Welcome and congratulations on your recent marriage. Lady Wesley Holbrook has told me all about your whirlwind courtship. What a charming way to begin a Season."

"How kind of you to say so," Tess managed. Why, Helena had coerced kindness from even this old dragon.

"Won't you complete a foursome with Mr. Grey and Miss Evesham?" the woman suggested in a tone that settled the matter.

The very last thing Tess wanted to do was dance, but refusing would have been beyond rude, especially in light of the princess's conciliatory overtures. The young couple to whom she referred stood nearby, tactfully pretending not to notice her hesitation. Tess and Charles joined them at the end of the double line of dancers.

Though she'd performed the steps since childhood, tonight the quadrille eluded her. When she linked her arm through Charles's, her elbow locked so tight he winced. As they circled one another, she trod on his foot, then missed Mr. Grey's outstretched hand during the crossover. A sense of urgency gripped her like a vise. She wanted only to race home and warn Fabrice.

"You're looking pale," Charles murmured as they circled the other couple.

"There's barely a breath of air in this room." She sounded tetchy, she knew. But dancing—how absurd when a murderer all but hovered at her back, ready to implicate her or perhaps make her his next victim.

"It's more than that." His fingers deftly slid from her elbow to her hand. He twirled her with an elegant flourish. "Did that Marauder business offend you?"

Oh, the man was far too astute. "Foolishness doesn't offend me." She tossed her head. "It bores me."

"Ah." He said no more but his expression pronounced her a liar. Indeed. She'd told so many lies and half-truths these past days, she herself barely remembered where the truth lay.

"May we go?" she asked when the quadrille ended and they'd bowed to their partners.

"If you wish. But it's scandalously early." He winked wickedly. "Imagine all the gossip about those newly married Emersons, who can't keep their hands off each other for the duration of a ball."

Chapter 17

Upon arriving home, Charles ushered Tess off to bed—her own—with a chaste peck on the cheek. He, meanwhile, sat up for hours sipping brandy—though not vigorously—and pondering Tess's troubling behavior tonight.

Perhaps he should have simply asked her why an innocent game of charades sapped the color from her face. Or, more to the point, why she'd stolen off to a London rookery at midnight two days ago and then lied about it.

Good grief, hadn't he given her sufficient opportunity to confide? Hadn't he gone out of his way to prove his loyalty, his good intentions, devil take it, his willingness to put aside personal qualms and walk through fire for her?

Apparently not.

Sleep eluded him while Tess's many demons teased and taunted. Alicia . . . the Midnight Marauder . . . two murdered prostitutes . . . Tess and her hothouse lilies. Among all those mismatched pieces, one stood alone, an ominous shape with the power to alter the nature of the puzzle: the discovered earring.

Charles wanted to believe a thousand people could have owned such an item. And indeed they could, had they traveled to the Americas where etched silver and coral were common among some of the Indian tribes. This one stipulation considerably narrowed the possibilities; in fact, when combined with a midnight ride to St. Giles and an abundance of hothouse lilies, it pointed in a single direction.

The very house in which he sat.

He awoke the next morning groggy and still in the clothes he'd worn to Almacks. Slightly trembling hands made shaving a risky endeavor. Yet it was neither lack of sleep nor brandy that put him out of sorts, but rather the dozens of unresolved questions buzzing in his brain, questions he was determined to answer this very day.

He paused briefly in the morning room, detecting no sign of Tess. From the window overlooking the garden, however, Fabrice's voice mingled with the housekeeper's as they discussed the day's grocery list.

Charles strolled out to the coach yard soon after to find Fabrice lying faceup on the ground, his upper torso hidden beneath the barouche.

"Making repairs?" Charles stuffed his hands in his trouser pockets, trying to look and sound idly curious.

"Oui." Fabrice wiped a rolled-up shirtsleeve across his brow and peered through the wheel spokes. "The axle is loose."

"That's dangerous. Glad you discovered it. You may be preventing a disaster. Tess's own parents died in a coaching accident."

"Oui." The servant grabbed a wrench from the batch of tools on the ground at his knee.

"You certainly seem to know your way around a coach. I wouldn't know a shaft from a bearing, I'm afraid."

"I learned as a child."

"Ah. I've often wondered, where are you from? Judging by your accent, you can't have lived in England very long."

"America," he replied without pausing in his task.

"One of the former French colonies? Quebec, perhaps?" Though a hunch told him different.

"Non." Taking up a mallet, Fabrice tapped the axle securely into its bearing. "Lousiane."

Yes, that would have been Charles's guess. "Always wanted to see New Orleans. I hear it's quite a town. Like nowhere else in the world, I'm told."

"I am from Baton Rouge." Fabrice dropped the mallet and tested the axle's fit by shoving his palm against it.

"I see. Do you miss it?"

The servant eased out from under the barouche. Pushing to his feet, he immobilized Charles with an animosity so raw it stole his breath. "Non. There is little to miss in a slave's life."

"I . . . I see." Duly chastised, he felt barely able to look Fabrice in the eye as he uttered the next falsehood. "Sorry. I didn't mean to pry."

"Monsieur asks many questions."

"I'm merely curious. I traveled for many years, so I know what it means to be far from home."

"Monsieur can know nothing of Fabrice's life." For several seconds the servant's eyes burned fiercely bright, a wordless story of despair and frustration. Then he turned away to collect his tools.

His unspoken reproach filled Charles with remorse. Fabrice was right, he could not know what it meant to be a slave. He'd never owned another human being, though he'd known other British officers who had kept native youngsters to polish their boots, care for their mounts, brew their coffee. All the same, Charles *had* helped turn free people into vassals under English rule.

Shamefaced, he mumbled an apology to Fabrice's back. He found little satisfaction in having achieved his goal, but in questioning Tess's manservant he'd learned something vital. A key puzzle piece had moved several degrees closer to the solution.

The earring found at the murder site could very possibly be of Natchez origin—an Indian tribe from the Baton Rouge area—and might just as possibly belong to Fabrice. Dear God, Charles wished otherwise, wished he could toss the trinket to the bottom of the Thames and forget all of it: the murders, the Marauder, and Tess and her damned lilies.

What had he walked into when he agreed to help her?

* * *

An impulse sent Charles searching out his old friend, the Viscount Kirkwood. He tried the man's rooms first. When the landlord heard him knocking, he yelled up the stairs about the 'lazy lout' not having come in last night and the rent being long overdue.

Despite the early hour, Charles next sought his friend at his club. His guess proved correct. After inquiring within, the porter ushered Charles into Bartles's drawing room, a masculine refuge of walnut paneling, leather and mahogany furnishings, and dark, heavy draperies.

He spied Kirkwood lounging in a dimly lit corner, his wrinkled suit looking as slept-in as Charles's own had that morning.

Even now, he wondered at his reasons for coming here. The viscount had never been more than a casual acquaintance. But perhaps that was the point. Perhaps Charles craved the objectivity of someone with nothing to lose or gain from the circumstances presently threatening his sanity.

Kirkwood spotted him over the edge of his newspaper. "Emerson. This is a pleasant surprise."

"I stopped by your rooms first. Did you sleep here all night?"

Kirkwood shrugged. "Wouldn't be the first time."

"Your landlord's looking for you."

"Not the first time for that, either. Home isn't exactly the safest place for me at the moment."

With a grunt of agreement, Charles settled into the overstuffed chair beside his friend's. "I know the feeling."

"What's the rub, old man? Honeymoon over already?" Kirkwood folded his newspaper and laid it on the Pembroke table beside him.

Charles shrugged and said nothing.

The viscount studied him. "You're so droopy-eyed you're reminding me of the time the bunch of us were gated for conduct unbecoming gentlemen in the Great Court at Trinity College." Kirkwood chuckled wryly. "We were so foxed we nearly burnt down the Master's Lodge. Lucky for us, men of good name aren't accused of drunkenness and arson, nor are they expelled. Not when their papas can fund new buildings and stock libraries. No, such fellows are gated for a night or two and forgiven."

"Good grief, I'd forgotten about that." Charles raked a hand through his hair. Even now the memory evoked boyhood insecurities. "I wasn't so sure of being gated and forgiven, as you put it, not at all certain my family name would see me through."

"Then that would account for your turning that peculiar shade of green when we were apprehended."

"No, the whiskey would account for that." He made a face. "I rarely drank whiskey after that night, and then only with the utmost caution."

Kirkwood laughed softly, crossing one long leg over the other. "Tell me, what's turning you green this morning, if not whiskey or boyhood mischief?"

Charles hesitated. The viscount's dry humor had already lifted his spirits a notch. But was he trustworthy? Charles looked into the other man's pale blue eyes, eyes that had always skimmed the world with a bored air, as if never expecting to discover anything extraordinary.

Detached. If any word summed up old Kirkwood, it was detached. Not aloof exactly—he wasn't as cold as that. But simply not . . . connected the way most people were. And that, Charles decided, made his old acquaintance the perfect confidante.

"Can I trust your discretion?"

"I am discretion itself, old friend."

"Yes, well, I have some questions concerning things that went on while I was away from England. And I wondered . . ."

Kirkwood nodded. "Ask away."

Charles steeled himself with a breath. "You told me you knew my wife. You probably have acquaintances in common. So I wondered, can you tell me anything about her sister's death?"

His friend's expression sobered. "Alicia James? Hasn't Mrs. Emerson told you?"

Charles shook his head. "I suppose she finds it too painful to speak about. My mother provided some of the details, but sketchy ones at best."

"What did she say?" The viscount sat up straighter, eyes sparking with interest.

"That Alicia ran off to what she believed would be an elopement, but in fact wasn't." Charles inclined his head and lowered his voice. "People were quick to judge, quick to assign blame. I hope you weren't one of them."

"Good grief, no." Kirkwood fell silent a moment. Then, "Did Mrs. Emerson, the elder Mrs. Emerson that is, reveal the identity of the scoundrel in question?"

"No. She has no idea who he was. Do you?"

"None whatever." Kirkwood set his coffee down and shifted in his chair. "Apparently the James family was rather tight-lipped. Who can blame them? And of course I've never been one to delve into gossip."

Charles nodded. "Tess knows, of course, but for reasons of her own, she chooses not to speak his name." He paused to signal a passing waiter. "Coffee, please. Strong." He looked in question at his friend.

"Too early for cognac?"

"I rarely indulge before four o'clock. But don't let that stop you."

"More coffee," Kirkwood told the waiter with a resigned shrug.

"Tess has barely spoken of her sister at all," Charles confided after the waiter walked away, "but I sense that Alicia's death still weighs heavily on her mind."

"I don't wonder." Kirkwood released a sigh. "I'm afraid your mother only told you half the story, old man."

Charles leaned over the arm of his chair. "Will you tell me the rest? Please. I can't be of any help to my wife unless I know what happened."

Kirkwood looked decidedly uncomfortable but nodded. "Apparently, after Alicia James's . . . heartbreak, shall we say . . . her uncle banished her from their home in Mayfair. Simply washed his hands of her. Rather harsh of him in my opinion, but hardly surprising. The geezer's of the old school. Simply couldn't brook modern standards of behavior."

"You don't have to tell me about Howard James." In fact, the last person Charles wished to discuss was Tess's uncle. "But what happened to Alicia after that?"

Kirkwood drew a breath. "You must remember that my information came not even secondhand, but third and sometimes fourth. Much of it may be based on rumor and sheer conjecture."

"I understand." Charles waved an impatient hand. "But what *happened*?"

His old friend pulled forward in his chair. "She left Mayfair and somehow ended up in Southwark where, apparently, she began working for a living."

"Working?" A sickening apprehension crept over him. "At what?"

Kirkwood gave him a pitying look.

"You can't mean . . ."

"The oldest profession. Sorry, old man."

Rage, sudden and savage, nearly propelled Charles's open palm into his friend's face. "Take heed when you attach implications like that to my sister-in-law's name.

Kirkwood blinked. "It isn't my intention to offend, merely to tell the truth as you asked to hear it." He paused as the waiter returned with a coffeepot and fresh cups. "Believe me," he continued when they were alone again, "I should rather cut out my tongue than make matters worse for you."

"No." Charles propped his elbows on the arms of his chair and lowered his head to his hands. "Forgive me."

"No need." Kirkwood leaned over and clapped his shoulder. Something in his expression indicated more to the story.

"You might as well tell me the rest of it," Charles said.

"That has to do with your wife, I'm afraid. You're sure you wish to hear it?"

Not at all sure, he nodded.

"I remember her from the old days." The viscount smiled. "A lively girl and quite lovely. I understood what you saw in her. But after her sister died she became a changed woman entirely."

"I don't understand." Or did he? All along, Tess had been lying and manipulating, and behaving not at all like the ingenuous young woman he had loved a decade ago.

"Her sister's death left her, well, disturbed."

"Of course it disturbed her," he snapped, his anger rising again. "Death has that effect on people."

"I don't mean in the usual way," Kirkwood replied, seeming unperturbed by Charles's retort. "Miss James's passing left Mrs. Emerson more than upset, more than grief-stricken. She was . . ." His gaze drifted to the window.

"What is it you don't wish to tell me?" But Kirkwood's taut expression conveyed the unsavory answer. Charles grimaced. "Are you saying Alicia's death left Tess unbalanced?"

"Unbalanced is too harsh a term. She became . . . confused, I believe. Fearful. Suspicious. Mind you, I'm only reporting what I heard. I'd been away in the country most of that year. But her friends became quite concerned about her, then frustrated when she turned them away. Most finally gave up."

"You believe Tess instigated some of the ill will shown her?"

"I'm sorry, old man. Perhaps I shouldn't have said anything." Kirkwood offered a grim smile. "It's none of my business. I just hate to see an old bloke like you in the doldrums."

Charles barely heard. Thoughts coursed through him like a foul wind laden with debris. Alicia, St. Giles, murdered prostitutes, Fabrice and his exotic earrings, Tess and her lilies.

He'd been searching for a connection, hoping to find none. Had Kirkwood provided the link he'd dreaded? Had Alicia's death driven Tess over the edge of sanity, impelling her to reenact her sister's fate again and again?

Could Tess, along with the enigmatic and often rancorous Fabrice, be London's Midnight Marauder?

"Charles, old man, are you all right?"

He shook his head to clear it. "Don't worry about me." He pushed to his feet. "Excuse me, Kirk. There's something I have to do, and I have to do it now."

"Before you go . . ."

Charles balanced on the balls of his feet, impatient to be off. Kirkwood looked up at him, uncertain, apologetic. "Do you think you might lend me few pounds, just till next Tuesday? I really need to get back into my rooms and the landlord, you know . . ."

Charles nodded and whisked out several bank notes.

"Becca, quickly, bring these two bags down to the foyer." Tess cinched the buckle on a third valise. Straightening, she smoothed the front of her traveling jacket and surveyed her bedroom. All in order.

They would be ready to leave within minutes, and none too soon. After last night's debacle at Almacks, she dared not risk remaining in London another hour. Not when Fabrice's earring had been found beside the second victim. He'd spoken of erasing all trails leading to them, but this drew a clear path straight to her front door.

Fabrice entered the room and relieved Becca of the suitcases. "The horses are hitched to the barouche, Madame. All is ready."

"Did you put my note in Mr. Emerson's room?"

"Oui." He crossed to the bed. Shifting one bag beneath his arm, he hoisted the third. "Mademoiselle Blair will be overjoyed at this surprise."

"Do we have anything special to bring her?"

He grinned. "You."

"Oh, I have an idea." She spoke to his reflection in her dressing table mirror as she tied her bonnet strings beneath her chin. "I'll bring that new bolt of blue moiré. It'll make a splendid frock for her."

"It was intended to be a frock for Madame."

"I don't need a new frock and the color will complement her eyes. Please fetch it from my dressing room." Then she noticed the three bags he already carried, one in each hand and one tucked beneath his arm. "Never mind, I'll bring it down. Now hurry and let's be off. Becca, please find Tanya."

The maid bustled out. Fabrice lingered, staring at her but saying nothing. She let out a breath. "What?"

"We are innocent."

"Of course we are."

"Then why are we fleeing?"

"Because someone is trying to make us—or at least the Midnight Marauder—appear guilty. If we stay, someone might connect that earring with you."

"Does not leaving also make us appear guilty?"

"Oh, I don't know." She tossed up her hands. "Leave or stay, either way we risk suspicion. But if another murder is committed while we're away, that earring will no longer have the power to incriminate us."

"Me."

"Pardon?"

"Me, Madame. The earring can only incriminate me. Not you." He set all three bags on the bed and crossed the room to stand before her. His tawny eyes held her in their catlike gleam. "If suspicion falls, it will fall on Fabrice. Madame will let it."

Her hands snapped to her hips. "I will not."

"No argument. Madame does not know about prisons and chains and the loss of freedom. You could not endure it." His mouth closed with a stubborn set, immobile, resolute. Behind it, Tess saw a world of repressed pain. With a shiver she recalled the glimpse he'd once allowed her of his back, permanently striped from an overseer's whip.

"All right. I won't argue," she promised. Neither would she allow him to bear the blame for a crime he didn't commit. For now, however, she'd provide him the comfort of believing she'd respect his wishes.

Minutes later, she picked her way carefully down the stairs with the bolt of moiré in her arms. The scene that greeted her in the foyer almost sent her running back up. Fabrice and Becca stood at attention, backs to the long console table. A third culprit, Tanya, peeked out from Becca's arms with a look of mixed apprehension and contempt. Before them stood a granite-faced Charles.

"What's the meaning of this? Where is your mistress going in such a hurry?"

Tanya blinked. No one answered.

"When was I going to be informed of this mass exodus?"

Tanya twitched her whiskers.

Charles's head swiveled in Tess's direction. "Ah, Mrs. Emerson. Going shopping, I presume?"

His gray eyes, scalpel sharp, held her frozen on the third step up from the landing. "I, uh . . ."

"Or perhaps a call on the Holbrooks. I do hope Sir Joshua hasn't taken a turn for the worse."

"No, he's fine."

"Glad to hear it." He strode closer, and Tess backed away until her heels hit the riser of the step above. He reached for the fabric. "Ah, I understand. You're off to your modiste, and you're bringing empty suitcases to fill with new dresses." He swung the bolt to the floor and leaned it against the wall.

"Not exactly," Tess mumbled. With her arms suddenly free, she resisted the urge to hold them up and shield herself.

"I'm sorry, did you say something?" Quite without ceremony, he captured her hand and tugged—not roughly, but enough to coax her down the remaining steps. "Let's talk, shall we? In the parlor. Now."

She cast desperate glances at Fabrice and Becca. Becca seemed about to chew a hole through her bottom lip. Fabrice targeted Charles with ill-concealed enmity. At the merest signal from her, her stalwart servant would incapacitate Charles and ensure her escape. Not daring to meet her dark angel's gaze lest he misinterpret her look as such a request, she trotted to follow Charles into the parlor.

He locked the door behind them, only to unlock it a second later. "You, out," he ordered.

Tess looked up at him, confused, until she felt a luxuriant, furry stroke against her ankle. She lifted her hem. Naughty Tanya had leapt from Becca's embrace and followed them into the room. The feline raised a disdainful glance at Charles, arched her back and hissed.

"Out." His jaw clenched. "Now."

Tanya's tail swished. Having made her point, she scampered into the hall. Charles shut the door and relocked it.

He turned and faced Tess with a smile that raised goose bumps. "Now then, Mrs. Emerson, I want answers. Neither of us leaves this room until I have them."

Chapter 18

"Don't you think you're being just the teensiest bit over-bearing?"

The moment the words left Tess's mouth, she regretted them. A kind of jolt went through Charles's facial muscles before they froze to a glacial scowl.

"I demand to know what's going on here. Start talking, madam. And it had better be the truth." Each clenched syllable brought him another step closer, his impatience pelting her like hail. She'd have sworn his shoulders expanded, his height soared. He made her feel not only small and vulnerable, but quite sorry she'd left her servants on the other side of that door.

Before she knew what he was about, he gave her bonnet strings a tug. The hat slipped askew and tumbled over her shoulder. He caught it and sent it skittering onto a side table. It slid against the wall and bounced to a stop.

"Now then." A forefinger danced before her face. "No more lies. No more elaborate tales. I want the truth or there will be consequences."

Consequences? The word frightened at the same time it set off an odd little spark. Never before had she encountered this side of Charles Emerson, the fierce soldier's side that couldn't be bargained with, couldn't be appeased without full surrender. She shivered.

"If you'd let me get a word in edgewise," she said with a show of indignation made flimsy by her trembling, "I'd already have told you I was on my way to Highgate Court. I have estate business to attend to." She hefted her chin in her best attempt to imitate Tanya's assertiveness. "That, sir, is the simple truth."

"That, my darling, is a bald-faced lie."

He seized her elbow and propelled her to the sofa. Her pulse hammered as she sat. He loomed over her, hands braced on the sofa's curved back on either side of her head. She felt trapped by the wall of his chest, the breadth of his shoulders, the muscles straining his sleeves.

"Dammit, Tess, the truth."

Her belly tightened in apprehension and something else, something that urged capitulation to that chest, those arms, the imperious line of those shoulders.

But surrender would mean explanations. The words eluded her. Charles believed the Midnight Marauder a vicious killer. Coupled with the countless lies she'd told him, how could he possibly believe anything she said now, no matter how true?

"I—I am on my way to Highgate Court," she repeated miserably. "Why won't you believe me?"

"That much I do believe." He straightened, his gaze never leaving her face. "It's the why I'm having trouble with. And don't try feeding me that 'estate business' rubbish, because I'm not swallowing it."

As he stepped back she felt more able to breathe, but not for long. He dropped down beside her and seized her hands. "I might not be your husband in actuality but, by God, Tess, you owe me the respect due a husband after all I've put up with."

Her hands shook beneath his larger, infinitely warmer ones. She knew the physical contact would reveal any untruth she attempted to utter. She stared mutely back.

"Go on, Tess," he challenged. "Tell me another tale. Make it a rich one. Tell me you're as ordinary as any other London lady, that you go about your daily activities with all the propriety of the other society matrons. Then tell me I'm raving, imagining things. Isn't that what you're going to say?"

"Yes. No." She gulped. "I wish my life *were* ordinary and boring. Good heavens, how I wish it."

"Why isn't it?" he whispered fiercely. "What sort of trouble are you in? Don't be afraid. I swear, no matter what it is, I'll help you fix it." He raised her hands to his lips, a gesture of undeserved affection that shattered her heart.

"This isn't something that can be fixed." The tears brimmed over.

"Trust me, Tess." Releasing her, he reached out and caught a teardrop on his fingertip. Suddenly he took possession of her face between his hands and pulled her to him. Against her lips, his mouth took up his demands with breath-stealing insistence. "Just bloody trust me. For once."

All the familiar fears—of trusting, depending, needing—rose up even as his tongue stormed her mouth. For several heart-stopping seconds she teetered, warring with indecision. The stakes were high, the risks impossibly great. It was her life's work, up against these surging feelings for the most honorable man she'd ever known.

Charles. Her undeserved champion. Despite her deceptions, he was still here, still bracing her with his strength while at the same time tearing down her last defenses. His lips eased and then pressed with renewed vigor against hers. Her passion burst free. She kissed him back, long and deep, groping for more of him, all of him, wanting to give all of herself.

"Will you lie to me now, my darling?" he asked, dragging his lips across her face.

The endearment traveled through her. Her fingers clenched the shoulders of his coat, bunching the fabric. "No. And never again."

She blinked to see him through a watery mist. "But there's so much . . . I don't know where to start. Or how. Come with me. Come to Highgate Court. You'll understand everything once you're there."

His sternness returned. He pulled away, holding her face

immobile between his hands. "You still insist on running away?"

"I know I haven't given you a single reason to trust me." She placed her hands over his. "Please try, just this once."

"Trust you?" With a laugh he brushed his lips across her brow. "Madam, in light of everything, that's a rather cheeky request, wouldn't you say? Though I suppose it's no more bizarre than anything else that's happened since you literally ran into me at Vauxhall Gardens."

"Then you'll come?"

His hands roamed her hair; his thumbs smoothed the length of her neck, raising new shivers. "All right, my dear, we'll run away to Highgate Court together. I'll trust you for just that long."

"Thank you."

"No need. It occurs to me that when someone runs away, they're often running *to* something. It's time I found out what that something is."

Charles peered out the coach window at rolling fields bordered by forested hills. They had passed a village some time back, a few scattered farms. Now, nothing but unbroken countryside, large and vacant.

The fragrance of lilies drifted beneath his nose. Like a persistent wasp, his old friend's words buzzed in his mind: *her sister's death left her disturbed.* Was Charles's decision to trust Tess ill advised?

What connection existed between her and the Midnight Marauder? Every instinct, every shred of common sense, assured him she could never harm another living soul. Not Tess, who coaxed vibrant blossoms from the most forlorn plants, who had coaxed his own weary spirit back to life these past days.

His gaze drifted to her face and then lower, to the graceful curves accented by her dark traveling clothes. Even after all the lies and manipulation, he wanted her. More than he'd ever wanted anything or anyone. Why should that be? Why indulge feelings for a stubborn, deceitful, infuriating woman with a knack for getting him into one predicament after another?

More to the point, what did he plan to do about her?

Well, travel with her to Surrey, for one. Secondly . . .

"I know about Alicia," he said to the aristocratic line of her profile. "All about Alicia."

She jumped as though jabbed with a pin. Startled, Tanya vaulted first into Charles's lap, then, appalled by her mistake, to the floor. Tess's purse tumbled after. Ignoring both, she scooted to the corner of the seat, putting as much space as possible between them. She glared saucer-eyed across the distance.

"Why didn't you tell me about her?" he asked quietly.

"Why didn't you tell me you knew?" At her feet, Tanya echoed the accusing question with a *yowl*.

"I'd hoped you'd come to me and confide, not only about your sister but all the strange goings on these past days." He watched a row of hawthorn hedges stream by his window. "Sadly, you didn't."

Her mouth twitched. "How long?"

"How long have I known? Since I first visited my mother. She told me most of the story." He almost mentioned Kirkwood, then thought better of it. Perhaps his source of information was a secret best kept, for the time being at least. "The rest I learned from an old friend who heard the details in the roundabout way people do."

"You mean he recounted all the horrible rumors?" Holding out her arms, she beckoned Tanya into them and hugged the cat to her bosom. Charles experienced an irrational pang of envy.

"I'd much rather hear the truth from you," he said. "And then you can explain some other odd occurrences as well."

Suspicion narrowed her eyes. "Have you been following me?"

"Oh, no, madam." He folded his arms. "My questions first. Then yours, assuming time permits."

"Yes." She sighed. "I suppose I owe you that much." She ventured several inches from her corner, but her stiff posture maintained a clear boundary between them. "I suppose you've learned that Alicia ran off to an elopement that never occurred, and that my uncle cast her from the house. After that—"

She broke off blinking, lips quivering. He instinctively reached to offer comfort but she brushed his hand away, a rebuff reiterated by Tanya's swatting paw. Far from offended, Charles understood by the grim set of Tess's mouth that she needed to find her own strength or succumb to grief.

In the next minutes her faltering statements confirmed both his mother's and Kirkwood's macabre tales of a gentlewoman's fall from grace, her subsequent illness and death. Then Tess fell silent, lips compressed and trembling. He waited. Finally, her pale face lifted. "There is more, but you'll understand once we arrive at Highgate."

"What about this fiend's identity?" he asked, tapping his fist against his open palm.

She lifted her hand, hesitated, then placed it over both of his. "Perhaps someday, but not now. I won't tell you for the same reason I've never told Fabrice."

"And that is?"

"Revenge. I won't have either of you compelled by honor to seek retribution. It wouldn't bring Alicia back, but I'd lose two people I . . . care about very much."

Care about very much. So that at least put him on equal par with her trusted servant. Lucky him.

"Very well," he conceded. "But one more question, and the rest can wait until we've arrived. How does all this fit in with your mysterious behavior these past few nights?"

"You *have* been following me." She made indignant noises in her throat. "How could you?"

He wasn't proud of his brief career as a spy, but neither did he intend to let her know how demented she could make him. He took the offensive. "Do not turn this around, madam. You've been sneaking out of the house in the dead of the night. And the places you've gone. Good God, woman, you might have been killed."

The last word echoed between them. Tess went utterly still. Tanya stiffened in her embrace.

"Y—yes, I know." She clutched her arms tighter until the cat squirmed. "The answer to that, too, rests at Highgate."

He scowled. "I'm beginning to think Highgate Court holds the secrets of the cosmos."

"For me," she said, "it does."

Tess watched in silence as Charles took in his first view of Highgate Court in the waning sunlight. His curious gaze scanned the front of the house, surveyed the lawns. What must he think? Probably that the place didn't warrant all the money she insisted she needed. Or perhaps that it was high time she used that money for improvements.

She grimaced when his gaze lighted on the sagging east chimney, again when he studied the paint peeling from the second story shutters. The house—a two-story Georgian affair of red brick, white columns and slate rooftops—had long since lost its grandeur. Not exactly shabby, but a far cry from the elegant country estate it once was. Ah, but Charles would learn soon enough that money went for far more important matters.

The sounds of female conversation drifted from beyond the south wing, from the old bowling green that had been turned into a laundry yard. Two of Tess's charges approached the front of the house swinging a basket of folded clothes between them.

Gwennie had been here nearly a month now. With satisfaction Tess noted the new roundness to her figure, the restored color to her cheeks. Gone was all hint of the frightening, hacking cough that had made pulling her off the streets so necessary.

By contrast, the signs of undernourishment persisted in the girl beside Gwennie. Yet even in Ellen, Highgate's newest arrival, Tess detected marked improvement. The girl's spare shoulders no longer poked so sharply beneath her frock, nor did the hollows of her cheeks drag as heavily at her features.

"You have company," Charles murmured beside her. "Funny, I don't remember you ever mentioning any cousins besides Helena."

The front door opened and four more young women sauntered onto the veranda. Raising a boisterous clamor of teasing and laughter, they failed at first to notice Tess and Charles on the drive. Then one's gaze happened to drift and she fell silent. The others ceased their chatter and stared. A tall brunette slipped back into the house, perhaps in search of Mrs. Rutherford.

Tess understood their reticence. Highgate Court never, ever saw visitors other than Tess, Fabrice and the Holbrooks.

"These can't all be cousins," Charles said.

"No, they are—"

"Aunt Tess!" The shout came from an upstairs window. Moments later little Blair dashed out the front door and down the steps, skinny shins pumping hard beneath a flurry of hems. She bounded across the gravel drive and vaulted into Tess's outstretched arms.

"Darling," Tess cried, catching her niece up and taking a step backward for balance. Her back groaned in protest—how her girl had grown these past weeks. Slender arms slipped around her neck while Blair's legs spanned her waist. Tess buried her face in a tangle of raven curls and held on tight.

As sweet, childish laughter heaved in warm puffs against

her neck, a lump pressed her throat. Ah, she'd missed this un-
ruly little bundle of a girl more than she'd realized.

She peeked at Charles from over the child's head. His eyes
blazed with curiosity.

"Blair, darling, go help Fabrice unload the coach," Tess told
her. "And see what I've brought for you."

The girl only held on tighter. Curls tickled Tess's chin as
Blair shook her head. "I don't care what you brought. I just
want you."

Her heart clenched. "Even if it'll make the most fetching
frock in a shade that matches your eyes?"

"A frock?" Blair's mouth twisted. "I don't need a new
frock, Aunt Tess. What I want is a riding coat and breeches."

"Breeches for a lady? And in that lovely shade of blue?"
Tess witnessed the determination in the child's face and
laughed. "Oh, why not? Why shouldn't little girls be as comfortable when they ride as little boys? All right, darling, a coat
and breeches it shall be."

"Thank you." Blair squeezed her neck.

"Feet down," Tess said and set the child on the ground.

Before she scampered away, she took notice of Charles and
pointed a none-too-clean finger. "Who's he?"

"Blair, this is Mr. Emerson. He's an old friend."

"Old friend?" She assessed him from head to toe as though
sizing him up for a new suit. "Why haven't I ever met him before?"

"Mr. Emerson's been away for many years, darling. He's
only recently returned to England."

"Does he knows about . . ." The child's eyes narrowed.
"You know . . ."

"I'm beginning to." Charles crouched to speak to her.
"How do you do, young lady?"

She shook his offered hand. "Quite well, thank you. And
you?"

"A bit confused, I must confess." He paused, craning his
neck for another glance at the house and lawns, at Gwennie

and Ellen who now stood beside Tess, their basket abandoned on the ground behind them. "Perhaps you might enlighten me."

"It's a secret of the highest priority," Blair replied in her most solemn voice. Charles flashed a surprised look; Blair's vocabulary always astonished people. "But Aunt Tess wouldn't bring you here if she didn't intend for you to know, would she?"

"No, I don't suppose she would," he agreed, matching her in seriousness.

"Do you swear not to tell?"

"Upon my honor."

"Pish! On pain of death."

"Blair," Tess exclaimed. Struggling to hide a grin, Charles held up his hand.

"On pain of death," he repeated in his gravest voice. "May I be drawn, quartered and beheaded should I ever betray your trust."

The child's satisfied air reminded Tess of the time Tanya stole a fish off the kitchen counter. "You've heard of us," she declared. "Aunt Tess and Fabrice, Aunt Helena and Uncle Wesley, Mrs. Rutherford and Reverend Coombs." She tapped her chest with her thumb. "And me, of course. We're the Midnight Marauder."

Chapter 19

Good Lord. Someone finally stole Charles Emerson's bluster. The fact that it had taken a five-year old to do the job didn't surprise Tess a bit, considering the identity of that five-year-old. Charles pushed to his feet in openmouthed, astonished silence.

She wasn't, however, fool enough to believe his unrelenting questions and plain bossiness would cease indefinitely. No, once he recovered from the initial shock he'd take up right where he left off: demanding, commanding—ugh—insufferable.

And completely justified, she had to admit.

"You and I need to talk," he growled. Beside her, Ellen flinched.

Oh, dear, her reprieve had ended much sooner than she'd predicted. She turned to Blair. "Darling, go and ask Fabrice to help you find that fabric. The blue moiré." The girl skipped away with Tanya loping after. Tess regarded Charles sheepishly. "We can talk in the house."

"Aren't you going to make the introductions?" He gestured toward Gwennie and Ellen.

Tess clasped their hands and drew them to her sides, though whether out of courtesy or self-protection she couldn't decide. "These young ladies are two of the Midnight Marauder's more recent victims. That is, if you still consider victim the proper word."

He scowled, but half-heartedly. "They look healthy enough

to me. Ladies." He bowed and then swelled Tess's heart by raising each girl's hand to his lips. "A pleasure."

Ellen blushed. Gwennie returned the pleasantry with a curtsy, but her attention had already wandered.

Tess followed her line of vision to where Blair stood chattering away to Fabrice, who was just now lifting the bolt of azure fabric from the barouche. He noticed Gwennie staring at him and waved. A snarl formed her response. Fists on hips, she stalked across the drive raising a ruckus of crunching gravel.

"Surely you're not planning to hand all that heavy fabric to this child," Gwennie accused in a tone that already declared Fabrice guilty.

"Mais non, mademoiselle." He looked offended. "Of course not."

"I *could* carry it." Blair bent her elbow to display a muscle only she could see. "I'm strong."

"Of course Mademoiselle is strong," he was quick to agree. "Fabrice could use your help carrying this basket. I will take the cloth."

"No, I'd best carry it." Gwennie snatched the bolt from him, grunting slightly beneath its weight. Fabrice moved to retrieve the burden but she hugged it to her torso. "I said I'd take it. You're likely to leave it where it'll get soiled. I suppose then I'd best come back and help with the rest, or nothing will find its way to its proper place. Never leave such things to a man, I always say."

Fabrice watched her set out for the house still muttering beneath her breath. Amusement played about the corners of his mouth. His mirth faded when he caught Tess studying him. He quickly resumed unloading the coach.

Hmm, she mused, *Gwennie and Fabrice. . . .* She wondered what had occurred between them when Fabrice came last week for the marriage certificate. Why, wouldn't it be splendid if—

"Let's go." Ending her speculations, Charles grasped her hand and started walking.

"Where?" She trotted to keep up.

"Not the house. I have a feeling it's much too crowded for my purposes. You tell me. Just make it somewhere we won't be interrupted until I'm satisfied that I understand everything. And I do mean everything, madam."

They circled the house, reaching the kitchen garden. On the other side of the wire and picket fence, two more of Tess's proteges hefted tin watering cans. Tess stopped and dug in her heels. The girls stared and traded whispers.

"We can't just run off," she said. "Mrs. Rutherford will wonder."

"Who is that? Another of your partners-in-crime?"

"Don't be absurd. She's the housekeeper."

"Then let her wonder." His grip as firm as ever, he hurried her the length of the garden and steered toward the tool shed. "She's obviously privy to your secrets. I should think that as your husband-presumptive I would be afforded the same courtesy you extend to your housekeeper, not to mention a tiny child."

"Stop pulling me." She tugged in the opposite direction. To her surprise Charles released her; she had to backstep quickly to keep from falling. They stood facing each other on a raked path beneath the fragrant shade of a pear tree. Tess inhaled deeply, drawing comfort from the sweet scent of ripening fruit. "You're quite right, you do deserve to know what High-gate Court is about. That's why I brought you here."

"Brought me? Ha! I left you no choice."

"I didn't think you'd understand, especially with . . . the recent developments."

He bent over her, gray eyes flinty and inescapable. "You mean the murders."

"Oh, Charles, Fabrice and I didn't . . . we never . . ."

He clasped her shoulders gently, warmly. "I know. Of course I know." Gathering her to his chest, he combed his fingers through her hair, pulling her careful chignon askew until the pins scattered and the tresses tumbled down her back. His lips nuzzled her forehead. In his protective hold, Tess felt the depth of his faith and instantly knew bitter remorse for every half-truth, every lie.

Strong, steady hands lifted her face. "I am beginning to understand. Insane though it sounds, you are the Midnight Marauder and this place . . ." He paused to glance back at the house, at the women now gathering their work tools in the garden. Mrs. Rutherford appeared in the kitchen doorway. Rag in hand, she waved but remained where she was.

Charles's handsome features smoothed. "This place is a haven for some very fortunate young women. Good God, Tess, why couldn't you have trusted me with this? What on earth made you think I'd object?"

Her throat tightened at the pain in his voice, at the wounded shimmer in his eyes. "I'm sorry. There were other matters to consider besides whether or not you'd approve. But please, not here. I know where we can be alone."

They continued past the stable yard and onto the riding lane that entered the forest. With each step beneath the thickening trees, Tess became very much aware of the man behind her, his heavy footfalls, his breathing, his hands that rose to steady her over each fallen branch or weed-choked boulder. Her back prickled in the heat of his presence, large and powerful and so very male.

The rushing of a brook soon became audible; the tangy scent of the sorrel lining its banks drifted on the breeze. Where forest gave way to meadow, Tess swept aside trailing willow branches overhanging the path.

Before them, a lawn of clover and buttercups stretched before a white clapboard cottage nestled against a hillside. Tess felt suddenly breathless for reasons quite apart from their trek through the woods. Charles's hand enfolded hers. He waited, patient and silent beside her. She regarded the cottage, not as a structure merely but as part of the secret life she'd led these many years.

The house had once served as a guest cottage, but in recent years its precious solitude had become her private haven. She often took Blair there for picnics, cherished times when she pretended her world revolved around the little girl and simple country life.

Would bringing Charles here shatter that illusion forever? Apprehension and anticipation mingled inside her. As dusk gathered, she felt more alone with him than ever before. More vulnerable. And not at all certain she was about to do the right thing.

"What a beautiful place," he commented softly, so close his breath stirred her hair against her cheek. "A scene out of a fairy tale."

Yes it was, with its curling ivy creeping up one wall and a riot of wildflowers spilling from the window box. But would he find the cottage as charming five minutes hence, or would learning the truth dispel every fairytale he'd ever believed in?

"Come." She led him by the hand as far as the stone doorsill.

"Aren't we going in?"

She sank to the stoop and drew him down beside her. "Not yet."

"All right." He studied her from beneath hooded lids. "We'll talk here."

She slid her hand free of his, suddenly needing even that small distance between them if she were to maintain any composure at all. "I hardly know where to begin . . ."

"You might try the beginning." He reclined against the door and folded his arms. "Just say it, Tess. I've yet to hear it from *your* lips. Even now you're afraid to speak the words."

"Yes, you're quite right. I am London's Midnight Marauder." She stopped, her heart fluttering wildly beneath her stays. Yet despite having never before uttered those words beyond her circle of accomplices, the earth did not now open up and swallow her whole. That gave her the courage to press on.

"Secrecy has always been my strongest weapon, for only secrecy can protect my girls. When they reenter the world, no one must ever learn of their former lives. And as you might well guess, secrecy protects me as well. There are those who would stop at nothing to put an end to my work."

"But then why the lilies? Why all the dramatics of creating this character that all of London knows about?"

Yes. Sometimes it all seemed the stuff of insanity, even to her. And yet . . . "I began inconspicuously enough. But it gnawed at me, the memory of Alicia's secret shame, her lonely death. Ah, Charles, London consists of two wholly separate worlds. There's the one we inhabit, and then there's the one where hungry people are desperate enough to do anything, anything at all to survive. Lillies were Alicia's favorite flower, if you'll remember. With a mysterious coach and hothouse lilies, then, I've attempted to build a window between those worlds, to force society to stop ignoring the tragedies that in many instances occur mere streets from their lavish homes."

"But what a risk you took in doing so."

"Yes, but you see no one—positively no one—ever suspected the Midnight Marauder might be a woman. Until you entered my life, that is."

"And when I did, you sought my help but evaded my confidence." She cringed at the tautness of his voice. "For the life of me, I don't understand why you lied to me. To *me*, Tess."

She swallowed a bitterness of guilt. "I lied because I knew that once my inheritance was secured, you'd return to your own life." She glanced at him quickly. "As of course you should. But I'm sorry to say that makes you an outsider."

"And what makes you so certain I'll leave?"

Despite the implications of his words—wondrous, startling implications—his question held clear rebuke.

"You left ten years ago," she blurted.

"You wouldn't have me ten years ago." His voice rose to a crescendo of frustration and a decade's worth of dashed hopes.

She tucked her chin. "I'm sorry."

"For dredging up the past or for having as little faith in me now as you did then?"

Ah, yes, she deserved that. "Both."

He pressed the heels of his hands to his temples. "Tess, I'd never betray you."

"I'm sorry," she said again, feeling wretched at having tossed the past at him, and at having ever doubted where she should have trusted. "I should have known you'd never be anything but honorable and loyal. I suppose faith is something that doesn't come easily to me."

"That, madam, is the understatement of the century." Plucking a pebble from the ground at his feet, he hurled it with bullet speed into a tree stump.

"You needn't be so snippy."

"No, I suppose I needn't." He flashed a wry smirk and relaxed back against the door.

"Charles, there is so much at stake. I had to be certain of you."

"And now you are?"

She hesitated before answering. "There are still so many barriers between us."

"Such as?"

"Emerson & Sons, for one. Do you even realize how your family's business contributes to the problems that make the Midnight Marauder so necessary?" She stopped, aghast at her own words. This was no time to cast blame, not on Charles or his family.

His head went down. "Yes, I do."

"You do?"

He pushed a grim chuckle between his teeth and nodded. "Up until now, redevelopment in London has always forced the poor from their homes with no thought as to where they'd go. I returned to England determined to change that, and I've devised plans that can help solve the problem." He smiled a little ruefully at his feet. "Pretty proud of them, I have to admit. I'll show you when we return to London."

Tess's mouth hung open. In the ensuing silence, the hissing

waters of the brook and the snapping of insects grew loud and conspicuous. Charles whooped with laughter.

"You've been like a cart careening out of control, Mrs. Emerson. I see I've finally stopped you cold."

"I had no idea."

"Of course not. I didn't tell you." He brushed her cheek with the backs of his fingers. "I've kept a few secrets of my own."

"But none as destructive as mine." She looked away, knowing self-pity rode such sentiments.

"Will you tell me who Blair is?" When her gaze darted back to his, he shrugged. "I've pretty much figured it out but I'd like to hear it in your words."

"She's Alicia's." Her throat compressed as it always did when she spoke of her sister. She bit down and swallowed, wondering how to proceed with details that sickened her so many years later.

"What of the girl's father?"

"He knows nothing about her and never will." The old loathing frothed inside her. "Not while I live."

He conceded this point with a nod. "And I suppose you still won't tell me his name."

"I believe it's wiser not to." Seeing the argument rise up in the squaring of his shoulders, she hastened to silence him. "What good would it serve? The villain is best left where he belongs, in the past. The fewer people who know his identity, the less harm he can ever do Blair."

"She's a beautiful child." He relaxed and reached an arm around her, drawing her against his side. "In fact, she reminds me of a certain lovely but terribly willful young lady I know." He pressed a kiss to her temple and held his lips there. "And she should no more be held accountable for the past than you should."

"Oh, Charles, really?" She nestled her face against his neck and reveled in the small miracle that he was still there, that he hadn't simply risen and walked away.

"Of course really." He shook her a little. "Do you think so ill of me?"

"No. Of course I don't. It's just that . . . I've grown so used to people thinking ill of me. And thinking ill of myself," she added in a whisper that would not be hushed.

"What have you to blame yourself for?" His hold tightened, fortifying her waning strength with his own.

"I might have prevented Alicia from leaving home. Or perhaps found her sooner than I did. She died having Blair, though the complications were a result of her illness, not the birth itself. I tried so very hard to save her, to nurse her back to health but—"

"Don't, my Tess." He spoke soothing tones against her hair, wrapping her in compassion, in the forgiveness she sought. "You've done right by your sister in raising her child, and in helping all these other women."

Relief spread from deep in her soul, radiating outward like ripples on a pond. "Thank you for not judging."

"Ah, Tess, I'm the last one to cast stones." An edge crept into his voice. "Not after ten years in the military—ten years of persuading myself that honor and duty were one and the same. Very often they are not. Sometimes they are exact opposites."

She opened her mouth to question this, but his severe expression silenced her.

"You must understand." His fist clenched. "We relocated entire villages in the name of duty. We never paused to consider how many generations had occupied a region, or how much their lives depended on tradition and the land."

"Charles, I'm sure you were only following orders." She slid a hand to his shoulder. "You can't be blamed for . . ."

He flinched at her touch. His face turned hard, relentless. "We simply took what we wanted, citing the king's authority with all the arrogance Englishmen can muster. We created poverty where none existed before. Sheltered village girls became camp followers while their brothers thieved, their mothers wasted from illness and their fathers drank themselves to death. Oh, yes, I told myself it wasn't my fault, that I was following orders. But what a lie. What an obscene, colossal lie."

"You're being far too hard on yourself. What choice—"

"Don't." His eyes burned. "I didn't confide to gain your sympathy, Tess. I've come to terms with my past—with the things I've done—and am making amends as best I can, here, where I have some power to effect change."

The anger drained from his features. "Forgive me. I only wanted you to understand the truth of who and what I am. It seemed only fair, considering." His mouth curved to something approaching a smile. Relief spread through Tess at the sight of it.

"There's nothing to forgive," she assured him. But there was still a matter of great importance that needed to be made clear between them. "Uncle Howard doesn't know about Blair. No one does, other than our Midnight Marauder conspirators. No one must ever know my sister bore an illegitimate child, for the child's sake."

She expected him to question how one might keep a human being a secret. Instead he nodded in agreement. "Of course no one must know. The society dragons would flay her alive the first time she showed her face in London."

"When she's older I'll concoct a story of taking on a ward. Perhaps enough time will have passed for people to believe it. For now, she's safe and happy here."

"Here," he repeated, "in this remarkable place. I never for an instant guessed its existence, though perhaps I should have. You, madam, are a remarkable, extraordinary woman." The admiration in his voice traveled like new life's blood through her. She felt suddenly younger, revitalized, exhilarated.

He grasped her hand. In the instant their palms met, an ember burst to life between their joined flesh. Tess didn't mean for the moan to slide from her throat but it did, and was quickly answered by a murmur from deep in Charles's chest. She couldn't have said which of them moved first; perhaps they both reached at the same time. She knew only that they'd suddenly become a desperate tangle of arms, seeking and greedy.

"Tess, my darling girl." Charles slanted his lips across hers, and as if parched and dying, they drank of each other, sharing breath and moisture and pressing for more. "Ten years," he breathed against her mouth. "So long. Too long."

Shoving aside layers of skirt and petticoat, he pulled her into his lap. His touch on her bared thighs elicited quivers that alternately chilled and scorched.

"Charles, I—"

"Oh, be silent, my Tess. If you push me away now I won't be responsible for the consequences."

That word again. Her limbs trembled. She shifted until she faced him, her torso pressed the length of his. Oh, she hadn't been about to push him away, not at all.

Those barriers she'd spoken of seemed suddenly gone, scattered and forgotten. Only the inconvenience of clothing separated them now. Charles's hands roamed her body. Her insides turned to liquid heat as he filled his open palms with the curves of her hips and waist, with her breasts' aching swell.

"Who the devil invented bloody brocade anyway?" he grumbled, searching in vain for the hidden hooks that held her carriage jacket closed. "How in the world . . . ?"

"It's easy." She released a hook with a flick, then reached to flip open his waistcoat's top button.

He acknowledged her dexterity with a rumble that dissolved her bones. His mouth dived for her throat, renewing those hot and cold quivers. She arched for him, raised her chin high, yielding all of her neck to humid, tingling kisses. His hands slithered inside her jacket but went suddenly still. His head came up.

"Another confounded layer?" He glared at her bodice. "Good grief, Tess, how many more?"

Desire made her giddy. She laughed instead of answering. Looking as though he'd reached an important decision, he shoved her jacket almost roughly from her shoulders. It landed in the clover with a soft thud.

She peeked through her lashes. Would he attempt more, here, beneath the twilight sky? Her breath caught at the scandalous notion. Charles's lips curled even as his arms encircled her. She felt a tug at her back and heard a little popping sound. The very top of her bodice slackened around her neck.

"I beg your pardon, sir."

Pop. Pop. Her dress drooped from her shoulders. Charles's smile became wolfish as he took full advantage of the widening view.

"Oh!" But her outraged squawk sounded extraordinarily like delight.

He grinned. "Perhaps you should show me into the cottage now."

"Good gracious, sir. Perhaps I should not."

Pop. His fingertips dipped inside her sagging neckline, burrowing between her linen shift and flesh. "I insist, Mrs. Emerson."

"But . . . Blair might wonder where we are." She sucked draughts of air as he grazed her nipple, teasing it between two fingers. "Sh—she might come . . . looking for . . . us."

"Does the door lock from the inside?"

"I s—suppose, but—"

Two more pops in rapid succession. Her bodice all but lay in her lap while his palm invaded her shift. He cupped her breast and she could have shrieked from the sheer erotic pleasure rippling through her.

"Would you rather she found us here? Those are your choices, madam. In or out. Tell me quick, Tess. I've waited ten long years and several frustrating, interminable days. I'm warning you, I've more than reached my limit."

She struggled for breath. "In. Let's go in."

He hoisted her in his arms and pushed to his feet, using the door at his back for leverage. Tess reached for the latch. The brass hinges groaned as she gave an inward push.

He stepped inside then hesitated. Lust-ridden shadows obscured his gray eyes. "I may loathe myself for this, but . . . you and I have been stumbling over each another these past days, not to mention ten years ago, trying to do the right thing. This feels right to me now, Tess. I haven't the slightest qualm. But are you quite sure? Because if not . . ."

"I am. I think. I mean—"

"Why did I ask?" He kissed her. And kissed her again. "My darling, your problem is you think everything to death. Trust your heart for once. Trust *me*."

She extended an arm, pointing to an inner doorway. "There's the most deliciously soft bed right through there. Take me to it and I'll show you how much I'm willing to trust you."

He took one pace before she stopped him. "Wait!"

"Dear God, what now?"

"The door. We need to lock it. We don't want to take any chances."

He stooped and she slid the bolt home. "Now then, madam."

She clung to his neck, her nerve endings pulsing with the realization that once through that bedroom door, their sham marriage would become infinitely less so.

Chapter 20

Charles stepped through the doorway, turning to accommodate the beautiful, exquisitely sensual and equally maddening woman in his arms. He kicked the door shut, then remembered he didn't have to. They were alone. No Fabrice, no Becca, no yowling Tanya. No one at all to disturb them . . . except Tess with all her damnable thinking.

The bed stood between two oblong windows on the opposite wall. Its brass frame clanged when Charles plunked her down. He grinned. "Ah, the essence of discretion."

"Do you intend to keep tossing me about, sir?" She pouted with lips gone soft and scarlet from their recent kisses.

"I most certainly do." He leaned over her, hands resting on disheveled locks of hair and effectively pinning her right where he wanted her. "Time to pay up, Mrs. Emerson, for all your lies and deceptions."

"And just how do you plan to seek retribution, Mr. Emerson?" The cheeky thing arched her neck in brazen suggestion.

His groin tightened around inner flames. He accepted the offer of tender flesh, nipping and kissing her throat till she squirmed beneath him. Grabbing a handful of skirt, he raised the hem to her knees, her thighs. "To begin with, I intend to take this."

"My dress?"

He nodded, flames licking to a blaze.

"Very well, then." She pushed his arms away and sat up,

turning her back to him with a purposeful air. "You'll have to work for it."

Damn. As many buttons as he'd done away with outside, at least that many remained, securing the dress snug at her waist. After fumbling with the first couple, he seriously considered ripping the rest free. Tess read his thoughts, or perhaps guessed by the sudden tension on the fabric.

"Don't you dare. I'm fond of this gown. If you damage it I'll be forced to demand compensation." She cast an appraising glance over one shamelessly bared shoulder. "That shirt, for instance."

Tearing rent the air, followed by the thudding of cloth-covered buttons hitting the hardwood floor. Tess's gown pooled around her hips.

"Now you've done it." Snatching her ruined bodice, she whisked it up over her linen shift in a show of modesty utterly belied by the wanton gleam in her eye.

Lust seared through Charles. Tess reached out, ignoring, or pretending to ignore, the way her dress slid lower over one breast. Her sheer camisole teased rather than concealed.

As her fingertips grazed his Adam's apple, Charles attempted to moisten his lips; his mouth felt like a desert. "What are you doing?"

Her smile widened. "This." With admirable skill, she opened his shirt's top button with a flick.

"You're rather good at that."

"Mm hmmm. Eye for an eye," she murmured, "or button for a button." She opened the next, and the next. Featherlight, her fingertips grazed his chest. A pectoral muscle twitched. When one button proved stubborn she frowned and stood, relinquishing her hold on her gown to gain the use of both hands. The garment slithered to the floor around her feet. "Oh, dear."

"I believe that's mine." He ogled the pert breasts beckoning through her shift. "Never mind, I'll have these instead."

Eagerness made him clumsy as he reached for her, and the hooked mat beneath his feet slid from under him. Catching the bed just before he fell, he shimmied up onto its edge and opened his arms to her. When she went into them he rolled, landing their entwined bodies headlong into a depression in the hissing feather tick.

"I finally have you right where I want you, Mrs. Emerson." He nipped at her lips, tugging at the bottom with his teeth. "And I'm yours to command."

Her expression turned sweetly uncertain. "I'd hardly know how."

"To what? Command me?" He started to laugh but a notion dawned. "Surely you can't mean that during your marriage you never . . ."

"Of course I don't mean that. Walter and I performed our duty as man and wife." She turned her face aside as though unable to meet his gaze. "But that's all it was, and it was rare at that."

He knew the grin spreading across his face was a stupid one, but he couldn't help it.

"Do stop smirking. You look like Tanya when she's cornered a poor little mouse."

"Sorry, it's just that . . ." He almost shared his immense relief that she had not, in fact, enjoyed a love relationship with Walter Hardington. But he realized in time that he didn't wish to discuss Walter Hardington or any other man for that matter. "I doubt any mouse could be as delectable as this." He traced his tongue along the underside of her chin.

Tess let out an *ahhh*.

"Or this." He nibbled her earlobe.

She giggled and half-heartedly tried to swat him away.

"Or . . . this." His fingers trailed to the edge of her camisole and delved inside.

Beneath him, Tess shivered, and ten years of pent up yearning nearly exploded inside him. That he maintained control at all paid tribute to his military training; he mentally recited marching drills to take the edge off his arousal. He'd waited an eternity for this and intended to savor every blessed moment of it.

Judging by the shakiness of his hands, he might have been that same eager youth of ten years ago. Somehow he managed to fumble clothing from a body that more than fulfilled a decade of fantasies, managed to peel petticoats and knickers from a tight little waist, sublime hips, down long, long shapely legs and—fling—onto the floor. He'd probably owe her new undergarments as well as a gown for the damage done. Or perhaps not, for he heard more than the occasional rip as Tess stripped his own clothing away.

With each scattered garment, she explored more and more of him, her lips curling at each discovery. "So muscular," she murmured. "Through your shirt, I hadn't realized just how so."

He gazed at her hands, slender and delicate on those muscles she admired. It made him feel . . . big. Masculine. The way a man should feel upon finding himself naked beside the woman of his dreams.

"My darling, you do know how much I respect you, don't you?"

"Of course, Charles."

"Good." Because for the next hour or so he planned to respect her not at all. Nothing—no part of her—would remain sacred or out of bounds. Nor—God willing—would any part of him.

He dipped his head and kissed a nipple as sweet as heated caramel, drawing its peaked tip into his mouth. Tess arched and moaned, and a shuddering, possessive pleasure filled him. She embraced him with arms and legs. Laughing, they rolled over and back, widening the hollow in the old mattress and filling it with secrets of the most sensual kind.

His hands adored her, revered her, claimed her with an impatience only just contained. The curve of her waist entranced him, the contour of her belly fascinated him. His mind reared dizzily at the soft purrs vibrating through her lips, at her fingers blazing trails across his chest, his back, his thighs.

While they mutually explored, his hand traveled to the moist nest between her legs, a seductive mystery unlocked with a light brush of his fingers. Trembling, Tess gasped and opened for him, setting him on the brink of his control.

She brought her lips to his ear. "Teach me."

He did. He taught her the many nuances of sensuality, beginning with the merest of touches and the heat of his breath, building layer upon layer of pleasure with hands and lips and tongue.

When he felt her tentative touch upon him, he covered her hand with his own and closed her fingers tight and firm around him, teaching her the rhythm of a man's indulgence. Moments later he stopped her abruptly, answering her unspoken query with a laugh of apology.

"Oh," she said with a nod and a grin. They laughed again, laughter that became kisses that roamed each other's bodies, that swept them from time and place and left only sensation. When Charles sensed her approaching a crest, he parted her wide and positioned himself.

"Charles," she breathed.

"Yes, my darling?"

"Don't . . ."

He tensed. Good God. Desperately he searched for adequate words to reassure her, to prevent her stopping what felt completely, perfectly right. Of all the times to pull away. For heaven's sake, they were practically. . . .

He realized she hadn't finished speaking. Her eyes were clenched. Her lips worked soundlessly, then audibly. "Don't . . . be . . . gentle."

Stunned, he gaped. As that last layer of propriety fell away, he gave her what she wanted, took what he craved. With a desperate thrust he entered her, not at all gentle but as she'd demanded. She cried out at the constriction of her muscles around him, so tight, so unused to being filled. Almost virginal. God help him, almost the way he'd left her ten years ago.

A surge of unabashed gratitude spurred his passion; elation

rode the tide of his lust. Perhaps she had, after all, felt something for him all those years ago that she'd never shared with another man.

As the thought melted into euphoria, Tess pushed against him, burying him deeper. Her cries turned raw. Alarmed, he nearly stopped dead. He opened his eyes to behold the throws of her ecstasy. The sight splintered his remaining control. His thrusts took on a determination of their own, fevered, frenzied, bringing him to a climax more crushing than he'd ever known.

Evening had chased all but the duskiest glimmers from the room. Listening to Charles's heart resume its normal beat beneath her ear, Tess thought, *What have I done?*

And then, *I don't care. I'm happy.*

No, not quite accurate. She cared very much about what they'd just done, about everything that had occurred since Charles first demanded explanations back in her London parlor. Being honest with him had been the most frightening leap of her life; it propelled her irretrievably from everything she'd based her life upon these past years.

He'd been so understanding, such a dear. And afterward. She filled her lungs with the scent of him. Afterward had been heavenly. Perfect. Thrilling.

No, the thing she couldn't seem to care about was the notion that she'd been weak. It simply didn't feel like frailty or depravity or any of the sins people had accused Alicia of and suspected in her.

"We have to go back."

The vibration of his voice against her cheek startled her. She thought he had dozed off. She, too, might have slept but had opted instead for the sweet pleasure of lying on his chest and listening to his breathing, his heartbeat.

She stretched and rubbed her palm over springy whorls of hair. Ah, this was contentment. For several more precious seconds she pretended it had taken permanent root in her life.

"Tess, did you hear?"

"Not yet." She resisted, closing her eyes to preserve the illusion that she and Charles might enjoy more than these few glorious hours together. "Blair won't come looking for us. Despite the fact that a darkened forest wouldn't deter her, Fabrice will have kept her occupied." She smoothed her hand back and forth across his chest, loving the hardness of it, relishing the memory of another quite solid part of him. She bit back a giggle. "He can be very understanding, not to mention perceptive."

"Who?"

"Fabrice, silly."

"Humph. At any rate, that's not what I meant."

"What isn't?"

He caught her hand and raised it to his mouth, sucking the tip of each finger in turn. Tingly goose bumps traveled her arm. "Are we speaking different languages?" he asked between nibbles, "or have our evening activities left us addlebrained?"

"Mmm. Lusciously so."

Gently he eased her onto the pillows and sat up. "Is there a lantern somewhere?"

"Beside the fireplace."

Sliding from between the bedclothes, he shuffled across the room, carefully picking his way through the shadows. Tess heard the tea tin she used as a tinderbox creak open. Charles selected a few lengths of charred linen and wrapped them round a chunk of obsidian flint. With a soldier's expertise, he struck steel to the flint, creating a spark on the first try. Within seconds he'd blown a small flame to life and held the glowing end of the tinder to the lantern's wick.

Climbing back into bed, he set the lantern on the table beside him.

"We must go back and soon, Tess."

"You already said that and—"

"No, not to the house. To London."

She lurched upright and tossed hair from her face. "Are you mad? I can't go back now. The murders, Fabrice's earring. I cannot let him stand accused of crimes he didn't commit. The best place for us right now is here, away from London."

Shoving at the pillows behind him, he propped his back against the headboard. "Tess, someone is using your alter ego to commit murder."

"Exactly."

"And that's exactly why we must return to London and speak with the magistrates. They're looking for the Midnight Marauder. Meanwhile someone else entirely is free to go on murdering."

"Dear Lord, I hadn't thought of it that way."

Charles resumed suckling her fingers as if disaster weren't hovering just over their heads. The sensation evoked spirals of pleasure. She forced herself to focus. "But darling, if heaven forbid . . ." She broke off. "Why are you grinning at me like that?"

"You called me darling."

"Oh, Charles really. If this villain murders again, our being here will prove Fabrice's innocence even if the earring is traced to him."

"And if, my darling, there are no murders while we're here and the earring is traced to Fabrice, no one will doubt his guilt."

The blood drained from her face in a dizzying rush.

Charles leaned to embrace her. "I don't mean to frighten you. Not that I quite understand your fears anyway. Your cousin's husband is a Member of Parliament. Surely he could . . ."

"If we must appeal to Wesley, we shall. Oh, but Charles, I fear what such a scandal would do to his future. I owe Helena so much. Neither Fabrice nor I wish to bring misfortune down around their heads."

"Sweet Tess. Always taking care of others." He pressed a kiss to her brow. "Very well. I believe we should bring one of the girls with us to London, to testify that the real Midnight Marauder has never hurt a soul. That should clear both you and Fabrice, and never mind the earring."

"Why do you wish to help Fabrice?" She stroked his face, the beginnings of his evening beard rough and reassuring against her fingers. "He hasn't been very nice to you."

"Neither has he done anything wrong." He let out a weary sigh. "And he is, for reasons that elude me, your friend."

"He saved my life once."

"The footpad you spoke of."

"Yes. And I saved his." She rested her cheek on his shoulder, discovering a surprising tension that hadn't been there moments ago. "Fabrice made his way from America to London without a farthing to his name. When we met, he was near to starving."

"I should think a man with Fabrice's wits would devise some passing clever schemes to keep from starving." His shoulder tightened to an uncomfortable angle beneath her cheek. A suspicion took shape in her mind.

"You don't understand him at all." She raised her head and met his gaze. "He's no criminal."

"He certainly doesn't shrink from crime when it comes to you."

"Oh, that little forgery. Are you still brooding over it?" She tsked. "You're partly right, though. He'd stop at almost nothing to protect those he cares about."

"I don't think I like the implications of that." He scowled. "To what extent does he care about you?"

"Don't be a dunce." She smiled and hugged him tight. "If anything, I do believe he's falling for Gwennie, and she for him."

"You mean the one who kept harping at him when we arrived?"

"The very same. She's sweet, isn't she?"

"I think they're made for each other," he mumbled, but his tension drained away.

She hid a grin. Charles had been jealous, actually jealous of Fabrice.

"We'll bring this Gwennie to London with us," he said. "Tomorrow."

"So soon?"

"Why wait?"

A weary sigh whispered from between her lips. "It's over, isn't it? The Midnight Marauder's secret will be out, and that will be the end of it. Highgate Court has seen its last pupils."

"Not necessarily. I overheard a conversation recently about the chief magistrate of St. Giles taking a stand concerning these murders. He sounds like a man who cares about justice. Perhaps if we go to him, he might be persuaded to keep our confidence."

"Or he'll clap us all in irons."

"My darling, whatever happens, we'll face it together. I'll be right beside you." He pressed her close, and she let him.

But, contrary to his intentions, his promise produced a sinking feeling. She'd come to depend more and more on this man's strength, his support. How easy to go on depending. Yet the longer she did so, the more deeply mired in her problems he'd become. And all the harder, in the end, to let him go as she knew she must.

He had returned home to join his family's business and begin life anew. To ensure success in his profession, he'd need a wife with connections, with the social influence to further his interests. Someone, well, like Helena. A woman like Tess—a social pariah loathed by his own mother and brother—would only thwart his future.

"You've done so much already," she said, backing out of his arms and trying to inject a believable optimism into her voice. "I couldn't possibly impose any further."

He shushed her with a finger to her lips. "Impose? Are you that much of simpleton?"

"I beg your pardon?"

"Dammit, Tess, can't you comprehend that I've fallen in love with you all over again?"

A burst of panic propelled her to the foot of the bed. She dragged the counterpane with her, holding it before her like a shield. "You mustn't say that."

"Why the devil not? It's the truth." He shifted beneath the

bed linen. Thinking he'd reach for her, she tensed to flee. But she was wrong. Charles merely reclined against the pillows and crossed his arms behind his head. His lips skewed to a knowing smirk. "I want to marry you, Tess. A king's ransom says you feel the same about me."

For a single moment of glory, her heart sang a joyous melody. But the moment passed and her soul and her eyes were left stinging with the reality he seemed unable—or unwilling—to accept.

"How we feel at this moment doesn't matter."

"Then you do love me."

"No. Yes. Charles, please understand . . ." She faltered, throat burning.

"Oh, Beatrice has nothing on you, has she?"

"Beatrice Aimes?"

"No, goose. Beatrice from Shakespeare's *Much Ado*, remember? 'It were as possible for me to say I loved nothing so well as you. But believe me not; and yet I lie not; I confess nothing, nor I deny nothing.' Poor Beatrice, too confused to see that Benedick was the only man for her."

She shook her head at him. "If you wish to compare us to Shakespeare, Romeo and Juliet is far more apt. Oh, Charles, the time is wrong for us, just as it was ten years ago. There are too many forces pulling us apart, and in the end they'll succeed. Again."

"What forces?" Consternation etched furrows in the brow she'd kissed and smoothed but minutes ago. "We're adults now, Tess. No one decides our fate but us."

"No? Have you forgotten the man murdering in my name?" Her voice threatened to crack. She looked away and swallowed, fearing a single glance at Charles might send her back into his arms.

"You and Fabrice have done nothing wrong."

"What of my uncle then? He has the power to undermine everything I'm doing here."

"Our marriage would solve that."

The simple suggestion broke her heart. She forced her gaze back to his. "Charles, look at me. See me for who I am."

"I see my beautiful, darling girl." For a moment, his eyes glistened like the silver depths of a waterfall.

She shook her head. "I'm an outcast. A nobody."

"No, Tess. Listen to me—"

"You listen to me." Why couldn't he understand? Why must he force her to speak of the hurtful truth that shaped her existence? "You are about to become an important man in London. I'd only hinder you. Hold you back. Drive potential clientele elsewhere."

"I don't believe that."

"No? Then what about your mother? She despises me." In a way, Blanche Emerson's animosity daunted her more than all the rest combined. It constituted the one adversity she and Charles couldn't face as a couple because seeing them together only fueled the woman's scorn. "I'm sorry, Charles, I cannot live with her disdain. I have Blair to consider. If your mother detests me, how will she feel about my sister's bastard?"

"That's my mother's problem," he retorted, anger gathering in his voice.

"No, it would be Blair's problem. I'd either have to hide my niece from my own in-laws or risk your mother destroying the child's reputation and self-esteem. I think you'll agree the woman is capable of doing the latter without so much as speaking a word."

Myriad emotions crossed his face as he studied her in the taut silence. She felt a chasm opening up between them, and in her heart. The pain of it threatened to send her into his embrace and simply believe, as he did, that they could ignore the many obstacles between them. But life had taught her differently.

"So," he said evenly, "you're saying you won't have me because of my family, even if I say the devil with them?"

"No, that is not what I'm saying." Obtuse man, why must he make this so difficult? "I'm saying there are too many factors threatening to tear us apart. That to even try at this point would be," she bit back a sob, "an exercise in futility."

"The hell it would, madam." Tossing aside the bed linen, he swung his feet to the floor with an angry thud. His naked body thus exposed, he combed the room for his discarded clothing without a trace of self-consciousness. He might have been alone in the privacy of his dressing room. Still, with a stab of guilt Tess averted her gaze. Though she adored every hardened plane and sculpted curve of him, he was not hers to admire.

"You can't toss me out again like last night's pudding, Tess. Not after what we've just done." He stepped into his pants and shoved his bare feet into his shoes. "There could be a child, you know."

She shook her head sadly. "I failed to conceive during my marriage. I have no reason to believe this time will be any different."

"Ah. How easy for you." He straightened, gray eyes hurling simmering fury down the length of his nose. "So once again you've made convenient use of me."

"No. Oh, Charles, you mustn't think that. These past hours have meant the world to me. If things were only different—"

"Things need not be different, Tess." His quiet severity slashed to her core. He stooped to retrieve his shirt, tugged it over his head and thrust his arms into the sleeves. "Only your perceptions need changing. You no more believe in me today than you did ten years ago. You were wrong then and you're bloody wrong now. And I intend to prove it."

As he strode from the room with the remainder of his clothing flung over an arm, she clutched the counterpane to keep from chasing after him, bit her tongue to keep from calling him back. What purpose would it serve? They could not change their lot with wishing.

Chapter 21

Fabrice tensed as the Honorable Samuel Crenshaw, chief magistrate of St. Giles Parish, lifted his steely gaze over the rim of his spectacles. "You mean to tell me that you—all of you—are the Midnight Marauder?"

No one, not Fabrice, Monsieur, Miss Gwennie nor Madame, spoke a word in reply. They had already explained a half dozen times at least.

"Anyone with an ounce of sense would toss the lot of you in Newgate and have done with it." The man's craggy fist slammed the scarred surface of his pine desk. A small silver and coral object clattered. Fabrice recognized his earring. "Do you think me daft?"

Fabrice wanted to groan, not out of fear of the man but because Madame had just stepped forward.

"Yes, well, you see, Mr. Crenshaw," she said, "we're not *all* the Midnight Marauder. I mean, there are actually more of us, although I suppose one could say we are the principal players. Of course Mr. Emerson had no idea until the day before yesterday, and Gwennie, well, she's actually one of—"

"Silence!" Peppered brows gathering like storm clouds, Crenshaw struck his hapless desk again. "Cease your yapping, Mrs. Hardington or Emerson or whatever you call yourself, and allow me to make some sense out of this balderdash."

"Well." Madame harrumphed and stepped back into line.

Monsieur Emerson glared at her. She treated him to an indignant pout.

Crenshaw cleared his throat. "Now then. Mr. Emerson, you claim to have had no knowledge of these goings on before this Saturday past?"

Monsieur nodded. "I've only been in the country a few short weeks, sir, and Mrs. Emer—uh, Hardington—didn't see fit to inform me of her activities until quite recently."

Madame's shoulders squared at his accusatory tone.

"Well, Mr. Emerson, it seems your return to England coincides with these recent murders." Crenshaw pushed his spectacles higher on his beakish nose. "What do you have to say to that?"

"If you're implying that I had anything to do with—"

The magistrate cut him off. "I'm implying, sir, that in light of the confession already made, you're all under suspicion. Can you supply a character reference?"

"My father is Richard Emerson—"

"Emerson & Son?"

"That's Sons with an s and yes, the same."

"Hmmm." Crenshaw scribbled some notes on a scrap of paper. "Richard Emerson built my house. An upstanding gentleman. If he can vouch for you, you're in the clear. But you . . ." A gnarled finger singled out Fabrice. "Who are you supposed to be?"

Fabrice opened his mouth but Madame was too quick. "He's not *supposed* to be anybody. He's my—"

She proceeded no further. The magistrate's hand shot up in warning. "I'm conversing with *him*."

"I am Madame Hardington's man-of-all-work."

A heavy silence descended while the magistrate alternately studied Fabrice and the earring. He bounced the ornament several times in his palm. For the first time since the interrogation began, a chill traveled Fabrice's back. If this man didn't believe their story, he might very well find himself bound for Australia as fast as Madame so often jested. Or worse, he might hang.

But if it came to either, he knew he would somehow manage to escape his bonds long before the ship left port or the rope circled his neck. No, what frightened him most were the consequences for Madame. She had endured much over the years but at least she had her comforts, her familiar surroundings, a few friends who cared for her. He dared not consider what would become of her if all that were whisked away.

Crenshaw dangled the earring between thumb and forefinger. "This yours?"

Fabrice nodded.

"Puts you right at the scene of the crime, doesn't it?"

"Non. It puts my earring at the scene of the crime. I never set foot in that alley."

"I'd advise you not to jest with me." A heated flush suffused the magistrate's neck. "You're my prime suspect."

"As we've told you," Madame interjected, "Fabrice is my servant. Anything he did, he did at my behest."

Fabrice resisted the urge to clap his hands over Madame's mouth. Could the woman never hold her tongue?

"In that case, Mrs. Hardington," Crenshaw said with a grim little smile, "that brings suspicion full circle back to you, doesn't it?"

Fabrice heard her gulp. He suspected they all heard it.

Crenshaw's bloodshot gaze swerved to Gwennie. Fabrice stiffened, rolling on the balls of his feet. He had already made a decision. If need be, he would grab the girl and run. Gwennie had not created this problem and he would be damned if she suffered for it.

She visibly shrank beneath Crenshaw's scrutiny. He once more adjusted his spectacles. "You look familiar."

Her chin came up. "I'm a whore, sir."

The man's face registered recognition, and suddenly Fabrice knew where, and under what circumstances, the two had previously met. A bolt of rage sliced through him. Though a murderer he was not, he would gladly kill rather than see Gwennie used in such a way again.

"She has begun a new life," he snarled, while a fiery possessiveness sizzled. "One worthy of respect."

"That's true, sir." Gwennie's hand curled around Fabrice's and gave a light squeeze. He understood. She wished to calm him before he made matters worse. The gesture banished his hotheaded wrath. He returned the pressure, but with a firm insistence that vowed to protect.

"Mrs. Hardington took me off the streets and brought me to her home," Gwennie told the magistrate. The hand in Fabrice's trembled slightly. "I'll never sell myself again."

Crenshaw studied her a long moment. "Are there others like you?"

"Yes, sir, quite a passel of us. We're learning skills such as teaching and the running of vast households. And dressmaking—oh, not plain stitching, sir, but true tailoring. Why, one of Mrs. Hardington's former students owns a shop right on Bond Street. Another opened an inn for quality folk in Brighton, and she's quite wealthy now. Imagine." She ended with a note of admiration and Fabrice thought, with such spirit, she could achieve anything.

"Yes, but did Mrs. Hardington force you to go with her?"

Fabrice braced for the answer. He *had* forced Gwennie into the barouche the night they found her. Between her ominous coughing and the danger of detection, they had dared not waste a moment plucking her from the street. If she renounced him now, he deserved it.

"Of course not, sir. It was my choice. And sir . . ." Pausing, she slipped her hand from Fabrice's and approached the desk. "I want you to know that it was the first time in my life—in my whole entire life, sir—that anyone ever gave me a choice. About anything."

Crenshaw's shrewd eyes narrowed. Moments passed. Perspiration trickled down Fabrice's sides. He remained poised to run, to fight if necessary.

Finally, the man behind the desk laced his fingers together and made loud cracking sounds in the knuckles. "Mind you,

I'm not saying I believe a word of this lunacy. Only a mob of Bedlamites would concoct a story the likes of this. But I've got no other leads on these murders. You, sir." Crenshaw nodded toward Monsieur. "Do I have your word as a gentleman that if I release the others, you'll take responsibility for their whereabouts?"

"You can depend on me, sir."

"Good. You two," his forefinger vacillated between Fabrice and Madame, "be warned. If either of you attempts to leave London before this matter is settled, I'll have a force on your tail quicker than you can cry Midnight Marauder. Now then, let's find a solution to this madness."

Two hours later, they were still inside Samuel Crenshaw's office. But instead of standing like the convicted before a firing squad, Charles and the others were helping the magistrate concoct a plan.

Tess's latest and quite absurd suggestion, however, had Charles reaffirming his conviction that he'd never met anyone more bull-headed in his life. The woman left him no choice but to resort to the military tactics he abhorred.

"You will not act as bait to catch the murderer," he ordered in his sternest voice. "You will stay home where you belong and let the law handle it."

"And who put you in charge?" she demanded with a superior tilt of her chin.

"Mr. Crenshaw did. I'm responsible for your whereabouts and you'll do as I say."

"Will I?" She dipped an impudent curtsy.

He wanted to shout. Seething, he looked to Crenshaw for assistance. The man offered a shrug and a scowl.

Charles turned back to Tess. "Your plan is out of the question."

"Why are you being so stubborn?"

"Why are you?"

"Because my plan is a good one."

He gritted his teeth. Tess had begun distancing herself from him ever since their tiff at the cottage at Highgate Court. Those few extraordinary hours might never have occurred. At first he'd credited her sudden fickleness to lack of trust, an unwillingness to believe in him. But that wasn't quite it. Tess was simply afraid—of love, of life, of her own vulnerable emotions. Like a wild colt in danger of hurting itself, she needed gentle but firm reassurances.

He attempted to relax his jaw. "I am not about to let you and Gwennie risk your lives in a reckless and harebrained scheme."

"Oh, pish."

He wanted to shake her till her teeth rattled. "There are a hundred better ways to go about snaring a murderer than letting you get yourself killed."

"For instance?"

He rounded on the magistrate. "Can't we lock her away?"

Brow creased in thought, the man rose, circled his desk and perched on its edge. "Does Mrs. Hardington have any enemies?"

"You obviously don't know me very well if you need to ask that." She released an ironic chuckle.

Charles ignored her. "What are you driving at?"

"Just this." Crenshaw pushed away from the desk and started pacing. "You've assumed the killer—if indeed the killer is someone other than Mrs. Hardington and her servant—"

"Would you please stop saying that," she exclaimed, her voice rising a full octave.

Crenshaw placed a finger in his ear and wiggled it. "You've assumed the killer is using the Midnight Marauder out of convenience, allowing the blame for his deeds to fall somewhere other than on himself. But perhaps our murderer is trying to incriminate Mrs. Hardington."

"Thank you for that sentiment," she said with no small

amount of sarcasm. "But no one except a few trusted friends knows I'm the Midnight Marauder."

"I believe that's the point, Tess," Charles said. "Mr. Crenshaw obviously believes someone else does know. Isn't that right?"

"Indeed. Which brings me back to my question. Do you have any enemies, someone who might want to do you harm?"

Tess's eyes went wide, and Charles knew she was mentally counting the possibilities. She had few friends among the *ton*, but with most it was a matter of avoidance, not vengeance. Only one person wanted—no, needed—her out of the way.

They spoke at the same time. "Uncle Howard."

Then Tess shook her head. "No, I can't believe he'd go this far. He wants my money, yes, but murder?"

"Money is the greatest motivator of all," Crenshaw said. "Who's this Howard fellow? Is it possible he's been following you, determining where you go and what you do?"

"I suppose it's possible." Tess's astonished gaze traveled from the magistrate to Charles. "Which makes all the more sense for me to be the one who—"

"You, madam, may consider yourself under house arrest," Charles all but bellowed. "Just as soon as I can return you there, that is."

She drew herself up, meeting him chin to obstinate, outthrust chin. "If you think I'm going to wait at home sipping tea while you take control of my life, you're very much mistaken, sir."

"Take control? Good God, woman, someone has got to. And incidentally, I happen to have the law on my side."

There were scores of other arguments he might have raised. He might have confessed that in all their years apart, his feelings for her had never diminished in the slightest, and that he wasn't about to risk losing her a second time. He might also have repeated that moment of insanity back at the cottage where, still immersed in the haze of their frenzied lovemaking, he'd blurted that he loved her and wished to marry her.

Like bloody hell. The resourceful little temptress would no doubt press her advantage, wrap him around her finger and coerce him into letting her help catch the murderer. Well, the devil she would. He needed her safe and no arguments about it.

"May I suggest a plan?" he said to Crenshaw.

"By all means."

He turned to Fabrice, sitting beside Gwennie on a bench against the back wall. "Please take Mrs. Hardington and Gwennie home. Then if you wish to help us, come back with the barouche. Alone."

Charles wasn't sure if Fabrice exactly nodded, but something in those odd gold eyes told him he had an ally he could count on.

By nightfall a day later they had set their plan in motion. Crenshaw enlisted limited help from the Bow Street Runners—limited due to the expense in hiring the private constabulary. Charles improved their odds. With his father's permission, he rounded up a half-dozen workers, men from some of the roughest sections of London. They in turn recruited several more each.

These were blokes who understood the alleys and back lanes of the city. Crime in such places was a way of life, but Charles believed his makeshift force capable of spotting intruders into their world.

He stationed most of them at key points: St. Giles, the docks, Stepney, Southwark—places frequented by the Midnight Marauder. Their job was to circulate through the neighborhoods, watching, listening, ready to close in if necessary.

The remaining men were to follow Howard James, literally become his shadow. Meanwhile, Charles and Fabrice traveled the streets at night in Tess's barouche, hoping to lure the killer into following them.

The first night proved uneventful. Howard spent the early

part of the evening playing bridge at his club before joining a supper party at the home of a bachelor friend. He retired to his town house near Berkeley Square shortly after midnight. Meanwhile, the neighborhoods under patrol remained relatively quiet, free of all but the usual minor crimes and misdemeanors.

Charles returned to Tess's house on Aldford Street drained and frustrated. After helping Fabrice unhitch the horses, he dragged leaden feet upstairs. A disturbing thought stalked him: supposing Howard James was not the killer. What then?

His hand had just closed around his doorknob when Tess's door swung open. He gave a start, then remembered how only a few nights ago he'd caught her sneaking up the stairs after one of her midnight jaunts. At least no more lies lay between them.

"Charles?"

A shaft of moonlight from the hall window outlined her body beneath her night rail, silhouetted the loose hair tumbling about her shoulders. Accessible. Touchable. He drew in a breath. "I'm here. What are you doing awake?"

"As if I could sleep." Ethereal in her flowing gown and streaming hair, she moved toward him with a faint padding of slippers on the hall runner. "What happened tonight?"

"Not a blessed thing."

Her disappointment was palpable in the stillness. "I'd so hoped all this would be over."

"It will be soon, I promise." He wanted to touch her, pull her into his arms to offer reassurance. But here in her London home, the boundaries of propriety crossed at Highgate Court loomed insurmountable.

"It's just as well I stayed home tonight," she said with a feeble smile. "Your solicitor came by."

"Kenneth?"

"Yes." She blew a lock of hair from her cheek. "He might have found a loophole."

"A loophole?" Staring at her lovely face, softly gilded by silver moon glow, he drew a blank.

"In the will."

"Good grief, with all that's happened I'd practically forgotten."

"Forgotten we're pretending to be married?"

Not the marriage, he thought, but the pretending. Forgetting that part of it at Highgate Court had been easy; had felt so damned good. The detail could easily slip his mind again with this scantily clad, moonlit wraith so close beside him. But aloud he asked, "What did Ken tell you?"

"He's found a precedent that might solve my problem." She sounded far more weary than excited. "It seems that since I am an adult of sound mind, I do have choices in the matter of the trusteeship. I can't avoid it, but since I'm technically still a Hardington, I can choose a member of my late husband's immediate family to supervise my finances. My stepson is abroad, but I believe we can locate him. If he agrees to help, Howard has no further claim on me." Studying her feet, she shrugged. "You might be off the hook quite soon."

The notion brought him no pleasure. "Can you trust this stepson of yours?"

"Gerald? I don't see why not. He has his own considerable resources and we always got on well enough. It's not as though he has any reason to do me ill."

"But you'll be trading one overseer for another. Surely that's not what you wish."

Her hands came up in a gesture of resignation. "I don't enjoy being treated like a child, but what choice do I have? At least I'll have the funds to continue as I've been."

"As the Midnight Marauder."

"Yes. And you'll be free to return to your business and your family."

He nodded, but her words burned in his gut. She seemed in such a hurry to send him packing. Despite all her reasons for denying their love, he'd been so certain her feelings matched his. Perhaps, after all, she'd only needed him to

elude her uncle. Perhaps he'd mistaken friendship and gratitude for more.

Perhaps, when she told him not to love her, he should have
taken her at her word.

"Good night, then, Tess." He started into his room, steeling
himself for a long, probably sleepless night alone. "Sleep well."

Her hand descended on his forearm in a gesture that
stopped him cold. Breath ceased as her fingers closed around
him, as she stood on tiptoe and raised her lips to his.

"Darling, don't let's each be alone tonight," she whispered
against his mouth.

His pulse bucked with an eagerness that threatened both
prudence and logic. He held steady long enough to search her
expression. What did she want? Perhaps only what she'd said:
to not be alone.

"Do you wish to come in?"

"Please." Her hand combed through his hair, leaving little
doubt as to her intentions.

"You'll share your bed with me but not your life." He grimaced, immediately regretting the accusation. How priggish
he must have sounded. He expected her to bristle. He saw the
gleam of a smile instead.

"Does that compromise your honor, sir?"

"I'm ashamed to say no, it does not." Catching her up in his
arms, he swung her through the doorway, eliciting a tumble
of soft laughter from her. "What kind of gentleman would I
be to deny a lady's request?"

Her laughter dissipated. She shook her disordered hair
from her face. "You still consider me a lady?"

He let her feet slip to the floor and gathered her to his
chest. "You'd be *my* lady if you weren't so hard-headed."

"I'll be your lady tonight." She kissed him quickly. "Beyond that, neither of us can make promises."

"As I said, hard-headed." Nuzzling her neck, he murmured,
"I suddenly remember you still owe me a gown."

"Indeed? I recall all debts being satisfied and then some."

"I'm afraid you're quite mistaken, madam." He backed her toward the bed until her bottom bumped the mattress. "I have nothing to show for my pains. But this," he fingered her flimsy night rail, "will do nicely."

The knowledge that she wore nothing beneath made him instantly hard. Hooking a finger into her neckline, he drew the garment away from her body and peered down her length.

Her breathing quickened, punctuated with gasping laughter. "Ah, good sir, must you take it?"

"I'm afraid I must." Her heavy-lidded gaze conveyed her desire to become his, albeit temporarily. Forgetting everything he'd ever learned of manners, he yanked the night rail from her shoulders and shoved it to her waist. She made a squeak tinged with shock and expectancy both. Without apology he cupped her exposed breasts, taking possession, reshaping the nipples to hard little morsels beneath his thumbs.

His body pounded in response to her soft moans. The notion of her naked body beneath his clothed one only made the demands more insistent. Grasping her beneath the thighs, he tipped her onto the bed. He worshipped each breast with his lips while working the night rail to the floor.

She wrapped trembling legs around his hips. He fumbled his trousers open, but hesitated before losing himself to pleasure. Even now, he needed to be sure she wanted this as much as he did.

She peered back, a spark of scandal illuminating the undeniable permission in her eyes. His eagerness turned savage. He didn't know if they were making up for a decade lost, or were spurred by a desperate need to fill whatever time Tess allowed them before she once more pushed him away. But he entered her with greed and impatience, building to a driving cadence that blotted out the night's frustrations.

Chapter 22

She awoke in his arms—a laborer's arms, solid and well muscled. Arms that had known years of punishing toil yet understood how to give pleasure, how to be gentle.

Gwennie sighed, her breath fluttering the sparse black hairs on Fabrice's chest. She adored that chest, had spent hours tracing its bronzed lines, kissing it, listening to the steady beat within. His chest was a haven of warmth and strength and now . . . all hers. Such was his promise, and she believed him.

His eyes were closed but his fingertips traveled her hip with a whisper's touch. His full lips parted, and she remembered their warmth on her body.

Smiling, she stroked the ebony hair fanning across the pillow, first with a single finger, then with the flat of her hand. Silently she vowed never to let him cut it.

The heat of his body and a delicious sense of safety lured her back to sleep. He met her with kisses at the edge of her dream, bidding her lie with him in a glen far from dingy London streets. Yet the tightening of his arms around her was too real to be imagined, as was the sugar-soft voice that drifted to her ear and curled about her heart.

"Je t'aime, ma petite."

By the end of the week Tess began to wonder if Charles's meticulous plans would ever yield results. If Uncle Howard had been spying on her all along, surely he'd know of this concerted effort to trap him. Perhaps he watched Charles's regiment set out each night, and secretly laughed.

The weather turned chilly that evening. As Charles prepared to leave the house after supper, Tess followed him into the foyer and helped him on with his cloak. He turned back around and grasped her shoulders.

Awareness coiled inside her. His touch was a heated reminder of their intimacy these past nights, except once when he'd returned home after she had fallen asleep. In the morning she had awakened to find him beside her, one solid arm draped possessively across her waist. She woke him with kisses and they had more than made up for their lost evening.

"Stay home," he admonished her now, just as he had every night previously.

"Will you never simply trust me?"

"Never." He pulled her close. "Which is why I've posted a constable outside. But lock the door behind me nonetheless."

"Be safe," she whispered into his collar. He released her and slipped out the door.

She turned to find Helena grinning at her from the parlor doorway. Wesley had joined Charles's patrol, combing the men's clubs and gambling hells, using his influence to uncover information about Uncle Howard's recent activities. Helena and Sir Joshua spent the evenings here, keeping Tess company and helping stave off the madness of waiting.

"I do hope that man of yours doesn't worry too much about you."

Tess tsked. "Charles is not *my* man and well you know it."

"If you say so." Helena shrugged, her smile turning impish. "My point is that he needn't fret. I've become quite the sharp shooter, thanks to my husband's excellent tutelage. With Father and me here, you're as safe as the crown jewels."

In the parlor, Sir Joshua and Gwennie sat side by side on the settee near the fireplace. Gwennie was conjugating verbs aloud from a French primer while Sir Joshua listened and offered occasional corrections. The girl had suddenly developed a fervent desire to learn the language. Tess didn't wonder why. Certain developments had not escaped her notice, and while she'd considered issuing a sober warning to her protégé, she realized doing so would render her the worst sort of hypocrite. In the end, she'd decided to trust Fabrice. He'd do right by Gwennie. After all, he never let down those he loved.

"This young lady's got a decent ear for languages," Joshua commented with a nod of approval.

Gwennie flushed at the praise. "Back home, whenever the local baron's daughter shopped in the village, she'd use lots of French words and wrinkle up her nose when no one understood. Mum always said proper ladies spoke French." She lowered the book to her lap. "Sure she never expected any of her own girls to learn it."

"Perhaps you'll visit her and show off your new skills," Tess suggested.

"Perhaps." A wistful longing entered her eyes. She lifted the cloth-covered volume. "Shall I continue?"

"I'm listening, child." In his none-too-steady hands, Joshua cradled an antiquated blunderbuss, a cumbersome pistol with which he planned to defend the household if necessary. As Gwennie recited, he smoothed his fingers back and forth along the buffed oak handle.

"You might be a sharp shooter," Tess whispered in her cousin's ear, "but I do hope your father's pistol isn't loaded." She shuddered at the thought of the thing misfiring in its present location.

"Of course it's loaded," he chided, reminding Tess of the selectiveness of his hearing loss. "How else do expect me to protect you?"

"Yes, well, why don't you set it on the table and we'll . . . we'll have a game of whist." She rummaged through the sideboard drawers until she found a deck of cards. "I don't suppose you've ever played, Gwennie, but I'm sure you'll catch on quickly enough."

As they settled around the card table, a knock sounded at

the front door. "Who on earth can that be?" Tess wondered aloud.

Becca's footsteps thudded down the hall to the front door. Joshua hurried across the room to retrieve his blunderbuss.

"Father, do put that thing away before you shoot yourself," Helena scolded. Paying no heed, he took up position beside the parlor doorway.

Becca entered the room alone, giving a start upon seeing the weapon aimed in her direction. Looking vaguely disappointed, Joshua muttered an apology.

"Just a messenger, ma'am. He left this." Becca handed a folded note to Tess.

She rose from the card table on pretext of using the brighter lamp beside the settee. In truth, she wished to skim the contents of this unexpected missive before the others saw it. If it contained disagreeable news from Charles, she especially didn't wish to alarm the elderly Joshua.

Reading, she sucked in a breath. Her instinct had proved correct, though not for the reason she'd thought. The note had come not from Charles, but from an anonymous author. The handwriting appeared deliberately cramped.

> *Tessa,*
>   *If you wish to prevent another unfortunate occurrence, be at Vauxhall Gardens tonight at midnight. Come alone, or be willing to bear responsibility for the consequences.*

The page fluttered in her hands. Only one person ever called her Tessa. Despite the attempt to disguise the handwriting, that single clue left few doubts. She crumpled the paper and tossed it into the hearth fire.

"What was that, dearest?" Looking only mildly curious, Helena shuffled and cut the deck with the dexterity of a gambling sharp. "A note from Charles?"

"Just so," Tess replied as calmly as she could. "He often

sends me little notes to keep me informed. I'm afraid there's nothing new. Becca, are the refreshments ready?"

"Oh, yes ma'am. I'll bring them straightaway."

"I'll help you. Gwennie, perhaps you'll assist us?"

Helena started to rise. "Do you need me, too, dear?"

"No, no. Stay where you are, we won't be but a moment."

Tess sent Becca on ahead to the kitchen but detained Gwennie on the service staircase. "That note didn't come from Mr. Emerson." She slipped an arm around the younger woman's shoulders and drew her into a conspiratorial huddle. "I need your help and your utmost discretion."

"Of course, Mrs. Hardington."

"Good. I must go out later, and I'll need your assistance in evading the constable watching the house."

Gwennie began shaking her head even before Tess completed the request. "You can't go out, ma'am. I mean, excuse me, Mrs. Hardington, but you promised Mr. Emerson and the magistrate you'd stay put."

"I know." Tess spoke in an urgent whisper. "But I've been summoned to Vauxhall Gardens and I dare not refuse."

"Summoned by who?"

"I can't say for sure."

"Who do you think?"

Though she would have preferred keeping this detail to herself, Tess couldn't demand Gwennie's cooperation without revealing the stakes. "You must swear not to alert my cousin or her father."

"I swear." Gwennie pressed a hand to her bosom. "Now who sent that note, ma'am?"

"My Uncle Howard."

Gwennie gasped. "The murderer? You can't possibly go. It's too dangerous. It would be madness."

"Not so." Tess tried to sound reassuring, to inject confidence into her tone. "My uncle has been under constant surveillance. If he's waiting for me at Vauxhall, at least half a dozen men will be ready to pounce on him. Besides, there's a ball tonight so there will be plenty of people about. I'm sure I'll be safe."

"I don't like this, ma'am. We should contact Mr. Emerson."

The suggestion produced a painful longing for the feel of his strong arms around her. Yes, Charles should know of this, should be close by when she confronted her uncle. But she dared not take the time to track him down. Uncle Howard's note said midnight, or another would suffer for it. Another young woman she'd failed to save; another Alicia.

"There isn't enough time." Tess glanced at either end of the staircase to ensure their privacy. "The note implied that if I don't go, another may fall victim. I can't let that happen."

"Lord in heaven. What are we to do?"

"It's nearly eleven now. In a little while I'll plead a headache and pretend to retire. After my cousin and uncle leave, I'll need you to devise a way to distract the constable. You might bring him some coffee, perhaps, and I'll sneak out the side gate."

"Perhaps we should tell your relatives about the note. Sir Joshua could accompany you . . ."

"And do what, shoot off his foot and mine with his blunderbuss?" Arms crossed, Tess shook her head. "Far better I go alone. Can I count on your help?"

"I don't like this one teensy bit." Gwennie's lower lip turned white with biting. "He said he'd kill again if you didn't go?"

"The note implied as much."

The poor girl's face contorted in an agony of indecision.

Tess lay a palm against her cheek. "Dearest Gwennie, how can I not go? I am the Midnight Marauder."

Gwennie nodded, eyes brimming. "Godspeed, ma'am."

Charles arrived home earlier than usual that night. Failure dragged at his heels. His men had trailed Howard James for hours and discovered him at nothing more sinister than cheating at cards. The old scoundrel had scooped his winnings into his purse and splurged on a hackney to convey him home not twenty minutes ago. The thought of facing Tess after another fruitless night slowed Charles's steps as he entered the main portion of the house.

All lay in quiet darkness. Good. He'd slip undetected into his own bedroom and break the disappointing news to Tess in the morning. But on his way to the stairs, he discovered a shaft of light spiking from beneath the parlor's closed double doors. Tess had waited up after all. Opening one of the doors, he stepped inside.

Light snores emanated from the sofa. Odd, he'd never noticed her snoring before. To his surprise, however, it wasn't Tess's slumbering form that greeted him but Gwennie's. She lay curled on the settee, a knitted afghan pulled to her chin. She looked so peaceful Charles considered leaving her there. Then he remembered the painful kink he'd got in his neck the last time he had slept on a sofa. He nudged her shoulder.

It took only one attempt. Gwennie's eyes popped open. Fully awake, the girl pushed upright and shoved dark hair from her face. Her alarmed gaze lighted on Charles. "Where's Mrs. Hardington? Is she with you? Is she all right?"

"She's in bed, I'd imagine," he replied, taken aback. He must have interrupted a particularly vivid dream. "Which is where you should be, young lady."

Her eyes became saucers. "No, she isn't. And you shouldn't be here either, not without her."

"What the devil do you mean?" He thrust his face closer. "Where's Tess? Please tell me she's somewhere in the house." But even as he made the demand, he knew the answer. "Good God."

"A—a note came. From her uncle. It said she had to go. Someone else might be murdered if she didn't. I didn't like it, sir, I told her so, but she didn't want anyone else to die . . ."

Charles shook her shoulders. "Stop babbling and tell me where she went."

Gwennie dragged in a breath. "Vauxhall."

"To meet her uncle?"

She nodded.

"The note was signed by Howard James?"

"I don't think it was signed, but Mrs. Hardington was certain he'd sent it."

"He can't have done." He sprinted for the hall. "When did she leave?"

"About half an hour to midnight."

"Ah, God. Oh, blast." He started shouting before he reached the kitchen stairwell. "Fabrice. We need the horses. Never mind the coach. It's Tess. We have to save her."

Chapter 23

As Tess paid her admittance and proceeded into Vauxhall Gardens, the lively confusion of a masked ball assaulted her senses. Mozart's *Magic Flute* comprised tonight's theme, and a bewildering assortment of winged lions, gilded birds and walking fish milled through the Grove. How would she ever find her uncle here?

Even those not in costume concealed their faces behind feathered and beribboned masks. A footman dressed as a gargantuan peacock offered Tess just such a mask, for which she was obliged to pay four pence.

Paper lanterns tossed patchworks of color from the trees and colonnades, adding an unearthly glow to the grotesque, fanciful and comical faces filling her view. Bearing right toward the Chinese Pavilion, she pulled up sharp at the sight of a countenance permanently frozen in laughter, only to turn away and be confronted by a distorted papier-mache sneer. Could either be Uncle Howard? Or perhaps that gentleman sporting a boar's head, conversing with the mermaid beside him.

Fighting a wave of dizziness, she changed course and headed to the Gothic Stage, the most central location in the Gardens. With her mask lowered, she pretended interest in the orchestra while waiting for Uncle Howard to approach her. Her apprehensions mounting like a house of cards ready to topple at the slightest touch, she lurched each time an elbow bumped her, a shoulder jostled her.

Charles. Only her trust in him prevented her turning on her heel and fleeing. Because of him, of his diligence, she knew she had little to fear, for of course he'd have directed a team of detectives to trail her uncle here. Because of Charles, she'd be safe.

The orchestra took up a tense melody that quivered across the first violins' strings, echoed by a flute's restless notes. It set Tess more on edge than ever. If only she might catch the eye of an officer she recognized. If only Charles would step out of the crowd, even for an instant, to offer a reassuring nod.

From behind, a whisper brushed her nape: *Tessa.*

She whirled, only to find herself face to face with an eagle in military uniform. As she gaped up at him, he and his scarlet-masked companion greeted her with inquisitive stares. She nodded an apology and drifted away.

She'd gone only a few paces when a cloaked figure stepped into her path. Through the slanting eye slits of a fox's head that concealed both face and hair, his gaze held her. Her heart prodded her ribs when he pointed a gloved finger at her, turned and pushed through the crowd.

He led her to the rear of the Gothic Stage, then vanished within the knots of masked partygoers spilling onto the Grand Walk. Tess threaded her way through, calming herself by again speculating who among the crowd might be Mr. Crenshaw's deputies or Bow Street Runners. The notion almost prompted her to wink in complicity, if only she knew at whom to aim the gesture.

A hand gripped her shoulder from behind. "Tess."

But even as the breath seized in her lungs, she recognized the contrast between that first hoarse whisper and this greeting—friendly, youthful, tipped with laughter. With a rush of relief she turned to behold a fellow Friend of the Bard Society member. "Nora, what on earth are you doing here?"

Too late did she realize the absurdity of her question. Nora Thorngoode realized it too, evidenced by a bemused expression she attempted to conceal behind a smile.

"Attending the ball, of course," she said. "Mama's idea, but I'll admit the evening hasn't turned out a thorough disaster—yet. What do you think of my costume?" She held out her arms and did a slow twirl, displaying the voluminous folds of an angel's gown. A hammered tin halo reflected points of light into her sleek, dark hair.

"It's lovely. It suits you," Tess replied after a cursory glance. Where had the caped fox gone? Was he waiting for her somewhere down the Grand Walk? Or had she squandered her one opportunity to ensure some poor girl's safety?

Had she failed again, as she'd once failed Alicia?

She turned back to Nora. "Have you seen my uncle?"

"Sir Joshua?"

"No, Howard James. Do you know if he's here?"

Nora held out her hands, an apologetic gesture. "Rather hard to tell who's here tonight."

Tess nodded and started to move on. Nora matched her stride. "Tess, what's wrong?"

"Shh, Nora, please. There's nothing wrong. I'm sorry, but I have to go."

"Go where?" Nora gripped her arm. "I don't like that look on your face. Has something happened?"

Tess cast an impatient glance at her young friend while growing dread prevented her answering. She tried to tug her arm free but Nora clung.

"Trust me, Tess," she whispered. "Whatever it is, perhaps I can help."

Trust me. Those were new words to her vocabulary, a notion once reserved for Helena alone but now . . . now she felt the very real possibility securely lodged in her heart, placed there—ah, so recently but irrefutably—by Charles. Still a frightening prospect, but a precious one as well.

She stopped tugging and looked, really looked into her friend's eyes and discovered there qualities she'd dared not believe in for so many years, loyalty not the least of them. "Nora," she said before the old doubts came crowding back, "there is something terribly, dreadfully wrong. I must continue down the Grand Walk to . . . to meet my uncle—"

"Howard James?"

"Yes. Look for me here in half an hour. If I don't return—"

Nora gasped.

Tess shook her head. "Please don't ask questions. Not now. If I don't return within half an hour, send for help. Will you do that for me, dearest Nora?"

The girl's eyes narrowed intently and Tess waited, knowing this was Nora's way of bringing matters into focus. Within moments, that naïve, slightly perplexed uncertainty Tess usually associated with Nora smoothed away, revealing an unexpected store of maturity.

She gave a steady nod. "I will wait here for you. Twenty minutes. And then I'm calling for help and coming in search of you."

They squeezed each other's hands. Then Tess started down the Grand Walk, wending her way through the crush until it closed behind her, blocking her from Nora's view and leaving her cut off and very much alone.

She continued on until the crowd thinned to a handful of stragglers too intent on their own clandestine endeavors to pay her any notice. A few paces more and . . . it came, a rasping summons from behind a marble statue some dozen yards away.

Tessa.

From around the stone goddess, the fox's head peered at her, it's queer hollow gaze holding hers a long moment. The sight sent her fortitude draining away in great bucketfuls, and she longed for the safety of the Grove, her friends, Charles's arms. But with a flick of his cloak the fox swept further away, leaving her little choice but to hurry after. A life might very well depend on her doing so.

Each step took her further from safety. Now far behind, the ball's distant hum accentuated the deadly quiet of the surrounding trees. The lighting grew sparse. In the deepening gloom, she lost sight of her quarry but plodded on until she spotted his white-gloved hand beckoning like a fluttering dove from a fork in the path.

With only the moon lighting her way, the disembodied snapping of brush and swishing of leaves sent her pulse galloping. A mournful breeze moaned through the higher branches, carrying with it the plaintive slapping of the Thames against its banks. Tess realized she'd gone farther than she'd thought. Amid the hoots and clicks of the forest, a tree limb cracked. She stumbled, groping to catch her balance against a tree trunk and scraping her knuckles in the bargain.

Up ahead, the sheen of a cloak's lining glimmered like quicksilver before whisking round a bend. She trotted to keep up. Chills traveled her back, raising goose bumps and an overwhelming longing. *Charles, are you here? Please be here.* Even if at this very moment he seethed with anger that she'd disobeyed him . . . even if he resolved to berate her until her ears rang.

Thoughts of him evoked a sense of security that astonished her even as it renewed her courage. With a jolt that nearly tripped her step, she realized Charles's presence in her life these past days had provided her the courage to step out of the Marauder's shadow and face her peers—and her fears—in ways she'd not dreamed of in a very long time.

She hurried on, guided by the flapping cloak hem. Just as she began to believe Uncle Howard had led her on a fruitless chase, she reached a small clearing ringed by tall birch and pine. A single lantern hung from a low branch; he must have readied it earlier. Hugging her arms about her waist, she stepped cautiously into its glow.

The clearing lay empty and silent, yet she sensed eyes watching from beyond the lamplight. She fisted her shaking fingers and pressed them to her sides. Her knees trembled. But from somewhere deep within, from the place that housed her love for the most honorable man she'd ever known, she found her voice.

"Why don't you show yourself, Uncle Howard? Just what is this all about, as if I didn't know."

"So, you've figured it out, have you, my dear?" A voice bearing little resemblance to the one she'd expected slithered from the trees mere paces to her left. Instinct sent her lunging to the right, heart thundering.

Looking wildly about, she tried to locate the owner of the voice, of a certainty not Uncle Howard's. Panic urged flight. She backed into a thicket that gripped her skirts in an impossible, thorny hold. While she thrashed for freedom, the murderer's laughter enveloped her, taunting and malicious.

"Ah, Tessa, dearest Tessa. This has been a long time coming." Undergrowth crackled at his approach.

Her knees buckled and she sank, hitting the ground in a heap of despair as the truth struck her a powerful blow. No one would save her—not Charles nor the magistrate nor the Bow Street Runners. They were elsewhere watching Uncle Howard, while here. . . .

"Are you not overjoyed to see me, then?"

His polished shoes filled her view first, then his dark-clad legs, long and lean like a spider's. Her fearful gaze traveled his torso to the fox's head perched on his shoulders. He cackled and removed the disguise.

"Sebastian Russell!"

"Surprise." A glacial smile burgeoned beneath glittering eyes, as hungry and rapacious as the beast he had resembled.

"It's been you all along, not Uncle Howard."

"How astute. You always were the smart one."

"What do you want?" Loathing frothed inside her, making her bold. "Isn't it enough that you destroyed my sister?"

He shrugged. "It might have been, I suppose, had you not become so intolerably nasty and vengeful."

Too quick for her to react, he crouched in front of her and curled his fingers round the neckline of her gown. Rage turned his features a murderous red. The reek of whisky stung her nostrils. "How dare you involve my family? How dare you blame me for what happened to your slut of a sister?"

"I only told them the truth," she snapped, spurred by outrage. "It wasn't vengeance, it was justice."

"Justice? Having me disinherited? Reducing me to little more than a beggar? Viscount Kirkwood? What damned bloody use is a title without means and money?" His voice rose to the brink of fury. His fist tightened and he shook her until she thought her neck would snap.

Abruptly his hold eased. His enraged featured cooled, leaving a look of calm, perversely civil regard. "Revenge is sweet while it lasts, isn't it, Tessa? But I didn't dare take mine while you had that dottering husband to protect you. And then when he died you all but disappeared from London. Now you're back and remarried, but Charles Emerson doesn't frighten me. He's no one of influence and besides . . . he's a dear friend of mine. Did you know that?"

The lantern swayed in the breeze, angling shadows that deepened and elongated Sebastian's sardonic grin.

Tess's throat closed. Charles and this monster were . . . friends? No. She didn't believe it; she wouldn't. But . . . if Charles *had* befriended this villain, wasn't it her own fault for refusing to confide, for failing to trust him with the entire truth?

"Why, yes," Sebastian gloated when she remained mute, "we're old university chums, Emerson and I."

"Charles Emerson would never befriend so vile a lout," she spat.

"Oh, but he did, quite readily. And I made a wager concerning you and I." His grip tightening to prevent her pulling away, he brought his lips beside her ear. "I wagered you hadn't told him about me. And you know what?" He sat back, grinning. "I was right. And then when the poor man felt the need to confide in me, I wagered, rightly again, that he wouldn't tell you. So you see, my dear, you and Charles have been your own worst enemies."

Horror wormed through her, cold and sickening. "If Charles confided in you, if he condescended to notice you at all, it was out of pity and because he'd no notion of what a beastly wretch you are."

A shove sent her reeling. Before she could scramble out of reach his hand slid into her hair. She tried to wrench away, only to provoke a burst of laughter. "Do not fret, dearest Tessa, I have no wish to besmirch your honor. I had my fill of James women long ago. Gutter wenches, the both of you. No, my only intention is to see you and your poor dead sister reunited. But of course, it won't do to have your crumpled body discovered beneath the shrubbery."

His hand tore away from her hair with a yank that produced tears. With bruising force he clenched her forearm and hauled her to her feet. Her skirt hem shredded free of the thicket. Sebastian gave a vicious jerk on her arm and spun her till her back came up against him. Something cool and cylindrical pressed her temple. Filled with icy, numbing fear, Tess shut her eyes.

"Want to know how you'll be remembered? After I shoot your brains out, I'll make it appear you'd come here to meet a lover, and when he jilted you, you took your own life. People will be oh so willing to believe it. They'll shake their heads and say you turned out just like your sister. Ah, those deluded, depraved James girls."

Deluded? Depraved?

His jeering triggered a rage, and rage sparked her courage. She loved Charles Emerson. She had too much to live for to allow Sebastian Russell to prevail. For so long she'd fought heavy odds for the sake of others. Now she'd fight for herself.

An image flashed in her mind, a technique Fabrice had once spent an afternoon teaching her. Lifting her foot, she slammed the edge of her heel into the hard bone of Sebastian's shin. He yelped, and when his hold slackened, she spun about and swung a knee to his groin. At the same time she sliced both hands at his arms, knocking them away. As he doubled over, she thrust her forefingers at his eyes. His shrieks in her wake, Tess ran.

Which way? She guessed she was somewhere between the Hermit's Walk and the Grand Walk, and a good hundred yards from the Grove. But she'd become all turned around, her bearings hopelessly lost.

She chose simple flight. Hefting her torn and trailing skirts, she wound in and out of hedges and trees, stumbling over rocks. Where no path existed she lashed through undergrowth, tugging her hems free of groping thickets.

Pounding footsteps sped her on. Panic sustained her when energy ebbed, though her legs burned and her lungs shrieked for breath.

Lights winked through the trees and Tess headed for them, knowing if she could only reach a populated area she'd be safe. Suddenly the trees gave way and she realized she'd found a main path. Should she yell for help? No, for she was still too far away from the festivities. Crying out would only alert Sebastian to her location.

The protruding paw of a marble panther snared her skirt, stopping her dead. Frantic, she beat at the stubborn fabric with her palm, her fist, tugging, pulling. It tore free and she lurched forward, nearly sprawling onto the Grand Walk. Using the momentum, she veered toward the Grove.

She'd advanced a few short strides when Sebastian crashed through the shrubbery behind her. Tess gathered her ruined skirts and ran for all she was worth.

Up ahead, figures came into view. She tried to call out but her aching lungs denied speech. All at once, an explosion shook the gravel beneath her feet. Tess tripped and fell, skinning her knees and palms raw. Her heart threatened to burst through her chest. Had Sebastian fired his pistol?

The sky above the river shimmered with blossoming light. Fireworks.

In the lull that followed, Tess thought she heard the impossible: her name shouted from the Grove. Charles? With a

burst of hope she sprinted but felt hopelessly slow, weighted
as if pushing through water. Sebastian's strides resounded
louder. She heard her name repeated up ahead while behind
her Sebastian's rapid footfalls and desperate panting drew
closer.

In the middle of the Walk, still dozens of yards ahead,
Charles's face appeared. He hailed. Then his features distorted. He raced toward her, shouting, but Sebastian's rasping
filled her ears. He was close, too close; he'd reach her long
before Charles.

Hope died when the demon's hand clamped her shoulder.
She went down and he on top of her, skidding on gravel that
tore fabric and stung flesh. She barely acknowledged the
pain, knew only the anguish of failure, of imminent death,
of the possibility that the person she loved most in the world
might share in her fate. All because of her foolishness. *Oh
Charles, forgive me.*

Another explosion rocked the ground. The sky glittered. In
the distance she heard shouts of pleasure, delighted applause.
Sebastian struggled upright and dragged her to her knees,
lodging his pistol against her temple. She shut her eyes, and
waited for the click.

Charles's profound relief at having found Tess turned to
choking terror as the man pursuing her—who was he?—
seized her from behind and the two of them tumbled in a heap
of arms and legs.

He pushed to a run that lasted no more than four strides before the glint of torchlight on steel brought him up sharp. He
stared—horrified—down the Walk as recognition mauled his
senses, as the elusive puzzle fell into place.

Sebastian Russell, Viscount Kirkwood. His *friend*.

All the time spent tracking Howard James—wasted. It was
Kirkwood that ruined Alicia. Kirkwood that committed the
recent murders. Kirkwood pressing a pistol to Tess's brow.

Charles didn't move, didn't dare even breathe. As Kirkwood hauled Tess to her feet, Charles tried to communicate to her with his eyes: *don't panic, I'll think of something. Be ready to run.* She met his gaze, eyes wide and shining with fear. But beneath her fright understanding peered through, and something more. Trust. And love, clear and unmistakable, arcing between them brighter and more certain than ever before.

His heart shattered. Why now? Why not weeks ago when they'd reunited; why not days ago when they'd joined their bodies in lovemaking and he'd all but begged her to be his wife?

But of course now, when they might lose each other forever. Everything became clear. He'd returned to England bearing a weight of guilt, and helping Tess had been part of his quest for redemption, a way to begin righting the wrongs. But—how could he not have realized—only one redemption existed for him. Loving her. Their years apart had amounted to so much wasted time, wrong decisions, mistakes. Only through loving Tess had he ever been, or would he ever again become, the man he wished to be.

God, don't let it be too late.

He met Kirkwood's gaze and wondered bitterly how he'd never seen more than boredom in those pale eyes. How had he missed the malice, the stone cold hatred?

"Let her go," he said, surprised at the steadiness of his voice when the very air that made speech possible seared his lungs. "It's over."

The blackguard's filthy snicker raised spots of fury and fear before Charles's eyes. "I might as well kill her, then, and have the satisfaction."

His gaze pinned on Charles, Kirkwood sidestepped toward the bordering trees, forcing Tess along with him. He held her in front of him like a shield, as if expecting Charles to pull out a gun and fire. Charles took a step toward them but froze when Kirkwood shoved the pistol with exaggerated force against her temple. She let out a yelp that was swallowed by another blast of fireworks. Kirkwood flinched at the report.

"Wait. Let's be reasonable." Charles held up a hand that shook. Thoughts raced through his mind and he struggled to sort them into a plan that might appeal to a desperate man. Fabrice had gone to collect Crenshaw at his home; the two should arrive at Vauxhall any moment. If Charles could detain Kirkwood long enough. . . "Tell us what you want. I'm sure we can work out an arrangement."

Kirkwood hovered beside a rhododendron, its scattering of scarlet blossoms a sinister reminder of the stakes. He seemed to weigh Charles's offer, cocked his head and said matter-of-factly, "I want her dead."

"Money," Charles blurted, remembering Kirkwood's financial woes. "We can deliver as much as you want, enough for you to live comfortably the rest of your life. In Paris perhaps, or anywhere."

"Trying to be rid of me?" Sebastian sneered. He winced as more fireworks detonated. The boom echoed like thunder. Pinpoints of light danced above the treetops.

"It's your chance to get away," Charles urged, stepping closer but stopping when Kirkwood's eyes flashed in warning. "You can start fresh. Name your price."

A gleam entered his erstwhile friend's eye and Charles seized upon a scrap of hope. The pistol eased a fraction from Tess's brow. Her lashes fluttered in a show of relief but she quickly refastened her gaze on Charles. Again he saw complete trust, felt the full thrust of it wash over him and fill his chest till it ached.

At length Kirkwood nodded. "Twenty thousand pounds, not a farthing less."

"Done."

"How soon?"

"Tomorrow, midmorning. So long as you release Tess at once."

A bark of laughter answered his demand. The gun resumed its ominous position. Tess stiffened, chest heaving with each audible breath. "If I let her go now," Kirkwood reasoned as though merely working out his afternoon social schedule, "all I'll receive tomorrow is a visit from the authorities. No, I believe I shall enjoy the pleasure of Mrs. Emerson's company until you deliver the payment and arrange my passage to France. I'll free her as soon as I board ship."

He waved the weapon at Charles. "Be a good bloke, now Emerson. Turn around and start walking. Tessa and I will follow you out, and rest assured my pistol will be lodged quite snugly against her back." He draped his cloak across her shoulders, making it appear as though he simply had an arm around her. "There we are, three old friends out for an evening. Let's go, shall we?"

Hating to lose sight of her even for a moment, Charles turned and trudged toward the Grove. His feet dragged as he grappled to concoct a plan, knowing it was imperative he do so before they reached the street, before Kirkwood bundled Tess into a coach and sped off.

That pistol contained a single bullet—a single chance to end a life. But might Kirkwood have another gun on him? If Charles only knew the answer, he'd devise some way to make Kirkwood fire that one and only shot—at Charles's own back if need be.

As they neared the Grove he saw few people about, most having gone to the riverbank to view the fireworks. That meant Kirkwood would proceed through Vauxhall's gates in a matter of moments. Precious few moments that would determine whether Tess lived or died.

As a sense of helplessness rose up inside him, an oomph and a grunt from behind sent Charles pivoting wildly. He witnessed Kirkwood's wide, vacant stare just before the scoundrel hit the gravel face first.

Even before he made sense of it, Charles dashed to retrace his steps. As he ran, Fabrice's compact figure took shape in the shadows beneath the trees. Tess was on the ground not far from Kirkwood, a bemused heap of skirts and petticoats.

Samuel Crenshaw stood above her, extending his hand to help her up.

Kirkwood began to move. His pistol lay inches from his hand and he reached out for it. Fabrice flung himself down on the man's back. They struggled, rolling, until a thrashing knee caught Fabrice in the gut. As the servant lost his hold, Kirkwood shimmied serpent-like on the ground. His hand came down on the weapon.

Rage, white hot and blazing, propelled Charles the last few paces and onto the prone man. The gun skidded away. As if of their own accord, Charles's hands found purchase around the other man's neck and locked. Thought evaporated, leaving him gripped in a blind, wordless horror at what Kirkwood had almost stolen from him—Tess, his heart, his very life.

Through the fury, voices shouted his name. Hands gripped his shoulders, tugging, prying. In the midst of the din he heard Tess's pleading voice, her entreaties. Tess—she was the reason Kirkwood must not live, did not deserve another day on earth. Reason enough for an honorable man to kill.

And yet. . . .

"Charles, don't. You mustn't. Please. I love you. Do you hear me? I love you. I've only ever loved you. Please don't kill him. Let the law have him. Don't let him destroy us."

Her pleas pierced the roaring in his head, but it was her love that penetrated the layers of wrath and appealed to his heart. The rasp of Kirkwood's constricted airways reached his ears and he realized how very nearly he'd committed murder. His grip slackened, slowly released. Fabrice and Crenshaw used the interim to each grab an arm and haul him off the sputtering viscount.

Tess. His beautiful girl stood before him, trembling lips forming a fragile smile, great blue eyes shimmering with courage and love and an adamant message; one he understood now his bloodlust had cleared. *No more killing*.

"Justice will do its work, Emerson," Crenshaw said, echoing her sentiments aloud. He clapped Charles's shoulder, then scooped Kirkwood's pistol from the ground. "He'll hang, mark my words. We don't want you swinging beside him, now do we?"

Charles clenched his fists at his sides and sucked draughts of air. He resisted the urge to deliver a swift kick to Kirkwood's side, opening his arms to Tess instead. She went into them and he gathered her close, crushing her far too tightly but making no apologies for it.

From over her head, he regarded Crenshaw. "How the devil were you able to sneak up on him like that?"

"Caught a lucky tip from a little birdie in the Grove. Or an angel, I should say." He winked.

"Nora," Tess exclaimed. She craned her neck around Charles's shoulder to peer into the Grove.

"Is that the lovely angel's name?" Crenshaw laughed, a low, satisfied sound. "No use looking for her, I sent her packing for her own safety. Put up quite an argument, she did. Had to threaten her with incarceration to make her leave."

"It was Nora who sent me down the Grand Walk, too," Charles told her. He pressed his forehead to hers and kissed the tip of her nose. "That's quite a loyal and brave friend you have there."

"Thank goodness she was here. She saved us both." She raised a puzzled countenance to Crenshaw. "That still doesn't explain how you and Fabrice appeared out of nowhere just now."

The magistrate offered a modest shrug. "Used to patrol the place for pickpockets in my younger days. Know it like the back of my hand."

Fabrice had just finished securing Kirkwood's hands with one of the villain's own trouser braces. Tugging on the bonds to ensure their adequacy, Fabrice gave a satisfied grunt and gained his feet. Though Charles hesitated to relinquish even partial hold on Tess, he held out his hand. "Thank you, friend. I hate to think what might have happened without you."

Fabrice's mouth quirked. He winced when they shook hands.

"No broken bones, I hope."

Fabrice flexed his fingers. "Non. Just a reminder of a job well done."

"That must have been some blow you delivered, to bring him down like that. Sorry I didn't turn sooner to see it." With no small amount of satisfaction, Charles surveyed Kirkwood's bruised and swelling jaw. "Where'd you learn to do that?"

"If Monsieur would like, Fabrice can demonstrate."

"So long as you needn't demonstrate on me."

The servant grinned. "I think there is much Monsieur and Fabrice can teach one another. But it is late and time for Madame to be home. Monsieur Crenshaw and I will deal with this baggage." He nudged Kirkwood, curled on his side on the ground, with the toe of his boot.

Charles brushed his lips across Tess's. "Would you like to go home?"

"With all my heart."

His chest constricted. Did her words convey more than a simple desire to be as far away as possible from Kirkwood? Now that the crisis had ended, was she willing to forget the past and begin a new life—with him? Was she finally ready to trust him with her heart?

In the kitchen at home, Tess summoned a smile for Gwennie as the girl applied salve to her skinned knees, elbows and hands and wrapped linen strips around the worst of her scrapes. Smiling wasn't so difficult a chore, really—she was too numb to feel much pain. Charles knelt beside her chair, holding his arms around her and grimacing each time Gwennie touched the wet cloth to her abrasions.

They had assured Gwennie of Fabrice's safety, which accounted for the cheerful tune she hummed as Charles helped

Tess from the kitchen and up the stairs. Though her bedroom door stood ajar, he seemed disinclined to go further than her sitting room.

She questioned him with raised brows. After all, he'd been a frequent visitor to her bed in recent days.

"I just want to hold you," he said. "Just to reassure myself that you're all right."

"Despite my many bruises, I'm fine. Perfectly fine."

"For once, I believe you."

They settled on the settee, he gathering her close and she snuggling her head on his shoulder. For a time, neither spoke. Contentment flowed through her. Life had never seemed so peaceful, so perfect.

"I'll take you on any terms you'll allow, my Tess, even if all I can ever be is your friend." His voice rumbled beneath her ear, enhancing rather than disturbing her contentment. "Never again will I abandon you, even if you wish me away. And if the Midnight Marauder continues to haunt the night, I'll haunt it with her."

"London still needs her Marauder, but I can't envision a life for that brave soul without her Courageous Crusader by her side." She raised her face to him. "Do you love me?"

He looked perplexed, endearingly so. "What do you think I've been telling you all this time?"

"Well, if you truly love me, you'll be willing to risk your reputation and run away with me."

"Are we still running away, then?"

"Yes, if you don't mind, to Surrey and as soon as possible." She hesitated, having never done this sort of thing before. It wasn't usually a woman's task, but she'd stupidly refused his suit on more than one occasion. She couldn't possibly expect him to ask again. No, this time it was up to her.

She squared her shoulders. "It's high time we had that wedding everyone thinks we had, don't you think?"

Her heart wrenched at the eagerness blazing in his eyes. "You're not afraid of facing my family or anyone else?"

"It's extraordinary what one sees down the barrel of a gun." Her trembling sigh released the tension of the past hours, the past decade. "I've wasted far too much time regretting the past and worrying about what people think."

She reached out to stroke his solid chin. "If your family never accepts me, what of it? I love their son and I intend to make him happy. What I faced tonight with Sebastian Russell makes them seem no more menacing than a pack of lambs."

Silent, Charles stroked her hair and studied her with a thoughtful expression. Why didn't he say something? Why was he beginning to look just a tad sheepish?

"I came within a breath of losing you forever," she pushed on, afraid of what his sudden reticence might mean. "For so long I've been brave for other people, but tonight I was brave for myself. I found the courage to fight Sebastian Russell because I didn't want to leave this world. I didn't want to leave you. I've been given not only a second chance at love but a third, and that's a gift I don't intend to squander."

As his silence stretched, her unsettling twinge of doubt grew into full-fledged fear. Was he remembering all her reasons for insisting a life together would never work?

If so, then pride and caution be damned. "Charles, I love you. I adore you. I always have. I've never loved anyone else. And I've never once stopped wanting you and needing you in my life."

"It wasn't a coincidence."

"What?" She blinked. After such a heartfelt confession, this was not the response she'd hoped for. "What wasn't?"

"Our running into each other at Vauxhall that first night." He smiled ruefully. "After ten years of trying to forget, of persuading myself I was better off without you, I came home searching for you. Determined to find you. Even though I believed you to be another man's wife, I had to see you." His gaze met hers with such heated longing she might have melted. "I scoured Vauxhall and every other place I thought I might find you. I'd have combed the entire country if I'd had to."

"And I ran away," she recalled, burying her face in her hands.

"You came back," he reminded her gently.

"I needed you."

"Don't ever stop."

And then she remembered. She had demanded so much of him already and had no right to expect more. But there remained one final boon to ask, something she hoped for with all her heart. It was the last possible barrier to their happiness. "There is someone else who needs you."

He brushed his lips across her temple, across the tender bruise left by Sebastian Russell's pistol. "Blair."

"She's a handful. I've spoiled her terribly. But she needs a father more than anything."

"Nothing would make me happier, except being your husband." He tipped her chin and kissed her full on the mouth, a wordless pledge to seal his commitment.

"We can say we adopted her."

"We'll simply say she's ours, just as you are mine and I am yours. If anyone ever dares malign her, they'll have me to contend with."

He disappeared behind a mist of tears. She reached her arms around him, determined to hold tight to this hero beyond imagining, a nobleman in the truest sense of the word, a man of honor, of family, of love.

"So, then," she whispered against his dampened shirtfront, "what do you say about running off to Surrey?"

"We'll leave tomorrow." He pulled her into his lap. Against her thigh, his desire pulsed, hard and eager. Her hands traced his back, his shoulders and sides, taking possession of every strong, masculine line. Lowering his mouth for a kiss, he emitted a groan that vibrated deliciously against her lips.

Barely breaking the kiss, he hoisted her into his arms, pushed to his feet and plowed a path to the bedroom. "Make that the day after tomorrow."

Please turn the page for a preview of
MOSTLY A LADY
by Lisa Manuel,
coming in April 2005 from Zebra.

"Help! Please stop. Oh, please. I need help."

But the wind battered the moors at a roar today, and Eliza's pleas were as quickly whipped away as uttered. She scrambled up the incline, her damp, muddied skirts doing their utmost to haul her back down.

Two endless, sodden, shivery days she'd spent here, and two pitch-black nights as well, huddled on the carriage seat beneath a pile of Elizabeth Mendoza's clothing. She'd found food among the scattered luggage—a loaf of bread, some cheese, a meat pasty that must have been bought the morning of the accident, for it was still fresh. There were a few apples as well. But Eliza had eaten sparingly, rationing like a miser in the event that no one would come for days and days. Even so, it was more than she'd eaten previously. She was still weak, too thin, but no longer plagued by the dizzying, heightened sensations of the starving.

Which made her wonder, as she struggled to reach the road before the rider passed out of view, had she made a rational decision the day Elizabeth died, or had her choices been shaped by an empty stomach?

Even before she topped the rise, the rider halted his horse and dismounted. Holding the reins in one hand, he stepped toward the incline, going quite still as he surveyed the wreckage. Eliza could make out little of him, half-hidden as he was beneath a woolen greatcoat. But even through the hair that blew incessantly across her face, she saw the cloak's three-tiered collar, its braided trim, its velvet lining. And his boots, buffed and only slightly soiled from his travels, were so well fitted as to form a second skin over the muscular swell of his calves.

A gentleman, then. Grabbing hold of a sapling and dragging herself, sodden hems and all, to the wall bordering the road, she steeled herself to play the role of a lifetime—the role that would save her life. She all but collapsed against the low barrier, catching her balance with the flats of her hands against the stones. It was then he saw her.

"By God." He ran toward her, cloak billowing behind and all around him like black flames. When he reached her she was still hunched and panting for breath, her bedraggled hair falling in her face despite an earlier attempt to secure it. From across the wall he reached for her. His hands, gloved and large, closed around her shoulders—around the shoulders of Elizabeth Mendoza's flowered muslin gown. Ever so gently, he raised her up.

"Madam, are you hurt?" A gaze the color of the Yorkshire hills at dawn, neither green nor gray but a shade in between, darted toward the carriage's awkward stance against the trunk of the rowan. "By St. George, what happened here?"

"The horses . . . they were going too fast, and the rain and the road, all muddy and pitted, and then the bend and the driver fell and . . ." She stopped, her head drooping and her teeth clamping her lip. She blinked and tried to stop the tears, quell the rising grief and guilt. And the numbing fear that she'd never manage this scheme of hers, that she'd been addled even to have thought of it.

The very thought started her shaking so violently the man's hands and arms shook, too, until his grip on her shoulders tightened and he straddled the wall to stand before her.

"It'll be all right now, madam. My name is Dylan Fergusson. I will bring you to safety. You'll soon be warm and dry and taken care of." His voice, husky, nearly a baritone, penetrated the wind and rolled over her like soft, sturdy flannel, making her believe, for a precious instant, that everything could and would be all right.

As if the gift of that voice weren't enough, he enfolded her to his chest, wrapping his cloak tightly around her, securing her in the shelter of his arms.

The tears became a torrent. Gentleman that he was, he went on holding her, patting her back and putting his solid presence at her disposal. Which of course only made her cry all the more furiously. It was the first time since Nathan died that anyone had shown her any kindness at all.

"Forgive me," she mumbled after some minutes into the second tier of his cloak's collar. He wore an open suit coat but no waistcoat beneath, only a fine linen shirt that smelled of an autumn meadow.

She was loath to pull her face away, to relinquish her first haven since her troubles began. Somehow she found the strength to lift her chin, straighten her shoulders, step back. "Forgive me," she repeated louder, more firmly this time.

"Not at all." He spoke with a soft brogue, and she realized it was this lovely lilt that softened a voice that might have been gruff and gravelly. His face, too, possessed an almost blunt, rugged quality smoothed by the fine arch of eyebrows beneath fireshot brown hair that wanted trimming. "You've been through a terrible ordeal," he said. "How long have you been stranded?"

"Two days."

"By God, and in the rain."

"Most of the time, yes. I stayed inside the coach, except when I tried to salvage the luggage."

He glanced over her head, not hard to do for one so tall. "Where is your driver? Your horses?"

"The linchpin and whiffletree broke, and the horses galloped away. We were headed south. They may be halfway to London by now." She ducked her head, not wishing to answer his first question, hoping he'd let it pass.

He did not. Removing a glove, he placed his hand beneath

her chin and raised it, and all Eliza could think as she met his concerned gaze was that there was a callous on the tip of his thumb, and how rough and reassuring it felt against her skin. How masculine in an honest, unpretentious sort of way.

"What happened to your driver?" he asked, his voice as gentle as a misty rain.

She shivered and turned her face to where the incline leveled. She'd rolled first the driver and then Elizabeth onto a blanket that first day and dragged them both there. Side by side she'd laid them, covered them with the only cloak she'd found and Nathan's old coat, and weighted it all down with stones. Thus she'd hoped, and succeeded, in keeping the buzzards away.

Mr. Fergusson followed the direction of her gaze, then looked back at her, one eyebrow upraised in a question that didn't need asking. She nodded. His gaze returned to the makeshift mound.

"Are there two deceased?"

Again she nodded. "The other was . . . my paid companion." She'd planned this story the first night, but stumbled over the voicing of it nonetheless. Lies had never come easy but this was the worst of all. This one sat like a stone inside her chest.

"How on earth did you survive unscathed?"

She felt a moment of panic. How indeed? What should she say? She began to open her mouth, hoping something believable would come out, when he shook his head.

"That you're standing here now is nothing short of a miracle, sure enough." His thick brows drew low. "Do you know of their families?"

The question startled her. Of course she didn't know a thing about the driver's background, and precious little about Elizabeth's. Mr. Fergusson eyed her, waiting and expectant.

"An aunt." She paused and thought back to the scant clues in Anselmo Mendoza's letter. "I believe there was an elderly aunt in York. They'd been recently hired, you see, and . . ." She cut short the fabrication, not at all feigning the sudden dizziness that made her teeter in the unfamiliar high-heeled boots she wore.

"Easy, lass." Mr. Fergusson's arm went round her waist and she once more found herself pressed to his solid torso. "I fear you may have been injured more than you realize. I won't rest easy till we get you to a physician."

For a wondrous moment she let him steady her, hold her. He didn't feel as she'd thought a gentleman would, not soft and purposeless but powerful, substantial, resolute. She felt a world of determination in the crook of his arm, tempting her nearly beyond endurance to remain against him forever, protected, cared for, no longer alone.

She eased away. "I haven't eaten much these last two days. I didn't know how long I'd be here and thought I'd best conserve."

"Pardon me for saying so, lass," he said with the beginnings of a smile that caused an odd flipping sensation in her stomach, "but I'd say you don't eat much most of the time. You're a mere slip of a thing."

Indeed. The corset she'd somehow wrangled her way into had delivered the same taunting message. She'd had to tighten and retighten the laces, yet even so whenever she moved the wretched thing twisted and gaped and poked where it shouldn't while her breasts kept disappearing inside. Where Elizabeth had been slender and graceful, Eliza was unfashionably gaunt.

Still, it took her aback that he should mention it. And when, exactly, had he proceeded from madam to lass? Had he sensed something amiss, some slovenly slant in her posture or tone of voice that proclaimed her less than a lady? Would a lady have leaned so readily against a complete stranger? Flames lapped at her cheeks.

"That was rude of me." He lowered his chin to search her face. Her first instinct was to turn away, hide her face in her hands. But the contrition in his misty hazel eyes held her immobile. His lips curved ruefully. "I'm very sorry."

In the next instant he shrugged out of his cloak, tossed it around her shoulders and tucked it tight beneath her chin. She all but disappeared inside its abundant folds, while the hem thudded to the soggy ground with fabric to spare. It felt, oh, like heaven, the velvet lining impossibly soft, incomparably warm with the lingering heat of his body.

But she slipped her arms free, intending to hand it back. "No, Mr. Fergusson, it's quite chilly and your suit coat will never suffice. You'll catch your death and I . . . I have a shawl in the coach."

He was already shaking his head. "No, lass, you keep it. This is considered bonny autumn weather where I come from. But you, now, you're as shaky as a newborn lamb."

He stepped closer, again tucking his chin as he regarded her in that familiar, intimate way of his. Eliza thought a lady might find his manner intrusive, might step away while issuing a firm warning to mind his distance. She didn't.

"Have you nothing warmer than this summer frock? You'll catch your death."

She shook her head, basking in his concern. There might have been warmer dresses in the piles she'd gathered, but she'd never dressed the part of a lady before. The corset had been difficult enough. This dress had few buttons and no lacings, a welcome respite for her cold and aching fingers.

She had, of course, searched for a black gown, for the widowed Elizabeth should appear in mourning. She'd found none among the scattered luggage. At first this puzzled her, until she determined it to be another clue to Elizabeth's immediate past. Her husband must have passed away so recently she'd only had time to have one mourning dress made—the one she wore.

"There's a village a few miles back." The young man's bare hand closed around her shoulder through the bulk of his cloak. "We'll stop there and hire someone who looks trustworthy to come and collect your baggage. Is there anything of value you wish to take now?"

"Only my purse and—" She started to add Nathan's rifle, but how could she possibly explain her attachment to the rusted old weapon? She shook her head, shivering again. "Just my purse. It's in the coach."

He nodded. Surely he recognized her awkward hesitations and sudden flushes for the signs of a liar. Or was he too much of a gentleman to read them accurately?

"Let's get it and be off. We'll need to search out the nearest undertaker as well. Your servants need a proper burial. What did you say their names were?"

She hadn't said. She'd thought up identities that first night, too, but when she opened her mouth now something entirely different, unexpected, appalling, came rushing out. "Nathan and Eliza Kent."

She very nearly clapped her hands over her mouth. And yet, those names made perfect sense. In order for Elizabeth to live, Eliza of course must die. And as for Nathan . . . she should have followed him into the grave ten months ago.

"A married couple?"

"Yes," she said, nodding, looking away. "Recently."

"Poor souls. I'll see to it suitable markers are made for their graves."

They had started down the incline toward the coach, his hand firm at the small of her back, a steady counterbalance to the uneven ground. Stopping short and nearly sending them both tripping over his trailing cloak hem, she gazed up into his face. "You'd do that, sir? You didn't even know them."

"I may not have, but I daresay Nathan and Eliza Kent deserve as good as anyone else. And I see no reason to burden an elderly aunt with the cost of it. When you write to her, assure her that her relations were well-tended."

"Thank you, Mr. Fergusson," she whispered.

He didn't reply; he merely took her hand to help her over the rocks.

Ah, his kindness made her throat throb with the desire to tell him the truth, made her wretched and ashamed. But then again, his generosity was offered because he believed her to be a gentlewoman. Had he known her for a plain commoner turned laundry maid turned almost-whore, he'd surely exact a lewd price for conveying her to the nearest village, then go on his gentleman's way while she returned to the Raven's Perch Tavern to decide whether to whore or starve.

At the coach she wrapped the cords of Elizabeth's reticule, the velvet one that matched the lovely carriage dress, around her wrist. She'd fretted over that frock, wondering what to do. What would people say about a paid companion wearing such expensive clothing?

She'd considered exchanging the gown for something less sumptuous, more appropriate for a genteel servant. But stripping those beautiful velvets from Elizabeth's cold body seemed an insufferable insult, an indignity the gentlewoman would never have forgiven.

Eliza so hoped she might have Elizabeth's forgiveness, not only for what she'd done thus far, but for . . . everything.

Mr. Fergusson found a small satchel among the baggage and handed it to her, "You might wish to fill this with necessities. I believe my horse can manage that much."

She packed a change of under things, stockings, an extra pair of gloves. She reached for a silver and gilt hair brush, then quickly shoved it inside when she realized the hair caught in its bristles didn't match her own sandy brown in the least. She stole a peek over her shoulder. Again, Mr. Fergusson made no acknowledgement of her odd behavior.

She selected a final item: an elaborate tortoiseshell trinket box that had been locked until she had tried one of the keys in Elizabeth's reticule. Inside she'd discovered money, a great deal, so much she hadn't bothered to count. Perhaps more importantly she'd found further clues into Elizabeth Mendoza's life: a copy of the bill of sale for Folkstone Manor and records of annuity and stock accounts that Eliza de-

spaired of deciphering. It didn't matter; she'd let Raphael
Mendoza de Leon handle financial matters.

She slipped the cache inside the portmanteau. After taking
a moment to twist her hair and pin it up, she secured a satin-
lined bonnet on her head. Then together she and Mr. Fergusson
made their way back up to the road. He secured the bag and
swung up into the saddle. Leaning low, he extended his arm.
Eliza took hold of his forearm with both hands, astonished all
over again at how muscular he was, how thoroughly solid. With
as much ease as if she were a child, he swung her up behind
him.

He twisted around to face her. "Perhaps it's time you told
me your name. You do have one, don't you?"

In spite of everything her life had been up until that moment, she found a smile for this man. "I do. It's Elizabeth
Mendoza de Leone." And then her smile withered away, consumed by her lying tongue.

This, too, went unnoticed. He grinned. "That's like music."

As he clucked his horse to motion, Eliza pressed her cheek
to his back and squeezed one last tear into his woolen coat.